GHOST OF A SMILE

Ghost of a Smile

STORIES

Deborah
Boliver
Boehm

KODANSHA INTERNATIONAL
Tokyo • New York • London

For Donald Richie and Edward G. Seidensticker
with maximum admiration,
affection, and gratitude

AUTHOR'S ACKNOWLEDGMENTS

With heartfelt alphabetical thanks for sustenance, assistance, advice, inspiration, recreation, and delight, to: Carol Applegate, Christopher Boehm, Dwight and Verna Boehm, Todd Fredell, Jim Gullo, Jeremiah (Jed) Gushman, Richard W. Gushman II, Sue Halpern, Mimi Hirsh, Francis Huxley, Pico Iyer, Hiroshi Kimura, Linda LeGrande, Katn Martin, Bill McKibben, Regula Noetzli, Elizabeth Floyd Ogata, Dirk Wales, and Nancy Way.
Thanks too to all the lovely librarians at the Vashon Island Library, for cheerful counsel and heavy lifting.

JACKET ART

Kyosai Kawanabe (1831–89): "Hell Courtesan" (*Jigoku dayu*). No. 9 from the series "Drawings for Pleasure by Kyosai" (*Kyosai rakuga*). Inscription: "Dreaming of cavorting skeletons." Used with the kind permission of the Taro Fukutomi Collection.

ILLUSTRATIONS

Takatsugu Torii

Distributed in the United States by Kodansha America, Inc., 575 Lexington Avenue, New York, NY 10022, and in the United Kingdom and continental Europe by Kodansha Europe Ltd., 95 Aldwych, London WC2B 4JF.

Published by Kodansha International Ltd., 17-14 Otowa 1-chome, Bunkyo-ku, Tokyo 112-8652, and Kodansha America, Inc.

Printed in Japan.

Library of Congress Cataloging-in-Publication data available

ISBN 4-7700-2531-9
First edition, 2000
00 01 02 03 04 05 10 9 8 7 6 5 4 3 2 1

Contents

If there is a theme that ought to be kept out of the ghost story, it is the charnel house. That and sex.

—M. R. James
London Evening News
April 17, 1931

It would be a mistake to suppose that supernatural fiction always seeks to produce fear ...

—Virginia Woolf
"The Supernatural in Fiction"

In 1808 the Japanese government legislated against ghost stories which featured flying heads, animal goblins, serpent monsters, fire demons, and accounts of the atrocities or manners of vicious women.

—Terence Barrow
Foreword to *Japanese Grotesqueries*
by Nicholas Kiej'e

THE SAMURAI GOODBYE

It is a melancholy truth that even
great men have their poor relations.

—Charles Dickens
Bleak House

Sometimes I imagine him walking these silent sloping streets in his beaver hat and caped greatcoat, trailing his long sepia-ink-stained fingers over the rough stone walls of embassy mansions and robber-baron estates. My grandfather, the genius—writer, painter, translator, polymath, president of the Asiatic Society, lover of women, collector of erotic ghost stories and supernatural *netsuke*. I never met the man; I know him as you do, from daguerreotype and anecdote, from biography and tribute, from that tacky TV docudrama, from his astonishing heap of work. And now here I am, following in his footsteps in the physical sense, at least: strolling the same slanted streets, reading the same inscrutable walls with my fingertips, trying to figure out what drew me back to Tokyo when I'm supposed to be drift-diving in the southwest Pacific, immortalizing the gaudy, gauzy lives of nudibranchs for a glossy new nature magazine.

"Any relation to the great man?" people ask, when they hear my name. I always used to answer "Yes," proudly, "I'm his grandson."

Then, a few years ago, people began looking at me askance as if to say, "At your age he had already published ten books and divorced five wives; what have *you* done lately?" Or else they'd turn coy, trying to show how well they knew the great man's quirks. "*Saraba*," they would say in parting, for that was one of my grandfather's idiosyncrasies, or affectations; he never said *sayonara*, preferring to use the raffish feudal form of farewell. I've never found the time to visit his grave, but I gather that's all there is on his tombstone in Yotsuya Cemetery: his name, the dates, and that elegant, archaic goodbye.

So, you're wondering, what *have* I done lately? Well, at the moment I'm a grad-school dropout in academic limbo: D.I.P. (Doctorate in Progress) or, more accurately, D.I.S. (Doctorate in Stasis) or, better yet, D.I.D. (Doctorate in Disarray). I suppose I could still go back and resume work on "'Bespectacled

Dwarves': Japanese Self-Image from the Edo Period Through the End of the Twentieth Century." The academic door remains open but the crack is growing smaller every day, as is my desire to return to that world of footnotes, backbiting, and hasty lunches of rancid falafel in Westwood Square. In the meantime, I support myself by hired-gun photography, filial free-loading, and the occasional raid on my inherited stock portfolio. I sometimes think I might like to be a writer; the trouble is, that's already been done.

I don't even have a steady girlfriend at the moment, much less a wife (or five), and unlike my larger-than-life forebear, I'm not six foot eight (but where I grew up—L.A., London, Tokyo, Rome—six-three wasn't such a disgrace). Nor is anyone likely to describe my face as "a devastatingly handsome cross between Apollo and the Dark Angel" (and a posthumous pox on the dizzy self-published poetess, one of my grandfather's extramarital conquests, who coined that pukish phrase). Those are just a few of the reasons why now, when Old Tokyo Types prick up their ears and say, "Oh? Any relation?" I shake my head and sigh, "No, alas, I'm afraid not. It's quite a common name in England, you know."

I have a letter in the pocket of my brown leather jacket as I walk the dark, diagonal streets on this chilly indigo night. The paper has the feel of old papyrus or mummified skin: dry, tissuey, barely clinging to molecular coherence. The stamps are wonderful and valuable too, no doubt. One is a reproduction of Tomioka Tessai's *Bodhidharma Riding a Tiger*, while the other shows Meigetsu-in, the hydrangea temple in Kamakura, in full flower, huge frothy billows of pink and blue like a baby shower gone berserk. The postmark is Karuizawa, the date is September 30, 1968, and the envelope is sealed with a fissured clump of wax the lusterless cinnabar color of old Chinese screens. (Sealing wax was another of my grandfather's stylistic furbelows, although I don't believe he ever went so far as to sport a pseudo-aristocratic signet ring.) The letter is addressed to my father, T. O. Trowe, Jr., and it is signed, of course, *Saraba*. This brittle piece of paper is my only portable keepsake of my grandfather, or my father, and I must have read it a hundred times. I know it by heart or, as the Japanese might say, I know it in my guts.

Third paragraph down, loopy scratch of sepia ink: *One thing I regret, as I near the end of this immensely interesting incarnation, is that I have never had an intimate encounter with the supernatural nuances of the night in Japan. The uncanny, yes, the enchanted, to be sure. But I never saw a footless ghost, I was never accosted by a* tanuki-*goblin masquerading as a priest, I was never seduced by a comely fox-woman with a bushy russet tail beneath her voluminous skirts. Fortunately, I believe in metempsychosis, so I can say with a blithe and hopeful spirit: Maybe in my next life.*

Poor Grandpa. The women flung themselves at his size-fourteen feet, the men worshipped the *tatami* he walked on, but the Japanese ghosts wouldn't give him the time of ... day.

Thinking those thoughts and a great many others, I started across an unlit bridge in the Akasaka district of Tokyo. The dragon-posts and arabesque embossing reminded me of Sacheverell Sitwell's description of the Bridge of the Brocade Sash, and I began to wonder what it would be like to be a not-quite-genius grandchild in that other gifted, flamboyant family. "Nobody comes to give him his rum/But the rim of the sky/Hippopotamus-glum," I recited out loud, and I didn't notice the woman crouching at the other end of the bridge until the sound of her crying roused me from my reverie.

I couldn't see the woman's face, but I could tell by her gold-buckled pumps and the cut of her gray wool coat that she was, as my class-conscious mother or my grandfather's immortality-rival Lafcadio Hearn might have put it, from a good family. A long loose sheaf of blue-black hair hid her face, and she was weeping helplessly, as if she had been walking across the bridge and had suddenly been overcome by grief or despair.

"Excuse me, Miss, are you all right?" I asked. The woman made no response, and her crying seemed to increase in volume. "Are you all right?" I repeated, using extra-polite verb forms so she wouldn't mistake my intentions. "Can I be of any assistance?" I could tell from the curve of her back and the shine of her hair that the weeping woman was young, and probably pretty, too. Maybe I would be able to cheer her up over a cup of tea or a glass of beer, and after that, who knew? Passion born of sorrow could be a beautiful thing.

Still the woman sobbed, and hid her face. "Please don't cry," I pleaded, but the woman just hunched her slender shoulders and wept some more. Maybe I should give up, I thought. My knees had begun to cramp from crouching for so long, and I stood up and stretched. "Are you sure I can't help you?" I asked, one last time.

Suddenly the woman stopped crying. Raising one small white hand, she pushed back the shimmering curtain of hair and lifted her head to reveal a face that was completely blank and smooth, like an egg. She had no eyes, no nose, no mouth, no features of any sort. I stood poleaxed with shock and disbelief for a few seconds, while the rational part of my brain posed logical questions like, "How could she cry without a nose, or a mouth?"

After a moment my mind made the transition from logic-fueled denial to unreasoning fear. I let out a shrill girlish half-shriek, then ran away as fast as I could, which, since I used to win schoolboy medals in both cross-country and the 440, was very fast indeed.

I ran for blocks, I ran for miles. I sprinted through dark secretive streets, past blue-roofed temples and vermilion shrines and topiary parks, past garden estates and fluffy-plastered condominiums, past gas stations and "convenience stores," now inconveniently closed. I saw no one along the way—no insomniacs out walking their miniature dogs, no night-shift joggers, no cruising taxis.

Please God, I prayed in a secular, opportunistic way. Please let there be someone to talk to, soon.

No more than thirty seconds later, I saw a light up ahead under a golden-leafed gingko tree. I slowed to a trot, and as I drew closer to the light I saw that it was an oil lantern, illuminating the stall of an itinerant noodle vendor. It struck me as an odd, untraveled place to set up a *soba* stand. At this time of night, most vendors were plying their trade outside train stations or in lively drunkenness-and-debauchery districts like Shinjuku and Yurakucho. Still, it was a godsend. (Thanks, God, I thought. I'll give you a jingle next time I need a favor.)

Alfresco food stands were among my favorite things in Japan, along with deep-mountain hot-spring baths, shrine maidens in long crimson culottes, and the mesmerizing sound of monks chanting mystic syllables behind crumbling snuff-colored walls. I also liked beer in amber bottles, salty seaweed crackers, the bitter salutary foam of ceremonial tea, and buckwheat noodles in any form at all.

"*Konbanwa*," I said as I ducked, still panting, under the calligraphed muslin curtains and sat down on a wobbly wooden stool.

"Good evening," said the vendor, with a friendly gold-toothed smile. "You look as if you've seen a ghost!"

"I don't know if it was a ghost," I said. "But I definitely saw *something*." The noodle man opened a long-necked bottle of beer and handed it to me, then busied himself behind the counter, scraping the cast-iron grill with a spatula, pouring a pellucid puddle of oil and spreading it around before adding chopped cabbage, carrots, and onions. When the vegetables were soft and slightly charred, he stirred in the precooked buckwheat noodles, scooped the steaming *yakisoba* onto a plate, doused it with a sweet thick soy-based sauce, sprinkled flamingo-pink shredded ginger and powdery green seaweed on top, and set the plate on the wooden counter.

"There you go," he said, flashing his gleaming dental work again.

"*Itadakimasu,*" I said, signaling for another cold amber bottle of Kirin. This is bliss, I thought. Perched on a stool on the edge of a fragile whirling planet, eating simple food, drinking sublime beer, with another human being to talk to or be silent with. The proprietor had been cleaning his griddle with the stainless-steel spatula, singing "Ginza Love Story" in a loud tuneful tenor with all the usual karaoke-balladeer flourishes. Now he leaned on the counter and looked at me with curious yellow-brown eyes.

"Tell me," he said casually, his bald head and metallic teeth glinting in the lamplight. "What was it that frightened you so?"

I took a bite of noodles and a big gulp of beer. Lots of Japanese people still believe in ghosts and apparitions and fox-bewitchment, I thought. This nice chap won't think I'm crazy.

So I told the soba man the story, complete with imitations of the girl's incessant sobbing, for (if I do say so myself) I have always been a rather good mimic. As I approached the denouement, the unveiling of that ghoulish unpunctuated face, my feelings of terror and revulsion returned. "And then she pushed her hair back and showed me ..." I stopped in mid-sentence, reluctant to put that incomprehensible image into words.

The noodle man leaned forward, and his benevolent smile suddenly turned into a menacing leer. "*Hé-eh,*" he said, baring his gilded teeth. "Was it anything like *this* that she showed you?" As he spoke he drew his hand over his face, and it became smooth and blank and featureless, like an egg. I screamed, and at that same moment, the light went out.

When I finally regained consciousness an hour or so later, I was looking up at one of the loveliest women I had ever seen. She was Japanese, with one of those classic pale oval Utamaro faces, medieval eyebrows, and a very modern magenta mouth, and she was dressed in subtle shades of pewter and khaki under a celadon-green smock. It turned out that this celestial vision was my attending physician at the Red Cross Hospital in Minami-Azabu. Evidently I had been found lying unconscious on the sidewalk in a puddle of beer, and taken to the hospital by ambulance, for observation. (The noodle stand and its owner had disappeared, of course, and all the neighbors swore they hadn't seen a soba vendor in that vicinity since the Occupation.)

Because this was my life and not some wishful escapist novel, it also turned out that the stunning doctor was newly married, to an absurdly handsome Japanese neurosurgeon. "Any relation to the great man?" he asked me in obnoxiously fluent English, when we were introduced. I was feeling too weak to fib, so I grimaced and said, "Unfortunately, yes." (Too bad we weren't speaking Italian; I've always loved hissing out *s-s-s-fortunatamente.*) "Well, saraba!" he said with a patronizing smirk as he left my room, his busy-man beeper abuzz, and then the bile-green door closed behind him.

After I got out of the hospital, I found a small stack of invitations addressed to my absent mother in the post-box of her small but expensive pied-à-terre in Akasaka-Mitsuke, where I was camping out. Art openings, lectures, receptions, strange-foreigner parties. Perfect, I thought. People to talk to.

I went out every night for a week, and when I told a few Japanese people what had happened to me, they all nodded sympathetically and said things like "Oh, how scary!" and "You must have had quite a fright," with no trace of sarcasm or doubt. At a tony soirée at the British Embassy, two solemn Japanese matrons told me that the Japanese word for "eggfaced monster" is *nopperabo,* and I filed that away under Information I Hope to God I'll Never Need Again. Later that night, after they had been hitting the champagne pretty hard, the same women (now giggling uncontrollably) shared their own personal ghost-encounter stories, whispered behind pale jade-ringed hands. I pretended to be impressed and reassured, but I couldn't help noticing that both yarns sounded suspiciously like borrowings from that classic volume, *Tales of Murdered Moonlight*, collected, annotated, and brilliantly translated from the Japanese by my ubiquitous ancestor, Thomas Oswald Trowe the Original.

The Americans were considerably more skeptical, and after being greeted with halitotic hoots of laughter from a gaggle of dissolute expatriates, I began saying that I had been hospitalized for anemia: my tiny, vengeful vampire-joke. I did, however, relate the genuine version to my mother when she rang me from her flat in Kensington.

That turned out to be a major mistake, because she insisted on sending me to see a psychiatrist named Neville Ruxton, whom she described in her vague way as "an old chum from Trastevere days, before you were born." Oh my God, I thought (the post-traumatic mind as runaway train), what if my mother had an affair with this slimy shrink? What if *he's* my real father? What if I'm not the great man's grandson, after all? The thought of being deprived of my deepest anxieties made me feel more anxious than ever.

But Neville Ruxton, as if you hadn't guessed, turned out to be a woman, named after a rich-recluse uncle by avaricious, profligate parents. (I was pleased to hear that the fawned-upon uncle had slyly left all his money to a foul-mouthed African Gray parrot named Dorcas.) When I told Dr. Ruxton about the faceless faces she looked smug and knowing, as if I had trotted in on all fours, furry naked body smeared with porphyric salve, carrying a blood-soaked white rabbit in my mouth and saying between guttural growls and bites of bunny *tartare*, "I don't know, Doc. I keep having these werewolf dreams."

"I wish every case were this simple," Dr. Ruxton said, manicured fingertips pressed together like the roof-beams of a Sepik River longhouse, the multiple facelifts (Mother's gossip) giving her skin an eerie Mongol tautness across the surgically-implanted cheekbones (gossip *ibid.*). Then, in a voice like treacle and lye, she pointed out that my story bore a remarkable resemblance to Lafcadio Hearn's retelling of the old folk tale known as "Mujina," and suggested that pretending to have had a supernatural experience was the only way I could make myself feel like my grandfather's equal, or even (she added with a that'll-be-the-day smirk) his superior.

"You've been a big help," I lied at the end of the hour. I wasn't in the mood to explain that I had never read "Mujina," nor did I see any point in spreading the greasy entrails of my second-generation inferiority complex all over the sage-velvet couch and the opulent ecru carpet. Besides, I had a plane to catch.

I jogged back to the flat, packed my motley leather-and-canvas bags, and headed for the Tokyo Interdimensional Space Station, also known as Narita Airport. At the airport bookstore, on impulse, I bought an overpriced paperback of Lafcadio Hearn's *Kwaidan*, subtitled *Stories and Studies of Strange Things*. By one of those uncanny coincidences it turned out to contain "Mujina," the story that Dr. Ruxton had obliquely accused me of plagiarizing. (According to my dictionary, a *mujina* is "a supernatural creature with shape-shifting powers." *Naruhodo*: Now I get it.)

I read the story in flight, while sipping ginger ale and nibbling Neolithic peanuts, occasionally glancing out my shoebox-window at the amazing diorama of cosmogonous clouds and Fauvist sunsets. Hearn's retold tale was so uncannily similar to what had happened to me that I got full-body goose-flesh, and I began to understand why Dr. Ruxton could have mistaken my account for a neurotic fabrication.

Maybe it was the sacramental sunscape, or the feeling of omniscience conferred by cruising so high above the cumulus curtain, but I had a major multilayered epiphany somewhere between the meal (a piece of halibut that passed all understanding) and the movie (some fireball-ridden absurdity which I watched intermittently with the sound off). I realized that ever since I was very young I've been worrying about being great—or rather worrying about *not* being great. My half-English, half-American father spent his life in the same futile dither; he died of a mutinous heart and a marinated liver when I was twelve years old, after an aggressively nonacademic but lucrative career in the recording industry in Los Angeles, London, and Tokyo. I realized, too, that from what I've read about my entirely English grandfather he never spent a moment fretting about whether he was going to be famous or rich or revered. He just pursued his own idiosyncratic quests and ended up becoming all of the above, not so much by default as by accretion. And finally, just before I fell asleep, hunched knees-to-chin like one of those poignant fossilized figures at Pompeii, it occurred to me that while I may have had an encounter with the supernatural nuances of the night and lived to tell the tale, I still didn't have the foggiest idea what to do with my own natural life.

—JOURNAL ENTRY

So here I am on the paradisiacal island of Sandovalle, midway between Vanuatu and Tokelau, living in a funky thatched-hut resort and diving daily with the person who is writing the text to go with my photographs. She's a

Tahitian-Irish ichthyomythologist and, as she puts it, "tadpole songwriter," who also happens to be the most attractive woman I have ever seen. (No wonder Gauguin went gaga.) The gold of her body, the gleam of her hair, the arc of her eyes, the curve of her mouth, the swell of her *pareu*, the velour of her voice, the scent of the flowers she wears even to sleep—everything about her drives me mad with desire and tenderness. How do I know what she wears to bed? I accidentally looked in her window one night as I was passing by: Peeping Thomas Trowe, the Third.

Even her name is a blossom, a cantata of vowels: Tea-ah-ré. (That's Doctor Tiare Teha'amana Faolain-O'Flynn, to you.) She's brilliant, of course, and funny and kind. She brings me roasted breadfruit and mosquito repellent, and last week when I stepped on a sea urchin she ducked behind a palm tree, then returned a moment later, shyly holding a leaf-cone filled with her own warm fragrant urine to take away the sting. She sings all the time, *sotto* that wonderful *voce*—one day it was "Moondance," the next a Monteverdi madrigal—and sometimes late at night she puts on a pale leotard and a long sheer skirt and dances on the beach like a dryad, or a *devadasi*.

Once I caught her staring at me with dreamy dilated eyes, a look I associate with poets on laudanum and women in love, and when I asked what she was thinking about she blushed like a half-ripe mango. Today, a major breakthrough. She asked me to come to her bungalow after dinner to read an article she's writing on seahorse myths, and I'm hoping we'll end up dancing in the moonlight, at the very least.

Incidentally, I'm beginning to think that I should stay away from cities. Not because of the hazards of the urban supernatural, but because pavement is not my sympathetic element. This morning the water was heraldic blue on the surface, malachite-green below. The opisthobranchs were in frilly translucent bloom, and Tiare and I swam for hours among the anemone mosques and brain-coral caverns, exploring the curving sonic highways and invisible-blueprint roads of the ocean floor. Whoever said that a sea is just a soggy desert had it completely backward. Deserts are enervated oceans, and seas are the grand oases of Earth.

On a more carnal note, what can I say about Tiare in neoprene, sleek and antic as an adolescent sea otter, long black hair streaming behind her like *Cupomedusae* tentacles or squid-ink silk? My carbonated lovesick sighs, her disciplined breath: our bubble-streams mingled as we bent our heads over a scarlet starfish or a pregnant male seahorse. ("The protofeminist nurturer," Tiare said later, with a mischievous smile). Once I almost bumped into a neon chorus line of *Flabellinopsis iodinea*, so mesmerized was I by the sinuous seal-shape undulating in front of me. I have always thought that a full-length wetsuit, worn by a graceful woman, is more alluring than anything in those *Naughty Negligées* catalogs that used to show up in my mailbox at UCLA, ludicrously addressed to "Professor Emeritus, or Current Occupant."

One of the many things I like about the ocean is that there are no legendary footsteps to follow in, no gigantic shoes to fill, no archives, no *curricula*, no impossible expectations. There's just vastness and mystery and color and movement and light, and a constant awareness that wonderment (or death) may be lurking behind every rock. And if that isn't a useful existential metaphor, I don't know what is.

There was music enough in the trees—the drowsy twitters of kingfishers, flycatchers, honey-eaters, and the small gray birds the natives call leaf-ghosts—but just for overkill I had brought along my portable CD player, programmed to croon "Tell It Like It Is" over and over, sweet bayou soul without end, amen. It was definitely Slow-Dance City, as one of my perennially dateless prep-school roommates used to say with a wistful, spotty-faced leer every time he heard anything even vaguely balladic on the radio.

"Nice," Tiare murmured as we danced a disappointingly decorous foxtrot. "The Neville Brothers, give or take a few siblings." Her eyes were closed, and her Tahitian-gardenia wreath was dizzyingly fragrant under my nose. (*Tiare*: her namesake flower.) To my dismay, though, her body wasn't touching mine except for the hands and occasionally the feet, when one of us lost our balance on the sand and accidentally trod on the other's bare toes. I kept trying to pull her closer, to fold her arms behind me and crush our torsos together at chest and groin in the subtle erotic tradition of the American high-school dance, but she resisted with surprising determination, as if I were the designated villain in some YWCA self-defense class.

The moon was full, and the broad silver stripe it cast on the cerulean water looked like a palpable, walkable road. Suddenly I wanted to ask Tiare to walk that illusory path with me, and all the other roads in life as well. In that moon-addled instant I saw getting married as an ultimate solution (World's Tenderest Lover! World's Greatest Husband! World's Most Flawless Father!). On a more immediate level, it seemed to be the only way to get Dr. Tiare Teha'amana Faolain-O'Flynn to stop dancing as if there were a roll of barbed wire between us. But just as I opened my mouth to propose, Tiare said, "Let's sit for a while."

The moment was lost, perhaps forever. As we hunkered self-consciously at opposite ends of a straw mat, instead of "I want to spend my life with you," I said lightly, "I don't know, I still think there's something slightly obscene about living in a climate so idyllic that the native language doesn't even have a word for 'blanket.'"

"Oh, but they do," said Tiare, who unlike me hadn't picked up all her knowledge of the local culture from breezy, superficial guide books. "They call it 'foreign mat for wrapping a chilly corpse.'"

"Lovely," I said sarcastically. "I'll remember that the next time I'm huddled under the covers in London on a frigid December night, alone and palely loitering."

Tiare didn't laugh, or even smile. She just looked at me, the planes of her extraordinary tropical face limned in moonlight. Eat your heart out, Gauguin old man, I thought.

"Listen, Ozzie," she said, and I saw her exquisite brown throat undulate with a nervous gulp, like a hummingbird chug-a-lugging sugar water. "There's something I probably should have told you a long time ago, but it didn't seem relevant until tonight." I was silent, for I knew that nothing good could ever follow a preface like that.

Tiare plunged ahead. "The thing is, I'm married, and I don't know if it's going to work or not. Right now we're separated—sounds like a Julia Child recipe for some egg dish, doesn't it?—but the truth is I don't know yet whether this particular soufflé is going to fall or not. God, that sounds so glib; metaphors always mess me up. Anyway, it was one of those grad-school romances, you know the kind, intense yet absentminded, and we've had some major problems adjusting to the logistics of life in the real world and the dynamics of a long-distance relationship. I mean, to be perfectly honest, which is to say far more honest than I had intended to be on this particular night, we're pretty much like strangers to each other these days. But we aren't seeing other people yet, although if we were, I'm sure I don't have to spell this out, I mean it almost seemed like adultery just to be *dancing* with you a minute ago, because I'm starting to feel so, um … never mind. It's just too soon, and too much, and too scary."

Not a word from me. I was the silence tree, the well of stillness, the mine of speechless ore. Actually, I was trying desperately to think of something sensitive and mature to say, but the only words that came to mind were "Damn! Blast! Bloody hell!" After a long moment, Tiare spoke again and this time instead of an earnest confessional tone, her voice sounded dreamy and trance-like.

"The people who live on this island believe that if you tell a really dreadful story on the first night of the full moon, the long-toothed ghosts will leave you alone for the rest of the month," she said. "It's a sort of preventive magic, I suppose. They call it something that translates very roughly as 'storytalk insurance.'"

"Blather in the face of fear," I said flippantly. I was still in shock from Tiare's unexpected revelation, for she wore no wedding ring, and I had chosen to perceive her as single and unattached. As for the hyphenated surname which I had found so fetching, there could have been any number of nonmarital explanations for that alliterative pageant of names.

"Blather? That's an awfully cynical, ethnocentric way to put it," Tiare said, but her tone was light. "So do you want to hear my little horror story, or not?"

"Hey, break a leg," said the World's Most Tender Lover.

Once upon a time, a long long time ago, on a beautiful island that has since been swallowed up by the waves, there lived a young princess named Deemah who was very much in love with her husband. Riahl was a famous warrior with a gift for wood carving, and between battles, when he wasn't decorating canoes and longhouses, he used to make little birds and animals for his wife's collection. Deemah spent her days gathering wild plants to make dyes for the cloth she wove from fibrous tree bark, and trying to imitate the songs of the brightly-plumed birds on her bamboo flute. In the evening, after the cooking fires had dwindled to small glowing coals, like the eyes of wild animals in the night, the two of them would repair to their sleeping chamber and reinvent the stars. It was a perfectly happy life for both of them, until the tall rough-bearded stranger arrived from another archipelago in his fine canoe of teak and mahogany, with a carved crocodile's head on the bow and a hold full of shiny stones and gold doubloons salvaged from the pockets of drowned Spanish sailors.

The visitor's name was Morro. He was a prince from Deemah's tribe who had been away for many years, and according to the rules of the island he could claim any woman he liked for his bride or his concubine, as long as she wasn't married to a member of the royal family. He looked around the fire at the great welcome feast the chiefs held for him, and he knew right away that he wanted Princess Deemah. There was nothing Riahl could say, or do. He was a great warrior and an accomplished craftsman, but he was not of royal blood.

After the feast Morro took Deemah aside and told her that she had captured his heart. He was a tall handsome man, with many shark's-tooth necklaces and several fine shrunken heads at his belt, but she just looked at him coldly and said, "I love my husband, and even if I were single I could never love a man like you." Morro laughed and his teeth, which were a bright bloody red from chewing betel nut, gleamed in the firelight like the fangs of a many-tailed demon. "What's love got to do with it?" he said, or words to that effect.

After that Morro cornered Deemah every chance he got. He told her of his deepening desire and gave her small gifts: a ceramic jar full of the best sago-grub marmalade, a cap of soft red and yellow feathers, a flute made clumsily by his own hand from a hollow worm-eaten branch. At first his desire was only that, the lust of flesh for flesh, but as he saw how pure and faithful Deemah was, his desire turned to love and he felt that if he could have this sweet, fascinating princess in his sleeping chamber every night, he would need no other concubines. But she refused him again and again, until he grew so angry and frustrated that he threatened to kill her husband while he slept.

Deemah looked at Morro as if he had just made a wise and noble suggestion. "Of course," she said, in her sweet voice. "I should have thought of that. I must confess that I am not unmoved by your charms, but I felt bound by my wedding vows. If you will just kill my husband tonight in his bed, then you and I can be together as you wish." Now, Morro was actually a bit of a coward who had never taken a human life, and the impressive-looking shrunken heads that dangled from his belt had been pilfered from a warrior who died of a heart attack in the forest. (To Morro's credit, he did try to revive the man with mouth-breathing before he stole his trophies.) But like many better and worse men before him, Morro was so inflamed by longing that he agreed to do exactly as Deemah said.

Deemah laid out her plan. She would sleep in her mother's palace that night, so Riahl would be alone in their sleeping chamber, under the mosquito net. She told

Morro that Riahl liked to go to bed with his straight, shoulder-length hair wet because he believed that bad dreams couldn't enter a wet head, and Morro nodded in agreement, for he too believed in sleeping wet-headed. This Riahl was a magnificent-looking man, and he sounded like a sensible one as well, but there was no choice. If Morro wanted Deemah, he would have to kill her husband. Morro reached out to stroke Deemah's slightly wavy waist-length hair, which was shiny and fragrant with coconut oil, but she shook her head and pulled away. "There will be plenty of time for that, and more," she said softly.

That night Morro sharpened his virgin sword, which had never tasted human blood. At the appointed hour he crept into Riahl and Deemah's sleeping chamber. It was very dark, but he lifted the mosquito net and groped around on Riahl's pillow. Just as Deemah had said it would be, the shoulder-length hair was wet. Morro felt heartsick at what he was about to do to the innocent Riahl, but then he remembered the look in Deemah's eyes when she said, "There will be plenty of time for that, and more." With one great blow, he hacked off his rival's head. It was surprisingly easy and unexpectedly elating, and he felt as if he had finally grown into his manhood. He would put Riahl's handsome head in the smokehouse and when it was shriveled and shrunken to the size of a baby coconut, he would hang it on his waistband, to show the world what he did for love.

Carrying the dripping head by its hair, Morro walked down to the beach, where Deemah had promised to meet him. The severed head left a trail of blood along the pristine white sand, but it was a moonless night and Morro didn't notice. While he was looking around for Deemah, a man jumped out from behind a palm tree, holding a fiery torch in one hand and a gleaming pearl-handled sword in the other. Morro screamed, for the man with the torch looked exactly like Riahl. Then he looked down at the head that hung from his hand and screamed again because the bloodied face bore the unmistakable flower-like features of Princess Deemah: the woman he desired, admired, and loved. Riahl and Morro sat down on the beach and wept like brothers, banging their heads together in grief, and then they pieced together the story, bit by bit.

When Morro threatened to kill Riahl—a threat he had not at first had any intention of carrying out—Deemah had evidently decided to substitute herself in order to save her beloved husband's life. She told Riahl to stand watch down by the beach with his sword at the ready, because (she fibbed) the royal witch doctor had told her that a certain three-headed sea demon was going to sneak ashore that night and suck the blood of all the villagers. Riahl was very superstitious, so he readily agreed.

Then Deemah hacked off her glorious hair, wetted it to conceal the difference in texture, and lay down to wait for Morro's sword.

"You can kill me if you like," Morro said, grabbing Riahl's blade and holding its sharp edge against his throat.

"No," said Riahl, heaving the sword down the beach as far as he could. "More killing will not bring Deemah back. I will treasure her memory, and perhaps, because men are men, I may even marry again someday, but no one will ever take the place of my darling Deemah. She was the love of my life, and I don't blame you for wanting her, too."

Just then a sentry came along, and Morro tearfully confessed to the inadvertent murder of Princess Deemah. The sentry wasn't certain whether it was a crime for one member of the royal family to kill another, even inadvertently, and while he went to rouse the tribe's magistrate from his bed of shiny ti *leaves, Morro got to his feet and gave Riahl a double-forearm embrace. Then he went down to the shore, climbed into his splendid canoe, paddled out into the dark ocean, and was never seen again. Some say the sharks got him, but there are those who still insist that Morro lived out his life on some lonely treeless atoll, a wild-haired, deranged monk ranting at the seagulls and chanting with the clams.*

Deemah's severed head was buried with her body, but a year after the murder her grave was opened and the skull was removed so Riahl could place it on his household altar along with his dead wife's flute, her hand-dyed robes, and all the bird and animal carvings that she had treasured so. Riahl never married again, but they say that he could be seen down at the beach on every full-moon night, dancing with a woman who would have been beautiful if she had only had a head.

This is a very ancient story, and I have told it to you exactly as it was told to me. May the gods bless your human spirit, and may your nights be free from ghosts.

It was just past midnight when Tiare finished her mesmerizing monologue, and the enormous moon above us was like hammered platinum, or silver mixed with gold. It illuminated the deserted beach with a light that was brighter and more naked than daytime, an X-ray polygraph light that made it impossible to tell a lie.

"I love you, Tiare O'Flynn," I said. I looked at her shining storyteller's face and wished I had brought my camera, and then I thought, No, I don't want a grimy lens between me and this perfect (which is not to say painless) moment.

"Earth to Ozzie," Tiare said, and I realized that I hadn't said "I love you" out loud, after all. In fact, I hadn't said anything, which was downright rude.

"That was a brilliant story, beautifully told," I improvised. "And quite startlingly relevant to us, tonight."

"Your turn," Tiare said. "One good fright deserves another." I've never been terribly good at command performances, and my mind went immediately, utterly blank. I thought of telling Tiare about my bizarre experience in Tokyo, perhaps defusing its power a bit by putting it into the third person ("Thomas Oswald Trowe the Third was walking across an unlit bridge ...") or even by pretending it had happened to someone else ("One night after midnight, a man was hurrying up the Kii-no-Kuni Slope when he perceived a woman crouching by the moat ..."). But even though I was prepared to promise to cherish Tiare forever, on the spot, I wasn't quite ready to deal with her possible ridicule, or disbelief.

"Hey, strong silent type," Tiare said, nudging me in the side. She seemed to have crept closer to me on the mat, or maybe I had unconsciously drifted toward the middle. "Are you going to tell me a scary story, or not?"

"Sorry," I said disingenuously. "I don't know any scary stories. I'm afraid I'm going to have to tell you a nice story instead."

"That's not fair," Tiare complained, but as she settled down to listen her bare arm brushed against mine, and she didn't take it away. I swallowed, and took a deep breath.

"Well," I said in what I hoped was a normal tone of voice, "this is something I saw on a newsreel on Japanese television a few years ago, and it really impressed me. It was a three-minute feature about a man—he must be close to seventy now—who has taken over a hundred thousand photographs of Mount Fuji. Twenty years ago he closed his photo-developing shop in Tokyo and moved to a town near the foot of the mountain so he could photograph it every day. That's his self-assigned full-time job: taking pictures of that one enchanted mountain. He leased a plot of vacant land at the base of the mountain, and he plants it with seasonal flowers and then uses the blooms as a foredrop, if that's a word, for his portraits of the mountain. Every morning he gets up at two A.M., puts on his beret, and drives to the foot of the mountain. Then he sets up his tripod and waits for the pictures to compose themselves.

"Anyway, he has made some extraordinary photographs, just staggeringly true, beautiful images. I remember one of a thousand cranes in frozen flight against the mountain, and another taken from one of the lakes at the bottom of Mount Fuji on a full-moon night, with the moonlight making a squiggly golden line from the shore to the oar of a rowboat, and another shot of the mountain looming above a riotous profusion of yellow flowers with the sky above filled with soft puff-pastry clouds, like a lemon-meringue sky, if lemons were blue. And at the end, the photographer said that when he went to live near Mount Fuji he destroyed all the slides he had taken in the twenty preceding years, and now he was thinking it might be time to destroy the hundred thousand pictures he's taken since then, and start over from scratch. The interviewer said, 'But why do you do this? Why this single-minded devotion to the image of one mountain, when we live in such a wide world filled with so many marvelous and photogenic things?' And the photographer shook his head and said, 'I don't know. You might as well ask the mountain.'"

Now it was Tiare's turn to be silent. The birds had finally gone to sleep, and the only sound was the rustling surf and the faint far-off shouts of some night fishermen diving for lobsters beyond the reef. "That's a wonderful story," she said after a long, electrified moment. "And you're a wonderful man." As I leaned toward her she jumped to her feet, thus saving me from the unpardonable gaffe of kissing a technically-married woman who was clearly dying to be kissed.

"What about you, Thomas Oswald Trowe the Third? Where do you go from here?" Tiare asked, looking down at me with her eyes strangely bright and her rippling river of black hair agleam with auburn highlights. She could have been Deemah the Princess, before she lost her head.

"I don't know," I said slowly. "I guess I'll just keep blundering along until I find my mountain."

"Good man," Tiare said approvingly. Then she added, suddenly playful and flirtatious, "Last one in the water's a rotten mongoose egg!" She sprinted down to the shoreline, shedding her hibiscus-patterned pareu as she went.

"Hey, wait," I called. I scrambled to my feet and followed her, stumbling out of my clothes as I ran, but by the time I hit the water Tiare was already in the midst of the silvery stripe of moonlight, draping her long wet hair over her breasts like Botticelli's *Venus* and beckoning me to join her on that shimmering mirage of a road.

I wish I could end it there, leaving you to think hot love and happily ever after, but I'm beginning to think I'm not what the Japanese would call a "*happii endo*" kind of guy. There was something strange going on, some trick of moonlight or imagination, and when Tiare raised her face to me it appeared suddenly smooth and uninterrupted, like a giant hard-boiled dinosaur egg. It was an optical illusion, of course. I knew that even as I screamed.

After a moment the lineaments of light shifted and her face returned to its beauteous human state, but the scream was already out, hanging in the dangerous air between us like a Damocles' sword of sound. I tried to explain, stammering out the whole unlikely story of that occurrence on the bridge in Tokyo, but the spell was seriously sundered. When I tried a cautious post-confession kiss, our lips felt rubbery and cadaverous. Tiare's mouth was tightly closed, and her arms were crossed upon her naked chest in classic *noli-me-tangere* body language: *I am a female fortress, and my moat is filled with crocodiles.*

"I may drop you a line after I sort things out with my husband," she said the following day as we stood on the steaming tarmac waiting to climb onto our respective cartoon-mouse airplanes (built, someone said, by two brothers in Dublin—Roy, I speculated, and Walt). It was not a long good-bye, just an awkward peck at the corner of that shapely mouth, a dizzying whiff of ginger from a farewell lei, a million unsayables left unsaid. Our second kiss, I thought morosely. And probably our last one, too. My heart was a sour heavy stone, my stomach a ferris wheel gone berserk. I tried to think of something light and curative to say ("Sorry, I had a Julia Child moment and accidentally mistook you for an egg dish" or maybe a Groucho-esque "You're certainly the dishiest egg *I* ever saw!"). In the end, though, I stuck with silence.

Tiare boarded first; there was a sign above the door of her aircraft that read THANK YOU FOR NOT SMOKING. She looked back at me and blew an unbearably ironic kiss off the tips of those fantastic golden fingers. "Thank you for not screaming," she said, and then she was gone.

—JOURNAL ENTRY

Tokyo again, free-diving in the dense gray air, getting the phantom bends when I emerge too quickly from the perilous depths of the subway. In lieu of deciding what to do with my life, I have taken a job that was conveniently vacated by Sam Sarkisian, a fellow dropout of UCLA's Post-Graduate Program in East Asian Studies who has decided with typical unexamined whimsy to try living as a *yamabushi* mountain ascetic for a year. So here I am, camped out in my mother's cozy, cluttered flat once again and working part-time at a big English-language newspaper as their reviewer-at-large, a position for which my primary qualifications would appear to be an immoderate fondness for books, food, and movies. I find the assignments almost sinfully easy and enjoyable, but I can't imagine spending the rest of my life blaring forth my highly subjective opinions on curries, memoirs, and apocalyptic *animé*. My reviews so far have been exceedingly charitable—so much so that I was recently warned by the chief copy editor to cut back on the superlatives and, I quote, to "show some claws once in a while."

All in all, things are going fairly well, but I do have to confess, dear Diary, that Dr. Ruxton was right about one thing: I was gloating a bit about my own encounter with the supernatural. It seemed like a lark, and a coup, and I felt a certain immature validation in having experienced something that had eluded my legendarily accomplished grandfather. She was wrong about my having invented or imagined those eggfaced ghouls, though. That was sheer, horrific reality. As for what happened with Tiare, that must have been hallucination, or rotten luck, or maybe just a subterranean fear of falling in love with a married woman—or with any woman at all. No, on second thought, I'm certain it was just a trick of the moonlight: a simple case of *trompe l'œil* or perhaps (forgive me) *trompe l'œuf.*

What worries me is that it happened again here in Tokyo, with someone I was in no danger of falling in love with, ever, at all. I went to an art opening in Minami-Aoyama last night, for lack of anything better to do. The walls were hung with large, livid oil paintings of what appeared to be either extraterrestrial cacti or priapic porcupines, and I was lurking near the punch bowl, nibbling happily on *kappa-maki* sushi and smoked salmon canapés, and sucking up the innocuous-tasting sunset-colored punch, like the incipient lush I am.

After a while a woman with the face of a medieval courtesan and a startling schizophrenic hairdo—short and spiky on the left side, long and silky on the right—came up to me and said in excellent English which had obviously been polished abroad, "Hi, I'm Fumiko. So tell me, are you shy, or reticent, or just plain antisocial?"

"Actually," I said impishly, to test her vocabulary, "I'm an anchorite."

"Oh, how exciting!" the woman gushed. "What network are you on, CNN?"

"No," I said, trying not to laugh. "I was joking. I'm really a writer."

"Oh!" Her face fell almost imperceptibly. "Well, that's exciting, too. I work in the creative field myself; I'm an advertising executive. So what do you write, novels?"

Instead of telling her about my abandoned dissertation and my fluke-of-luck newspaper job I said, from the depths of my unconscious, "Mysteries, actually." And even as I said the words they seemed to become true, or at least possible: the pre-tadpole novelist, me.

At any rate, we hit it off reasonably well, and it looked as if the end of my involuntary-anchorite dry spell might be in sight. The physical attraction was undeniable, so when Fumiko invited me back to her place to see her portfolio, I said "Sure, why not?" I was feeling randy and reckless and pleasantly befuddled by several mugs of that rosy insidious punch, concocted from cranberry juice, guava nectar, ginger ale, and "many, many gin," as the white-coated Japanese barman had informed me conspiratorially. By then, though, I was already a goner.

We walked the few blocks to Fumiko's stylish slate-and-saffron flat in a glittering Harajuku high-rise, and while she was in the amber-lit bathroom doing the mysterious cabalistic things that women do before sliding into bed with tall, dark, intoxicated strangers, I turned off all the lights and lit a candle that was next to the bed. I was lying on the ash-gray polished cotton quilt, watching the ceiling do its tipsy psychedelic twirl, and after a few moments Fumiko emerged in an ivory lace teddy and struck a pose direct from the pages of *Naughty Negligées*. I looked up at her and let out a loud, convulsive gasp, because by some trick of angle or candlelight her already rather concave face appeared suddenly seamless, slick, and alarmingly devoid of apertures.

I didn't scream this time, to my credit, but even though Fumiko's appearance immediately returned to normal (which is to say extremely sexy and appealing), I simply couldn't go through with the mutual-seduction ritual. I kept thinking, suppose she's on top of me, pinning me down, and her features suddenly disappear and don't come back? It was not an aphrodisiacal prospect, to say the least, so after a half-hearted nuzzle or two I stood up and babbled out some shameless, desperate excuses. (I believe I may have invented a jealous wife, or a communicable disease, or both.)

"Another impotent foreigner," the medieval beauty sneered as I stumbled toward the door, buttoning my pants on the run like some vaudeville buffoon, and I didn't stop to argue. I just wanted to get the hell out of there before her face started looking like breakfast again.

Don't worry, I see the pattern here. I know I have a problem, but I'm actually more concerned about the illusion than the reality. It would almost be easier to deal with a world in which all the women I approach really *are* faceless ghouls than one in which they only appear to be. When I called Dr. Ruxton just now to schedule an emergency appointment she said, "In the meantime, you might want to go back to the place where you saw the first, um, manifestation." I could just imagine the patronizing speculations she was scribbling on my chart: *Attention-getting fantasy … Nervous exhaustion … Pathetic attempt to one-up his famous grandfather.* I'm not looking forward to seeing her again, but I can't think of anyone else to talk to.

After a busy but absurdly diverting day of review-work—a sumptuous meal at a new Indian restaurant called Pondicherry, sandwiched between reading *Bosie* in a classical-music coffee shop and watching *Fantasia 2000* in a plush Shinjuku theater—I was about to head home when I remembered Dr. Ruxton's suggestion about returning to the scene of the fright. I took a cab to the Kii-no-Kuni Slope and got off by the same brocaded bridge where I had seen the weeping, faceless girl. As I started across the bridge I could see a female figure in kimono coming toward me, and every muscle in my body tensed in anticipation. But it was just a middle-aged woman with a sad, kind face. She was carrying a bunch of dried poppy-pods wrapped in pink paper and humming under her breath, and she took no notice of me.

One down, I thought as I trotted through the residential streets. One to go. I had been dreading my confrontation with the sinister noodle man, but when I got to the corner where his stall had been and found nothing but a crumpled stop sign I was oddly disappointed. So now what? That question was answered for me by the honk of a horn.

The car was a black BMW 540i sedan with dark-tinted windows, and when the enigmatic glass slid down I saw Dr. Neville Ruxton behind the sheepskin-covered wheel. "Were you checking up on me?" I said suspiciously and she laughed, her unnaturally taut skin like a Noh drum, or a death mask.

"No," she said, "it's pure coincidence, I assure you. I live nearby. Can I give you a lift somewhere?" Suddenly I felt very tired, so I climbed in without protest.

The lush smell of the butterscotch leather was restful and reassuring, and I closed my eyes and listened to the pleasantly soporific strains of *Pavane Pour une Infante Defunte*. I had expected to have to make small talk, so Dr. Ruxton's companionable silence was a pleasant surprise. I wasn't in the mood to chat just then, and it would have seemed improper to discuss my worries with the meter off, so to speak.

After driving for about ten minutes we stopped at what I assumed was a traffic light, and I sat up and opened my eyes. We were parked in a narrow, unlit *cul-de-sac*, and Dr. Ruxton was slumped forward with her head on the steering wheel. Heart attack! I thought in a panic, as I shook her padded-silk shoulder.

"Dr. Ruxton!" I shouted. "Are you all right?" Slowly she raised her head, and the face she turned to me was pale and smooth and featureless. No eyes, no nose, no mouth.

"Of course," I whispered, but I didn't scream or even gasp. Instead, I reached out and touched that blank white surface, and what I felt under my fingertips was not like skin at all; it was exactly like chilled vanilla pudding, after the tensile membrane forms over the top. I waited for the optical illusion to dissolve, but after a moment I knew that this one was real. With the faceless face still staring at me in that creepy, eyeless, imploring way, I opened the car door and jumped out, grabbing a tuft of the soot-colored carpet as I went.

I ran all the way to my flat at full speed, without looking back. I had only one desire: to climb under the quilt, pull the covers over my head, and fall into a dream-free sleep. I didn't think I was losing my mind, but I was a bit frightened by the way that reality and unreality seemed to have merged. I remembered a novel I had read years ago, called *The Ordeal of Gilbert Pinfold*, by Evelyn Waugh. I didn't like it much, actually, but the subject matter suddenly seemed very relevant. The book was Waugh's *roman-à-clef* account of his own skirmishes with hallucinatory illusions, but his were auditory, as I recalled, and they went away when he stopped drinking his dinner and gobbling handfuls of extra-potent sleeping pills. I hadn't taken so much as an aspirin in months, and my drinking was confined to the odd bottle of beer or a few glasses of punch at parties.

There was a pay phone in the lobby, and I used it to call Dr. Ruxton at home. She answered on the first ring, sounding very mellow and relaxed, and I wasn't surprised to hear that she had not gone out that evening. "Just checking," I said cagily. "I thought I saw you somewhere, that's all." I reached into the pocket of my leather jacket and fingered the corroborating tuft of carpeting, and then I hung up.

Next I peered into my mother's post-box, and when I saw a salmon-colored envelope I had a moment of irrational hope that it might be a missive of love and forgiveness from Tiare. But it turned out to be a hand-delivered note from Sam Sarkisian saying that he wasn't cut out to be a mountain ascetic, after all, and would be reclaiming his cushy reviewer's job the following Monday, if that was convenient for me. Baroque apologies followed, along with a promise to take me to his favorite sushi hangout, Kamei-Zushi in Ryogoku, in the very near future. His treat, of course.

"Thanks for nothing, Sam," I said as I dropped the letter in a cuspidor, adding with perfect hypocrisy, "You chicken-shit dilettante bastard, you."

As I headed for the wrought-iron elevator with my mind in a fair degree of turmoil, I heard a familiar sound: the Japanese concierge muttering in her little sitting-room off the lobby, interspersed with fragmented chants and the brassy ringing of a small bell. Violating every canon of international etiquette, I crept to the door and peered through the crack, for I was suddenly curious.

The concierge, a worn but still pretty woman in her sixties, looked up with a weary smile. "Welcome home," she said.

I stammered out a rude question, and she replied, "Oh, I was just chatting with my ancestors, telling them about my day and consulting them about my foolish worries." I could see a stack of tangerines on the altar, along with two doll-sized cups of tea, still steaming.

"I find this communion very comforting for my spirit," the concierge added. "Better than a priest, or a psychiatrist." She laughed, and then she asked, "Are you going to sleep now? I could brew some fresh tea if you like."

"No, thank you," I said, my entire body vibrating with the thrill of sudden certainty. "I just remembered, there's someplace I need to go."

I found the place right away, by the light of a striptease moon: modestly draped in clouds one moment, brazenly naked the next. I had always pictured the scene in daytime, the way it was portrayed in that overdone docudrama, with the heaps of expensive flowers, the piles of pedantic mash-notes, the awestruck hordes of great-man groupies loudly quoting their favorite epigrams from *The Collected Works of T. O. Trowe*. But at ten P.M. the only sound was the subliminal twitter of a few insomniac crows in the cryptomeria trees, and I had the mossy green labyrinth of Yotsuya Cemetery all to myself. I sniffed a familiar scent on the breeze—the acrid aroma of cheap joss combined with the faint fecundity of rotting flowers—and it occurred to me that I should have brought an offering: a single stick of some exotic incense, a vending-machine can of saké, a bottle of Guinness stout.

I wandered through the maze of graves, rounded a corner, and there it was, a rough-hewn rectangle of amber stone quarried from the banks of the Kamogawa River, adorned with a single bouquet of limp daisies and smudged with charcoal where the grave-rubbers had indulged in an orgy of fan-club frottage. And there, in the Olde English type my grandfather used on his calling cards, were the famous words:

Thomas Oswald Trowe
May 26, 1898 ~ October 1, 1968
Saraba

I felt a strange upheaval in my viscera, as if I had just given birth to myself. "It's me, Granddad," I said. "Sorry I'm late." I didn't feel a ghostly presence, exactly, but when I closed my eyes I could sense my grandfather's spirit inside me, where it had probably been all along. I began talking very fast, the way people do when they're terribly frightened, or deeply moved.

"I heard a story the other day that I thought you might enjoy," I began a bit stiffly, but before long I was sitting cross-legged on the walkway in front of the grave like some male Scheherazade, telling Tiare's tale of Riahl and

Morro and Princess Deemah and what they did for love. From there it seemed natural to segue into my own story about the eggfaced horrors, but I was suddenly reluctant to flaunt my supernatural exploits. I felt a rush of fondness (and pity, too) as I pictured my grandfather lurking about in country graveyards after midnight, trolling for ghost-fish with his own wide-eyed receptiveness as bait, but never snagging so much as a spectral minnow. And then one night his undistinguished grandson goes out for a stroll in post-modern Tokyo, miles from the nearest cemetery, and the faceless goblins come tumbling out of the woodwork.

In the end, that was the tone I took: self-deprecating wonderment. I even managed to imply that the shape-shifting mujina had only appeared to me because of the paranormal groundwork he—the real, true, one and only T. O. Trowe—had done before I was born. And then as I was telling him about the Dr. Ruxton-impersonator, I had one of my famous multilayered epiphanies, the kind that grabs you by the throat and takes your breath away.

I thought, first, about that letter in my pocket, the one in which my grandfather wrote "I believe in metempsychosis," which was his literary way of saying reincarnation. I had never paid much attention to the fact that I was born on the same day he died. As a child it had just seemed like bad luck that he wasn't around to take me to festivals and buy me indulgent presents, while in adulthood I had made a cottage industry out of being, ferociously, Nobody's Grandson At All. But what if there were some significance in that coincidence, in the final ebb of one body and the simultaneous surge of another? Japanese folktales were full of such mystical continuities, across-the-board transmigration of spirits, or exchange of vessels.

And then the second layer of my epiphany hit me like a ton of bricks: what if my grandfather, in whatever dimension he now inhabited, had supernatural powers of his own? Was it possible that he had taken the form of the egg-faces to scare me into being true to myself, and to his memory? Or maybe he was just lonely and cold in the afterworld and wanted the kind of grandson he deserved, one who would visit him once in a while and share a few stories about the bizarre, comical beauty of life on earth. Either way, I had a feeling that the ghouls had served their purpose, and would not be visiting me again.

"Forgive me," I said out loud, with tears streaming down my face. "I've been stubborn, and stupid, and selfish, and slow."

"No," said a husky voice. "You've just been human."

I jumped in surprise, half-expecting to see my grandfather materialize as a footless ghost, dressed in his trademark brown kimono and clove-colored beret, smoking a long brass-bowled pipe filled with an aromatic mixture of licorice root and tobacco. But the owner of the voice was female, and not only did she have feet, they were startlingly shod in deep purple boots with brilliant green shoelaces that matched her leather gloves. Above the luminescent footwear hung a layered assortment of jewel-hued skirts and tunics and jackets in topaz, amethyst, and emerald. The anarchic assemblage of fabrics and colors gave her an ambiguous look; she could have stepped off the runway of one of Japan's avant-garde designer's shows, or she might have been a bag lady, come to rob the drowsing dead of their unpeeled tangerines. The woman carried an enormous canvas satchel, and in one green-gloved hand she held a bouquet of daisies, a fresher version of the wilted ones that lay atop the gravestone.

"You're the grandson," she said. It wasn't a question.

"Ozzie Trowe," I said, holding out a hand which I realized too late was still wet with snuffles. Fortunately she was wearing those extraordinary grass-colored gloves, so she didn't notice.

"Cassio Kline," said the woman. She smiled for the first time then. Instead of gazing into her eyes, which were a deep sage or sorrel color, gray irradiated with green, I did that nasty superficial thing men do: I assessed her as a potential sex partner, assigning points to her legs and lips and what I could see of her fashionably mummified figure. This woman appeared to be just a notch above average in all the visual lust-producing categories—not a drop-dead beauty like Tiare, by any means—but there was something about her that rang more subtle bells in my head. That slightly crooked smile, for one thing, which seemed to hint at mischief, and warmth, and amused intelligence.

We bantered a bit to establish that her name wasn't Cassie O'Cline, and I learned that her full name was Cassiopeia, thanks to amateur-astronomer parents, but that anyone who called her that to her face was risking serious damage to life and limb. She explained that she had been doing a Ph.D. at Michigan, working on a dissertation about folkloric motifs and death legends in the work of three writers: my grandfather; Lafcadio Hearn; and their lesser-known female counterpart, Lady Sarah Edgeworth-Sugioka, an

Englishwoman who became a Buddhist nun after her aristocratic Japanese husband committed *seppuku*.

"Believe it or not, she died on the day I was born," Cassio said, and I felt the thrill of compounded coincidence.

"So now you're a professor?" I asked blandly, but my mind was racing.

Cassio Kline made a rueful face. "No, so now I'm a private detective," she said. "I'm afraid I haven't lived a very logical life." She told me that she had always been ambivalent about the academic route, but hadn't known what else to do with her life. She had come to Tokyo on a grant to gather supplementary materials for her dissertation, and by some complex conspiracy of circumstance, as she put it, she ended up helping a Zen temple in Shiga Prefecture regain some stolen art works, and then she helped a family find their missing daughter, who was being held prisoner in a doomsday cult in the mountains. Now she was working on the unsolved mystery of a female pop star who had apparently disappeared into thin air after a concert at the Budokan.

"Or maybe I should say into *thick* air," Cassio quipped, "since it happened in Tokyo." She added that the cases were coming in faster than she could handle them, and she was thinking of advertising for a partner, someone who spoke better Japanese than she did and had some basic photography skills, which she lacked and didn't have time to acquire. She may as well have held up a sign that said, HELP WANTED, ONLY PEOPLE NAMED OZZIE TROWE NEED APPLY.

"Shame on you," I said playfully, "bailing out on academia. You may be solving crimes and saving lives and making people happy, but think of all the scintillating monographs you're depriving the world of." Somehow I knew even as I spoke those words that I wouldn't be going back to UCLA, and that from then on D.I.D. would forever stand for Doctorate in Dumpster. I felt strangely excited, and it occurred to me that Dashiell Hammett—one of my literary heroes—had paid his dues as a lowly gumshoe, too.

"Hey, screw academia," said Cassio Klein with surprising vehemence. "And the hell with my parents, too, if they can't understand that I'd rather be Nancy Drew than Susan Sontag, not that she isn't totally admirable, and awesome. But after all, it's my life, and who knows? It may be the only one I have." After that I had no choice but to share my own ambivalent-dropout story, and then I went on to tell her about my lack of direction, the loss of my idyllic job and, finally, about the parade of eggly apparitions.

"Do you think I'm making this up?" I asked at the end.

Cassio shook her head. Her hair was a bright brownish-gold, like her eyes, but most of it was hidden under a moss-colored Borsalino hat exactly like the one my mother's latest underage lover, Fabrizio, was wearing when I collided briefly with them last year in Positano—*sfortunatamente*.

"I think anything anyone believes is probably true, on some level," Cassio said slowly. "After all, as your grandfather said in that famous interview, 'Human existence is at best a fragile construct of imagination, faith, and fairy dust.'"

"Faërie dust," I mused, pronouncing it the old-fashioned way.

"Yes," she said. "That too." We were silent for a while, the two or perhaps the three of us. Then Cassio said, "I can see him in you, you know."

"Good," I said. "I think he's been there all along, but I was too chicken to face it." (Which came first, the chicken or the egg?)

Cassio looked perplexed. "Really? Why? I'd be thrilled to have such a fascinating relative."

"Well, it may sound silly, but it isn't easy being descended from a household word, when you know there's no way you'll ever reach those heights yourself."

"Hey," Cassio said reprovingly, "first of all, you don't know what you might turn out to be. And secondly, millions of people manage to live grand, full, productive lives without ever becoming a household word. I mean, at the risk of sounding like the Maid of Amherst, if everyone in the world were a household word, the din would be unbearable."

"You're right," I said, but I think we both knew it wasn't quite as simple as that.

"So what's the deal with your accent?" Cassio asked. "I mean, one minute it's pure Oxbridge, the next it's sort of San-Fernando-Valley-meets-*Braveheart*. Is that what they call mid-Atlantic?"

"I never thought much about it," I said. "My prep-school roommate used to call it the man-without-a-country brogue."

"I don't know," said Cassio. "It sounds to me as if you have more countries than most. But listen," she said, holding out her hand to show me the small dark confetti-sized spots on the viridian leather, "it's starting to rain. Do you suppose we could continue this conversation somewhere with a roof overhead where we could get a pizza or something? I forgot to eat dinner tonight 'cause

I was working late, and then I felt a strong urge to come here and bring some fresh flowers. But anyway, what are your plans for the next hour or so?"

I started to say "No plans at all," but something made me decide to stay. I still felt a curious need to console my grandfather, for however rich and mysterious his afterlife might be, his official human existence (unlike mine) was at an end. And there it was, the final layer of my epiphany parfait. For the first time in my illogical, conflicted life I realized what a gift it is just to be alive, with a body to walk around in, hard choices to make, and an immediate future to fill with work, adventures, mistakes, and various sorts of love.

"I think I'm going to hang out here for a while longer," I said. "But would you have time for tea or something tomorrow?" In Japanese, the phrase "tea or something" can imply romantic interest, and I trusted her to know that I didn't mean it that way. Cassio Kline wasn't really my type, but I felt I could talk to her for hours, or days.

It was raining harder now. The sky was the color of blackened catfish, and the moon seemed to have vanished forever. I turned up the collar of my jacket, and wished I had worn a hat.

"Actually, caffeine tends to make me crazy," Cassio said, "but a cup of something sounds good. Maybe hot lemonade. I'll give you a call tomorrow." I started rummaging in my pocket, hoping to unearth a pen and a scrap of paper, but Cassio put her hand on my arm.

"Don't worry," she said. "I'll find you. I'm a private detective, remember? Well, I'll leave you Trowes alone for now. Sayonara!"

She raised a green-gloved hand in farewell, opened a large teal-blue umbrella, and began to thread her way among the wet, shiny tombstones, her purple boots like giant eggplants in the tall grass.

"Sayonara," came my automatic reply, but after a moment I felt the need to make a correction, or an improvement. "No, wait," I said, with the rain streaming down my face. "Saraba!"

Cassio turned and smiled that complicated smile. "Ah," she said appreciatively, "the samurai goodbye. So you like the old ways, too?"

"Yes," I said, proudly. "I do. I guess it must run in the family."

THE FIRE DOWN BELOW

Erotic love is a madness.

—MURIEL SPARK
Symposium

aizo Taka, a.k.a. The Grape Gatsby, had made a fortune in the international stock market. *Insider trading*, some newspapers called it, in righteous indignation. Other papers, notably those whose publishers he had entertained at his pastel villas in Hanalei, Zushi and Rapallo, dismissed such remarks as unfounded innuendo or (coyly) sour grapes.

In addition to a thousand-acre vineyard near Kagoshima, Daizo Taka also owned a vast cattle ranch in Hokkaido, a twelve-room pied-à-terre in Akasaka, a walled estate in Kamakura, those airy pink-washed villas by various seas, and an abandoned monastery near San Gimignano, straight out of *The Name of the Rose*, which he planned to turn into a winery someday. In addition to real estate, Daizo Taka liked to collect things that were beautiful and expensive: grape-colored jade, antique tea bowls, glossy mercenary women.

He had been married once, before he became wealthy. Aya was a teacher of *koto* and classical dance, and she died giving birth to their only child, Kiyohime. Daizo had never forgiven his daughter for causing the death of his beloved Aya, for that was how he saw it.

He gave Kiyohime every imaginable privilege and luxury, but he saved his affection for bar hostesses, hunting dogs, and grapevines. Kiyohime Taka—the name means "Princess of Purity"—grew up to be very pretty, exceedingly willful, and impossibly spoiled. She was noisy and mercurial by nature, given to whoops of joy and hoots of laughter. ("Most unladylike, even for a dragon-child," the servants whispered. "*Most* un-Japanese.") She was also inclined to throw a tantrum—complete with earthy multilingual curses, for she had been educated since kindergarten at international schools in Kamakura and Tokyo—any time anyone refused to bend to her will, or her whimsy.

Just after she turned sixteen, an occasion which was celebrated with a lavish all-day party at Tokyo Disneyland, paid for but not attended by Daizo Taka, Kiyohime decided that it was time to stop being a virgin. She was curious about the mysteries of what her French-Barbadian friend Eulalie Gray called "carnal congruence," and she also thought it would be a good way to hurt her father, whom she despised. He had lectured her time and again about the importance of "saving herself" for marriage: for marriage, he always implied, to a man of aristocratic lineage whose illustrious forbears would thus become Daizo's ancestors as well, by wishful extension. Daizo was terribly self-conscious about his humble origins, and he knew that while it was possible to purchase a castle and even a title in Great Britain (he had seen the ads, in the back of high-class English magazines), impressive ancestors were one thing money couldn't buy.

By the time she turned eighteen, Kiyohime had had twenty-six lovers, or co-conspirators. From each of them, on the cusp of what was often their first non-solo sexual experience, she had procured a signed statement to the effect that they were sitting "naked and tumescent" in such-and-such a love hotel (Infidelity Inn, or Chateau Desire), gazing across a blue-mirrored room at Kiyohime, who was slowly getting undressed in front of them. Here she would dictate florid descriptions of her own "ripe contours and voluptuous valleys," language inspired by the hyperthermic American romance novels she had read secretly with a flashlight, under her pale pink quilt, in preparation for those marathon afternoons.

"Why do I have to write all this weird stuff?" the chosen boy would ask between labored inhalations, for Kiyohime's partners always found the amanuensis-prelude alarming and arousing, in nearly equal parts.

"Oh, I just want to show it to Eulalie," Kiyohime would say casually, and the boy's reluctance would vanish at the thought that Eulalie—the convex cocoa-colored goddess—might read his scribbled words and decide that *she* wanted him, too, on some other decadent, rainy, oyster-colored afternoon.

Kiyohime's plan was to accumulate at least thirty of these epistles, each one written in a different trembling male hand. Then, on the inevitable day when her father brought her husband-to-be (selected without consulting her, of course) to the big house in Kamakura, she would casually toss the letters onto the immense carved-oak table in the Western-style drawing room.

"Excuse me," she would say to the prospective bridegroom and his snooty upper-class parents, "but I think you might want to take a look at these before you make your final decision."

Everything was proceeding on schedule. Kiyohime was a senior in college, the locked brass box in which she kept all her secret treasures was overflowing with shocking letters, and Daizo Taka was beginning to make noises about finding a suitable husband for his "little girl." But then something unforeseen and disastrous happened: Kiyohime fell in love.

About a mile from the Takas' estate in Kamakura, on a high wooded hill, there was a very old temple which belonged to one of the more refined and ascetic sects of Buddhism. Daizo Taka was a generous patron of this temple, although he didn't attend the services. Once a month, a couple of monks were sent to Daizo's house to pick up donations of rice, vegetables, cash, and grapes (in season). This was a coveted assignment, for the Takas' cook always prepared a big pot of sukiyaki made with corn-fed, beer-massaged Kobe beef for the monks, most of whom were ambivalent vegetarians at best and were happy to succumb to their primal craving for animal protein. During and after the sumptuous meal, the convivial Daizo would pour glass after glass of wine from his Peregrine Vineyards, named after his favorite bird of prey.

"Liquid rubies," the tipsy monks would sigh, for intoxication makes every cliché seem profound.

Later, the monks would totter dizzily home in their noisy clogs, listing forward at a sharp angle like not-so-tall ships propelled from behind by a stiff wind. "We aren't drunk," the monks would reassure each other. "No, we definitely aren't drunk. Our tongues are just relaxed, that's all."

One night two of the monks returned to the temple so inebriated from Daizo's Kagoshima wine that they never made it to their cells. They were found by a newspaper boy the next morning, asleep beside the gateless gate, reeking of beef and perspiration and sweet grapes turned to bile.

After that the abbot decided that the coveted task of collecting Daizo Taka's offerings would be permanently assigned to Anchin, who was the most serious, self-abnegating monk in the temple. Anchin was a staunch teetotaler, a sincere celibate, an unhypocritical herbivore. Unfortunately, he was also the best-looking of all the monks—tall and lithe and muscular, with luminous amber skin, limpid tea-colored eyes under thick boomerang-shaped brows, a high-bridged nose, and a startling *satori*-smile: a phosphorescent revelation of perfect teeth and cosmic joy. Kiyohime had never paid much attention to the monks who came to the house ("impotent beggars," she called them derisively, while the servants shushed her and muttered about bad karma) but when she saw Anchin for the first time she felt an uncanny sense of connection. He's the one, she thought with absolute conviction. This is the man I want, to love and be loved, in purity and passion, forever.

On Anchin's first visit, Kiyohime spied on him from behind a sliding *shoji* door. Then she sat down in her room and had an imaginary conversation with the monk, about foreign novels and Noh plays and how much she hated her father. On his second visit, she stared at him from behind a Chinese screen (wild geese in the moonlight). After he left she lay down on her futon and fantasized about holding his hand as they walked through a meadow ablaze with orange azaleas.

Finally, on Anchin's third visit, Kiyohime came out and was introduced. She had spent three hours getting ready, and was wearing her most subdued kimono (smoke-blue origami cranes on a lichen-colored ground). One of the female servants had helped to arrange her hair in a lacquered medieval pompadour, and Kiyohime fancied that she saw the monk's clear eyes widening with instantaneous attraction when she entered the drawing room. Afterward she sat in a steaming bath and recalled the delicious details of their meeting, reliving every word of conversation, every graceful gesture, every flash of eye contact. Later, when she went to bed, she tried to have an erotic fantasy about the monk, but to her surprise the best she could do was to picture them walking hand-in-hand through a field of poppies.

When Anchin arrived for his fourth visit, Kiyohime was sitting next to her father in the tea-room, dressed in her second-most-subdued kimono (pale blue moon-rabbits on a dark blue ground). In her official capacity as lady of the house, she whisked the radiant monk's tea in the slow-motion choreography she had been taught as part of her mandatory preparation for marriage. And when she saw him watching her supple alabaster wrist with unmistakable admiration, she felt happy that she had taken all those tedious lessons in *cha-no-yu*, the ritualized tea ceremony.

After Anchin left, bowing deeply from the waist as if to avoid meeting her shining eyes, Kiyohime went to her room and pretended that the monk was lying there beside her. She closed her eyes and imagined the feeling of his shy, sculpted mouth on hers. Then she pictured them undressing each other with maximum wonderment and making wild, perfect, poetic love.

Kiyohime had had crushes and cravings before, and she had never had any trouble fulfilling them. Japanese males of her age were singularly unconcerned about disease or morality, and they were perennially whipped into such a frenzy of randiness by the semipornographic comics they read and the R-rated foreign movies they sat through two or three times in a single night, that she had only to raise an eyebrow and they would follow her to the Purple Swan Chalet or Libido Lodge with heaving chests, surreptitiously pinching their forearms every block or so to make sure it wasn't just another heavy-breathing comic-book dream.

But the obsession with Anchin was different, for Kiyohime didn't merely want to seduce the monk. She wanted to marry him, and live with him forever. She wanted to watch his face grow old, she wanted to cook his rice to sticky perfection, she wanted to sit with him in a mountain hot-spring bath in winter with macaque monkeys chanting in the snowy trees, and faraway sounds of *samisen* and avalanche. She wanted to have his children, and mend his clogs, and pour his saké. And when the time came, she wanted to bury his ashes and mourn for him till the day she died. But first, she had to get him alone.

The chance came sooner than expected. One rainy day in late April, just after the last soggy cherry blossom had fluttered to the ground, Daizo Taka called his daughter from the office. Kiyohime had purposely stayed home from school because she knew that this was the day the monk would come, and she wanted to compose her mind, her face, and her costume.

"*Moshi-moshi*," her father shouted into his speakerphone, "I can't get away today. Would you please greet the monk, and give him the bags of food and rice from the storehouse, and serve him something good? *Macha*, of course, and maybe some of those cherry-blossom rice cakes from Kobayashi Confectioners. There's a fresh box in the pantry."

"I'd be glad to, Papa," Kiyohime said demurely, but her father had already hung up, for Japanese telephone etiquette does not require closing statements or long goodbyes.

The meeting went perfectly, up to a point. Anchin arrived right on time, dressed as always in a black mesh robe over a white under-kimono, while Kiyohime looked otherworldly in a not-at-all-subdued kimono of iridescent silver silk embroidered with pink and blue hydrangeas. It was too early in the year to be wearing summer flowers, but the kimono was so becoming that Kiyohime had looked in the mirror and said, in English, "The hell with seasonality!"

She performed the tea ceremony with the grace of a temple dancer, and the conversation meandered through topics as diverse as rice embargoes, fertility rites, and the Temptations of the Buddha with the ease of a stream flowing around boulders. At the end, as they were saying goodbye in the high-ceilinged entry hall, Kiyohime suddenly felt that she would die if she had to live another day without declaring her love, or without gleaning a hint of Anchin's feelings for her. She had been subtle all afternoon; now she would be bold.

"Anchin, have you ever been with a woman?" she asked. The monk looked at her gravely with his lambent hazel eyes, and then he gave a quick heart-stopping smile.

"There are many lives in any life, and many men in any man," he said solemnly. With a small sardonic bow, he slung the heavy bags over his strong shoulders and set off along the cobblestone path that meandered through the lush yet understated garden, down to the main road.

Kiyohime ran to her room and cried for hours, until she finally fell asleep in dehydrated exhaustion. She didn't feel rejected, exactly; just mystified, lovesick, and aflame with impatient appetite. In the days that followed she began to neglect her studies, and avoid her friends. The boys she met in class and at coffee shops bored her now, and she no longer cared about adding scandalous letters to her secret stash, or clumsy one-day lovers to her life list. She bought a calendar with a picture of Anchin's temple in autumn (leaves the color of crematorium flames, or roses) and she began to count the days until the monk would come again. Time had always flown by for her in a formless hedonistic rush, like an emergence of fruit bats heading for a mango grove, but now she seemed to see the shape of every second: slow-moving, oblong and gray, like sedated bacteria under a microscope.

Finally the day for Anchin's monthly visit rolled around. "If you like, I could serve tea to that boring monk again," Kiyohime said offhandedly at breakfast as she was spreading lingonberry jam on a piece of toasted white bread sliced Japanese-style, two inches thick. Kiyohime knew that her father had a new mistress in Tokyo, and she suspected that he would prefer to work late and then spend the evening at his moll's apartment. She could just picture the decor: hot-pink vinyl couches, zebra-skin throw rugs, Siamese-cat sculptures, an aquarium full of garish, neglected, overfed fish kidnapped from some faraway Micronesian atoll.

"Are you sure you wouldn't mind?" Daizo said, his face brightening.

Kiyohime made her trademark moue, carefully designed to give an impression of filial self-sacrifice. "It's the least I can do, after all you've done for me, Papa," she said piously. "You selfish, lecherous, hateful old bastard," she added in English, after the door had slid safely closed behind him.

On this day, as an experiment, Kiyohime decided to abandon the formal style of dress and try something a bit more liberated. She suspected that the monk preferred kimono to Western garb (too bad, because no male had ever been able to resist her black jersey off-the-shoulder minidress), so she assembled the sexiest kimono-costume she could think of. It was inspired by a scene in a recent samurai movie in which a young shrine maiden, sworn to virginal celibacy, succumbs to her obsessive longing for a magnificent one-eyed swordsman. The swooning maiden (played by a fifteen-year-old pop singer) had slowly let down her long straight hair, scattering pins on the *tatami* of the seedy inn where the two forbidden lovers had rendezvoused against their better judgment. Then, while the samurai watched her through the eye that wasn't rakishly hidden behind a black eyepatch, she slowly removed her scarlet *obi* and her indigo-and-white wave-patterned cotton *yukata.*

Kiyohime was able to duplicate this outfit exactly from her own vast wardrobe, and after she had tried it on and seen how fetching she looked, she decided that she had better give the servants the rest of the day off, just to be safe. (Or rather, just to be reckless.) She took a languorous bath, got dressed, brushed her glossy black hair, and tucked a crimson silk camellia behind one small, shapely ear. Then she spread out her bedding—the thick under-pad, the white cotton sheets, the cherry-blossom–colored quilt—on the tatami floor of her bedroom, ready to receive her guest. There was no question in Kiyohime's mind of Whether, only How and When, for she felt that if she didn't get the monk into bed on this day she really might die of desire.

When Anchin came to the door, Kiyohime greeted him with a graceful forehead-to-the-mat bow, then raised her head and let her long, loose hair fall around her like spring rain. She knew how charming this gesture looked, for she had practiced it several times in front of her full-length mirror.

To her chagrin, the monk simply bowed and said, "It's been a while" in his deep, rough voice. Kiyohime wondered whether he might be a bit dense, or naïve. Surely any ordinary man would have recognized the significance of the casual bath-house costume and the unbound hair. But he *is* a monk, Kiyohime reminded herself. That was part of what made him so exciting, and so irresistible.

"I'm afraid we've run out of tea," she said disingenuously, for there was enough tea in the pantry to give every monk in Japan insomnia for a week.

"Water will be fine," the monk said agreeably.

"Unfortunately the well is contaminated, and we don't have any bottled water," Kiyohime said, barely keeping a straight face at the enormity of that fib. "So I'm afraid we'll have to drink, um, grape juice."

"Anything is fine," said the monk, placing his palms together under his chin.

Kiyohime's father had once told her that monks were theoretically not allowed to drink alcohol but that the rule was relaxed when they went out to collect donations. (This was just after the two rowdy young monks had gone staggering off into the night singing "My Way" in phonetic English between slugs from a bottle of sparkling burgundy.) Even so, she decided it would be safer to pretend to be serving the virtuous Anchin a nonalcoholic beverage.

"One bottle of grape juice, coming up," she said.

After three glasses of what was in fact a plummy red Chardonnay, Kiyohime was feeling dizzy, languid, and uninhibited. Anchin had matched her sip for sip, but he still sat in meditation position with straight spine, relaxed shoulders, and feet on the opposite thighs, nodding politely and making wry, allegorical remarks. Kiyohime took one more gulp and decided she couldn't wait another minute. "Look," she said, "I can't bear this ambiguity any longer. Do you find me attractive, or not?"

"The hummingbird may admire the cactus flower," said the monk, "but it dares not drink the nectar."

"Oh, please, spare me the metaphors!" Kiyohime said. She seemed suddenly to have no control over what she said or did. The next thing she knew, she had crawled around to the monk's side of the table and was sitting back on her knees, not entirely steadily, staring at his amazing, luminescent face.

"I want you," she said, gazing into his impassive golden eyes. "And not as a plaything, or a novelty. I want you now, but I also want you tomorrow, and the next day. I want us to spend our lives together, forever." She took a deep breath. "I've never said this before, to anyone," she began, and even as the monk was saying "Please, don't," with genuine anguish in his voice, she said "No, I can't help it, I'm afraid I just really, really love you a lot."

Anchin scrambled to his feet, upsetting his wine glass. The grape-colored liquid formed a vaguely heart-shaped pool on the tatami, but neither of them noticed.

"I'd better go," Anchin said. "Please forgive me." He seemed distressed, and distracted. His normally serene, contemplative exterior was in disarray—as was Kiyohime's yukata, which had fallen open to reveal a plush parabola of breast.

No man alive could resist *this*, she thought, and she pulled her scarlet sash, like a rip cord. The yukata dropped away and she stood there, naked and candescent, every schoolboy's midnight dream incarnate. But the monk just kept edging toward the door, his eyes filled with panic.

"Please stay," Kiyohime said urgently. "You *have* to stay."

Anchin replied with equal fervor, "Please, if you really do care about me, you'll let me go and never see me again." Then he flung himself through the door, leaving behind the bags of rice, barley, and turnips, and the fat envelope full of ten-thousand–yen bills. He even forgot to put on his wooden clogs.

Kiyohime stood in the entry, naked, with wild, electrified hair like some demented ghost from *Tales of Moonlight and Rain*. Anchin was running as fast as he could in his bare feet, down the long path to the great wooden gate, while Kiyohime stared forlornly after him, holding his clogs in her hand and wishing she could somehow reconstitute the man from his footgear.

She sat down on the polished wood of the entry hall, feeling sad, and heavy-hearted, and very, very dizzy. Suddenly her sadness turned to rage, and she felt as if her body were being torn apart, heated to the point of molten oblivion and then annealed into some violent alien form.

When she looked down at herself she saw not the expected moon-colored landscape of fertile female flesh but rather a seething mosaic of shimmering red and black and golden scales, laid thickly over the pulsating muscles and sinews of a gigantic dragon with obsidian eyes, razor claws, and breath like a blowtorch, fast and fatal. The shock of seeing herself literally transformed into her own emotions was too much; the young woman named Kiyohime Taka lost consciousness and the deranged dragon took over.

The dragon knew the monk not as a person or an object of love, but as a quarry to be pursued and seized and punished, although for what crime or transgression, it wasn't sure. The furious beast burst through the door, breaking the frame with its huge torso, and flowed down the garden path and out onto the broad tree-lined street that led to the temple. The dragon had four stubby legs, but it could move like a snake too, on its swollen scaly belly, and that was how it was moving now.

When the temple came into sight the dragon could see the monk Anchin ahead, running up the long flight of stone steps and catapulting through the door beside the gate, and it increased its pace. Upon reaching the gate the dragon found that its body was too large to fit through the opening, so it simply swarmed over the wall. There was no one in sight, and something about the manicured tranquility of the temple grounds calmed the dragon down for a moment, but then its unreasoning stalker's blood began to roil again and it went looking for the monk.

Behind the kitchen there were a number of large cast-iron pails, like double-size garbage cans, where the monks stored their rice and barley and millet. The dragon sniffed around these cans, for it had caught the scent of the monk. The pheromonal aroma was strongest at the last can, and the dragon nudged it gently with its pyrotechnic snout. Cautiously, thinking a fellow monk might have come to rescue him, Anchin lifted the lid and peered out.

"You!" cried the dragon. The word came out as an inarticulate roar, and that single blast of flaming breath burned away all the shapely flesh from the monk's handsome face. He screamed, a horrible tongueless shriek, and collapsed back into the can still alive from the neck down. The enraged dragon wrapped its powerful body around the iron pail and squeezed as hard as it could. One of the young apprentice monks, who was watching in horror from a tower window, said later that the metal became so hot that it glowed reddish-orange, like the setting sun in winter, and he could actually hear the sounds of sizzling flesh, melting marrow, and de-ossifying bone. And then the dragon uncoiled its great body from around the still-glowing pail and raced away, over the temple walls and down to the river. It leaped into the water with a great hiss and billow of steam, and that was the last anyone ever saw of it.

When Daizo Taka came home around ten o'clock that night, after an evening of sex and *shabu-shabu* with his frisky young mistress, he found his daughter sitting in a huge puddle of water in the middle of the parlor, dressed in a rumpled wave-patterned yukata with a sodden scarlet sash and the lapels overlapped the wrong way, left over right, in the style reserved for corpses. In one hand she held a pair of sewing scissors, in the other a bloody straight razor. Her lovely long hair lay on the floor in soggy sheaves like hastily-harvested rice fronds, and there were livid nicks all over her shocking naked scalp.

"Thank you for taking care of me for all these years," Kiyohime said, bowing so low that her scabby hairless head touched the tatami. Daizo was startled, for that was the formulaic speech made by brides as they prepared to leave the family home for the last time. Kiyohime looked up at her father, and he saw that her eyes were red-rimmed and dull. She seemed dazed and vacant, like a dreamer who is still half-asleep.

"With your kind permission," Kiyohime said, using curiously archaic language, "I would like to renounce this illusory world of temptation and disappointment, and become a nun."

Daizo was surprised, but not entirely displeased. Thanks to the servants' gossip, he had an inkling of the nature of his daughter's social life, and he had already given up hope of marrying her off to some prestigious descendant of a feudal lord or of the prehistoric gods. He had learned just a few hours earlier that Michi, his mistress, was pregnant with a male child—so he would have an heir all: after all: a fine son who might someday marry a docile, well-mannered girl of impeccable pedigree.

"My daughter is a nun," Daizo murmured, trying out the words on his tongue. It had a good sound, a classy sound, and it could only help what some of the less friendly newspapers—the same ones who had dubbed him The Grape Gatsby—insisted on calling his "moral credibility gap."

"Go with my blessing," Daizo said munificently. "But first, tell me one thing: why did you have to shave your eyebrows off, too?"

Kiyohime put her hand up to her face and ran her fingertips over her singed eyebrows, like a sightless person reading the embossed numbers on an elevator panel. Suddenly it all came back to her—the love, the flames, the burning flesh—and she began to weep, softly at first, and then more loudly, until she was shrieking uncontrollably in sorrow and horror.

Those dream-screams woke Kiyohime up, and after a few minutes of dreadful, dry-mouthed disorientation she realized that her dragon rampage had been a nightmare. A horrible mutant nightmare, she thought, obviously midwifed by her recent reading of the legend of Dojoji, in which something very similar happens to a girl and a monk.

"Omigod," Kiyohime said in English. She put her hands up to her face, and found her nose still small and human, her eyebrows intact. Her hair was falling around her like spring rain, not lying on the floor in soggy sheaves. And her father was still out, cavorting shamelessly with his airhead mistress.

It was odd, Kiyohime thought, how she had been able to read Daizo's mind in the dream. (He had seemed almost human somehow—certain proof that the entire episode was fiction.) She wondered if she might be developing some clairvoyant powers, like her friend Eulalie, who had an uncanny knack for predicting the winners at Wimbledon, or the next song the DJ was going to play at their favorite disco in Roppongi.

Just then the phone began to ring. Kiyohime waited for one of the servants to pick it up, but after the second shrill ring she realized that she had given them the night off so she could be alone with Anchin. Ah, she thought melodramatically, the optimism of youth! She felt curiously philosophical about what had happened; it seemed more interesting than heartbreaking, and she wondered whether the dream had had some sort of cathartic or curative effect.

The nearest telephone was in Daizo's study, a wood-paneled cavern decorated with photos of his houses, his dogs, his grapes. There was even one small picture of his daughter—wearing black mouse-ears and flashing the V-sign—taken at her sixteenth birthday party, the one he had been too busy to attend. As she walked into the study, Kiyohime decided to try out her newfound powers of prediction.

"It's Anchin, calling to say he forgives me and still wants to be friends," she said aloud, but she wasn't sure whether that was a genuine hunch or merely wishful thinking. She picked up the phone and waited, as they do in Japan, for the other person to speak first.

"Moshi-moshi," said a young female voice. "*Kochira wa Gureii desu ga, Kiyohime-san irrasharanai desho ka?*"

"Eulalie!" Kiyohime exclaimed joyfully. "I had a feeling it was you."

"Hello, DoDo Darling!" Eulalie said, switching to exuberant Bajan-flavored English. "Listen, this is so exciting, I can hardly breathe. I met these two fantastic guys today, at Tower Records in Shibuya. They're roadies for Porlock, can you believe it, and they're here for the sold-out concerts this weekend, the ones we couldn't get tickets for. They're plenty fresh and nice, as we say back home, and after this summer they're going to be starting grad school, somewhere lah-di-dah like Princeton or Yale, I forget which. Their hair is longer than mine, but they aren't like the scruffy roadies you see in movies, with nasty nose rings and bad tattoos. I mean of course they have tattoos, but theirs are really gorgeous, they got them in Tahiti. And anyway, everyone has a tattoo these days, even my mother's nerdy accountant. I mean, even *me*. And you're going to get one too, right? You promised, as soon as you decide on the design. Actually, I wouldn't mind getting another one, maybe a Tantric serpent climbing up my calf. Anyway, not only did these incredibly cool guys give me tickets to the concert tomorrow—Saturday, right?—but I've got backstage passes too, for both of us. And it gets better, because guess what? I'm meeting them in Roppongi tonight at ten, and we're going to go to Hell and dance and eat all night. Their treat, of course. And not only that, it's practically guaranteed that some of the guys from the band will show up later, maybe even John Donne Dillinger himself!"

Hell was the most popular disco in Japan, if not in all of Asia. It had a selective admission policy (that is to say, snobbish and superficial) but Eulalie and Kiyohime were on air-kissing terms with the European doorman, and he always opened the velvet rope for them. "Right this way, my beauties," he'd say. "If only I were ten years younger, I'd go in there right now and dance with you myself."

The girls never had to pay a cover charge, but the problem was that everything on the menu was so expensive that, once in, they would have to subsist on a couple of bottles of Evian water, at five hundred yen a pop. Sometimes they remembered to pack a few snacks in their bags—Men's Pocky-brand pretzels dipped in dark chocolate, or the energizing honeydew-flavored candies called Melon Collies—but even then they would end up gazing longingly as waiters wafted by with two-thousand–yen artichoke-and-Asiago pizzas the size of a tea-saucer, or huge heaps of maddeningly aromatic garlic-marinated shrimp that would have cost them two weeks' allowance, combined.

"Kiyo? Darling? Are you there? Say something! Are you in shock from this incredibly exciting news? Blink twice for 'yes'!"

Kiyohime had been listening to Eulalie's euphoric monologue with a strange feeling of detachment. She should have been thrilled—after all, Porlock was one of her favorite groups, and as recently as her sophomore year in college she had made a collage, for art class, composed entirely of photos of John Donne Dillinger, the group's tall, poetic, copper-haired lead singer and chief songwriter. (Sample lyric: "You've really started to grow on me/Like mold on a baseball glove/It started out as lichen, but now/The spores are sown for love.")

But Kiyohime was still a little dizzy from the wine, and dazed from the dream. And while her consuming passion for Anchin seemed to have evaporated, or gone up in flames, she didn't feel ready to jump right back into the whirl of discos and late nights and "safe" (but really reckless) sex with men she hardly knew, and didn't love at all.

Even after Eulalie's hard-sell of the evening ahead, Kiyohime still just wanted to crawl into bed and think about the marvelous complexity of life, and love, and the dreaming mind. Surely there must be some reason why she had had that amazing dragon vision. Was there a lesson to be learned, some profound insight about controlling your passions, and thinking about the other person's feelings? Or was it something simpler, and more obvious?

"Sorry, Eulie," she said at last. "It's just that I drank too much wine, and I'm feeling kind of sleepy and weird, so I don't think I would be very good company tonight. The concert tomorrow sounds great, though."

Ominous silence on the other end of the line. Then: "You know that huge, enormous, unspeakably gigantic favor you owe me?"

"Oh, Eulie, you wouldn't."

"Sure I would. You owe me big-time, darling, and I'm calling it in tonight. It's for your own good, you know—we're going to have the most fantastic time in the history of the world, and I refuse to let you throw this chance away. And think of the Grape Gatsby's face when you tell him you're dating a long-haired tattooed American roadie for a heavy metal rock group. Can you *imagine*? And who knows, you might fall in love with one of them and decide to get married. Wouldn't Daizo just absolutely die?"

That was the clincher. Kiyohime sighed, "Okay, you win. See you in Hell!" She ran to her room, took a quick shower, then jumped into her disco clothes—the black jersey off-the-shoulder minidress, of course. Hot pink L.A. Gear aerobic shoes to wear on the train, strappy high-heeled red-and-black sandals for dancing. She tossed the latter into her big black mesh Lancôme bag along with everything else she might need for a long rock-and-roll night: money, mouthwash, sleepshirt, raincoat, extra panties, Walkman, mix tapes, an assortment of condoms, and something sensational to read on the train: her diary.

She left a note for Daizo—"Gone to slumber party at Eulalie's, back tomorrow"—and gave him Eulalie's cell phone number. Then she set out for the Kita-Kamakura train station.

It was one of those sweet balmy June nights, the air faintly fragrant from temple gardens and the invisible but not-so-far-off sea. Kiyohime didn't take the most direct route to the station, because there was something she needed to resolve. The destructive-dragon dream still felt so real that she was afraid that maybe, on some weird metaphysical or astral plane, it might really have happened. She needed to know that Anchin was safe and alive and unsinged, before she could go off and enjoy her hedonistic heavy-metal fantasy come true.

The antique wooden gate to the temple where Anchin lived was closed for the night, but there was a low, child-sized door next to it for late returnees. Kiyohime ducked through the elf-door, wishing it didn't squeak quite so loudly. She had never been inside the temple, which covered nearly an acre of ground, but she seemed to have some memory or psychic notion of the layout. She found the metal storage-pails, just as she had dreamed them. They were cool to the touch, and when she gingerly opened them up, one at a time, she saw nothing inside except grain. No incinerated bones, no steaming flesh, no gilded teeth.

That was all the proof she needed. Feeling absurdly relieved, Kiyohime was starting across the courtyard toward the gate when she heard a human voice reciting mystic syllables. It was the Hannya Shingyo, the Heart of Great Wisdom Sutra, which Kiyohime's mother used to chant every morning in front of the family altar. Kiyohime recognized the words first, then the voice, and she knew she had to go and see him, one last time.

Anchin was saying his Buddhist prayers in his sleeping quarters, a small round-windowed outbuilding beyond the communal kitchen. (As the most senior of all the monks, he had long since graduated from the austere dormitory where the younger monks slept lined up on straw mats like not-quite-enlightened sardines.) When Kiyohime crept closer, she could see his form outlined through the open window: the strong upper body, the graceful skull beneath the skin. Thank God that skin was still in place. Even though it had just been a dream she felt she had somehow had a close call with the dark forces of life, and she was glad that she—and Anchin—had survived.

As she looked at the monk's solemn chanting profile she didn't feel the old rush of selfish schoolgirl longing, the urge for instant gratification. Rather, she felt a deep human tenderness, and a sincere hope that he would find happiness and completion as he trod his chosen path.

"I'll always carry a torch for you," she whispered as she turned away, but she knew it probably wasn't true.

Kiyohime's chosen path led down the hill to Kita-Kamakura Station, and from there into Tokyo, to Roppongi, to all the exotic promise of a night in Hell with a bunch of bright, creative, good-looking American rockers. The dream was still with her, sliding through her veins like molten lava on the move, and as she pictured the dragon she had been, if only in her mind, it suddenly hit her.

A tattoo! Of course! That was the message the dream was trying to send her. She had been born in the year of the dragon, and she was meant to have a dragon tattoo. She knew just where she wanted it, too: on that pale private delta of skin at the base of her spine, where it would only be seen by lovers, doctors, massage therapists, and servants. And the tattletale servants, of course, would rush off to report the scandalous sighting to Daizo Taka, who would go totally berserk and ricochet off the walls.

That was a truly delicious prospect: the final stake through the heart of her respectable marriage prospects. Yet even as she was standing on the geranium-bedecked station platform reveling in that wicked fantasy, even after she had boarded the sleek platinum train that would carry her to "the most fantastic time in the history of the world," Kiyohime still wasn't in her usual ebullient night-life mood. On the contrary, she felt curiously calm, reflective, and wise.

Maybe this is a sneak preview of maturity, she thought. That reminded her of something she had read somewhere, and transcribed into her diary:

"Growing up is a dance, just like the mambo or the cha-cha: one step forward, two steps back. The trick is to enjoy the lively process, in both directions." That made sense. The disappointment with Anchin was a step back, but she had grown through the experience, and she felt like a full-fledged woman now. Or at least a full-fledged girl.

And then she remembered something else she had read in a book, or heard in a movie: "The night is young, and so am I." Suddenly, as abruptly as she had seemed to turn into the flesh-melting dragon, Kiyohime was restored to her giddy hedonistic self. She put on her Walkman, pressed Play, and began to sing along with her favorite oldies anthem: *The time to hesitate is through/No time to wallow in the mire/Try now we can only lose/And our love become a funeral pyre/Come on baby, light my fire …*

"Oh perfect, 'Try to set the night on fire'!" Kiyohime said out loud, as the dark urban villages rushed by outside the train window. Sometimes life was just too sweetly symmetrical for words.

AN ITCHING IN THE HEART

Faithful to this feeble magic, he would invent,
so that they might not happen, the most atrocious particulars.

—JORGE LUIS BORGES
Ficciones

The time was late afternoon, the place was a rococo coffee house near the Ginza, the light was the color of lemon marmalade. "The Japanese have been characterized for centuries as an exquisitely polite race," the living legend was saying in her husky yet musical voice, "but I hadn't been in this country for more than a week before I concluded that much of their so-called courtesy is strictly formulaic."

Spyro Suginami sat in silence, listening. That was what the legend paid him for, among other things: to listen and nod and, he suspected, to look beautiful in the gilded light of afternoon, the Greco-Japanese planes of his face creating a lean primeval geometry evocative of poetic warriors and licentious gods. Spyro was talkative by nature, even garrulous at times, but now he was concentrating on keeping his mouth shut. He always blamed his attacks of compulsive candor on his Greek blood, just as he rationalized all his social inversions and reticences with, "Hey, what can I tell you? I'm part-Japanese." Sometimes he wished he were pureblooded something—Japanese, Greek, Nigerian, Scottish—and other times he thought that all blood was pure blood. But mostly he just wished for a more varied pool of ancestors; that is, for a wider selection of ethnic stereotypes to blame for his own gaffes and eccentricities.

Like Lafcadio Hearn, Spyro Suginami had a Greek mother, but his father was Japanese. At elementary school in California the crueler children used to call him Zorba the Jap; in junior high, before he began to grow and started lifting weights like a maniac, they called him Zorba the Geek, which he considered an improvement, as racist epithets went. Now he was tall and muscular and shockingly good-looking, and everyone called him Spyro, or Suginami-san.

Spyro grew up in Redwood City, went to college in Palo Alto, and sowed his wild rice in San Francisco. (That was his own little ethnic joke, for he had early learned the value of self-mockery and the power of the preemptive strike.) He thought of himself as a casual California guy, and although he spoke Japanese fairly well he felt as foreign in Tokyo as he might have felt on Mars. More so, perhaps, for he had a curious affinity for those livid Martian seas, that merciless sand, those promiscuous moons. After working for several years as a copy editor on a travel magazine in New York, Spyro took a trip to Japan, to rub noses (as he put it, deliberately mixing his cultural metaphors) with his heritage.

One day on the subway he struck up a conversation with a glamorous woman in her mid-sixties who turned out to be from Atherton. "Why, we're practically next-door neighbors!" she exclaimed, and Spyro smiled politely and thought, Yeah, nothing between us but two miles and a hundred million dollars. The woman invited Spyro to an embassy party, and he went, out of curiosity. His favorite writer was there, and after Spyro had helped her scrape up a lox-and-caper canapé which she had dropped on the Aubusson carpet, she asked him to be her editorial assistant.

It was an interesting, lucrative, ambiguous job. He had enjoyed it enormously at first, but one afternoon a month earlier he had suddenly seen his employer as a desirable woman (he blamed his samurai blood, his Aegean hormones, his reckless soul). Since then his life had been a torturous whirl of insomnia, vertigo, throttled declarations, and nervous hiccups.

"It's like having hives on my heart," Spyro told his Swedish-Japanese friend Gunnar Naganuma, who worked as a translator at Kyodo News Service.

"Maybe you should drink some calamine lotion," said the laconic Gunnar.

The living legend—that was what the English-language newspapers called her, though sobriquets always made her cringe—was named Ursula McBride, but she wrote under the non de plume Murasaki McBride. She had lived in Japan for thirty years, since her twentieth birthday. Her first book, *The Parboiled Heart*, a boldly erotic ode to hot-spring inns, was published when she was twenty-five (the same age Spyro Suginami was now), and she had published a book a year ever since. They had nearly all been bestsellers in Japan, and had found a respectable audience in the U.S. among Japanophiles, Japanophobes, and general-interest readers who enjoyed her intimate revelations and irreverent observations about Japanese culture.

She wrote fiction, too, strange stories of doomed love, cruel fate, and paranormal coincidence, like the imaginary novels in *The Trick of It.* Murasaki McBride's heroines drank dry champagne, ate dark-chocolate truffles, and wandered through fields of lupines the color of gumdrops, while her heroes wore tuxedoes to breakfast and kilts to bed. It was light, loopy fantasy, but because the author's nonfiction books were so well respected, critics hailed the novels as allegories and parables and metaphoric musings on the carnival absurdities of life. All this successful work had made Murasaki McBride reasonably rich, and relatively happy. She had never married, but even the savage Japanese press acknowledged that she was far too attractive to be labeled an Old Miss, the quaint Japanization of the Occidental pejorative "old maid."

Spyro had heard a scurrilous rumor, via the foreign-community gossip mill, that Murasaki McBride was something of a man-izer: a serial seductress with a short romantic attention span who "used men for her pleasure," then tossed them aside the minute they began to bore her. But aside from occasional letters in masculine handwriting marked *Personal, Private, and Confidential*, and two or three huge, costly bouquets of tropical flowers delivered by Arisugawa Floral Designs, Spyro had never seen any evidence of his hard-working employer's man-devouring side. Still, it was an exciting thought.

Murasaki McBride took a sip of tea (Earl Grey, two sugars, half a pitcher of cream) and continued her monologue. "When I first arrived in Tokyo, a million years ago, I was expecting to be dazzled by the famous Japanese *politesse.* So I was more than a little surprised when people I barely knew started dropping in on me unannounced at all hours of the night—just as I was sitting down to dinner, or getting ready to take a bath, or even climbing into bed. Not that Americans don't do the same thing, of course, but somehow one expects more sensitivity from the Japanese. And they don't just reserve that sort of behavior for strange foreigners, either. I've heard a number of stories of philandering Japanese husbands who suddenly turn up as if nothing had happened, after a silent absence of ten or twenty years. Not a single phone call, not one lousy postcard. Just '*Tadaima,* I'm home! Is the bath water hot?'"

"There's something I have to tell you," Spyro said. He wanted to say *I think I love you, I know I want you, I've never been so attracted to anyone in my life. This isn't what I would have planned, at all; I always pictured myself with a tall young blonde, a cross between a Valkyrie and a fashion mannequin, but now all my fantasies focus on you and me. I see us in a wind-swept room in an old hotel on some whitewashed Greek island—you know, Mykonos,* The Magus, *azure skies and ouzo oceans—stuck together like a two-headed one-souled beast, a heavy-breathing hydra of part-Hellenic passion. (Oops, sorry, I know how you hate alliteration and hyperbole. You call them counterfeit poetry, but what can I say? I'm Greek, I'm Japanese, I'm myself, and I like lavish excess and the lush momentum of echoed sounds.) And you don't need to worry about the age difference, or the future, either. After this year I'll always be less than half your age, and I promise to take care of you in your dotage, although I suspect you'll probably outlive me, or wear me out.*

But of course he couldn't say any of those outrageously inappropriate things, so what he said was this: "Actually, you know your comment just now about philandering Japanese husbands who show up out of the blue? That reminds me of a ghost story my father once told me. The story wasn't original—I think my dad probably read it in some musty old book—but I suspect he added a few touches of his own." Spyro paused deferentially. He had never told Murasaki McBride a story before, and he wondered if he might be overstepping his job description.

"I love a good story," said Murasaki McBride with a wave of her hand, the ringless long-fingered hand that Spyro had been fantasizing about every night for a month. He kept imagining that talented, prolific hand fumbling with his shirt buttons, speed-reading the serpentine Braille of his zipper, burrowing in his front pants-pocket like a marsupial looking for mice. Oh, shit, he thought. Now it has to be *good?* Spyro took a deep breath, closed his eyes, and pictured a street of old wooden houses under a starless treacle sky.

Once upon a time (Spyro began, for he knew Murasaki McBride liked the classical approach) there was a man named Rokunosuke Tanto. He was a gambler, a womanizer, and a drinker of whiskey. He always had some reckless entrepreneurial scheme in the works, and he always had at least one mistress. Bar hostesses, masseuses, florists, greengrocers' assistants, the white-gloved girls who bow to customers at the top and bottom of department-store escalators; he would take them out for a cheap bowl of curry-rice, and they would take him back to their shabby working-girl rooms, with the Hello

Kitty towels and the pastel lingerie hanging from the clothesline like strange hybrid tulips. These young women were looking for a little adventure before settling down to a boring marriage, and they didn't worry about virtue or reputation because they knew there were surgeons in Tokyo who would restore their maidenheads to a virginal state before the ceremony, for a fee of twenty thousand yen. They liked Rokunosuke because he was wiry and self-confident; they liked him because he spent money like water; and they liked him most of all because he had a wife.

Rokunosuke's wife was named Kazue. She wasn't a classical Japanese beauty—her forehead was too aggressive, her chin too unassuming—but she had the most gorgeous long, thick, straight, shiny blackberry-colored hair Rokunosuke had ever seen. He had married Kazue for her hair (she was a maid at a hot-spring inn at the time, he a traveling salesman who made his real money by cheating at cards), while she had married him to get away from the dirty dishes and saké-soaked robes and adultery-stained sheets, all the sordid detritus of human appetites. But an odd thing happened after the wedding: Kazue and Rokunosuke fell in love. This unexpected idyll lasted for perhaps five years, and then Rokunosuke began to stay out later and later until finally he stopped coming home at all.

He's playing mah-jongg, Kazue told herself. He's visiting his mother in the country. He's working late, he's drunk in the gutter, he's passed out on the train platform with his head in a pool of caramel-colored vomit. These reassuring fantasies would help her to make it through the weeks, one night at a time, but of course she knew all along that he was in some lurid love hotel or tacky little barmaid's room, making tipsy staccato love by reflected-neon light, with the Star of David he wore on a gold chain around his neck brushing against the other woman's mouth the way it used to brush against hers. ("I just like the shape," Rokunosuke had said when Kazue asked why he had chosen that particular ornament. "Stars always give me hope.") In Japan, male adultery has always been a fact of life, if not a sacrament, and Kazue never dreamed of asking for a divorce. She kept busy with the little house and the miniature garden and her freelance work as a kimono seamstress, and she prayed that someday her beloved Rokunosuke would tire of his giggling henna-haired mistresses and come back to spend his old age with her.

One night Kazue was sitting at her dressing table, brushing her glorious hair, when she heard the front door slide open. "Tadaima," said her husband's voice. "I'm home." Kazue rushed to greet him. She didn't ask where he had been for the past two weeks, or why he hadn't bothered to call to let her know he was alive. She just said, "Welcome home, dear. Would you like a bath, or perhaps a bowl of *ochazuke*?"

Rokunosuke stood awkwardly in the entry, and as Kazue watched his strong shoulders twitching nervously inside his apple-green sports jacket, she was reminded of abandoned puppies trying to escape from a paper bag. She had found several such bags, discarded on the grounds of a nearby temple. The monks were too busy seeking enlightenment to be bothered with unwanted animals, and Kazue's landlord forbade pets, so she always took the dogs to the animal shelter, then returned to the temple to pray for their tiny souls. "Actually," Rokunosuke said after a moment of excruciating silence, "I just came by to get some things. But maybe I will take a quick bath, as long as I'm here."

And so while Kazue packed her husband's clothes and papers into two heavy striped-cardboard suitcases, being careful to fold the shirts the way he liked them (sleeves inside, collars buttoned) and trying not to splash tears on his neatly ironed white handkerchiefs, Rokunosuke lolled in a hot bath, drinking warm cheap saké straight from the bottle. He thought about Rumi, the Ikebukuro bar hostess who was waiting for him outside in her snazzy red Mustang. He pictured her pale peony-breasts, her enchantingly crooked teeth, and her incredibly full lips, which always reminded him of the inflated polyps on branches of kelp. When he and Rumi first met, Rokunosuke used to bite her lips till the blood flowed, half-expecting to hear a percussive pop as the air rushed out, like seaweed crushed under a fisherman's boot. "You're a wonderful kisser," she would say afterwards, discreetly sucking on her injured mouth, and her throat would undulate gently as she swallowed a pungent mouthful of her own blood.

Rumi had just inherited a ranch near Sapporo, and she and Rokunosuke were going there to raise cattle and drill for oil and prospect for gold. (No gold or oil had ever been discovered in the area, but Rokunosuke couldn't look at a patch of vacant land without thinking of it as a possible source of precious metals, or Sweet Light Crude.) He stared down at his small, flaccid penis, floating in the water like an off-grade turnip, and he thought: That silly-looking little thing has ruled my life since I was sixteen. And then he started thinking about Rumi again, with her schoolgirl face and her courtesan's tongue, and he decided that it hadn't been such a bad way to live a life, after all.

Back in the entry hall, there was another awkward silence. Kazue knelt on the landing, while Rokunosuke stood with a suitcase in each hand. "I don't know when I'll be back," he said. "I don't even know *if* I'll be back."

"I'll wait for you forever," Kazue said, staring at the floor. "No matter what happens, I will always be your wife." She touched her forehead to the mat so that Rokunosuke wouldn't see her tears, and when she raised her head he was gone. He had left the sliding door open, and she heard the sound of a car door slamming, giddy female laughter through an open window, the confident throb of a V-8 engine, the squeal of a tire set free.

Kazue put on her wooden clogs and walked out into the immaculate garden. She looked up through the branches of her favorite maple tree at the cloudy coffee-colored sky with its few low-wattage sparks of light, and she remembered what Rokunosuke had said: *Stars always give me hope.*

"Intermission," Spyro said, pantomiming a parched throat. He took a sip of his tea (English Breakfast with lemon, no sugar), found it tepid and tasteless, and beckoned to a waiter for a fresh pot. They were sitting on the top floor of La Traviata, a famous coffee house on a back street of the Ginza. It was housed in a free-standing stone building, covered with vines like the old house in *Madeleine*. The interior was a labyrinth of polished dark wood, spiral staircases, burgundy velvet banquettes and beveled windows, giant prisms that cast dismembered rainbow stripes on tables, faces, silver teapots. For many years the musical playlist at La Traviata had been exclusively operatic, but the place was under new management, and a placard in the front window proclaimed: ALL BAROQUE, ONLY BAROQUE, BAROQUE FOREVER! When Spyro began his story the music in the background had been Handel's Suite No. 2 in D. There had been a brief, exuberant C-minor tinkle of Corelli in the middle, and now the stone walls resounded with the Concerto in D for trumpet, strings, and harpsichord, by Telemann.

Murasaki McBride was looking directly at him. The trajectory of light was lower now and her face was in partial shadow, but Spyro could see that she was smiling. Her face had a soft, ripe look and her mouth was curved in a beatific half-smile, and he gulped at the sudden dizzying thought that she might, perhaps …

No, he told himself sternly, she's probably just enjoying the story. Just then Murasaki McBride spoke. "I'm really enjoying your story," she said dreamily, and Spyro sighed.

Outside on the street, the shapely willow trees that punctuated the pavement bent (but didn't break) in the early-autumn wind. People with breeze-ruffled hair jostled for position on the narrow sidewalks: salarymen in sober blue suits, schoolgirls in middy blouses, delivery boys with white caps and tall clogs, balancing a stack of bowls of hot noodles or sushi with one hand while steering a bicycle with the other. White-gloved chauffeurs polished Infinitis and Nissans and listened to the prime-time sumo matches on bright yellow Walkmans while they waited for their bosses to emerge from meetings with other tycoons, or from trysts with their flashy mistresses. Somewhere far away an optimistic vendor of roasted sweet potatoes (for it really was too early to be peddling that winter snack) called "*Yakiiiiiimo*" as he pulled his steaming barrow through the streets, hoping that someone with a slow metabolism or a craving for a quick bite of nostalgia would flag him down. A man in a tuxedo climbed out of a double-parked Audi 5000 and strutted toward a small restaurant which he obviously owned, holding in each hand an amber jar of Creap, the nondairy creamer whose name has afforded Westerners so much merriment.

"Creap in both hands," Murasaki McBride muttered as she looked down at this curious tableau. Spyro recognized the variation on the metaphorical Japanese phrase "flowers in both hands," and he smiled complicitly before resuming his reverie.

He was thinking about the moment when he had first realized that he was in love with his legendary boss. He had come to work one day at ten A.M., as he always did, expecting to find Murasaki McBride sitting at her computer dressed in the prim, voluminous retro–Mother Goose style she favored for working at home: long ruffled skirts, high-necked blouses, *faux* ivory brooches, hand-woven shawls. But she was nowhere in sight, and he walked through the big airy Japanese-style rooms, treading silently on the *tatami* like a cat, or a ninja, and wondering if something might be wrong.

"Uh, Ursula?" he called. She had insisted that he call her by her real first name, and he tried to comply, but as he confided to Gunnar Naganuma, it felt a bit like being asked to call Queen Elizabeth "Betty Lou."

"In here," Murasaki McBride called in a strangely subdued voice. Spyro looked through the door into her Western-style bedroom: all blue and white, Balinese batiks and eyelet lace, with polished-mahogany antiques. The "sexy, eccentric authoress," as one Japanese tabloid magazine insisted on calling her, was still in bed, with her great cloud of hair (auburn, with a narrow stripe of silver at each temple) hanging down around her shoulders. She was wearing an ivory satin bedjacket over a matching nightgown, her bronze-rimmed reading glasses were halfway down her nose, and she was snuffling.

"Do you have a cold or something?" Spyro asked, lurking shyly in the open door.

"Come in, sit down," Murasaki McBride said, making a fluid hula-like gesture with her right hand. Spyro sidled in and sat in an ikat-upholstered rocking chair.

"Shall I make you some tea?" he asked nervously, for he had never been in his employer's bedroom before. There was a housekeeper—an angular, frowning Frenchwoman named Françoise who dressed entirely in rusty un-chic black, like the repressed abbess of some vaguely kinky convent—but Spyro sometimes performed a few small domestic duties. He didn't mind at all; his salary and benefits were so generous that he would have happily swept the chimney, or picked fleas off Doku and Fungus, the two mushroom-colored cats.

"No, thanks," said Murasaki McBride, "I'll be getting up in a minute." She blew her nose again and gestured at the thick book that was lying beside her on the bed.

"*A Place of Greater Safety*," Spyro read out loud. He hadn't heard of the book, but he recalled seeing the author's by-line in one of the curmudgeonly, opinionated British magazines his employer subscribed to.

"I was reading all night," said Murasaki McBride. "I just finished a moment ago."

"Oh, was it sad?" Spyro asked, suddenly making the connection between the tears and the book.

"Terribly sad. Tragic, in fact," Murasaki McBride said. "It's about the French Revolution."

"Oh," said Spyro. He knew nothing about the French Revolution, except some vague cartoonish phrases: "Let them eat *brioche*" and "Off with their heads."

"All those lively minds," said Murasaki McBride, half to herself. "All that lovely wit, all those mothers and fathers and daughters and sons and lovers, all that complex life chopped off at the neck after an obscenely unfair trial. What a waste, what a shame, what a terrible, bloody way for a story to end!"

"But how else *could* the book have ended? I mean, it's a true story, isn't it?" Spyro said, playing the literal-minded sounding board.

"You're right, it *is* true, and it's a brilliant book, quite perfect in every way. No, you're absolutely right. Mankind doesn't need to learn to write better stories. We need to learn to *live* better stories." Murasaki McBride looked up at him, wiped her eyes, and smiled her dazzling book-jacket smile.

That wasn't when Spyro realized he was in love with her, though. It was later that day, when he saw her standing by the window rubbing her long pale neck, obviously thinking about the guillotine, that it hit him like a *yakuza* punch to the solar plexus: Holy shit, I love this woman, and I want her to love me. It was as sudden, and as simple, and as impossible as that.

And so (Spyro continued after the tea had been poured and sweetened) ten years passed like a dream, one day at a time. Rokunosuke never found any gold or oil, and he soon lost interest in the messy idea of cattle ranching. He and Rumi broke up after a couple of years and then he just drifted around the country, hoping every morning that he'd make his fortune that night, hoping every night that his luck would change the following day. He went from woman to woman, and some liaisons lasted an hour, while others lasted a year. Rokunosuke never wrote or telephoned his wife, of course. Kazue had said she would be waiting for him, and he believed her.

Finally, he wandered back to Tokyo. It was one of those fresh chilly late-fall nights, and as Rokunosuke got off the train at Kita-Senju he turned up the lapels of his worn green jacket. He only had one of the striped-cardboard suitcases now, and it was filled with dirty laundry and expired lottery tickets. He had hoped, if he came back at all, to come back a success, but now he was so tired that he just wanted someone who was as familiar as breath to say, "Would you like a bath now, dear?" And after that he wanted to gaze up at the muted urban stars, drink some warm saké, and sleep for a long, long time.

The first thing Rokunosuke noticed as he opened the battered bamboo gate was that the house was in extreme disrepair. Shutters flapped in the wind, there were more gaps than tiles on the roof, the garden was overgrown, and one of the maple trees had died. *I wonder if Kazue's been ill*, he thought. *She always took such good care of the garden*. But he was relieved to see that she was still living alone, with no man around to fix things. A sudden horrible possibility occurred to him, and he quickly put it into words, to make sure it couldn't be true. "I wonder if Kazue might be dead," he said out loud.

Rokunosuke slid open the glass door and stepped into the *genkan*. The house was dark and there was a musty odor, a smell like mildewed tatami and salty pickles kept too long.

"Tadaima," he called, and after a moment a light went on down the hall. "I'm home!" he called again, perching on the edge of the step and untying his shoes. He left them where they dropped, one pointing north, one pointing south, for he knew that Kazue would straighten them so they both faced the door, ready to step into the next time he went away for an evening, or a lifetime. He could see the light of an oil lamp coming toward him down the long hall, splashing the shredded-paper *shoji* screens with shadow and light, and he wondered what had happened to the electricity.

And then there she was, his faithful wife, looking exactly as she had when he left, only happier. "Welcome home," she said, as if he had gone off to work that morning and had come home right on schedule.

"Tadaima," Rokunosuke repeated for the third time. He wanted to laugh out loud with joy at finding Kazue alive and unchanged, but he knew that would be unseemly. It occurred to him that he should have brought her a present, a good-luck amulet from some famous temple or a bath-towel bearing the name of a popular hot spring, but he knew she wouldn't mind that he had returned empty-handed. She had never expected anything from him, so she had never been disappointed.

Later, Kazue turned down the lamp and spread out the futon. It was tattered but clean, and Rokunosuke was touched by how poor she had become in his absence. They slipped under the covers and made love, slowly and silently. It was the first physical contact they had had since his return, for traditional Japanese couples do not exchange hugs at the front door, even after ten years apart. Rokunosuke's Star of David brushed against Kazue's face (women always loved that, for some reason he had never understood) and then her lips parted and she took the pendant in her mouth and held it there very gently, like a cardinal fish incubating its translucent microscopic heirs. After that he moved even more slowly and carefully above her, because he didn't want his precious gold chain to break.

Later still, when they were getting ready to go to sleep, Kazue said, "Good night, dear," and kissed him on the forehead, the way his mother used to do. Rokunosuke felt a strange thrill go through his body, and it took him a moment to recognize the sensation as love. I'll never leave this woman again, he thought. This is where we belong: my body, my soul, my heart, my mind, my tiny tyrant, and me. But all he said was, "'Night."

Rokunosuke slept later than usual, until the late-morning sun came through the half-open shutters and made his head feel like an overripe melon. He opened one eye and was surprised to see that Kazue was still asleep, too, with her *yukata*-covered back to him and her glossy hair coiled on the pillow like a lacquered serpent. She had always been an early riser and he was mildly disappointed that she wasn't up making his breakfast, washing his laundry, and aligning his pointy-toed shoes. But then he remembered the slow-motion poetry of the night before and he thought, Ah, she wants more, the randy wench. Feeling very loving and potent, Rokunosuke reached out and put his hand on Kazue's shoulder. "I have a special wake-up call for you, my darling," he whispered, and then he leaped out of bed and screamed in horror because—

"Please forgive me, Spyro," Murasaki McBride interrupted as she stood up and began to button her lemongrass-colored Issey Miyake jacket. "I know this is the most atrocious timing, and I'm absolutely dying to hear how your lovely story ends, but I really have to run. I promised to do an interview at NHK, and I had no idea it had gotten so late. Do you think you could come over to my house tonight and tell me the rest?"

"Your house? Tonight?" Spyro echoed stupidly. The suggestion was unprecedented, although by no means undreamed of.

"Yes, unless you have something else planned." Murasaki McBride was giving him that mellow laudanum-look again: the soft loose mouth, the flared nostrils, the heavy marble eyelids. "You might bring something to drink, too," she said. "Something delicious, and decadent."

Spyro's heart was pounding. This is it, he thought, the Invitation to the Dance. He wasn't sure the living legend returned his love, but perhaps she shared his hives. Something delicious and decadent? A very dry champagne might be good, since Murasaki McBride liked the classical approach. Champagne, truffles, a darkened room; epic kisses, Canon in D on continuous play, the doorbell disconnected, the phone left off the hook.

Spyro saw his famous employer off in a turquoise taxi (the color of the Adriatic Sea, he thought giddily, the color of my grandfather's eyes). As she slid into the doily-draped back seat he said, trying to be polite and considerate and Occidental, "Shall I give you a call tonight, just in case you change your mind?"

"Do you want me to change my mind?" Murasaki McBride asked. She smiled mischievously, a smile he had never seen before, and then she was gone, leaving Spyro with a mouthful of half-formed retorts and reassurances.

She's so attractive, so accomplished, so ... *available*, he thought as he watched the taxi roll away between the yellowish-green willow trees. He could tell from the movement of Murasaki McBride's head that she was talking to the driver in her fluent, playful Japanese, and he could tell from the angle of the driver's head that he was amused and impressed. Spyro felt oddly let down, for it was a bit of a shock—a disappointment, even—to have the object of his impossible desire become suddenly possible. She hadn't exactly said, "I want you, baby," but the implications were as clear as they ever are.

Spyro felt a strange pre-coital sadness, a sense that this unlikely romance was doomed, that it was over before it began, that the more ecstatic their momentary union might be, the more desolated he would be by the inevitable dissolution. And what if the gossip was true, and she really was a philanderess with a short attention span? When she got bored and sent him away he wouldn't just lose his peace of mind, he would lose his wonderful job as well.

"Shit," he said out loud, "I think I'm about to ruin my life." And then after a moment he grinned and executed one of those jubilant gestures (clenched fist pulled back and in toward the waist) that pro bowlers and action-movie underdogs always make when they bowl a perfect frame, or triumph over some absurdly exaggerated adversity. "Yeah," he added. "And I can hardly wait."

Spyro went back into the coffee shop, put in a request for the "Brandenburg 3-in-G" to calm himself down, sat down in a small back booth, and ordered a cup of black coffee, just in case he might be required to stay alert all night.

"Excuse me," said a voice, in American English with a strong Eastern-Seaboard accent: heady, nasal, and urgent. "You'll probably think I've totally forgotten my manners, but I was sitting in the booth behind you a while ago, eavesdropping shamelessly, and I don't think I can go on living if I don't find out how that fascinating story ends." Because it had been a fateful sort of day, Spyro knew before he looked up that the voice would belong to a tall young blonde, thin yet voluptuous, sultry and smart. She would be holding a copy of *The Iliad* (in Greek, of course), and she would ask him to take her dancing in Roppongi tonight, thus forcing him to choose between the woman of his wildest fantasies and the woman of his most inappropriate dreams.

But, as Spyro saw when he raised his eyes, he was wrong. The American voice belonged to a large, pleasant-looking woman with a puffy pink face, fluffy gray hair, and a wide gold wedding band embossed with tiny roses. She wore a purple beret and a rather snug dress of strawberry-colored jersey, and Spyro was suddenly reminded, with an unexpected tweak of homesickness, of the overstuffed pincushion in his mother's sewing box.

The woman introduced herself as Marion Farradine ("But please call me Mare, everyone does"). She explained that she was an amateur folklorist—"That's a housewife who reads a lot of fairy tales," she said ruefully—with a special interest in the supernatural and in oral tradition. "So I'd be ever so grateful if you could share the rest of your father's marvelous variation on 'The House Amid the Thickets,'" she said, barely managing to squeeze her scarlet-upholstered bulk into the banquette across the table.

"Uh, sure, yeah, okay," said Spyro, marveling at the nerve, and the openness, of his fellow American. Oh well, what the hell, he thought, it'll be good practice for telling the story tonight. He had recovered from his attack of qualms about the assignation with Murasaki McBride, and once again he was feeling excited, and chosen. "Do you by any chance remember where

I left off?" he asked, and his new acquaintance reminded him about Rokunosuke's horrified scream. "Oh, that's right. Thanks, Mrs. Farradine. Oh, I'm sorry"—for she was wagging a plump, stern finger at him—"I mean Marion. What? Oh, sorry: *Mare*."

So anyway (Spyro continued), Rokunosuke stared in horror at the dreadful thing lying on the futon. Under his wife's beautiful black hair was a skinless skull with a prominent forehead and a disappearing chin, and under her bamboo-patterned robe was a skeleton with fragile-looking bones the color of old piano keys. The room was suddenly filled with a sad and terrible stench, a fetid smell of stale calcium and wormy earth. Rokunosuke gagged and ran to the bathroom, where he splashed some water on his face and stared at his haggard, cynical, disillusioned reflection in the dusty mirror. Maybe it was an illusion, he thought, and that gave him the courage to tip-toe back to the bedroom. Sure enough, the bedding had been folded up, the shutters were thrown open, and the room smelled the way it always had: like sunlight and straw, like cryptomeria sachets and Kita-Senju smog.

Rokunosuke got dressed. He heard Kazue clanging pots in the kitchen, and he went to tell her about his bizarre vision. She was standing in front of the stove, trying to light the gas with a long wooden match, her hair loose like a cape over her cotton sleeping-robe.

"Good morning, dear," Rokunosuke said. His wife turned to face him, still holding the match, and when he saw the skull beneath the hair and the skeleton beneath the cloth, he knew that this was neither a dream nor a hallucination. With a cry of anguish and fear Rokunosuke ran from the room, and a second later he heard Kazue running lightly down the hall behind him. "Wait, darling!" she called in her sweet voice, but Rokunosuke leaped into his neatly lined-up shoes and rushed out of the house without looking back.

Rokunosuke had read all the old ghost stories, and he was certain that such things happened all the time. Like traffic accidents and wasting diseases, though, he never expected them to happen to him. He understood dimly that his wife's soul must have wanted to keep her vow to wait for him forever, and he realized, vaguely, that only he could put that restless soul at ease. He half-walked, half-ran the four blocks to the neighborhood graveyard. There, in a far corner, shadowed by a mossy rock wall, he found what he was looking for, inscribed on a cheap granite tombstone:

KAZUE TANTO, WIFE OF ROKUNOSUKE
Born October 12, 1943
Died June 23, 1984

"Oh no, that can't be right," Rokunosuke moaned after a moment's calculation. June 23, 1984 was the day after he had run off to Hokkaido with Rumi. Had Kazue been taken suddenly ill? Had she died of a broken heart? Or had she killed herself, then regretted it and returned to the derelict house to wait for him?

Rokunosuke knelt down on the grave. "Please forgive me, my dearest wife," he said. "I never deserved you, not for a single minute." He reached behind his neck and undid the clasp of his gold chain. After cradling the Star of David in his palm for a minute, polishing it with his thumb, Rokunosuke dug a small hole in the sparse grass above the grave, and buried the necklace. "I know you always liked this," he whispered. "It's my only treasure, and I want you to have it forever." He chanted *Namu myoho renge kyo* (the only religious phrase he knew) over and over, until his jaw was stiff and his head began to throb. "Forgive me, Kazue," he said again, and then he stood up and walked unsteadily to the gate of the graveyard.

Rokunosuke started to head toward the train station, for he knew now that he was finished with Tokyo forever. Afte a moment, though, he decided to go back to fetch his suitcase. There wasn't much in it, but it was all he owned. The house had been a rental, and Rokunosuke realized with an involuntary shudder that it must have been left empty all these years because it had gained a reputation for being haunted.

As Rokunosuke came around the corner by the futon shop, he saw the smoke. A moment later he heard sirens, and screams of panic. He thought of the skeleton standing by the stove holding a long match, surrounded by straw and wood and paper, and he turned and began to walk rapidly in the other direction, away from the fire.

Rokunosuke had no idea where he was heading, but he had a vague vision of an uninhabited island set in a gray-green sea, a simple place where a man could see more of the stars and try to live an honest, harmless life.

Maybe I'll become a monk, he thought. Just then he caught sight of a long-haired young beauty in a red miniskirt and white rubber boots, hosing down the sidewalk in front of a flower shop, and he stared at her exquisite oyster-shaped knees and thought, Well, maybe not.

When Spyro had finished, Marion Farradine sat quietly for a long moment, staring out the window at the heathery lavender dusk. A nice touch, Spyro thought; a sort of silent applause.

"Thank you so much," his new acquaintance said at last, turning to face him. She had a pudgy pudding-face, but her eyes were clear and intelligent. They were an unusual grayish-violet color, like the smoky crepuscular light outside the leaded windows of La Traviata.

"It was so kind of you to take the time to tell me the rest of the story," Marion said. "I know it's short notice, but would you like to come over and have dinner with my husband and my daughter and me tonight? We live out in Denenchofu. Company housing, but it's quite nice."

Aha, Spyro thought, the daughter. Young and tall and blonde, an ectomorphic Viking, bright and passionate and definitely not twice my age or ten times my fame or a hundred times my fortune. And not a notorious man-eater, either. But then he realized that he had no interest in meeting any other woman, not even the tall pale goddess of his immature dark-skinned dreams.

"I'm sorry, I have a date," he said, and then he thought, Holy shit, I really *do* have a date. Not an appointment, not an interview, not an audience, but a genuine prime-time date, with the woman I think I love and know I desire, all inequality-equations aside. Spyro had a sudden chilling vision of Murasaki McBride—no, of Ursula—at home, at that very moment, standing by the window and rubbing her swanly neck and thinking, *What have I gotten myself into? He's half my age, he works for me, he isn't my type, I just want to be his boss and his mentor.* Then Spyro remembered the molten look he had seen on her graceful aging face. He was a fairly astute reader of expressions, and he felt certain that women's faces don't melt like a *croque monsieur* unless they have strongly unprofessional, non-Platonic feelings for the person they are looking at.

"A date?" Marion Farradine raised her feathery gray eyebrows and smiled. She had squarish ivory teeth, like Japanese chess markers without the black calligraphy. "Well, whoever she is, she's a very lucky girl." Spyro elevated his thick, dark Spartan-samurai eyebrows in return. If you only knew, he thought.

A few minutes later, as he stood in the darkening street waving the amateur folklorist off in a persimmon-colored taxi, Spyro began to laugh. "If *I* only knew," he said out loud. Whistling what he could remember of "La Marseillaise," he set off to find a magnum of dry champagne, a gigantic box of dark-chocolate truffles, and the biggest bouquet of gumdrop-colored lupines the Ginza's fancy florists could provide.

THE BEAST IN THE MIRROR

I saw a werewolf with a Chinese menu in his hand
Walking through the streets of Soho in the rain.

—WARREN ZEVON
Werewolves of London

I'm not the first *sumotori* to fall into disgrace, God knows. There was a grand champion who was banished from the sport a few years ago because of a shady-money gambling deal; now he's a pro wrestler, enjoying his new notoriety as the Kagoshima Krusher. When I first came to Tokyo, I remember being shocked to find the sumo magazines full of rumors about fixed matches, flaps over smuggled handguns, and sordid sex scandals—including a head-in-the-oven suicide attempt by a neglected sumo wife whose high-ranking husband was carrying on a very public affair with the aristocratic-looking beauty who reads the news on Channel Three.

But those cases are different from mine, as different as day from night, as sunspots from fog, as bouillabaisse from *crème caramel.* Gambling, womanizing, reckless immature behavior: those are the follies that sumo-flesh is heir to, but in my case the problem was the flesh itself. The flesh, and the blood, and the fur … but wait, I'm getting ahead of my tale.

I suppose the story begins on the balmy day in October when I was "discovered" on the playing fields of Kapiolani Park in Waikiki. Our team—the Diamond Head Demons—had just won a hard-fought victory, 43–37, and my white rugger uniform was covered with a colorful mixture of volcanic dirt, grass stains, and the blood of the Maui Monitor Lizards (our plucky but doomed opponents that day). I was chugging a post-game bottle of Beck's when a sleazy-looking white man approached me.

"Excuse me," he said, proffering a lurid lime-green business card which identified him as a sumo scout for a certain stable. "Do you speak English, by any chance?"

Instead of replying, I stared at the stranger in my best noble-savage manner, letting him feast his tiny eyes on my languid tropical features, my coconut-oiled curls, my cappuccino skin, my huge ambidextrous hands, my Sistine muscles.

"So do you speak English, or not?" the man repeated nervously.

"Like a bloody native," I said, affecting what I hoped was a posh-sounding English accent, like Ian Richardson's evil Prime Minister in *To Play the King*.

"Oh, great, that's a big relief, 'cause I don't speak a *word* of Samoan," gushed the scout.

"That's quite all right," I said acidly, "because neither do I. I'm not from Samoa, I'm from Anonymous Island. But I do speak French and Tahitian and English, in addition to the language of my island. Not only that, but I'm majoring in American Studies up at UH Manoa, and after I graduate I'm planning to go for my Master's in Comparative Culture." I guess I might have been bragging a bit, but I was only nineteen, and I didn't like being patronized.

"How ironic," said the scout. He was a pale fat *haole* guy in a truly vile aloha shirt accessorized with glistening white patent leather shoes and matching belt, and he wore one of those embarrassing matte-black toupees that makes the wearer appear to have a decomposing vole on his head. I wondered how he had gotten mixed up with sumo, of all things. I couldn't picture him as an athlete, except maybe a double-digit bowler, so I figured he must be in it for the reflected glamour, or the finder's fees.

"What's ironic?" I asked, totally deadpan, after I had opened another green bottle with my perfect white teeth. No sissified pop-tops for me.

"Oh," said the scout with a chuckle, half to himself. "I was just thinking that if you do get into sumo you'll have to learn to speak in a slightly more, shall we say, *basic* style for the post-match interviews."

I scratched my ribcage with both hands and grunted like an orangutan. "How's that?" I said, and the scout's pasty face brightened.

"Perfect," he said. "They'll love you." He wasn't quite as dumb as I'd thought at first, but he wouldn't have known irony if it fell on his foot.

He launched into the sumo hard-sell then, and I somehow allowed myself to be talked into going over to the Halekulani—my nominee for the loveliest hotel on the planet—to join the head of the sumo stable in question for a late-afternoon drink at the House Without a Key. The stablemaster's name was Ukemochi Oyakata ("Oyakata" being the customary title for stablemasters, retired wrestlers who stay in the sumo world, and yakuza bosses alike) and he had apparently been an illustrious grand champion, under the ring name Kurokami, before he retired.

"Will you be there?" I asked the scout, knowing he wouldn't get the reference to *Love and Death*. To my relief, he mumbled something about having a previous engagement with a sponge cake. At least that's what it sounded like, and I didn't ask him to elucidate.

The stablemaster turned out to be a handsome, stocky, hoarse-voiced man with a short kinky perm and enough gold in his teeth to pay off my student loans. While an earnest *nisei* guy in a pink golf shirt provided more-or-less simultaneous translation, the former *yokozuna* talked about the promising lowness of my center of gravity, the advantages of "ambidextrosity," my need for additional upholstery in the midriff area, and the remarkable aptitude of my countrymen for the sport. (He too assumed I was Samoan, but I let that misunderstanding slide.) Then he offered me free room and board at his stable in Ryogoku—"*lots* of board," leered the translator, poking a jocular elbow in my ribs—and a chance to become rich and famous and triple my body weight over the next few years. It still seemed like a joke to me at that point, so I said, "If I decide to quit, do I get to keep the fat?" but the spoilsport go-between refused to translate that question.

As I left I said coolly, "Let me think about it." The whole thing seemed pretty unreal, and the truth was, I wasn't eager to give up my life of school, rugby, outrigger-canoe paddling, weight training, and working nights as the assistant *sous chef* at Frangipani Bar & Grill, the best Franco-Pacific restaurant in town. I tried talking to my rugby coach, an albino pirate named Jake (no hyperbole there; he really was a pirate in the seas off Sumatra years ago, with an AK-47 instead of a cutlass). Jake just laughed and flashed his diamond tooth-stud. "No way anyone wants *you* to be in sumo, dude," he said. "Not with those washboard abs."

Finally I called my dear, sweet, linebacker-sized mother, on that paradisiacal island which must remain anonymous here. Predictably, she said, "Oh my darling son, this is the work of the gods! You have been chosen, you must not pass up such a chance."

It turned out that Nonnie, Mami's younger sister who lives on Maui, had sent her reams of clippings about a Samoan-Hawaiian football player who made it big in sumo and built his parents a classic *nouveau riche* house with eight bedrooms, twelve bathrooms, and a ballroom-sized laundry area complete with big-screen TV, hot tub, and two extra-large "washer-dryer condos," as my Auntie Nonnie said when she related the story on the phone. I knew she meant combos, bless her not-quite-bilingual heart.

"Okay, Mami," I told my mother, after a lengthy discussion of pros (she wanted me to go) and cons (I didn't want to). "I know you just want me to buy you a fancy washing machine, but maybe I'll go over and give it a whirl. To tell you the truth, I've always wanted to visit some of those places Lafcadio Hearn wrote about, and Isabella Bird, too."

"What's that about Larry Bird?" said my mother. Mishearing things seems to run in our family, but it was a terrible long-distance connection, as well.

"Not Larry Bird, Mami," I said. "Isabella."

"*Isabella?* Oh no!" she cried. "I knew if you went to the city you'd end up with some trashy white girl!"

That's when I said goodbye, gently, and hung up. Actually, there was a trashy white girl in my life at the time, off and on: Kellianne Kewshaw, the languid blonde surf goddess who tended bar at Frangipani and modeled for a local T-shirt catalog, while talking endlessly about her pipe dream of going to New York to take Broadway by storm.

That evening I went to work in my XXL chef's whites, driving my extra-small, extra-old Toyota with the GIVE BLOOD: PLAY RUGBY bumper-sticker. (Now, *that's* ironic.) On my dinner break I saw Kellianne flirting ostentatiously with the restaurant's new owner. He was one of those slick, ponytailed, Corvette-driving L.A. types, the kind that has a closet full of Armani and After Six, and a medicine chest full of male-hooker scent, sex toys, and designer drugs. I'd heard via kitchen gossip that he had made millions executive-producing schlocky films, and even after he'd put a small fortune up his nose, he still had a good deal of cash left over. Apparently one day he went in for a past-life regression session (which is like a *lomilomi* massage for the ego, if you ask me) and his PLR guru told him that, in addition to having been Cleopatra's favorite lover and Rasputin's right-hand man, he had been a valiant Hawaiian warrior during the reign of Kamehameha the First.

So did he react to that revelation by making a generous donation to the Hawaiian sovereignty movement, or to some local charity? No, he flew his

Learjet to Honolulu and bought a trendy, exclusive restaurant for six million dollars. I felt physically ill when I saw him tucking his business card into my supposed girlfriend's overripe cleavage, and my stomach did a triple gainer when she responded by tucking *her* card coquettishly into the front pocket of his Hugo Boss slacks.

Later, when Kellianne asked me what was going on, I said airily, "Oh, I've decided to go to Japan to be a sumo star." I always told myself (and everyone else) that I did it for my mother, but the truth is that if Kellianne Kewshaw hadn't been treating me like fermented iguana-shit on that particular tropical night, I probably wouldn't have gone.

When I first arrived at Ukemochi Stable, my fellow sumotori exclaimed over my muscles, my curly locks, my prodigious *membrum virile*, and my stomach—which was, as Jake the Pirate had pointed out, as flat as a boogie board but considerably more muscular. Most of all, my new Japanese colleagues seemed to be impressed by my body hair. Fur, they called it: *kegawa*. I went along with the joke by pretending to be a knuckle-dragging baboon, which by coincidence is the position assumed by both wrestlers before a match commences.

I was drowsing in my tiny, flimsy-walled room that first night, enjoying the dreamy jet-lag delirium, when there was a knock on the door. It was Sachiko, the stablemaster's only child, a rare beauty with the face of an enchanted princess. She was dressed in a sea-colored kimono, a muted gray-green shadow plaid bisected by a smoke-blue obi patterned with stylized clouds, and her lustrous black hair was pinned up carelessly, as if she had done it without looking in a mirror.

"Come with me," said this vision of unselfconscious loveliness.

Anywhere, I thought. Any time, gladly.

I followed her to the communal bath, which was a large dimly lit room with frosted-glass windows and several shower heads and low spigots on the pseudo-pebbled wall. Sachiko (that's not her real name, of course) sat me down on a stool, and then she proceeded to shave my chest and back. In the space of a few minutes we went from being strangers to an almost conjugal intimacy, without a word, and it was oddly soothing and very sweet.

I had had quite a few girlfriends and sex partners, but I had never fallen in love so fast, or so hard. By the time Sachiko had sheathed the razor, I was ready to marry her, on the spot. I couldn't tell how she felt about me, but (to be honest) I had always been something of a chick magnet, and I blithely assumed that she would eventually be mine.

I didn't even question why I had to lose my body hair; I understood that it was a requirement of training, like eating a huge beery lunch before a mid-afternoon nap so the food would turn to fat. After that I kept the hair off with a weird Japanese device, a sort of long-handled lint brush with magnetized Velcro instead of bristles. I didn't understand the principle, but it worked like magic.

On my second night in Japan they put me in a smallish *tatami*-matted room with another recruit, a tall rangy guy from Shikoku whom I'll call Gonzo (that really is a Japanese proper name, with a long "o" at the end, although it didn't happen to be *his* name). Gonzo was a former collegiate wrestling champion who had spent an exchange-student year in Albuquerque, New Mexico, of all places. He spoke fairly good English; that is, he knew a lot of swear words, pickup lines, and heavy-metal lyrics. It turned out that he had some body fuzz, too, so we would depilate each other every night after dinner while we listened to rock and roll on his portable stereo. Besides the collected works of AC/DC, Led Zeppelin, and Monster Magnet, Gonzo had a CD by a new English group called Oleo Strut, and I used to chant one of their lyrics when I did my sardonic hairy-ape imitation in the hall. *I looked in the glass/And what did I see?/That the beast in the mirror/Was me.*

"Too bad the beast didn't have a Depilomatic," Gonzo said once, holding up the instrument of torture and flashing the toothy, vacuous smile of a TV pitchman. Japan has some truly bizarre commercials, as you probably know. Sophia Loren tooling along on a motor scooter, Sylvester Stallone hawking pork snacks, fifteen flatulent schoolboys in a communal bathtub. At one time they even had giant billboards of Woody Allen, of all people, modeling dapper menswear for Seibu Department Store.

"Yeah," I quipped. "Why be a werewolf when you can be a Chihuahua?" But by the time I finished explaining about Mexican hairless dogs, the wit, such as it was, had gotten lost in the old cross-cultural shuffle.

Gonzo was in love with a girl back home in Uwajima, a florist's assistant named Chie, and I was smitten with Sachiko, the boss's daughter, even though we hadn't had a single moment alone together since the night she shaved my furry torso. Gonzo and I used to talk about our feelings for those two women while we rubbed the Depilomatic over each other's wide backs and convex chests and burgeoning bellies; I'm sure a psychologist would say that was our unconscious way of defusing any sexually ambiguous thoughts we might have had. I once read an article in the London *Spectator* in which a Fleet Street journalist, just back from Tokyo, compared a typical Japanese sumo stable to an English public school. He called the ritualized feudal world of sumo an "endomorphic Eton," but while everybody knows that the samurai of old were great practitioners of "comrade love," I never saw or even heard of any homoerotic activity in a sumo stable.

That was almost three years ago, when our hearts were young and ... carefree. Things have changed a bit since then, to put it mildly. In spite of having gotten such a late start (many of my colleagues had joined the stable right out of junior high) I shot up the sumo ladder at record speed, exceeding all expectations, including my own. I made good money, I won some prizes, and I attracted my share of rabid fans and good-looking groupies. I suppose I had begun to take my success for granted, and then one day, in the most bizarre way imaginable, my snug little world simply fell apart.

As I write this, I am holed up in my secret hideout, an apartment several blocks from the stable which I have rented under an assumed name for the past year or so. I still sleep at the stable most of the time, but this is where I keep my books, my music (Mozart, Metallica, Mark O'Connor), my sound system, my free weights, my refrigerator full of coconut milk, dried breadfruit, and *poi*. And, since I refuse to be reduced to a gastronomic (or ethnic) cliché, my Nova lox, Carr's Biscuits, and Oxford marmalade as well.

This is also where I used to come to seethe. Like the time I let my attention wander for a nanosecond and lost a crucial playoff match in the most ignominious way: my opponent simply stepped aside and let me blunder past him, out of the ring and into the lap of a diminutive slick-haired politician who was indicted the following day for bribery. I also used to come here to exult—to high-five myself, so to speak. Like the time I won both the Technique and Fighting Spirit prizes in the Fall Tournament, and knew that my promotion to the third-highest rank, *sekiwake,* was assured. But best of all were the hours I spent listening to music and dreaming of becoming *ozeki,* marrying the adorable Sachiko, and building my mother a snazzy house in the lush fragrant foothills of Anonymous Island, where all the sport fishermen, pearl smugglers, and trust-fund satyrs live.

I used to rehearse the scene in my head back at the stable, too, while the sumo hairdresser tried to subdue my curly sternum-length hair with handfuls of *bintsuke* (a thick, aromatic brilliantine; if you're familiar with a heady perfume called Secret of Venus, you know approximately how it smells). The hair-taming wasn't an entirely pleasant ritual, and once or twice I actually said "*Itai*" ("Ouch") as my forcibly-straightened curls were being scraped into a fat topknot culminating in a gingko-leaf shape—an archaic hairdo worn only by wrestlers above a certain rank. I'll never forget the thrill of looking in the mirror and seeing my face crowned for the first time with that imposing, atavistic 'do.

Anyway, in the fantasy, I would drive my mom out to the magnificent house, with orange and magenta bougainvillea spilling over the lava-rock terraces like sunset-colored waterfalls. She would say, "What are we doing here, son? I left my laundry soaking in the stream." And I would say, "Well, Mami, I thought you might need a place to put your snazzy new washer-dryer combo." Then I would hand her the house keys, with a big gold ribbon attached.

I remember, back when things were normal—it seems like a previous incarnation, but it was only ten days ago—that once in a while, late at night when I couldn't get a taxi, I would be walking home from a publicity-date with some perky young pop star, or from a karaoke blowout with a couple of vaguely gangsterish *tanimachi* (sumo slang for big-spending patrons), or from a stolen hour of passion with my married lover, or from a safe-sex fling with some irresistible sumo groupie—anyway, on my way home I would pass the public bathhouse. I knew it must be closed, but there was an odd play of light and shadow against the smoked-glass windows, and I heard a weird sibilant murmuring, like the wind through a stand of bamboo.

The owners are probably just cleaning up, I always told myself, but on some reluctant subliminal level I knew that the sounds were not janitorial, and the shapes glimpsed through the glass were something other than human.

A small mystery, that. Nothing to lose sleep over, especially when I was busy worrying about whether I would do well enough in the next tournament to attain the elusive ozeki promotion, at last. But now I know what goes on at the bathhouse late at night. That's just one of many things I know, and wish I didn't.

Like *The Hound of the Baskervilles*, it all started with a dogbite. One night around two A.M. I was walking home alone from a torrid tryst at a high-class love hotel called Amorata Inn. The woman I'd been cavorting with—a stunning Siberian-born fashion model, who was flying back to Paris the next day—had declined my suggestion that we actually *sleep* together that last night (something we had never done) so I was feeling singularly empty, disappointed, and disgusted with myself. Irina and I had met at a disco in Roppongi and had immediately fallen into one of those intense, unabashedly bestial three-day affairs, the kind that leaves you feeling sated but not really satisfied, no matter how many times you make love. She never pretended that it was anything but a purely physical connection, and I suspected that she had just been curious about how it would be to go to bed with a man of my size. Or maybe she wanted to add a sumotori to her life-list of exotic conquests.

My mind was in turmoil that night for a number of reasons. I was feeling guilty about cheating on my married lover with a gorgeous, glamorous, and possibly promiscuous model. (Irina claimed to be coming off a long sexual drought, and I was careful about using a condom every time, but still, you never know.) I felt perpetually guilty about fooling around with a married woman in the first place. And I was seriously conflicted about that particular married woman, for reasons I'll explain shortly.

In addition to my multilayered parfait of guilt, I was feeling angry and betrayed because a female sumo reporter—a flirtatious brunette from San Francisco who had her own column in one of the English-language papers—had done a fawning interview with me, then turned it into a vicious article in which she misquoted me right and left, questioned my "heart," and boldly predicted that I was just a flash in the sumo pan who would never be promoted to ozeki. I shouldn't have been surprised; I knew there would be repercussions when I not only rejected her suggestion that we continue the interview over a bottle of wine at her place in Yokoyamacho, but declined her coy offer of a rain check as well. (I was actually fairly attracted to her, physically, but I knew she had already slept with two other guys in my stable, and I wasn't interested in being another notch in her notepad.) Still, I never dreamed she would have the nerve to slander me in print.

So anyway, I was more than a little upset, and when a yappy little cur started barking at me outside the bathhouse, that was the last straw. The dog was one of those ridiculous lap-ornaments, the kind that looks like a cross between a tasseled lampshade and a mole with a manicure. I think it might have been a Pomeranian mix of some sort; it was better groomed than most humans, complete with red-lacquered claws, and I wondered what an obviously pampered pet was doing out on the street in the middle of the night.

I was planning to ignore the dog, but when it followed me down the street, still yapping hysterically, I lost my cool. "Buzz off, flea-bait," I said, and then I gave a menacing snarl and held up my hands with the fingers flexed like a B-movie vampire. Instead of fleeing with its fluffy tail between its sawed-off legs, the dog dug its gaudy nails into my *zori*-shod foot, then sank its teeth into my leg.

"Ouch," I said. "That hurt! You mangy little bastard," I added. I gave the pest a swift and none-too-gentle kick, which sent it yelping down the nearest alley.

I looked down and saw a spot of blood just above my ankle, but I didn't think anything of it. I guess I haven't mentioned that I'm six foot seven and weigh close to 340 pounds—the former thanks to my island genes, the latter the result of large quantities of poi, beer, sleep, and *chankonabe* stew. So the wound, if you could even call it that, was pretty far from my center of consciousness.

The nightmares began that same night. I remember thinking as I relived those dreams the following morning that they were curiously cinematic, with some astonishing special effects reminiscent of Paul Schrader's *Cat People*: green-violet night vision, I-am-a-camera shots of running through the underbrush, languid slow-motion ballets, distorted sound. I blamed the sudden change in the texture of my unconscious on my recent penchant for eating seaweed crackers and Morinaga caramels before bedtime. But even after I stopped indulging in that indigestible late-night snack, the dreams continued, growing increasingly more horrific. It never occurred to me then that they might be something other than nightmares, and there was no physical evidence to point me toward that bizarre, unthinkable conclusion.

Aside from the dreadful dreams, life went on as usual. The stable got a new recruit, a stupendously well-built, sweet-natured Tongan-Hawaiian guy named Tama Leighton, whom I immediately nicknamed Tamale. He didn't speak more than ten words of Japanese, so I gave him a crash course in sumo etiquette, neighborhood hangouts, and the delicate art of being a gigantic *gaijin* in Japan.

I knew I couldn't protect Tamale from all the hard knocks that come with being a new recruit, although I did say "Knock it off" to the stable's highest-ranking wrestler, a perennially cranky ozeki whom I'll call Onizato, when I caught him hazing the newcomer one idle afternoon. Oni had about as much imagination as a bottle cap, so he was playing the same lame sadistic trick on Tamale that he had pulled on me when I first arrived. He ordered him to shinny up the stable's "*daikoku-bashira*"—the massive polished-treetrunk pillar that stands off to one side of the practice arena—and then, while hanging on for dear life, to repeat over and over in a falsetto voice, "*Hototogisu! Hototogisu! Hototogisu! Hototogisu!*" ("Cuckoo! Cuckoo! Cuckoo!")

It was a stupid prank when Onizato did it to me, and it was stupid now. I told the foul-tempered ozeki, though not in so many words, to lighten up and get a life. Then I took poor, trembling Tamale out for a between-meal snack of sixteen Mos Burgers (that's only eight apiece, and they were tiny). Tama Leighton was a nice kid, and I was sorry when he had to throw in the towel after only his third practice. It wasn't a lack of heart or motivation; he had an old knee injury from playing football, and when someone did a twisting *yoritaoshi* throw on him, that fickle joint just gave way.

One morning toward the end of that week, I was shocked to read in the newspaper that the lady reporter—the frustrated seductress who had done her best to trash my reputation—had been found dismembered in an alley in Roppongi with several vital organs missing, including the heart. Even though I vaguely remembered dreaming about her the night before, I felt no sense of guilt, or connection. Then, several nights later, I wakened suddenly from a particularly nasty nightmare.

In the dream, I was chasing a pack of wild dogs. After I had caught and killed them one by one (not for food, just for fun), I went and loitered outside a pub called Café Society. I had seen a juicy young girl go in, and now I was watching her, furtively, through the window. She was sitting in the rosy lamplight, reading a cartoon anthology and drinking a glass of orange soda. *The window opens like an orange/The lovely fruit of light*: I remembered that line from Apollinaire much later, for when I was in my lycanthrope incarnation I thought only of flesh, and blood, and ecstasy.

The girl had round white arms, like those huge *daikon* turnips you see in country markets, and I was mesmerized by the absentminded way she kept putting one arm behind her head to play with a renegade tendril of hair—a sort of Japanese *peot*—next to the opposite ear. She was plump and fey and double-jointed, and I knew I had to have her. When she finally came out, humming *La Vie en Rose*, I leaped on her and dragged her back into the alley. I snapped her neck in one quick move, the way the feral yellow-eyed cats on my island used to do with those big tropical rats, and then ...

No, that's enough; there's no possible redemption in regaling you with the grisly gastronomic details. I figured out later that while I was doing those awful things they were being imprinted on my memory, and I would ordinarily have recalled them later as dream-sequences, or nightmares. But this time something—the sound of a siren, or a change in my cursed molecules—catalyzed a return to consciousness.

I woke up and found myself sitting in an alley in Kinshicho, with my mouth full of turnip (no, it was a human arm), and what I thought at first was a torrent of catsup running down my chest. The girl's other limbs (pale glimmering skin, bright terrible blood) were scattered lewdly around the alley, and when I looked down at myself I saw that I was ... well, put it this way: I was not myself.

I must have passed out from the shock, and when I came to, the girl's body had disappeared. The only evidence of my bloody bacchanal was a few burgundy splotches on the asphalt and a clear plastic coin purse with a picture of a cartoon raccoon on it, which had fallen from my victim's pocket. Without a qualm of guilt or remorse I took out the money—four hundred measly yen—and tossed the purse in a nearby dumpster. Just then I felt a great shudder pass through my involuntarily-borrowed body and when I looked down I had returned to my own outsized-sumotori shape, with my muscular big-bellied bulk encased in a blue-and-white cotton *yukata* made from cloth printed with the name of Orochiyama ("Giant-Serpent Mountain"), an ozeki from a stable that was affiliated with mine.

On the way home, feeling sick to my very soul, I passed that eerie bathhouse. It was dark, but the door was open, and there seemed to be no choice but to go in.

"This way," said an irresistible voice. It wasn't a human voice speaking a particular language, but rather a sort of extrasonic emanation.

"All right," I emanated in reply, and I followed the invisible soundless presence into the big communal bathing room. I had been there before, when I first began exploring the neighborhood, so I knew that there were several small sunken tubs and one large one, big enough to accommodate (as the old joke goes) thirty or forty very close friends. When my eyes adjusted to the absence of light I could see that there were figures lounging in the large pool and leaning against the walls, and after a few minutes I began to identify them.

That silly lapdog was there, glaring at me with the same simple-minded hatred, but it was no longer the size of a shaggy shoebox. It was larger than a mountain gorilla now, standing erect, and its obscene red-lacquered nails were as long as steak knives. There were hordes of demon-cats with sharkish teeth and scythelike claws. They too walked on two legs, as did the six-foot rats and the cockroaches the size of water buffaloes, and all the animals had the light of evil in their bloodshot eyes. But terrifying as these horrid bloated beasts might be, they were like cuddly stuffed toys compared to their humanoid compatriots.

At first I saw them only as vague forms shrouded in steam. It was a normal bathhouse scene: a group of undressed men submerged in hot water, some with damp towels draped over their heads or twisted around their temples. But then my eyes became accustomed to the dimness and I gasped in horror, for they were not men at all. Some of the nonhuman creatures in the steamy bath had two heads; some had multiple noses or mouths, while others had faces with no features at all, like giant hard-cooked eggs with the shells removed. Several of the monsters had transparent horns growing out of their heads. Suspended in clear liquid inside those horns, like macabre paperweights, were tiny living embryos: chickens and rabbits and toads and, unless I was mistaken, one or two incipient human beings. Perhaps I should have run screaming into the street, but I felt no fear; I knew those unholy aberrations would do me no harm, because I was one of them. Indeed, aside from that creepy cur, no one paid any attention to me at all.

Over in the corner, almost obscured by the billowing fog, was a square bath originally designed for mothers and their babies. I crept over, thinking I might wash my hands under the nearby taps. (My clothes, skin, and fingernails were already pristine, for some reason; I never did figure out the metaphysical logistics, or the hygiene, of transubstantiation.) To my surprise, the bath had been converted into a sort of stewpot filled with *oden*—the poached dumplings, seaweed, vegetables, and tofu which were one of my favorite street-food snacks. After a moment, though, I realized that the morsels in this pot were not made from the usual innocuous ingredients.

Floating in the broth, just beneath the rainbowed archipelago of oil-drops that shimmered on the surface, was a hodgepodge of horrifying snacks. What I had at first mistaken for a pork-and-vegetable dumpling was a single steaming gonad; a short-stemmed tree mushroom was actually a parboiled human penis; and small squares of textured tofu turned out to be tidily-diced bits of cerebellum. I was wondering whether I would have found this display appetizing in my cannibal-ghoul incarnation, when a twelve-foot-tall apparition who looked exactly like a typical salaryman (blue serge suit, brush cut, gold-rimmed glasses) aside from the fact that his face appeared to have been turned inside out, came and stood beside me. He bent over to survey the selection, and then with one flashlight-sized pinkie raised he plucked out a little bouquet of human toes bound together by a glossy ribbon of *konbu* seaweed, dipped it in a vat of what looked like Chinese mustard but could have been some particularly putrid bile, and popped it into his bloody maw of a mouth.

Okay, I thought, I've seen enough. I was one step away from the door when a huge presence loomed in front of me, blocking the exit. It was the Pomeranian from hell, the creature whose vengeful bite, I now realized, had doomed me to this gruesome double life.

"Sorry, pal," smirked the dog, the nasty sentiments communicated by that same soundless telepathy. "But the bite wouldn't have taken if you hadn't been a festering swamp of guilt, so don't blame me. If you had been living right, it would have just left a little scab."

Reiko—mother of Sachiko, wife of my stablemaster—wasn't a wicked woman at all, just a lonely, passionate, ill-used wife from a generation which recognized few options for women beyond marriage, child-rearing, and perhaps some genteel part-time teaching of the tea ceremony or flower arranging. Reiko's husband, my stablemaster, had been a legendary womanizer when he was single, and he didn't let his marriage vows cramp his style one iota. Reiko was the daughter of an elder statesman of sumo, a third-generation luminary of the sport, the former grand champion Botanyama. The match, which was a purely political alliance-forming device, was arranged through a go-between. After the wedding ceremony the groom rushed off to meet his favorite mistress, a former bar hostess who ran a chain of high-priced drinking clubs on the Ginza, without even taking the time to deflower his shy new bride.

All the sumotori loved Reiko—the *okami-san*, as we called her. (It's surely no coincidence that a stablemaster's spouse and a female innkeeper are both addressed as okami-san, for the job descriptions are remarkably similar). The lower-ranking sumotori helped with the menial tasks, including shopping and cooking, but Reiko was responsible for organizing all the domestic aspects of the stable. She also served as an *ad hoc* psychotherapist for the wrestlers when they became depressed as a result of homesickness, injury, failure, lack of obesity, or some romantic setback.

One day I went with Reiko to the fish market, where she patiently taught me how to recognize the appropriate ingredients for chanko-nabe in preparation for my first stint on kitchen duty. (I never did tell anyone that I had professional cooking experience, for fear of being stuck on KP forever, so my instructors just thought I was a remarkably quick learner.)

On the way home Reiko asked if I would like to have a cup of tea at Peer Gynt (a local coffee shop popular with sumotori, who pronounce the name "Pea-ah Gin-toh"). I agreed, thinking she was just being kind or, a bit more cynically, that she might want to practice her English, which was quite good aside from some confusion about adjectives and adverbs. Reiko was an exquisite-looking woman—if you're familiar with that famous woodblock print where a woman is sitting in an alfresco wooden bathtub under a cherry tree in full bloom, you've seen a face exactly like hers—but I was already madly, if chastely, in love with Sachiko, and I thought of Reiko as a kindly okami-san (not to be confused with *ōkami,* which means Big Wolf) who was just doing her duty as the stablemaster's wife. On some fantasy level I may have viewed her as a prospective mother-in-law. But even though she was very attractive, I never once looked at her with lust, or longing.

Reading romantic semaphore has never been my strong suit, although rather than being slapped for being too forward, I have more often been shoved petulantly in the chest for being hopelessly obtuse. And so it was with Reiko. The signs of her nonmaternal interest in me were all in place: prolonged eye contact, special treats left beside my pillow, fresh flowers in my room. But at the time I had no inkling whatsoever, not even when Sachiko whispered to me in the hall one day, "Sorry, but I have been forbidden to talk to you for a while." Not that we ever talked much anyway; she always seemed to be avoiding me, but I thought that was just her Japanese shyness.

Shortly after that Sachiko simply disappeared. I heard from various sources that she had gone to Kyoto to study art history, or to Nagoya to study weaving, or to Akita Prefecture to learn the alchemy of brewing indigo dye, and I was hurt that she had left town without saying goodbye. One day while I was still smarting from this imagined rejection, Reiko asked me to come with her to pick up some gigantic bags of rice which, she said, had been donated to the stable by one of its many patrons. "I need your strongly arms," she said in English, and I said, "Sure, no problem."

Reiko led me to her dark green Miata, which was parked around the corner from the stable and we sped out into the country toward Narita Airport. How naïve was I? Well, put it this way: when we pulled into the subterranean parking garage of the euphemistically-named Catnap Inn—a vast suburban love hotel which was evidently patterned on Castle Howard in Yorkshire, down to the last rococo turret—I simply assumed that the rice was a gift from the generous proprietor.

Somehow we ended up in a tawdry, garish room: red satin, pink mirrors, circular motorized bed. Even then, it wasn't until Reiko began to unpin her chignon and shake out her shimmering sable hair that I finally understood. My stablemaster's wife had chosen me to be her lover, and there was no way to refuse without causing her to lose face. So I took her in my arms and made deliberately clumsy, selfish love to her, trying to keep my heart and mind from becoming involved, wondering if Sachiko would ever forgive me, doubting it, even weeping a few large warm tears which Reiko clearly mistook for signs of emotional sensitivity, or rapture.

I could have walked away after that first time. I might have had to quit sumo, or move to another stable, but my heart was still my own—or rather it still belonged to Sachiko. But it was one of those heavy-aired, dove-colored days in early June, perfect weather for illicit sex, and Reiko was clearly determined to use the afternoon to make up for half a lifetime of romantic neglect and humiliation. She insisted on making love again and again, and by the third time we had begun to fall into something—love or lust or quicksand—and the feelings were getting deeper and more intoxicating by the minute.

By the time we pulled up in the *cul-de-sac* behind the stable and began unloading the bags of "donated" rice (which Reiko had actually purchased at a grain shop on the way home), my only thought was: When can we do that again? The answer turned out to be: Tomorrow, and the next day, and the day after. That's how it started, years ago, and while I never stopped idealizing the absent Sachiko as my one true love, I knew her mother was my true desire: my animal mate, my lower-primate destiny, my angel-faced ticket to purgatory.

Yet even though Umekochi Oyakata was a lousy husband, even though he and I had never had anything but the most superficial relationship, I still felt guilty about bedding my stablemaster's wife. It just wasn't the sort of thing one ought to do, and I knew Mami would be shocked and disappointed if she ever found out. Still, it was such an addictive pleasure that the only things I really used to worry about were getting caught, or being blackmailed, or getting kicked out of sumo. It never occurred to me that the punishment for my transgression would be so grotesque, and so fatal.

I was always pretty good at science in school, and I remember being captivated by the poetry of physics, and higher math: black holes, quarks, chaos theory. But nothing in Introduction to Astrophysics (which I aced, by the way) could have prepared me for a bewitchment in which I could take on the forms of other people, then change back into myself with no evidence of my grisly crimes on my clothes, in my mouth, or under my fingernails.

Remember when I said that I looked down, after killing that poor innocent young girl, and saw that I wasn't myself? I meant that literally. As I discovered when I looked at my reflection in that shard of blue mirror-glass, not only was I someone else, but that someone else was a startlingly familiar face. (The terrible teeth, however, were those of a predatory killing machine, a cross between a tiger and a barracuda, and the hands were tipped with big-cat claws.)

The person whose form I took was a popular and not untalented American movie actor, with fair hair, perfect features, and a four-letter surname. Why him? I can only guess that it was because I had seen his face on a magazine cover earlier that day and had wondered, briefly, what it would be like to be short and blond and cute.

As for the how, I asked the monstrous Pomeranian about that during our telepathic chat at the bathhouse, but he was no help at all. He just bared his hideous fangs and sneered, "Wouldn't you like to know, fat boy."

I think that was when I realized how serious my predicament was. There was no way I could go on living as a monster, hoping every day that I would somehow snap out of it before I killed too many more people, and dreading every night. If I had no control over the shapes I took during my bloodthirsty rampages, how long would it be before I looked down and found myself in the shape of my beloved Mami, munching on some hapless nocturnal noodle-vendor? The thought was unbearable, and I could only think of one solution.

I'm really just killing time here, so to speak, writing down what happened to try to make sense of it one last time. I can feel the poison working now, threading its insidious way through my engorged arteries, sending my immune system into hysterical air-raid formation, numbing my lips, taming my unruly brain. Back on Anonymous Island we call it *malua;* it's made from a combination of *kava* liquor, tattooing ink, and the supertoxic liver of a *nualoa* blowfish, all pestled together by intoxicated shamans in the sacred volcanic mortar dropped from heaven two million years ago by the Goddess of Anger, Tuatuaroli. That magical mortar is hidden high and deep in the jagged green velour mountains of the island that I love, and will never see again. Ironically, it was my own dear Mami who gave me the sealed clamshell full of malua when I first left for Hawai'i.

"This will keep my darling boy safe from rats and cockroaches," she said. And then she added, only half in jest, "They say it works on evil women, too."

I've already mailed a note of apology and explanation to my mother, along with my will and my bankbook, and I'm planning to burn these unexpurgated pages before I go. The only thing I'll leave behind is an all-purpose plea, black ink on crimson paper: FORGIVE ME, PLEASE, EVERYONE. In the absence of a detailed suicide note, people will probably assume that I was despondent over the downward curve in my career: all those bouts that I should have won easily but didn't. Sometimes an Utamaro face in the audience would suddenly remind me of Sachiko, or Reiko, breaking my concentration for the split second needed to send me stumbling out of the ring, hopping pathetically for balance before finally crashing onto the hard band of sand in front of the ringside seats while the affluent front-row spectators giggled behind gold-ringed fingers, and brushed sand and gladiator-sweat from their expensive but oddly ill-fitting clothes. I would never have taken my own life over anything so petty and ephemeral, of course, but better that the world should think I'm a weak-willed quitter than that anyone should realize the truth about my monstrous crimes. My Mami is the gentlest creature on the planet, and I think she might really die of shame and anguish if she ever found out what her darling son had done.

The curious thing, considering what an athletic, sexual, corporeal sort of life I've led so far, is that I don't regret snuffing out my physical plant so much as terminating my brain waves. All that arduous education, all those joyful insomniac nights of reading until I truly couldn't see straight, all my unique adventures and gaudy mistakes. I would like to believe that the soul goes on, in some improved form, and I hope that next time, if there is a next time, I won't screw up quite so badly.

I've done a fair amount of reading about the Japanese supernatural in recent days, over at the Japan Foundation reading room. What I've learned is that I wasn't really a werewolf at all, just a flawed, hedonistic guy who had the bad luck to get himself turned into a virulent shape-shifting ghoul. *Well then,* you say reproachfully, *If you weren't really a werewolf, what was all that loose talk at the beginning about flesh, and blood, and fur? Where did the fur come in?*

Ah, yes, the fur. Surely you've heard the story of the man in fifteenth-century Austria who was found running naked on all fours through the streets of Salzburg on a moonless night, with a freshly-harvested human spleen in his mouth. Three policemen stopped him on a dark wooden bridge carved with gargoyles and cherubs and oak leaves.

"What's all this, then?" the constables said briskly, shining their oil lamps into the crusty face overhung with blood-soaked hair, then recoiling in horror from the lunatic eyes, the grimy purplish skin, the jagged yellow teeth caked with carrion-plaque.

"I am a werewolf," the man-beast told them in a weird strangulated voice, and the wine-colored organ dropped from his mouth as he spoke. "Please kill me now, before I do any more harm."

"A werewolf? But where is your fur?" asked the literal-minded policemen.

"Can't you see?" cried the Werewolf of Salzburg, his thin lips bright with blood. "The fur is on the *inside*."

That's how it was with me, too, I think: the fur-lined beast of Tokyo. If only someone had invented a Depilomatic for the soul.

I hear police sirens outside now. I don't know if they're here for me, but just in case, I've eaten the last of the malua, washed down with some coconut milk. My lips feel petrified, and enormous; if I looked in the mirror I would expect to see not my own mournful tropical reflection but something resembling one of those uncanny monolithic statues from Easter Island. It grieves me greatly to leave a world which is filled with so many sweet and marvelous things, and I find myself hoping frantically, like a small sleepy child being dragged away from a riotous, sparkling amusement park, that I'll get a chance to return to this lovely little planet, very soon.

So what have I learned from my life as a sumo werewolf, the benighted *loup-garou* of Ryogoku? Nothing terribly original, I'm afraid; just the same old boring rules that no high-spirited young man wants to follow. Don't let feeling good become a substitute for doing right. Never go to bed with a woman you can't hold hands with in public. Borrow your values from poets and philosophers, not from beer ads and action movies. And, of course, beware of devil-dogs.

I know, I know; you weren't expecting a coda. It's like going to a funeral where the corpse suddenly sits up and asks the organist to play "Take Me Out to the Ballgame." So now you want an explanation, right? Fair enough.

Apparently when the paramedics broke the door down (Reiko called them when I didn't answer the phone, bless her heart) I was very near death. At the hospital they pumped my stomach and put me on life support, but the doctors gave me less than a five percent chance of survival. Then—I heard this later from a bouncy little nurse named Kiki—Reiko showed up with a thermos full of some murky liquid ("the color of roses mixed with spinach," as Kiki put it) which she insisted on dribbling into my mouth for hours on end, a few drops at a time. The easygoing nurse figured a little folk medicine couldn't hurt, so she didn't tell the doctors. And then, after three days of touch-and-go during which I coded a record seventeen times, I miraculously woke up, more or less intact.

Meanwhile, the official story put out by the stable was that I had tried to kill myself by taking some potent Polynesian poison, which my mother had sent me to use on rats, because I felt I had let my supporters down with my sloppy sumo of late. In Western culture the "goodbye cruel world" approach is generally considered cowardly, inconsiderate, and vaguely embarrassing, but Japan has traditionally embraced self-destruction as a reasonable, even noble, alternative to sticking around and facing the messy music. The tabloids played up the samurai-suicide aspect, and overnight I went from goat to hero. (Fortunately the scribbled account of my crimes had fallen behind the desk in my apartment, so no one saw it.)

While I was lying comatose, there was another scandal at the stable, which quickly pushed "SUMO SUICIDE ATTEMPT" off the front pages of the hyperventilating tabloids. Three days after I was hospitalized, the stablemaster's long-time favorite mistress went on a daytime talk show, ostensibly to promote a little recipe booklet she had compiled, called *Delicious Midnight-Snack Recipes from the Ginza*. Apparently someone gave her several large shots of whiskey to calm the butterflies in her stomach, and she ended up getting extremely tipsy and announcing on the air that she had been the love of my stablemaster's life long before his empty charade of a marriage, and that she had borne him two strapping sons, and was pregnant with a third. She added, as a reckless afterthought, that she did wish he wouldn't keep his stash of illegal guns at her place, because the children were forever wanting to play with them.

She was still sobering up in the Green Room when the shit hit the fan. The super-staid Sumo Association announced that Ukemochi Oyakata, the former yokozuna Kurokami, had been stripped of all his titles and benefits, and banished from the world of sumo forever. (He subsequently turned to acting, specializing in police dramas, and has done rather well, from what I hear. Who knows, maybe it was a relief to stop living a lie.) And then, in a hell-freezes-over shocker, the Association's spokesman added that the new head of Ukemochi Stable—the inheritor of the venerable title of Ukemochi Oyakata, a name which had once belonged to her father, grandfather, and great-grandfather—would be the wronged wife, Reiko.

I don't know how to express what a radical departure from tradition this was. Imagine that the most hidebound anti-Semitic, homophobic, racist, male-only country club in the United States suddenly decided to admit a woman who was half-Jewish, half-African American, and one hundred percent Lesbian. At any rate, Reiko eagerly accepted the unprecedented offer, for she was after all a fourth-generation sumo child who knew as much about the sport as anyone on earth. She started divorce proceedings against her disgraced husband immediately, and when I finally opened my eyes and began to breathe on my own, she asked me if I would like to run the stable with her. It sounded at first like a business opportunity, and it took me a moment to realize that it was a proposal of marriage.

I think Reiko knew what my answer would be, but I was touched by the offer, and she was very understanding about my need to take my life in another direction. We're friends now (more than friends, actually: business partners) and I was happy when she remarried recently, to a just-retired sekiwake from a rival stable, a much younger man whose sumo pedigree runs almost as deep as hers. I suppose I loved her, in my inconstant philandering way, but she deserved far better, and truer, than me.

As I was getting ready to leave the hospital, alone, I had some unexpected visitors. First came my former roommate Gonzo and his apple-cheeked true love Chie, who wanted to invite me to their wedding. (I declined, but sent a gift.) Gonzo had decided to drop out of sumo since his career was going nowhere, and he and Chie were planning to open their own flower shop back in Uwajima, specializing in extravagantly colorful tropical blooms imported from Tahiti.

Then, as I was sitting in the mandatory departure-wheelchair with nurse Kiki at my side, waiting for the elevator to take me back to the world, who should come floating down the corridor but Sachiko, dressed in a hand-woven blue-and-white ikat kimono, looking lovelier than ever. My jump-started heart did the old fool-for-love flipflop at the sight of her, but it sank a moment later when I learned that she, too, had come to invite me to a wedding. Her face glowed like a Chinese lantern as she told me shyly that she had just become engaged to a smart, kind, talented young man who was an apprentice with the famous Demon Drummers of Sado. (That was where she had been all that time: on Sado Island, studying weaving.)

Kiki discreetly went off to the loo, to give us a few minutes alone. I knew it was pure male ego, but I couldn't help asking whether Sachiko had felt something for me that night when she shaved my torso, and afterward, or whether it had just been my imagination.

"I'm very flattered by your interest," Sachiko began, and that was when I knew that she had never seen me as a romantic prospect. I didn't feel heartbroken so much as amazed and appalled by my own stubbornly myopic male vanity. I tried to stop her from elaborating, but she insisted on adding some words that haunt me still.

"To tell the truth, you were so large that you scared me," Sachiko said, looking down at the floor. "And you always acted very kind and gentle, but—forgive me for saying this—once or twice I thought I saw something strange and dangerous in your eyes."

Yes, I thought ruefully: desire, and egotism, and unreciprocated infatuation.

I took a cab from the hospital back to my secret apartment. On the way we passed one of those mesh-shrouded building sites, and I noticed a sign: COMING SOON: ANOTHER LAWSON STATION! Then I did a double take, for the new construction was on the lot that had until recently been occupied by the spooky bathhouse, official hangout of the most gruesome ghouls in Tokyo. So where had they gone? Back to hell where they belonged, I hoped. Or maybe they were just biding their time, and when the new building was completed, they would stage their midnight revels in the world's most beguiling convenience store, amid the tamarind popsicles and the Holiday Dog chocolates.

There was so much going on that I had hardly thought about the reasons behind my abortive suicide, but I could feel, in my marrow, that the spell was no longer in effect. Still, I found it unbearable to be in Tokyo after what had happened, and I didn't even entertain the idea of returning to sumo—even though, as a Japanese journalist suggested in a telegram sent to me care of the stable, a comeback attempt could have been a "fine human interest angle, indeed."

Hastily, I packed up my things for shipping, said a few good-byes, and issued a combination retirement announcement and public apology for the trouble my suicide attempt had caused. Using an assumed name, I also hired a private detective to find the families of the two women I—or rather, the Beast—had killed. (I could only pray there hadn't been other victims that I didn't know about.) Then I hopped on an Air Melanesia plane and went back to my island.

Once I had finished making anonymous, untraceable payments to the relatives of the victims, there was just enough of my sumo savings left over to buy Mami a stacked washer-dryer combo, in breadfruit green. She loves it, and it is the marvel of the modest village where we live, together, in the same three-room, thatched-roofed house where I was born. The neighbor ladies line up to wash their bright-flowered pareus and "I Got Lei'd in Hawaii" T-shirts, while the giggling children stand on each other's shoulders to peer inside at the vertiginous cosmic drama of the spin cycle.

They call me the Rugby Priest now, because I coach rugby all over the island. As for the second half of my nickname, that comes from the fact that I completed the rigorous shaman's training up on Mount Ala'aloa, and have been admitted to the priesthood of our native religion. My late father was planning to be a priest until he fell in love with my mother and became a deep-sea fisherman instead, so I'm following in the footsteps he almost took. The traditional belief-system of our island is uncommonly sweet and simple; it's all about nature, kindness, dream interpretation, and wishful thinking, so there's nothing that sticks in my religious-anarchist's throat.

Celibacy is a requirement for the priesthood (that's why my father dropped out), but fortunately, or unfortunately, that isn't a problem for me. Although there was no damage to my other faculties—and, thank the gods, no loss of brainpower, for I still love to read, and write, and think—the powerful poison did have a deleterious effect on my sexual functions. My celebrated *membrum virile* now hangs perpetually harmless and deflated, like a windsock in the Sahara on a still day. Irreversible nerve damage, the doctors said; my libido was destroyed as well, so being chaste is a piece of cake.

I keep reminding myself that I had more than my share of passion, romance, and ecstasy in my day, and although it was difficult at first, I'm starting to feel increasingly comfortable with the role of asexual holy man. (Actually I still look big and strong and athletic; I've been working out and watching my diet, and I'm almost back to my rugby-playing weight of 275. It's just that I no longer have the proverbial pistol in my pocket.) It's almost too perfect: I'm like a man with no mouth, no food, and no appetite, who has taken a job in which eating is strictly forbidden.

To be honest, this isn't how I thought "happily ever after" would look, but it's so much better than the alternatives—death, or coma, or serial killing in Tokyo. Reiko's home-brewed combination of pickled *umeboshi* plums, Chinese herbs, and a number of secret ingredients, (patent pending, so I can't divulge the recipe; suffice it to say that I expect my marketing efforts to save lives all over the Pacific)—at any rate, that miraculous potion not only turned out to be an antidote for the deadly poison I had ingested, it may also have cured me of my beastliness. Or maybe that reverse transmogrification was due to something else entirely. Whatever the explanation, I am eternally grateful to have been restored to myself, and eternally sorry for the lives I took. The murders may not have been my fault, exactly, but they happened on my watch, and (short of turning myself in to the police and going to prison, which wouldn't do anyone any good) I take full responsibility.

This is like a second incarnation for me, in a way, a chance to make amends and try to do things right. Sometimes, when I'm with Mami, sharing a dinner of fresh-caught parrotfish, purple sweet potatoes, and coconut-and-seaweed salad, or when I'm watching one of my youthful rugby teams kicking the butts of some cross-archipelago rivals, or when I perform a birth-blessing or soul-speeding ceremony for one of my fellow islanders, I feel that this time I may just be able to get the hang of it. I had my taste of fame and fortune, in a small way, but I seem to be happiest doing elemental things: standing out on the reef fly-fishing with my father's old bamboo rod, or watching the splashy pink-and-orange sunsets from my childhood treehouse, or helping Mami fold the clean laundry. She uses the washing machine every day but she still hangs the wet clothes out to dry on a line strung between two coconut trees because she likes the smell of sun-dried cloth and also, she told me apologetically the other day, because she prefers to use the automatic dryer's circular cavity as a repository for green bananas.

These days, when I look in the mirror, I don't see a beast, or a man with strange and dangerous eyes. Rather, I see a man with the fur on the outside, a man who's trying very hard to be as good as he can. I still do penance every day, in my secret heart, but I know that you have to forgive yourself before you can forgive anyone else. Loving others is easy; the tricky part, for me, is going to be learning how to love myself.

HUNGRY GHOSTS IN LOVE

I have heard of the magical incense
That can summon a soul from the gloom;
I wish that I had some to burn tonight
As I wait by my lover's tomb.

—From an ancient Japanese song

Call me atavistic, but when I find myself in a scary spot I often look to the past for courage and inspiration. Like the time I was on the island of Kulalau, researching my usual semi-frivolous bouillabaisse of travel stories (one on totemic costumes, another on the local penchant for erotic gravestones, a third on a supposedly aphrodisiacal herb called, by delicious linguistic coincidence, *amatti).* A territorial war broke out between the Clan of the Yellow Moth and the White Shark Clan, and I somehow ended up being taken hostage by a gorgeous young Moth Clan warrior—an ordeal I survived by practicing the timeless advice my grandmother Leda once gave to my mother, just after the publication of Leda's scandalous article "My Days (and Nights) with Mr. Pancho Villa." *Remember, darling girl,* she said, *all bandits are gentlemen at heart. Act like a lady, and they'll treat you like a goddess.*

Leda's advice worked like a charm on the Moth Clan warrior, whose name was Raadi Ulonggo. He was one of the most magnetic men I had ever met, and by the time the uprising had been quelled we were what my mother Lilio would have called a torrid twosome. The affair didn't last long, not due to any diminished attraction but simply because I had to go home and do my work, while Raadi had devilfish to catch, angel-masks to carve, and ancestors' skulls to worship.

We did stay in touch, though. He didn't have a telephone at home and he said he wasn't allowed to get calls at the school where he taught, so I would call him at the Red Ginger Inn at a prearranged time every week. Then one day the desk clerk told me that on his way to take my call, Raadi had been ambushed and shot by a member of the Blue Snake Clan. I could hear bloodthirsty shouts in the background, and I hung up the telephone feeling sick, not just for the senseless waste of a beautiful life and the personal loss of my dream-lover, but for the murderous cruelty of clan warfare, on any scale. I was house-sitting on Maui at the time so I cycled over to the nearest church in Kipahulu, a small white-frame chapel in a grove of dizzyingly fragrant yellow plumerias. Kneeling in front of the art-naïf altar, I mumbled an incoherent secular prayer through my tears. Then I lit twenty-six candles, one for every short year of Raadi's life. "Rest in peace," I whispered. "My lovely moth, my fatal flame."

Act like a lady, and they'll treat you like a goddess. Useful advice, to be sure, but the situation I found myself in five years later, on a lonely mountain road in the rugged part of the Japan Alps known as the Valley of Hell, seemed to call for an entirely different sort of maxim. Demure behavior was unlikely to impress the ravening bears which, I imagined, were about to leap out of the forest and shred my tender flesh. No, I needed something more along the lines of "Nothing to fear but fear itself." What I *really* needed was a stun gun or a nice cozy taxicab, but I was alone in the deep dark boonies and the last cab I'd seen was in front of Kyoto Station, several hours earlier.

It had all looked so easy that morning, as I sat reading a secondhand guidebook over sourdough toast and ginger marmalade. (I still haven't managed to develop a taste for the traditional Japanese breakfast of fish, rice, seaweed, a raw egg, and *miso* soup.) I was sitting on the verandah of my little wood-and-paper house in Ohara, outside of Kyoto, gazing at the green and golden geometry of ricefields and the verdigris-frosted roof of an abandoned temple across the way, feeling immoderately grateful for my tiny place in the universe.

Aside from what my mother might have called a serious lack of Vitamin L (for Liaisons, I had always assumed), my life was going fairly well. I loved my rented house, I had just leased a snazzy car, and I had a seemingly endless supply of glamorous, challenging travel-writing assignments. I had only to pick up the telephone and I'd be off to Tuscany or Moorea, Provence or the Outer Hebrides, everything first-class and all-expenses-paid, to write about whatever struck my fancy for an appreciative audience of literate and increasingly mobile Japanese travelers. Those trips took time to arrange, though, and I needed to get out of town right away.

"There are many interesting myths associated with the old wooden inns in the mountainous hot-spring area known as the Valley of Hell," the guidebook said. "According to one story, every year on the tenth day of the tenth month the ghost of a chambermaid who killed herself for love appears at the hot-spring baths down by the river, singing a mournful medieval song and searching for her faithless swain. It is popularly believed that the ghost has strangled several men whom she mistook for her inconstant lover, although no actual fatalities have ever been documented. Still, the legend remains strong, and male guests who are courageous (or foolish) enough to bathe at the inn on that night are required to sign a waiver agreeing to hold the management blameless for anything, however dreadful, that might befall them there."

Now, *that's* my kind of travel story! I thought. Not that I gave the slightest credence to ghosts or to the supernatural in general, but I was absolutely convinced of the inherent romance of outdoor hot-spring baths. I had been wanting to write about their steamy mystique for ages, and now at last I had my angle: The Haunted Hot Spring. Not only was it an excuse to get out of town on that very day—which, as luck would have it, was the tenth day of the tenth month—but I had been feeling somewhat tense and high-strung that week, and there are few things more restorative than a soak in a hot-spring bath. The moon would be full, too: a huge marmalade-colored October moon.

I phoned Maruya-san, the endearingly accommodating editor of a classy bilingual travel magazine in Tokyo called *Odysseus*, and told him the idea. "Great," he said. "Let's set it up for next year."

"Next year?" I echoed. "But I want to go today."

"Then go," he said. "Just keep track of your expenses, and we'll reimburse you for everything, within reason."

I always kept an overnight bag packed and ready, along with my trusty Explorer's Bag, a dark blue canvas labyrinth of pockets, cavities, and secret compartments into which I crammed my laptop computer and an assortment of pens, notebooks, and dictionaries. I only had an hour and a half to get to Kyoto Station, park my car, and catch the train, so I quickly threw on my autumn travel uniform: a long-skirted Delft-blue dress, leggings, thick socks, and my navy-and-taupe suede hiking boots. I left a vague note on the door for the unwelcome (and, I might add, uninvited) visitor who was my reason for wanting to vacate the premises, while another note went under the doormat for the neighbor who would be feeding my portly black-and-white cats, Gifu and Piggott. I nuzzled the kitties goodbye while they squirmed impatiently in my arms. Then I jumped into my little car, an almost cartoonishly sporty celadon-and-cream "Tadpole" roadster (christened, I suspected, by the same marketing genius who came up with the unforgettable Nissan "Parsley" Sedan) and sped off down the dusty road toward Kyoto Station.

The guidebook said that Yomogi Sanso, the purportedly haunted hot-spring inn, was an hour by bus from the Kawanakacho train station, high in the Japan Alps. Simple enough, but the book had neglected to mention that the last bus left at six P.M. while the last train—the one I was on—arrived at 6:45. There were no cabs at the tiny station, so I went to a public telephone and tried to call the inn. The line was busy, and after I had re-dialed several times to no avail I remembered the sepia photos of my beautiful eighty-year-old grandmother Leda climbing a precipitous Himalayan peak with a strikingly handsome young Sherpa in tow. (I'm sure to this day that they were lovers, but she would never admit it, even on her flower-strewn deathbed.) I may as well hoof it, I thought. I mean, what's the point of wearing hiking boots if you don't take a hike once in a while?

So hoof it I did, enjoying the sparkling air and the sweet cheeps of bird-song, automatically composing a bit of florid travelogue text as I marched along. ("The last shreds of burnished rose, glacéed apricot, and smudgy charcoal were fading from the crepuscular lavender sky ...")

Fortunately I had plenty of time. It was only seven o'clock, and the ghost wasn't due until sometime after midnight. Not that I had the slightest expectation of seeing an actual specter, for I was an official nonbeliever when it came to ectoplasm. I just wanted to be on hand to chronicle the ghost's nonappearance in the bemused tone that had become my hallmark, along with a slightly baroque vocabulary and a predilection for idyllic islands, plush landscapes, and four-star hotels.

But then an odd thing happened. The last shreds of burnished rose, etc., really did fade from the sky, and it was suddenly quite chilly and unexpectedly dark. Pulling on my thickly-quilted cotton ski jacket dispelled the chill but did nothing to relieve the disturbing darkness. I could make out the outlines of tall trees on both sides of the unpaved road, and the gravel seemed to give off a faint ambient glimmer. After a while that faded, too, and the only evidence that I was still on the road was the crunch of small stones under my boots. The only other time I had experienced such absolute darkness was in those bottomless caves on Saipan, the ones that are so deep that even the most advanced spelunkers have to explore them on oxygen, like scuba divers.

You can lie to heads of state and customs agents, but always be honest with yourself. That was another of Leda's words-to-live-by, handed down to my mother and passed along to me. All right, I thought, I'll be honest. I'm scared out of my wits. I can't see a blessed thing, I don't know how much farther it is to the inn, I only have the stationmaster's word that this *is* the road to the inn. What if he sent me in the opposite direction by mistake? What if there are beasts in the forest? There could be murderous bears, or rabid raccoons with claws like narrow knives ...

At least I wasn't raised to be superstitious, I told myself, trying to look on the bright side. My heart would be stopping for good right about now if I believed—as everybody used to, in Old Japan—that there is a sinister shadow world populated with a pantheon of malevolent demons, ghouls, and shape-shifting monsters.

I tried all sorts of devices to keep my spirits up: singing old Ricky Nelson songs, composing a semi-objective journalistic account of what I was experiencing, thinking about a creepy bug-movie video I had recently watched, called *Twilight of the Cockroaches*. (I also rented the remake of *The Fly* the same night—the one with Jeff Goldblum as the world's sexiest, most poignant housefly—in an attempt to cure myself of my insect-phobia. Needless to say, that particular double bill did not have the intended effect.)

I finally managed to distract myself from the fear in my gut by fretting about logistics. I had blithely assumed that I would be staying at the "haunted" inn that night, but I hadn't taken the time to ascertain whether Yomogi Sanso was still in business, much less if they had a room available on such short notice. How could I have been so unprofessional? Easy: I was in a rush to catch a certain train and to get out of my house before the man I didn't want to see showed up. Still, I really should have checked the accuracy of that antiquated guidebook before heading for the Valley of Hell.

Extrapolating from the one-hour bus ride, I calculated that it would take me approximately four hours to walk to the inn. My heart sank, and I weighed the merits of returning to the station and trying again the following year. But then it occurred to me that Leda wouldn't have turned back. (Neither would my mother, unless she was sure there was a tall glass of bourbon and a pack of Turkish cigarettes waiting at the train station. And maybe a tall Turkish man, as well.) *One bloodied foot in front of the other, one bloody step at a time*: that was the way Leda made it back alive from the Congo after she was mauled by a tiger cub in a game preserve.

So I kept on walking, one bloodless step at a time. The fear was growing inside me, though, and I realized with a shock that I, the intrepid professional traveler, was actively afraid of the ambiguous darkness of night. Holy cow, I thought, trotting out my trademark vocabulary. Not only am I a hardcore entomophobe, I'm a nyctophobe as well. But what a way to find out, alone on the road to nowhere, with nary a moon in sight.

Then I remembered that I had a penlight in my bag. Brilliant! I thought as I switched it on, and even though the torch only illuminated the road directly in front of me, I found that weak firefly-shaft of light enormously comforting. I quickened my pace, thinking about the hot tea and scalding bath that awaited me at the inn. The straps from my bags were cutting into my shoulders and I was beginning to wish I had left my seven-pound laptop at home, but now that I had a source of light the night seemed reasonably friendly again. It even occurred to me that this forced march, this trial by darkness, might provide the always-elusive first line of my story: "I didn't encounter any ghosts on the road to the Valley of Hell, but I did tangle with some hobgoblins of a purely psychological nature ..."

After about half an hour, the soybean-sized bulb in my miniature flashlight began to flicker and hiss. "Oh no," I said, "please, no." The flashlight sputtered one last time, and I brushed away tears of fear and frustration as my eyes adjusted to the resurgent darkness. And then, half a panicky heartbeat later, I saw the single most welcome sight of my entire well-traveled life.

Off to the left, up a short path, was a tile-roofed gate lit from above by a parchment-shaded oil lantern. A temple! My life was saved. There would be a kindly old priest and his twinkly little wife, or maybe a young couple with two or three rosy-cheeked children peeking around the sliding doors at the bright-haired barbarian. They would have a telephone and a car, and they would almost certainly offer to drive me the rest of the way to the inn.

It was only 8:30, so I would get my story and my sybaritic moonlight soak after all.

As I trotted up to the picturesque gate, I felt suddenly brave, adventurous, redeemed. Another ordeal survived, I thought triumphantly, choosing to forget the unseemly tears of a few moments before. The name of the temple was written in rain-blurred calligraphy on a wooden plaque above the gate, but I'm ashamed to say I couldn't read it. I can read *hiragana* and *katakana* and a few indispensable *kanji*, of course, but I've always been too busy—or perhaps just too lazy—to learn how to read Japanese beyond a precocious-kindergartener level.

The gate was closed and bolted, but there was a low wooden door on one side of it. I climbed through, carefully ducking my head. In front of me was a cobblestone slope lined with gingko trees whose leaves were just beginning to turn a lovely parchment-gold, and at the top of the slope was a graceful antique temple with swooping roofs and bell-shaped windows faintly lit from behind.

Home free, I congratulated myself, as if it were an accomplishment rather than a gift from the gods, and with a sudden burst of energy I sprinted up the slope. There was no doorbell, so I slid open the door, stepped into the stone-floored entry, and called out "Excuse me!"

"*Hai!*" The voice was low and masculine, and it seemed to come from far away. The kindly old priest, I thought fondly. While I waited for the elderly cleric or his diminutive fairy-tale wife to come tottering out to greet me, I looked around the entryway. There was one pair of shoes, straw pilgrim-sandals with white cloth straps, and in one corner was a carved wooden staff topped with a stylized lotus flower. Against the far wall was a mahogany *tansu* chest with polished brass fittings, and above it hung a yellowed scroll, a comical depiction of a teapot with a bushy tail dancing around while a group of townspeople in eighteenth-century costumes looked on. That tableau was familiar, somehow. I seemed to remember having read a story about a supernatural *tanuki*—a type of raccoonish badger-dog—that could turn into a dancing teapot on demand. I had often wished that my own dear, spoiled, indolent cats could be trained to perform simple household tasks, but I couldn't see the appeal of frolicsome pots and pans.

"I'll be right there," called the male voice, closer now, and I could hear the sound of bare feet running along polished wood floors. I suddenly thought about how disheveled and disreputable I must look, but I didn't want the old priest's first impression of me to be as Vain Barbarian with Mirror and Hairbrush in Hand. So I just smoothed my hair, moistened my lips with my tongue, and ran my forefinger under my eyes to wipe away any teary dribbles of mascara. And then there he was: the priest of that lonely antique temple, looming above me on the landing.

We gazed at each other for a long moment. The priest opened his mouth and closed it again, and I did the same. When neither of us seemed to be able to produce a sound, we gave up on speech and just stared at each other with eyes wide and mouths half-open, poleaxed with wonderment.

An hour later, the priest and I were sitting at a low table in a pleasant room overlooking a lantern-lit garden, eating crisp translucent slices of *nashi* pears and crunchy rice crackers, drinking hot green tea, and carrying on an animated, mirthful conversation. We still couldn't stop staring at each other, because the priest of that remote mountain temple was not a kindly old person at all. He was a charismatic, strapping young man of thirty-five or so, with the most extraordinary eyes I had ever seen. This was it, the romantic miracle I had been waiting for since I was fourteen years old: True Love at First Sight. And I had no doubt from the way he was looking at me that the priest was as knocked out as I was.

What did we talk about? Everything, and nothing. Our favorite flowers, our favorite pickles, whether virtuous acts should be broadcast or kept a secret, the relation between fate and coincidence. The priest had never ventured outside Japan and his tastes struck me as a bit outdated—atavistic, even—but those things didn't matter because we had an electrifying rapport that transcended petty matters of language, background, or nationality.

It wasn't a lightweight conversation, though we did make a lot of silly jokes. Or rather, I made silly jokes and he made wry, subtle plays on words. We would be laughing uproariously one moment and the next we would both fall silent, gazing at each other with such intensity that I found it impossible to take a proper breath, and had to get by with shallow gulps of air. We talked about the sequence of events that had brought us together, and I pointed out, with shameless self-congratulation, that if I had chickened out and turned back when the going got rough, I would never have knocked at his door: The Door (I thought melodramatically) of Destiny.

The priest told me his name was Gaki, and I told him he could call me Jo because I hated watching anyone struggle to Japanize my full name, Josephine. Nor did I want the newfound love of my life to be calling me "Josefuiinu" when we eventually got intimate, partly because it takes so long to say and partly because "*inu*" means dog in Japanese.

As I stared at Gaki-san's face, I felt my heart swell with the purest, most primeval sort of attraction. I usually look first at people's mouths—the eyes seem too naked somehow—but there was something so hypnotic about Gaki-san's eyes that I couldn't tear my gaze away. His brows were remarkably thick and shapely, and seemed to wrap halfway around his smooth shaven head. The absence of hair made his large, lucent tea-colored eyes even more compelling, and his other features were a symphony of curves and convexities, firm flesh over elegant bones. The truth is, I didn't dare look at his mouth after the first glance, because I found it so desirable that I was afraid I might do something rash or inappropriate like leaning across the table and kissing him, which would ruin the delicate courtship ballet and remind him that I was an impulsive, culturally illiterate foreigner, not at all a suitable soulmate for a refined Japanese priest.

As I may have hinted already, I'm not only a third-generation travel writer. I'm also a third-generation woman of passion, and after an hour or so of soulful stares and intoxicating conversation I was beginning to wonder when I was going to get to touch him, this man I now wanted more than anyone I had ever met. And then a terrible thought occurred to me. Maybe the soulmate link existed only in my imagination. Perhaps he was just being polite to the strange foreigner, and the reason he was staring at me was simply because he had never seen anyone with blue eyes up close before. Oh no, I thought, he could be married, and there could be a wife sleeping in one of the back rooms of the temple, the petite, impeccably Japanese mother of his apple-cheeked children.

There was only one way to find out: I had to ask. That was another thing my Grandmother Leda told my mother when she returned from her first safari in 1934: *Never beat around the bush.* No African-savanna play on words was intended, alas. Leda was a courageous feminist pioneer, a fine reporter, and a brick in every way, but she had a curious post-Victorian aversion to frivolous wordplay.

"Um," I said, "if you don't mind my asking, who lives here besides you?"

The priest looked at me quizzically. "Just me and Pimiko," he said.

Pimiko? Of course: the flawless wife. I could picture her in every exquisite detail. Long black hair, delicate small-featured face, graceful body wrapped in an elegant kimono, fluid mistress of all the Zen-influenced arts I had made such a mess of: dropping the tea whisk, spilling the *sumi* ink, snipping my flower stems too short, then furtively trying to Scotch tape them back together. "I see," I said glumly.

"Would you like to meet her?"

"No, that's all right, please don't bother waking her up on my account."

The beautiful priest laughed, the most luminous full-faced laugh I had ever seen. "That's all right," he said, "she spends most of her time sleeping anyway." That remark baffled me, since the only Japanese wife I knew complained constantly about overwork and sleep deprivation, but before I could respond Gaki-san had left the room. I felt sick to my stomach, because this disappointment seemed to confirm what I had long feared: that it was my fate to have brief, doomed affairs, that I would never marry, would never know genuine love, would never find a man who wasn't just a passionate playmate (or someone else's husband) but a true friend and ally as well.

The door slid open and I held my breath. "Miss Jo, meet Pimiko," said the priest in his deep voice. When I looked up, eyes full of dread, he was standing over me holding a small biscuit-colored kitten with cornflower-blue eyes. He tried to get the kitten to shake hands with me, but it swiped at his sturdy forearm with its tiny claws, jumped down, and ran away.

"*That's* Pimiko?" I said, trying to keep the relief from showing in my voice.

"Yes, what did you think, that Pimiko was my wife?" Gaki-san laughed again, a hearty booming laugh, and I shook my head in an exaggerated way to demonstrate the sheer absurdity of such a thought. "No," I said huffily, "I thought maybe she was the housekeeper."

"No such luck," he said with a maddening grin. "I live here alone. I don't mind the housework, and the solitary life does have its occasional advantages." I assumed he was talking about privacy, and I thought this might be the breathtaking moment when he led me off to his priestly sleeping chamber. (I imagined a patched futon laid out on the floor, a window opened to the frosty garden, the air fragrant with incense and mandarin oranges.) Instead he said, "Do you have the time?'

"It's nearly ten," I said, glancing at my watch, which has stars and crescent moons instead of numerals, on a midnight-blue face. I've always had a thing about the semiotics of sorcery, dating back to the first time I saw *Fantasia* at age three and said to my mother, "Lilio, I simply must have that hat!"

"Well," said the priest, "if you want to get to the inn by midnight, we probably ought to leave right now."

"Oh," I said unenthusiastically, for I had completely forgotten about my assignment. I thought of saying, "Forget the haunted hot spring, I'd rather stay here with you," but I was afraid he might not respect me if I didn't appear to be conscientious about my work. Besides, it was a potentially great story, even without the ghost. "Will you come with me?" I asked.

"Gladly," he said, "but I'd better warn you that my vehicle is not exactly the latest model." We put on our shoes and jackets, and he led me outside to a detached barn. I saw then that his "vehicle" was a wooden cart, which he quickly hooked up to a sleepy-looking gray donkey named Suzu.

"I've been meaning to buy a car," my sweet priest said, "but I'm waiting for them to invent one that runs on hay." Then he laughed his amazing whole-souled laugh, and the night seemed to explode with stars.

Once she was fully awake, Suzu the Donkey moved much faster than I would have expected, and we arrived at the inn well before midnight. I couldn't help wishing the trip had taken longer, because I was enjoying the legitimized closeness of sitting next to Gaki-san on the seat of the cart, our tingling arms tangential, our thighs barely touching, our chilly breath mingling in a cloud of sentient ambiguity. The priest held a large paper lantern which illuminated the road for several yards ahead of the donkey's clip-clopping hoofs, and it occurred to me that the temple hadn't had a telephone, or flush toilets, or electricity.

We hardly talked at all on the way to the hot spring, except once or twice when he asked me if I was cold. I always said "A little," knowing he would tuck the shared blanket around me while I closed my eyes and inhaled his intoxicating incense-tinged aroma. Finally we came to the top of a ridge, and Gaki-san reined in the donkey.

"That's Yomogi Sanso down there," he said, pointing to a dark, sprawling compound of two-story wooden buildings set on either side of a rushing river and connected by a covered wooden bridge. At precisely that moment the fat yellow-orange moon, which had been obscured all evening behind thick clouds, sailed into the clear part of the sky and I could see the natural hot-spring pools along the river bank, steaming in the cold night air like giant vats of noodles.

"But there are no lights at all!" I said, my voice strident with anxiety. "There's no way everyone could have gone to bed already, I mean this is supposed to be some major supernatural occurrence!"

"Let's go down and see what's going on," Gaki-san said calmly.

What was going on at the unilluminated inn was precisely nothing. There was a sign on the firmly bolted front door which, Gaki-san told me, announced that the inn would be closed from September 15 until March 31. (I could read the Japanese numerals, but that was about all.) In case of emergency, the owners could be reached at such-and-such a number, in far-off Kumamoto. There wasn't a word about the tenth day of the tenth month, or about the chambermaid's ghost. I felt a quick rush of disappointment, but then I thought, Wait a minute, if I hadn't gone on this wild ghost chase, I would never have met this wonderful man.

"Well," said Gaki-san, rubbing his ungloved hands together. "As long as we've come all this way, what do you say to a moonlight swim?"

No one can ever take that away from me: the memory, clear as water, of that irresistibly lovable man standing on the banks of the river, slowly removing his priest's robes. First the padded woolen jacket, then the heavy indigo cotton *koromo* (like a kimono, but with a fuller skirt), then the two layers of under-kimono. And there he was, surprisingly lithe and muscular, dressed in nothing but goosebumps and a white cotton loincloth. He plunged into the chilly water with his back to me, and a moment later I saw the loincloth floating on the surface, like bandages unwinding from a poorly-wrapped mummy.

The next move, obviously, was mine. I took a deep breath and shed my own jacket, then my dress, shoes, socks, and leggings. I stood there for a moment, shivering convulsively in my brassiere and underpants. Fortunately they were newish lace-trimmed satin from Victoria's Secret, gray on ivory, not mismatched oddments held together by mildew and safety pins, like some of the carbon-dated lingerie that lurked sea-monsterishly in the uncharted depths of my underwear drawer. I wasn't quite ready to shed those last bits of insulation, not so much out of modesty as because it was so damn cold. I took another deep breath, and waded cautiously into the frigid water.

It was a shock, to be sure. The chill literally took my breath away, but at least my heart didn't stop. The priest had been treading water with his back to me ever since I had stuck my icy toes into the even icier water, and now he swam over to where I stood submerged up to my neck, my teeth chattering like demonic castanets.

"I know," he said. "This is ridiculously cold, but I thought we should try it just for the contrast, and the discipline. Enough is enough, though. Let's jump into the *rotenburo,* quick!"

I tried to say "Gladly," but my frozen lips wouldn't cooperate, so I just nodded. I got out ahead of him, which meant that I didn't have to worry about hypocritically averting my eyes from the place where his loincloth should have been. But then I noticed peripherally, with a mixture of relief and disappointment, that he had put the loincloth on again.

My teeth were still chattering audibly as I ran the short distance across the smooth rocks and plunged into the nearest hot-spring bath, which bubbled up from a mineral-rich spring below the ground. The radical change in temperature was another shock to my system, but after a moment the warmth began to kick in and I felt a sensation of absolute and total well-being. *I can't imagine feeling better than this*, I thought. I heard a splash behind me, and then I felt the priest's gentle hands on my shoulders. *Actually, on second thought, perhaps I can.*

Slowly he turned me around so that I was facing him through the ethereal steam. What I saw in his eyes frightened me a little, in the way that pure romantic possibility is always slightly alarming to someone who has spent her life compromising in matters of the heart. Gaki-san didn't say anything at first. He just drew me toward him, and when we were so close that I couldn't focus my eyes and his already beloved face was swimming before me like a phantasm, he said, "I think you know how I feel." And then at long last, he kissed me.

There are no words in my vocabulary to describe that moment. I've squandered all my superlatives on run-of-the-mill sunsets and mediocre men, and all I have left is wonder and breath. Kissing Gaki-san was pure *ahhh*, the openest sound the human mouth can make, the most receptive feeling the human heart can support without dying of rapture. Did I undress myself? I think I must have, because all I remember is being naked and standing there, heart-stoppingly close but not quite touching, like in one of those silly teenage tease-me games. Except this wasn't a game. I think we both knew that once we let our bodies touch we would be lost to the world for weeks, and we wanted to savor the anticipation for as long as possible.

Gaki-san's kiss was like life support and oxygen, it was like all the fruit in the world. When he pulled his mouth away, saying "Wait! Did you hear that?" I gave a little moan and put my hand behind his neck to try to pull him back. "No," he said, resisting. "Listen!"

I listened, and a moment later I seemed to hear a faint snatch of vocal music, an old-fashioned song without words—all breath and tremolo, as if the breeze itself were singing. A moment later I saw something materializing in the thick gauzy air. At first I thought it might just be the roiling steam from another of the open-air baths, but as I gaped in disbelief the steam-cloud began to take on a perceptibly human shape. I could see planes of more substantial mist that seemed to translate into a spectral sweep of hair, a translucent trailing kimono, a sad bewildered face.

The kiss has made me delirious, I thought with a shiver, but when I turned to look at Gaki-san I saw that his face wore a complicated expression: a combination of fear, belligerence, and resolve. I remembered then that the ghost supposedly preyed on men at the hot-spring baths. Was it possible that Gaki-san was seeing the same illusion I saw, and thought the vengeful chambermaid had come to get him?

"Close your eyes," he said, his voice strangely harsh.

"Why?" I asked.

"Just close them, now!" he hissed with shocking ferocity. I scrunched my eyes closed, like a child playing hide-and-seek. "Don't open them until I tell you to," Gaki-san added. "If you open your eyes, our love will die."

I closed my eyes even more tightly, thinking, *Our love, oh my God, he said "our love"!* I managed to resist the urge to peek, but I was aware of some sort of change going on in the water, as if Gaki-san were thrashing around. There was an odd sense—how shall I put this?—that he was occupying more space than before. And then I heard a terrible low growl, not so much animal as bestial, followed by a shrill female scream. The water churned again and I thought I heard Gaki-san say something, but it didn't sound like Japanese or any other language I had ever heard. There was another soprano scream, not quite so close by as the first, and after a moment the stirred-up water seemed to subside into its normal quiescence.

I heard Gaki-san sigh, and then I felt his warm lively lips on mine, but I still didn't open my eyes. After a long moment the priest whispered "You can look at me now, Jo-san." He was standing there in front of me, with only his spellbinding face and shining shaven head showing above the water. There was nothing in the air around us except for the benign shapeless steam from the hot-spring pools: no blood, no ghosts, no monsters. The reporter in me wanted to ask "What on earth happened just now?" but the woman of passion just wanted to be kissed again.

Like all beguiling, addictive, potentially deadly drugs, sex has its downside. But it has its miraculous side as well, which is probably why I've never quite managed to give it up. In fact, I've always suspected that part of the reason some religious adepts take vows of celibacy is because the most sublime sort of sexual rapture can do a really wicked and confusing imitation of spiritual enlightenment. Meditation is all very well, but I have to confess that I've never felt more in and of the moment, more connected to the fluid mystical matrix of existence, than when I was in the throes of a mad affair: sensual pleasure as mock *satori*.

Yesterday we were monkeys, tomorrow we'll be memories. The only true reality is Now. That was one of my mother's original profundities, hatched, no doubt, in some subversive whiskey-soaked spy haven in Budapest or Istanbul. She was right, though. Yesterday and tomorrow are the ghosts that haunt us all, and we sometimes spend so much energy on guilt and nervous anticipation that we have no time left over for simply being alive. But on that full-moon night, in the steaming riverside pool with Gaki-san, I was like a single-celled organism in the very best sense. No emotional baggage, no ambivalent thoughts, no hidden agendas. I was a vessel of sheer desire, and my only wish was for closeness and completion.

"There's no one here," I whispered. "It's only you and me." Our faces were so close that our eyelashes were touching, and the vaporous plumes of breath came out of our half-opened mouths in perfect unison. Had I been capable of rational thought I might have seen that as a metaphor for the merging of souls, but I was out of my head with desire, and all I could think about was closing the last gap between us. I had reached the point where kissing stops being delicious foreplay and turns into sadistic torture. On some level I was probably aware that I was a slave to my hormones and to the antiquated mammalian mandate to increase our flawed but charming tribe, but that didn't make the urges any less imperative.

So when Gaki-san lowered his eyes and began to descend on my mouth again I said, "Please, I can't do this anymore, I need to be closer to you." Gaki-san put his arms around me and squeezed so hard that I thought I heard one of my ribs crack, which seemed appropriately Adam-and-Eve-ish, somehow.

"We're as close as two people can be, aren't we?" he murmured. "You're inside my heart, and I'm inside yours, and when I look into your eyes I feel as if I'm swimming in the deep blue lagoon of your soul. Isn't that enough?"

Don't even think about saying it, you crude American wench, I warned myself, but of course my headstrong self, hell-bent on instant gratification, didn't listen. "I'm sorry," I whispered. "I know I'm not enlightened, but I really, really need to have you inside me in a more, um, tangible way, too."

Gaki-san looked stricken. "Oh no," he said. "I had no idea. I can't mate with you, it would be ... *chimeiteki*." I didn't know the word, and it wasn't until I looked it up in my Japanese-English dictionary, several lifetimes later, that I discovered it meant "fatal." In the meantime, I hazarded a guess.

"Do you mean you're sick?" I said incredulously, for he hardly seemed a likely carrier for a sexually transmitted disease.

"No," said Gaki-san, "that's not it. That's not it, at all." He went charging out of the water like a terrified water buffalo, and when I looked up through prismatic tears of humiliation I saw him shaking himself dry on the bank above, looking as magnificent as a god and just as unavailable.

We rode home in the donkey cart in excruciating silence, the two of us huddled at opposite ends of the seat under separate small blankets. Back at the temple, I retreated to the clean but shabby guest room after a mumbled "Good night." No eye contact, certainly not a kiss; I had somehow managed to ruin the most promising love affair of my life before it began. Feeling as if I had swallowed a large cold stone, I changed into my flannel nightgown, unpacked my laptop computer, and climbed under the patchwork cotton quilt. Pen and ink on paper might have been more in keeping with the preindustrial ambience, but I needed the comforting glow of that radioactive screen.

"Dear Gaki-san," I typed, but that was as far as I got. I didn't know what had gone wrong, so I didn't know what to apologize for. Had I been too forward, too fast, too Occidental? I felt the sick familiar chill of heartbreak as I realized how desperately I wanted this man in my life, even if I never got to experience the sweet illusion of sexual connection again with him or with anyone else. I felt, in that mad moment, that I would rather live with Gaki-san as monk and nun, than to live with anyone as man and wife, or squire and squeeze. (Yes, anyone: even my dear vanished Raadi Ulonggo, even that tender, hilarious flamenco-dancing architect in Seville, even the exiled White Russian composer on Salt Spring Island who wrote poignant *a capella* cantatas based on whalesong.)

Life had handed me the magic muffin on a plate, and I had turned it into a sordid heap of crumbs. The reverse Rumpelstiltskin, that was me, busily spinning gold into straw. To be fair to myself, I also had a small gift for making something out of not very much: artichoke soup out of thorns in the heart, amusing articles out of disappointing trips to polluted places, a modest, ephemeral sort of poesy out of some decadent luxury-hotel brunch. I may have been a washout as a soulmate, but I could still write a presentable sentence, most of the time.

I closed my eyes and waited for the first words to come. That was what I liked most about writing: the seance and the seizure, the feeling that the keyboard under my fingers was a sort of literary Ouija board. Publication was just a pleasant side effect and a way to pay the bills, but it was the channeling process that made me feel chosen, and alive.

"Ah," I said, as the words began to take shape, like a ghost in the mist. I put my hands on the self-same keys and to my surprise, my fingers began to type what might have been the beginning of a novel: "Big moon, rushing river …"

Big moon, rushing river, mountain full of monkeys. In the same steaming pool where fugitive samurai once came in disguise to recover from their wounds, a man and a woman sit in silence, half-submerged, eyes closed, minds attuned to the music of time. The man has broad shoulders, cryptic eyes and a minstrel mouth. A wet cloth is draped over his effulgent shaven head, and he is humming an old brothel tune. The woman's long hair smells vaguely of almonds and peaches; it is carelessly pinned up with ivory combs in the shape of swans, and her pale breasts float on the water like disembodied triangles of tofu. He is a traveling monk, sworn to the celibate road, she a divorced designer of iridescent raincoats who lives for sensation, gossip be damned. Perhaps later his overheated blood will send him sleepwalking to her room in the inn, and they will embrace wildly, transparently, like ghosts in heat, with no witness but the myopic moon. For as Japanese novelists have known for eons, there is more potential for erotic abandon at a hot-spring resort than anywhere else in the world ...

Wait, time out, I hear Gaki-san's footsteps coming down the hall. He's probably just going to use the bathroom, that curiously primitive wooden-lidded hole in the ground. But no: the footsteps have stopped outside my door. And now the door is sliding open, and I have stopped breathing, possibly forever. The only reason I'm still typing this nonsense is because I want to appear busy and occupied, self-conscious poseur that I am. Okay, this is it. I can feel Gaki-san standing in the open door, and I'm going to turn and look at him right ... now.

We were like beasts that night, but we were like angels too, Gaki-san and I. The explosive collusion between our bodies seemed to be a sort of cellular semaphore for the sparks in our souls, and the wildfire in our hearts. I wasn't planning to tell this part of the story (as my passionate but always circumspect grandmother used to say, *There are times when the most eloquent word in the world is an ellipsis*) but because of the weird way things turned out, I really think I have to.

So, flashing back a bit: I turned to look at Gaki-san, expecting to see him standing in the door dressed in a rumpled sleeping kimono. I was totally unprepared for the vision of ecclesiastical elegance that greeted my eyes. He wore a gold silk kimono under a sheer robe of scarlet voile trimmed at hem and cuffs with gilt brocade, and on his head was a stiff black mesh hat in a style I associated with shrine priests or medieval courtiers. In one hand he held a calligraphy brush and a cinnabar-lacquered box, while in the other was a tarnished bronze bowl full of glowing charcoal briquettes. Even from ten feet away, I could feel the delicious heat.

"May I come in?" he said, almost shyly, and of course I said, "Yes." I thought he had come to Talk Things Over, so I was perplexed when he handed me a small blue ceramic pitcher in the shape of a bird, with its beak as the spout.

"Go fill this with water," he said. (No please, no *kudasai*, no *onegai shimasu.*) I padded down the cold wooden hall, my visible breath preceding me like a ghostly lady-in-waiting, until I came to the pump-handled faucet outside the bathroom. I filled the bird to overflowing, then put a few drops of the icy water on my fingertips and pressed them to my tired eyelids. As an afterthought I took a sip of water and spit it out, remembering the dragon-mouthed fountains at the gates of Shinto shrines where visitors stop to rinse the tawdry taste of self from their mouths before asking the gods for some selfish, impossible favor.

When I returned to my room Gaki-san was sitting in the middle of the floor in meditation posture. As I approached he opened his eyes, took the pitcher without a word, and began grinding a jet-black ink stick in a recessed oval stone embossed with *chinoiserie* arabesques, adding a trickle of water every few moments.

"All right," he said when the inkstone's bowl was nearly overflowing with dark, lustrous fluid, lacunaed here and there with opalescent rainbow shimmers. "Take off all your clothes."

I thought you'd never ask. Of course I didn't say that, or anything else. I just pulled my blue flannel nightgown over my head as matter-of-factly as I could, then stepped out of my lace-and-satin panties. When I stood naked before him this time I felt a bit shy, because he was still dressed in his opulent, intimidating costume and it is a basic precept of civilization that the clothed person has the advantage in most social situations. I had no idea what was going on, but for once I wasn't craving a specific sensation, or outcome. I was just waiting to see what would happen and thinking joyfully, This is my life, and it's incredibly interesting right now.

"Close your eyes," said Gaki-san. "This may feel a little cold at first." I closed my eyes, and waited. After a moment I felt something cold and wet moving down my shoulder. For the briefest of instants I thought it might be Gaki-san's gelid tongue, but then I realized that it was the brush, laden with chilly black ink. What on earth was he doing? Another vague image surfaced, of a scene in a grainy old Japanese horror movie I had seen once on PBS in Honolulu, in which a priest painted sutras on the body of a blind lute-player to protect him from angry ghosts. Unfortunately, he forgot to paint the ears and the ghosts literally ripped them off. Could this be some sort of charm to protect me from the chambermaid's peevish ghost?

I felt the brush running down one arm, then the other, then down my back, then across my chest. When it finally began to circle first one breast, then the other, I gasped in awe at the intensity of my suddenly resuscitated desire.

"Now stand up," Gaki-san ordered. He painted the rest of my body and my face, including the ears. By the time he finished I was no longer capable of normal respiration, and my chest was heaving uncontrollably.

"All right, open your eyes," Gaki-san said. I obeyed, feeling as if I had been long gone, and far away. When I looked down at my body I saw that it was covered with fluid, serpentine calligraphy. The only thing I recognized was the sinuous Sanskrit character for "a" or, I prefer to think, for "ah," which I had seen on scrolls in many of the temples I had written about.

"Can you draw this?" In one fluid motion Gaki-san painted that same character on the cover of my new moss-green notebook, then handed me the brush. I memorized the simple swoops and swirls of the character, then opened the notebook and drew a slightly shaky facsimile on the inside of the cover.

"Perfect," said Gaki-san charitably. "Now just draw that same character all over my body, the way I did on yours." His voice was so cool, his demeanor so dignified, his aura so priestly, that I suddenly had a startling thought. I had been assuming that he had forgiven me, and that we would end up spending the night together. But maybe this whole ritual wasn't leading up to some transcendent body-and-soul confluence at all. Perhaps it was just protection against the ghosts, and after we were both suitably decorated with mystic scriptures we would chastely put our clothes on and return to our solitary beds.

As I watched Gaki-san step out of his splendiferous robes, I felt almost nauseated with longing. He was wearing a red silk loincloth, and when he showed no signs of removing it, I said, "Shall I begin?"

"Please," he said, kneeling in front of me. I knew then that there was no romance in our future, because our faces were just inches away and he didn't show the slightest interest in bridging that breathy gap with a kiss.

I began painting the "ahs," timidly at first but with a growing sense of assurance and elation. *Lovers are a dime a dozen,* I told myself (quoting an epigrammatic ancestor, of course), *but love is hard to find.* I loved this remarkable man, although I knew he would probably never be my lover. It was a bittersweet thrill to be painting spidery symbols on his warm golden skin on the tenth day of the tenth month, in front of a bell-shaped window limned in moonlight. Unrequited desire aside, I felt perfectly at home in the marrow of that exotic moment, even if I had no idea what I was doing, or why.

I painted Gaki-san's arms, legs, back, and chest, trying not to perceive them as components of a sensuous male body but rather as inert canvases for my childish but improving calligraphy. I painted his face, trying not to see it as the face of the man I desired but rather as an intriguing arrangement of features, a logistical challenge to my paintbrush.

"And now, the ears," I said, wondering whether he had seen the film. (*Kaidan*, that was it, or maybe *Kwaidan*.) Now that I thought about it, there had been a timeless tone to all our conversation, with none of the usual pop-culture references to books, movies, television, songs.

Gaki-san was silent the entire time, his eyes downcast as if he were lost in meditation. Finally I finished decorating his perfectly masculine neck, with its prominent tendons and undulating Adam's apple under silky amber skin, and nothing was left un-inked except for the area beneath the red loincloth.

This has nothing to do with sex, I told myself, it's just another bit of human canvas to cover. But that didn't stop my hands from shaking as they slowly unwrapped the iridescent crimson silk from around Gaki-san's strongly muscled loins. I wouldn't dream of describing what I saw when the loincloth fell to the floor, or how exciting it was to be touching that lovely fertile realm with the tip of my trembling brush, any more than I would want him chatting with some stranger about the shape of my breasts, or divulging how he felt while he was covering them with tender Sanskrit "ahs." Suffice it to say that my desire wasn't diminished, even slightly.

"I guess that does it," I said after the last breathless flick of the brush. Gaki-san opened his eyes and looked straight at me, and I felt as if I had just been electrified by a million volts of desire. "Do you know what this was for?" he asked.

"To protect us against angry ghosts?" I said. Gaki-san looked as if he might be about to offer some sort of explanation, but after a long pause he just said, "That's close enough." He put his robes back on, picked up the calligraphy tools, and left the room without meeting my naked gaze, sliding the door behind him with a jolting thud. Oh no, I thought, he didn't even say good-night. After a moment I heard his muffled faraway voice chanting a Buddhist sutra, and it seemed like the most alien sound I had ever heard.

I flung myself down on the futon and began to weep. I felt sick, rejected, and totally alone. Here I am at last, I thought, at the bottom of the misery pit. This is what happens to foreigners who stay too long in Japan.

That bleak epiphany made me cry even harder. I must have been snuffling rather loudly, because I didn't hear the door slide open. Suddenly I felt strong arms lifting me up and Gaki-san was there in a rumpled sleeping kimono the color of maize, holding me tightly and whispering, "I couldn't stay away from you, I'm so sorry if you misunderstood. I've never stopped wanting you, it's just that it's very difficult and dangerous for me to be with you right now." I didn't know or care what he was talking about; we were together, and that was all that mattered.

There's really nothing new to say about sex, or passion, or making love. The words that spring to mind are oddly mercantile, and scientific: merger, congruence, fusion. "Miraculous" might work if I hadn't overused it quite so shamelessly in the past ("The chef does a miraculous *crème brûlée* ...") and the same goes for "rapturous," "blissful," and "ecstatic."

But we humans are a naturally curious and voyeuristic species, and I'm sure you must be wondering: how was it? Since I've dragged you, my phantom reader, along this far, through all the ambiguities and misunderstandings, I should at least tell you that *it*—that is, what transpired between Gaki-san and me that night, between our illustrated bodies and our sublimely empty minds—was simply, unbelievably, indescribably wonderful. And there you have it: the woman who gets paid by the adjective, tongue-tied, dumbstruck, and at a total loss for words.

A torrid twosome, lost to the world for weeks. That was the scenario I envisioned, but since nothing had gone as I expected, I shouldn't have been surprised when Gaki-san brought me breakfast in bed early the next morning (rice, seaweed, miso soup) and then announced that he had to leave on a journey.

Before I could embarrass us both by begging to go with him, he said, "Your bus will be passing by in about half an hour, so you have time for a quick bath. I heated up the water for you."

He was kind and shy, he was obviously thinking about me, but I was consumed with panic. "I need a kiss," I said, hating myself for needing anything. He gave me a dutiful little fadeaway kiss, a miserly tight-lipped peck that seemed to negate all the voluptuous open-mouthed passion of the night before.

"Couldn't we make love one more time, for the road?" I pleaded in a horrid tone of craven desperation. "I don't need to bathe, I'll just get dirty on the train."

Gaki-san stared pointedly down at the arms that were draped possessively around his neck and I noticed that while he had washed off his temporary Sanskrit tattoos, mine were still more or less intact, if a bit blurred from the night's activities. "Please forgive me, but I have some things to do," he said, gently disentangling my arms as if I were some lewd octopus-woman, and then he left the room. Men always leave, I thought.

So that was it. A night of wild, perfect, soul-swallowing love, of two people saying all the things that anyone could ever wish to hear, and the next morning it's soup and rice and See you later. As I climbed out of the tangled bed I noticed that Pimiko, the little beige kitten, was asleep on top of my soft suitcase, her forepaws curled up and her long vibrissae trembling with each exhalation. Suddenly I felt a surge of homesickness for my own cozy home and my own somnolent cats.

Oh well, I thought, if this turns out to have been a one-night stand, it was surely the most thrilling dalliance in the history of romance, and even though I felt as if someone had just made *teppan-yaki* out of my heart, I don't regret the experience for an instant. Maybe I would even try to write about it someday, in a tastefully elliptical way: How I Spent My Pre-Halloween Vacation, by a third-generation fool for love.

Bathed, dressed, and packed, etched-silver jewelry and Mink Brown mascara in place, I began to feel like myself again. (Actually, I had only been able to find one of my Zuni hoop earrings, but I figured the mate must be in my bag somewhere.) "Goodbye, Pimiko," I said, and the kitten half-opened one brilliant blue eye, then let it slide closed again. I wondered who would take care of her while her enigmatic master was away, wherever he was going.

Gaki-san was standing in the entryway looking exotic and remote in a round bamboo hat so large that it completely hid his face. He wore a black robe over two layers of white under-kimono, white cotton leggings, and straw sandals, and he carried a wooden staff with a carved lotus blossom at the top. It seemed like many months ago that I had seen that staff and those sandals in the entryway, and I found it hard to believe that I had only spent twelve hours at the temple. My insatiable lover now seemed as distant as a stranger, like some faceless pilgrim I might pass on the street.

That's what I hate about men, I thought, they're totally different in the dark than they are in the daylight. It's as if they go through some weird internal metamorphosis at dawn, like emotional vampires.

I was sitting on the landing, lacing up my boots, when Gaki-san lifted his hat and looked up at me. His mesmerizing eyes were still hidden but I could see his lips moving as he said, "I know this isn't what you expected, and I apologize. I do love you, and I meant every single thing I said last night. I'll be waiting here for you next year, on the tenth night of the tenth month, and I promise that nothing will have changed. But please don't come here in the meantime or try to contact me in any way. A year flies by, you'll see. We'll be together again in no time."

He bowed to me then, nose to knees in the exaggerated Japanese way. That impeccably polite bow was like an arrow through my heart, for even though we had shared hundreds of the most intimate kisses imaginable I felt I needed a goodbye kiss in order to go on living. But Gaki-san just bowed again, so low that his height was cut in half.

"*Osaki ni*," he said. "Please excuse me for leaving ahead of you." And then he was gone, closing the door behind him.

"I'll be true to you, I promise!" I shouted, but that didn't seem like a satisfactory ending. I needed to hear him say, "I will, too."

Leaving my laces untied, I grabbed my bags and ran down the walk to the gate, only to find the country road deserted. Gaki-san hadn't had more than thirty seconds' head start, but he seemed to have flown away or vanished into thin air. Very confusing indeed, I thought as I walked along the road—that perfectly ordinary road which had seemed so terrifying the night before. Then I smelled diesel exhaust and an ancient pale green bus stopped in front of me.

"Where are you going?" asked the driver. He was an elderly man with skin the color of roasted pecans and a dazzling metallurgic smile, not just the usual gold-capped teeth but a scattering of silver and bronze ones as well. I wish I knew, I thought as I boarded the bus. But I just said, "I'm going home to Kyoto."

"Ah," said the old man, with a cryptic gleaming smile. "Back to the real world."

Autumn, Winter, Spring, Summer. Days passed, then months, then entire seasons, but no matter how busy I was, no matter how diverting my surroundings, I never went an hour without thinking about Gaki-san. My heart was safe in its carapace of confounded love, and I barely looked at another man. They were around, of course, everywhere I went. A footloose mystery writer in New Zealand; an exuberant magazine editor in New York; an Oxford-educated botanist who moonlighted as a witch doctor specializing in the exorcism of Oceanic tree spirits; a sensitive tuna-fishing mogul in the next seat on a flight from Guam to Yap, wearing a "Flipper" T-shirt under his palomino-colored silk suit.

By some grisly fluke I even ran into the uninvited visitor whom I had managed to avoid back in October by fleeing to the Valley of Hell. He was a successful documentary film producer, and on paper he looked like the perfect man for me: smart, witty, well traveled. In person, though, I felt an inexplicable revulsion when I was around him. I didn't like his musky aroma, or his multiple earrings, or his faddish barbed-wire tattoos, and his repeated declarations of some sort of Kismet-like attraction only intensified my unease. We literally bumped into each other at the San Francisco airport, where we were both buying gift-wrapped loaves of sourdough bread. Our chat was mercifully brief, and as he dashed off to catch his flight to Zagreb he called over his black leather shoulder, "Dream about me tonight, okay?"

Ooh, yuck, I thought, and I actually shuddered. Romantic chemistry is one of the great mysteries of life, but another puzzler is how people can have the density of ego not to realize that their interest isn't reciprocated in the least.

Even with men who didn't actively repel me, I felt none of the usual tugs of temptation, no stirrings in the viscera or the imagination. Gaki-san had never asked me to be faithful, but I couldn't imagine wanting to be with another man when someone so rare was (he had said it himself) waiting for me. Even though I was exceedingly busy during those months, somewhere in the center of my being there was a gallstone, or a heartstone, a hard knot of unslaked appetite and unrequited desire. And at the center of that stone, like a pickled plum inside a rice ball, lurked a tiny malignant ball of doubt.

I tried to ignore the questions that popped into my mind almost every night before I fell asleep. Does he really love me? Why all the mystery? What happened at the hot-spring bath while my eyes were closed? Why couldn't we have a normal long-distance relationship, talking on the phone for hours and visiting each other every few months, at least? Why did we both have to be painted with Sanskrit runes before we could make love? Why did he rush off the next day without even walking me to the bus, and how did he manage to disappear so fast?

I carried a miniature calendar with me as I flew around the globe, and I marked off the days, thinking *One bloody foot in front of the other, one bloody day at a time.* A year flies by, Gaki-san had said, but somewhere around April the trajectory of time seemed to freeze in place and I woke up one brilliant daffodil morning to the realization that I couldn't wait another six months to make contact. What I really wanted to do was to jump in my car, drive nonstop to Gaki-san's temple, and fall into his arms.

Instead I sat down and composed a letter, laboriously written in kindergartenish *hiragana* with an occasional triumphant *kanji*, plucked from the dictionary. Since I didn't know Gaki-san's last name, or the name of the temple, or even the name of that dark lonely road, I asked my neighbor Yumi (sleep-deprived housewife and cat-minder *extraordinaire*) to write on the envelope, "To the priest Gaki-san, at the old temple with the parchment lantern, near the bus stop, on the left side of the road from Kawanaka-cho to Yomogi Sanso Inn, Valley of Hell, Japan Alps."

"That's a very weird name, 'Gaki,'" Yumi said. "Are you sure it wasn't something else?"

"Yes," I said, "I'm sure." Yumi gave me a quizzical look, so I made up a story about having asked an aged priest for directions when I got lost en route to a hot spring and being invited in for tea. To make it sound more legitimate I said, "Actually, I'd like to thank his wife, too, so would you mind writing 'To Pimiko-san' on the envelope as well?"

"Okay," said Yumi, picking up my fat-tipped brush pen. For some reason that spurious, inspired detail seemed to set her mind at rest.

Several weeks later, the letter came back harshly stamped "Return to Sender, Undeliverable, Addressee Unknown." I was crushed, but not entirely surprised. I guess the address was just too vague, I thought. I'll just have to wait and see him in person.

Sometime in May, I was en route from Boston to Tokyo after researching some light stories (Filene's Basement feeding frenzies, Italian restaurants in the North End, Japanese expats in Cambridge) for a new magazine called *Tabigarasu*. It was a full flight and I found myself seated next to a woman, younger than I, who was on her way to teach anthropology and English at a small women's university in northern Japan. She would also, she explained, be gathering material for a dissertation on the folklore and legends of the area. I couldn't help wondering what a grad student was doing in first class, and she confessed over the coquilles Saint-Jacques that she was "kind of a reluctant robber-baron heiress, of sorts." That was the way she talked, all apology and modification; I figured it was a side effect of not having to work for her spending money. She didn't look like a typical spoiled-heiress type, though. She wore her walnut-colored hair in an unembellished ponytail, and she was dressed in a simple denim skirt and a cotton fisherman's sweater. No chunky gold, no murdered fur, no diamond-and-lapis tiaras.

We ordered all the same things: swordfish instead of steak, salad instead of soup, mineral water instead of wine. We agreed that the movie selection was atrocious, and when we turned on our reading lights after dinner and both took out mysteries by Minette Walters (she had *Sculptress*, I had *The Ice House*), that clinched it. We were clearly on the same wavelength, so we put our books away and settled in for a long chat.

During the second hour, as the sky turned inkstick-black outside our tiny windows, we got onto the subject of my bizarre experiences in the Valley of Hell. It was the old strangers-on-a-train phenomenon, I suppose, but there was something so warm and genuine about Amalie Aldrich (that was her name) that I felt I could trust her with my deepest secrets. She had already told me several intimate things, about one ill-fated affair with a married friend of her father's and another with a famous professor at Harvard, also married, a messy saga which she concluded by saying ruefully, "Well, that's enough about my shameful follies. I just hope there are some single men in Sendai."

My own confession started out as an expurgated travel-narrative, but I soon found myself telling Amalie about all the mysteries and inconsistencies of my trip to the Valley of Hell. At first I pretended that the priest had just been a sexless good Samaritan, but eventually I ended up confiding to this disarming stranger that I thought Gaki-san was the love (and the lover) of my life, and I was counting the days till we could be together again.

"Wow," Amalie said when I finished. "That's quite a tale. You ought to write it up."

"Oh no," I said. "I couldn't do that, at least not for publication." I didn't mention that I had been chronicling it all along in my journal as a kind of catharsis, or exorcism.

It was an inordinately long flight, with a stop in L.A., and by the time we got to Narita we were like old friends. Sometimes those time-in-a-bottle encounters turn sour toward the end, but I felt that Amalie Aldrich was someone I wanted to know forever. She struck me as the perfect female confidante, something that had been missing from my busy, rootless life. We exchanged phone numbers and e-mail addresses, and at the end of the customs line we gave each other a friends-for-life hug and said goodbye.

St. This, San That, Santa Someplace. There was a curiously non-secular tone to my itinerary over the next months: all those obscure saints, all those palmy alabaster resorts with a thin veneer of luxury over the economic inequity and civic unrest. I sometimes felt a sense of alarm when I sat down to crank out yet another paean to another purportedly perfect island, as if I might finally have used up my quota of metaphor and hyperbole and would never again be able to describe an incendiary sunset, a Lucullan brunch, a "romantic moonlight cruise." But of course I always came up with something suitably extravagant, and no one seemed to notice that I was repeating myself shamelessly. *I* noticed, though, and every time I typed "sublime" or "gorgeous" or "delightful" I half-expected the computer to beep reprovingly and announce, "Sorry, that account is overdrawn."

One still, sticky, windless night in August I was sitting on my couch in Ohara, watching some giddy garbage on television with Gifu and Piggott curled up on either side, when the telephone rang. "Hello?" I said, wondering who would be calling at ten o'clock at night. My pulse quickened at the thought that it might be Gaki-san, at last.

"Josephine? It's me, Amalie. Sorry I haven't been in touch but I warned you, I'm the world's worst correspondent."

"Amalie! I'm so glad to hear from you. And I haven't written, either, so there's no need to apologize. How's everything up there in Sendai?"

"Well, the big news is that I've found the most fantastic informant, one of those old blind soothsayers—female, of course—and I've been spending all my free time taping conversations with her because she really is quite alarmingly ancient. She's been telling me the most astounding things, things you simply don't find in books."

"That's terrific news," I said. "And what about your other quest? Are there any single men in Sendai, after all?"

"Oh, that." Amalie laughed. In the background I could hear music, some sort of tinkly harpsichord concerto. Behind that was a sharp clicking sound which could have been an Irish step-dancing class but which I happened to know was a neighborhood volunteer going from house to house banging the wooden clappers that for centuries have reminded people to turn off the gas and stifle the fires before retiring to sleep in their flimsy wood-and-paper bedrooms.

"Actually," Amalie continued in a voice that sounded almost coy, "I haven't had much time for a social life, but there is one kind of attractive man, who seems to be more or less single, wonder of wonders. The thing is, I don't think he really sees me as a woman, exactly, if you know what I mean."

I knew exactly what she meant. "Is he Japanese?" I asked.

"No, actually he's American, from Boston of all places, though I gather he spent his summers at Newport, sailing yachts. He's a post-doc philologist trained at Harvard, a few years ahead of me. I must have walked past him a million times in Harvard Square. Isn't that just too ironic, though? I *would* have to come all the way to Sendai to be rejected by a Harvard guy."

"What? You made a move and he rejected you?"

"Oh no, I could never be that bold, but he just doesn't show any interest, you know? I mean I'm sure he must have a beautiful Japanese girlfriend, that type of guy always does. But never mind that. The real reason I'm calling is to share some things my informant told me, because they seemed almost shockingly relevant to the story you told me on the plane. It seems that ..." Amalie launched into a monologue that went on for at least twenty minutes, and after that we wished each other all the best and said goodbye.

I sat on my couch staring unseeing at the television news in front of me, the rapidly dissolving images of flood and salmonella and newborn pandas at a zoo. The theme of Amalie's startling revelations had been simple, and chilling: I should never return to the temple in the Valley of Hell, under any circumstances. I had been lucky to escape with my life in the first place, and only a fool would take that risk again.

Apparently the old woman concluded from what Amalie told her that Gaki-san was some sort of evil phantasm, and she said it was surely not an innocent coincidence that the word *gaki* means "hungry ghost" in Japanese. She described that area of the Japan Alps as a notorious hotbed of supernatural activity, adding that that was why it was so sparsely populated. Amalie made me promise not to go back there under any circumstances, and I reluctantly agreed. Her concern for my welfare was obviously sincere, and I began thinking again about all the unexplained mysteries, paramount among them Gaki-san's refusal to see me for an entire year.

But no sooner had I hung up than my feelings of love and trust and longing came surging back, and I decided that I would keep my October 10 date with Gaki-san, no matter what. I had never been a believer in the supernatural, and in retrospect I thought the chambermaid's ghost must have been an optical illusion, like those ambiguous religious images that appear on a tree trunk or in an unwashed window. All the talk about hungry ghosts sounded like a load of superstitious nonsense, and my only fear was that Gaki-san might not be there to greet me.

Late September found me in hot, muggy, insect-infested New Guinea, doing a story for a magazine called *In Vogue Japan* on "Cannibal Fashion." This involved traipsing around the more civilized parts of the jungle with a photographer and a translator, interviewing media-savvy chieftains who wore penis shields and feathered headdresses, and regal, stunning women with polished hyena bones through their noses and shoulder-length earlobes, like ropes of pulled taffy. My favorite "model" was the wild-haired, clay-painted warrior who had replaced his nose ring with a yellow ballpoint pen and was proudly sporting a partially-inflated "Happy Birthday" balloon (red, with blue letters) in place of his penis gourd.

Forty years ago my mother had done a similar story, but in those days "cannibal" was an anthropologically (and anthropophagically) accurate term, not sensationalistic nostalgia. Still, it was all very atmospheric, apart from the ravenous man-eating bugs. And even though I knew I was practicing a patronizing, opportunistic sort of pseudo-anthropology at best, the assignment was a welcome respite from writing about cornucopian hotel buffets and supernal sunsets.

On my last day in Port Moresby I was sitting at the thatched-roof bar in our raffish hotel, drinking a nonalcoholic Monsoon Julep, when I was called to the telephone in the lobby. It was Maruya-san, my old friend from *Odysseus* Magazine, asking me if I could possibly arrange to stop over on Kulalau to do a story about an annual bacchanal called the Festival of Flowering Flesh, for which he already had the photographs. I refused at first, because I was so sick of traveling that I just wanted to go home and hug my cats until they gasped for air. As I was about to hang up, though, it occurred to me that I had never visited Raadi Ulonggo's grave.

"Okay, I'll go," I said. "But only one night, and I want to stay at the Red Ginger Inn."

"Done and done," said Maruya-san. I loved that man.

You can make the case for Monument Valley or Mount Fuji or the Rock Islands of Palau, but I happen to think that the Kulalau Archipelago in Kulanesia is the most artistic geological phenomenon on earth. You don't really get a sense of its majesty from the ground; it just seems like a cluster of singularly picturesque tropical islands with sparkling black-sand beaches ringed with turquoise water, while the inland hills are perennially abloom with hibiscus, plumeria, and the intoxicating white and yellow ginger blossoms. Seen from an airplane circling to land at the rustic airport, though, the beauty spread out below reduces even the most eloquent and jaded travelers to an inarticulate intake of breath.

The Republic of Kulalau consists of one main island, about the size of Manhattan, surrounded by thirty-eight smaller islands, each joined to the mainland by a glittering spoke of mica-flecked black sand. Traditionally, each island belonged to a separate clan while the main island was considered communal property. There were originally forty clans and forty islands, and the problems began when a hurricane destroyed two of the smaller islands, forcing the displaced residents to move onto other islands.

"Think of it as a really bloody version of musical chairs," Raadi had told me when I asked him to explain the clan warfare. "We no longer have enough islands to go around, so instead of learning to coexist people embrace the stupidest, most barbaric solution, which is to eliminate the two extra clans. Only, of course, they aren't too thrilled about being eliminated."

After I had settled into my airy sea-view room at the Red Ginger Inn, I changed into a dress that Raadi had always liked—a sleeveless, square-necked purple cotton sundress with a tiny waist and a very full calf-length skirt—and went down to the desk. The open-air lobby was filled with orchids and the breeze from the ocean blew through, smelling of fish and salt and sunken ships. There was no blood in the air this time. The displaced people were sharing a village on the leeward side of the main island, and the clans had made a temporary peace.

The desk clerk was not the willowy young man I remembered from my first visit, the one who had told me when Raadi was shot. This man was shorter, stockier, and older, but he wore the same pleasant, welcoming smile.

"Excuse me," I said, "but could you please direct me to the graveyard where Raadi Ulonggo is buried?" The man's friendly face seemed to freeze, as if he had just bitten down on a caramel and couldn't open his mouth. While he stared at me in silence I explained, in a veiled euphemistic way, about my friendship with Raadi.

"Ah," said the man, prying his jaws apart at last. "I see. So you aren't a reporter? All right. You have a car? No? In that case, I will arrange for someone to take you where you wish to go."

The driver who showed up half an hour later was a taciturn gray-haired man, dressed in a crisp white cotton shirt over the traditional knee-length cloth wrap the Kulalauans call a *kamikka-mikka.* "Hello, Miss," he said, and that was it. I was glad not to have to make small talk as we drove across the island, because I needed time to sort out my feelings about visiting Raadi's grave.

Until I met Gaki-san, Raadi Ulonggo was the closest thing I had found to the love of my life. Once we got past the armed captor/resentful hostage stage, we had discovered a surprising rapport which blossomed, after uncounted hours of conversation, into an exuberant, affectionate affair.

Raadi had gone to high school in San Francisco, and had attended Stanford on a football scholarship for three years. (I was startled to hear that he had supplemented his meager allowance by selling sperm to a fertility clinic in San Jose.) He returned home for his mother's funeral, and then the hurricane came and clan war broke out, and he never went back to college. When I met him he was working as a fifth-grade schoolteacher at a private elementary school and playing acoustic guitar at night in a Moth-Clan band called the Seagods. (I suggested changing the band's name to Moths to the Flame, and he laughed.) Raadi was so much younger that I never thought of our relationship as having any lasting potential, but I believed that we genuinely cared for each other, and I had grieved sincerely when he died.

"This is it, Miss," said the driver as he stopped the car, an old grasshopper-green Jeepster. I peered over the front seat, looking for a meter.

"May I pay you?" I asked.

The man waved his hands and grimaced in disgust, as if I had proposed something obscene. "I am Moth Clan," he said solemnly. "I do this out of love, not for money." He drove off in a cloud of curry-colored dust, and I was left standing on a grassy anvil-shaped bluff above the sea, at the gate of the loveliest graveyard I had ever seen.

Overhead, small white birds with bright red feet and matching beaks were circling with angelic grace, and the vivid expanse of green was ringed with trees laden with purple frangipani blossoms, the deep *murasaki* color of my dress. Most of the gravestones were amorphous natural boulders, gray or tan or snuff-colored, with the name and dates of the deceased written in some sort of waterproof colored chalk, but there were a few of the "erotic tombstones" I had written about five years earlier. These were rocks roughly hewn into shapes that suggested two people in close naked embrace, and were reserved for couples who had died on the same day, whether in an accident or during one of the wars. Planted around the stones were green-and-garnet hedges of *amatti*, the spearmint-scented "aphrodisiac herb of Kulalau," which was sold in its dried form at the airport gift shop as tea, sachets, and potpourri.

I wandered through the forest of stones, lamenting the shortness of some of the lives and feeling a pang of envy when I saw a handsome pair of anthropomorphic lava-rocks bound together with braided rope and inscribed "Tikko and Puua, True Love Forever." All the men I had ever loved had either disappeared, dumped me, or disappointed me in some irreparable way, so it seemed unlikely that I would ever rest in peace under a communal gravestone, erotic or otherwise. No, I would probably end up like one of those fictitious hungry ghosts Amalie had talked about, still looking for love in the next dimension.

As I scanned the inscriptions I saw Calvins and Clementines, Baatis and Luellos, but no Raadi Ulonggo. I was beginning to think I might have been dropped off at the wrong graveyard when I noticed a sapphire-and-white kingfisher perched on a large smooth putty-colored stone at the seaside edge of the cemetery. I walked over, gazing out at the dazzling view of azure sea and leafy green islands, each connected to the main island by a long, high spit of charcoal-colored sand. When I got to the big rock the bird gave me a curious look and abruptly flew away. That was when I saw the inscription calligraphed in pastel chalk:

RAADI ULONGGO
BORN 1969, DIED 1995
LIFE IS SHORT, BUT POSSIBILITY IS INFINITE

I knelt in the damp grass and placed a bouquet of hastily-picked plumerias in front of the gravestone. "Dear Raadi," I murmured, as if I were writing a letter out loud. "I've missed you very much, and I'm truly sorry that you're gone. I won't pretend that I haven't fallen in love with someone else, but I've never stopped caring for you, and I feel that if you had lived we would have been really good friends, at least. You were such a kind, bright, magnificent young man, and even if I didn't agree with some of your methods, I always respected you. That's why I hate war, because it robs men of their youth and innocence, and deprives the world of the wonders those young men might have accomplished, and of their cheerful company. I know you believed in reincarnation, and I wonder if that kingfisher just now might have been you? If it is, I hope that you're having a good time flying around in the sky, and that you're catching lots of fish or worms or whatever it is that kingfishers like to eat."

Just then I heard a noise behind the gravestone and when I looked up Raadi Ulonggo was standing there smiling down at me, larger than life and twice as beautiful. I had always wondered what I would do if I ever saw a ghost, and now I found out. I screamed, and then I fainted dead away.

Back in my hotel room, drinking cold hibiscus-flower tea the color of Beaujolais, everything was easily explained. On that day in 1995 when the desk clerk told me that Raadi had been shot, I had assumed he meant "shot and killed." In fact, Raadi told me, he had been so seriously wounded that his relatives had gone ahead and erected a gravestone, but then he amazed everyone by emerging from his coma and making a slow but complete recovery.

"But why didn't you let me know you were alive?" I had gone from joy at finding out Raadi was still on earth to indignation that he had left me in the dark all this time. "And why didn't you take down the gravestone when you recovered?"

"I figure I'll need it soon enough," Raadi said with the sly bad-boy smile I remembered. "And I didn't know you thought I was dead, I only knew that I never heard from you again. Forgive me, but I figured you had just been using me as a toy boy, I mean a boy toy, not that I felt that way when we were together, not at all, but when you didn't even send me a get-well card ..."

"Well, I did light twenty-six candles for your immortal soul," I said. We both laughed, and that seemed to clear the air. Raadi told me that he had had a few girlfriends since he saw me last, but that he had never met anyone who understood him as well as I did. "Come over here," he said, patting the seat on the couch beside him, but I shook my head.

"Oh, right," he said coolly. "You were saying at the graveyard that there's someone else. Who is he, some bestselling writer or genius professor or big-shot businessman, or what?"

What could I say? I wasn't exactly sure who Gaki-san was. I only knew that I had promised to be true to him, and I couldn't allow myself to think about breaking that pledge at this late date, when October 10 was only a couple of weeks away. I was powerfully attracted to Raadi, not just because he was seriously gorgeous—tall, bronzed, curly-haired, with broad, generous features and a joyous smile—but also because of who he was, and how we had been together.

But to take up with him again, and then to go see Gaki-san the very next month? That was too much like something my mother would have done. If I began to let the pursuit of physical pleasure dictate my every move, the next thing I knew I'd be slumped over the bar at some seedy hotel mumbling "Buy me a drink, dreamboat?" Being faithful to Gaki-san for an entire year had become a major symbol: the magical talisman that would keep me from turning into my mother, the once-promising writer turned barfly-seductress.

"So, you were telling me about the man in your life," Raadi prompted.

"He isn't any of those things you mentioned," I said. "He isn't rich or famous or powerful. He's a Japanese Buddhist priest who lives in an old-fashioned temple up in the mountains, in the middle of nowhere. At this point I honestly don't know what's going on between him and me, but in the meantime I promised to be faithful. It's weird; I love him, but I love you too. I mean, I always did, but I thought you were gone."

"I'm alive and well and full of desire, so come over here, now," Raadi said, but I just shook my head sadly, no.

Raadi offered to escort me to the Festival of Flowering Flesh, but I knew that would be asking for trouble. Instead, I went with a guide who accosted me in front of the Visitor's Bureau, a hugely pregnant woman whose long black braid was tied with blue-tinged snakeskin (Snake Clan! I thought). She spoke barely any English, and her guidance consisted of grabbing me roughly by the upper arm and pointing at some object of interest while saying, "Now look you here, Missy."

Somehow I managed to fill a notebook with scribbled impressions of the whirling dancers, the flower-carpeted streets, the colorful clan costumes, the stirring pagan drumbeats. At one point as I was standing under a banana-leaf awning drinking fresh guava juice and eating a fast-food plate of crab-and-seaweed salad, I caught a glimpse of Raadi in the eddying crowd. He was dressed in a short raspberry-colored kamikka-mikka and a shimmery clam-shell vest with a large pair of gossamer moth-wings attached, and it was all I could do not to run after him and leap into his big, strong arms.

The real festival began at midnight. Every year on that one night, from twelve until four in the morning, people were allowed to pair off with whomever they desired regardless of marital status, clan affiliation, or gender. (By law, though, the desire had to be mutual.) Shortly before midnight Sigella, my guide, asked me if I wanted to watch people pair off, as if romantic dalliance were a spectator sport. "No," I said, for Raadi had asked me to meet him on the beach in front of the Red Ginger Inn at twelve-thirty. "I think I'll call it a night."

I walked back to the hotel through the jostling, high-spirited, wildly costumed crowds, trying not to think about what would soon be taking place on every horizontal surface on the island, and no doubt against some vertical ones as well. I had serious reservations about the idea of free love on one night a year. It seemed like a dangerously anarchic rite, and I couldn't believe that it wouldn't lead to the dissolution of marriages and families that otherwise might have endured quite nicely. But there was a giddy throb of sexual intoxication in the air, and when I tried to concentrate on my feelings of love for Gaki-san, my sweet, enigmatic soulmate-priest, all I could see was the image of Raadi in his opalescent moth-wings, waiting for me on the beach.

Back in my room, I couldn't seem to catch my breath. To go to meet Raadi would be to turn into my mother, a woman incapable of being faithful to anyone, but the force of irrational desire was so strong as to be almost unbearable. Slowly, unable to meet my own eyes in the mirror, I changed from my khaki cotton fact-gathering dress into a sheer silk sun-dress printed with pink and lavender hibiscus flowers. I brushed out my hair, put on some rose-colored lip gloss, and headed out the door.

When I got to the elevator I had a sudden vision of Gaki-san saying, "I think you know how I feel," and instead of pressing the down button I picked up the house phone and called the front desk. The maintenance man arrived three minutes later. He was a pleasant, soft-spoken older man in a yellow jumpsuit with a white orchid embroidered on the pocket above his name, Miilio. When I told him what I wanted he showed no surprise at all, and on impulse I explained my dilemma, without mentioning any names.

"I see," Miilio said. "I understand your feelings very well. I once took a twelve-hour sleeping potion on the Night of Flowering Flesh to keep myself from going off into the hills with a charming young woman who worked at the restaurant here in the hotel, because I knew it would be the end of my twenty-year marriage, one way or another."

That story gave me strength, somehow. After Miilio had tied my arms and legs to the rattan chaise longue with the soft cords from my dressing gown, he wished me luck and left me alone with the fragrant trade winds blowing through the room. I must have cried myself to sleep, because I awakened to the intoxicating smell of coconut oil and tropical flowers and the sound of a familiar voice saying gently, "I had no idea you wanted me so much."

"Oh, Raadi," I murmured sleepily. "You can't even begin to imagine how much I want you." I kept my eyes closed, just to be safe.

"Then may I untie you? Please?" I could feel the air around him trembling slightly, as if he were a newborn butterfly drying its wings.

"Better not," I said. "I don't think I can be trusted tonight." He was standing so close to me that I could smell the various layers of his deliciously natural scent: the coconut oil he put on his hair, the ginger and plumeria blossoms in his head-lei, the dried seasalt on his feet, the Tahitian beer on his breath.

Once again, my resolve began to waver. After all, a lot can happen in a year. Gaki-san could have died, or gotten married. Or else *I* could die tomorrow; the airplane might crash into the ocean, and this unique moment would have been lost, my self-denial all for naught. I was knee-deep in rationalizations when Raadi spoke. "Let me know what happens with your priest, as soon as you figure it out," he said.

"All right," I said, feeling slightly relieved that I had been forced to do the right thing, after all. "I'll call you when I know." I still didn't dare to look up at his face; I loved it too much.

"Don't call me, just come if you can. I'll be waiting for you."

"Waiting to do what?" I asked. I was still just a reckless breath away from saying, "Forget my priest, forget ethics and promises; this is the Night of Flowering Flesh and it's a crime to waste such lovely mutual passion." I was just an overheated heartbeat away from citing the song that has paved the way for so many broken vows: *If you can't be with the one you love ...*

But I didn't say those things, and Raadi placed his warm fingers on my lips for the briefest instant, then pulled them away. "Waiting to do anything you want," he said, and then he was gone, closing the door behind him.

"Raadi!" I shouted a second later. "Come back and untie me!" but I guess he didn't hear. I felt empty, sad, and deeply disappointed. I suppose I had been half-hoping Raadi would ravish me through my bonds so I could have my love both ways, all the pleasure with none of the guilt, but I respected him even more for walking out the door.

Somehow I survived the night and even managed to get some sleep. At dawn Miilio the maintenance man came and untied the cords, murmuring that it had been a long night for him, too. Two hours later I was at the thatch-roofed airport, standing in line to be weighed (a necessary preliminary to making seat assignments for small airplanes). As the line shuffled forward, I noticed a tattered newspaper lying on the floor. I picked it up and opened it at random, and the first thing I saw was an ad for a post-festival dance to be held at the wishfully-named Clan Peace Pavilion, down by the beach. DANCE UNTIL DAWN TO THE MUSIC OF MOTHS TO THE FLAME (FORMERLY THE SEAGODS). DRUMS: SAAMOLI MALUKKA; BASS: SUEZZI KOLLO; PIANO: NULLI TREOTTI; GUITAR: RAADI ULONGGO.

Oh, I thought, my heart swelling with fondness, he changed the name of the band! If it hadn't been so close to October 10 I think I might have cashed in my ticket and run back to Raadi right then. Instead I stepped on the scale and exchanged smiles with the attendant. He was an obviously hung-over young buck wearing an inside-out orange tank top, a crumpled head wreath of spiky green ferns, and a dreamy, sexed-out smile.

Seated next to a taciturn Carolinian man whose thigh was larger than my torso, I declined the flight attendant's offer of a betel-nut chew and peered out the window. I wonder if I'll ever come back, I thought as the plane flew over that radial blossom of islands with its clans of moth and mouse, snake and owl, butterfly and snail. Once we were aloft I opened the newspaper again, and this time I noticed the date on the masthead: September 20, 1995. Five years ago, exactly. I couldn't help shivering at the coincidence, because that was the day Raadi Ulonggo was shot. I shivered again a moment later, when it occurred to me that it was very odd indeed that a five-year-old newspaper would be lying on the floor in the spic-and-span Kulalau Aerodrome.

Amalie was still stewing over Brian, the guy from Boston. He had finally asked her out to lunch but only, she was convinced, because he wanted to pick her brain about her secret informant, who also happened to be an informal expert on Brian's academic specialty: the intricate staccato dialects of Northern Japan. Under the circumstances, I couldn't very well tell her that another of my favorite lovers had turned out not to be dead, after all, or that he seemed to want to have some sort of continuing relationship with me. Nor did I feel it would be diplomatic to mention that I loved Gaki-san even more now that I was back in his country, where the temple roof across the fields from my cottage served as a constant reminder of the wondrous night we had spent together. Not that I needed reminding, for that memory was indelibly imprinted on my most secret cells.

"You aren't going back to that creepy temple next week, are you?" Amalie asked at the end of our conversation.

"It isn't creepy but no, probably not." An off-white lie, veering toward beige.

"Well, just to be safe, let me tell you what my soothsayer said you should say if you need to find out whether someone is really an evil spirit in disguise." She told me the archaic-sounding word, and I obediently wrote it down on the inside cover of my green notebook, biting my lip to keep from laughing out loud.

Love isn't merely blind, it's deranged and demented as well. That was one of my mother's more pessimistic aphorisms, coined after my glamorous, irresponsible ski-bum father went out to buy a copy of *Sports Illustrated* and never came back. As I drove through narrow, rustic villages, past patchwork fields and houses wreathed with strings of dried sardines, breathing the increasingly pure and revivifying air, I couldn't help thinking that I might be proving the validity of her cynical theory. I had just devoted a year of my life to a passively monogamous relationship with a man with whom I had spent one marvelous but mystifying night, a man about whom I knew next to nothing in a biographical sense, a man whom a soothsayer suspected, on the flimsiest of hearsay evidence, of being an evil specter in disguise.

That last part always made me chuckle, it was so absurd, but I still couldn't get past the question of why we had to be apart for an entire year. I seemed to remember Gaki-san's saying something along the lines of "Buddhists make lousy pen pals," but surely he could have picked up the telephone once in a blue moon. And then it hit me: maybe this separation had been a test of my character, and if I passed he would consider me a worthy life partner.

Oh, well, I thought fatalistically, I'll know soon enough. Gaki-san had said October 10, and I was planning to knock on his door at one second after midnight on that date. As it turned out, I was half an hour early so I sat in my car with the heater on, listening to Van Morrison's *Greatest Hits*, watching the clock, and checking my reflection in the flip-down mirror every few seconds, as if it might have changed.

Finally it was midnight, but I forced myself to wait until five past so I wouldn't appear too eager. I locked my luggage in the car and walked slowly up the cobblestone slope, savoring the silence, the sweet spicy smell of autumn, and the nervous anticipation. Taking a deep breath, I slid open the door and called out a timid greeting.

No response. "Hello," I called again, more loudly. I heard the reassuring creak of a door at the rear of the house, and after what seemed like an eternity there was the sound of unmistakably male feet running along on polished wood floors. And then there he was: the lovely priest of this antique temple, looming above me on the landing saying, "Welcome! Welcome! Welcome home!"

Gaki-san's kisses were rougher than I remembered, but he smelled exactly the same, like incense, warm skin, and cryptomeria sachet. He was dressed in his pilgrim garb, the big hat and white leggings under a short black robe. As he led me off to the guest room I said jokingly, "Did you just get back from a one-year trip?"

"Yes," he said. He seemed oddly taciturn, but I figured that we were both just tired and anxious. Feeling a sudden need to prove that ours wasn't merely a carnal attraction, I said, "Can't we go in the other room and talk for a while? I'd love a cup of tea."

"Plenty of time for that later," Gaki-san said shortly. His voice sounded unnaturally low and hoarse, and I figured he must have caught a cold on his long journey.

"Do you mean that you don't have to rush off in the morning?" I said.

"No," said Gaki-san, and his voice seemed to soften. "I can stay forever. Can you?"

"Yes," I said, wondering if I had just gotten betrothed.

And then we were in my old room and he was tearing off my jacket, unbuttoning my dress, nuzzling my chilly breasts. (Biting, too; he hadn't done that before, and I didn't really care for it.) He began kissing me on the mouth in that newly rough but not unexciting way, and I immediately metamorphosed into the woman of passion, with no shame or inhibitions and only the barest rudiments of common sense.

"Wait," I said, as he was kneeling above me, naked now except for his big bamboo hat, his split-toed socks, and his pilgrim leggings. I found his half-undressed state very erotic. He almost seemed like another species, and I was reminded of one of those florid paintings where Zeus swans around and somehow (I've never quite grasped the mechanics) manages to ravish every maiden in sight. "I mean, I don't want to stop, either," I said. "But don't we have to paint the Sanskrit on each other?"

"No need for that," he said in that harsh, guttural voice. He was fumbling with the buttons on the skirt of my dress, bending to kiss me almost savagely on the mouth each time he got another button undone. I caught sight of his eyes under the hat for the first time then, and they were not the clear, bright eyes of the man I loved. There was something cloudy and calculating about those eyes, something furtive and sly, something not priest-like at all. Something, in fact, not quite human.

"Wait," I said, stalling for time. "Let me undress you first." I tried to sit up.

"No!" he growled, holding me down with two strong hands on my shoulders.

"Well, at least take off your socks and stay a while," I said. My tone was playful, but I was beginning to be afraid.

"NO!" he shouted. When I heard the anger in his voice I threw caution to the winds and shouted "★★★★★," the magic transformation-reversal word Amalie had taught me, which I have sworn never to reveal to anyone. In that instant the hands on my shoulders turned into huge furry paws with sharp curved scimitar-claws, and I closed my eyes and screamed, long and loud.

Running footsteps sounded outside, then the door was wrenched open so violently that it came out of the grooves and fell to the ground with a crash. I heard a high-pitched voice shouting something in a language I had never heard—or wait, maybe I had heard it, once—and I opened my eyes in time to see a great furry beast in a priest's robe charging out into the hall. I caught a glimpse of a long snout under the big hat, and I heard the four-footed creature's claws scrabbling on the smooth wood floors as it ran away as fast as it could.

I sat up in a daze, looking around for my rescuer. Just then the oil lamp in the corner of the room went out, and the room was plunged into darkness. "Who's there?" I asked in a small voice. I was thoroughly bewildered, and nearly speechless with terror.

"It's me, Gaki," said the shrill voice.

"Then who was that—that *thing* in the hat?"

The voice gave an eerie falsetto laugh. "That was a tanuki," it said. "What did you think of his imitation of me?"

It was better than the imitation of yourself you're doing right now, I thought, but instead I said, "What's wrong with your voice? And why did you turn off the light?"

"It's a long story," sighed the disembodied voice. "You might be happier in the long run if you just went home right now and forgot you had ever met me."

"Not a chance," I said. "I've been faithful to you for an entire year, and I think I have a right to know what's going on."

Another sigh, out of the darkness. "All right," said Gaki-san. "But first you'd better get dressed, because when you hear what I have to say you may want to run screaming into the night."

I followed him down the unlit hall to the room where we had sat drinking tea and making sparky jokes that first night. I could see only the vaguest outlines, a door here, a table there, and when he sat down across from me I could just discern that he was wearing the same outfit—pilgrim hat, robe, leggings, and split-toed socks—as the tanuki. (There would be plenty of time to sort out that horror later, and to face the extremely bizarre fact that I had very nearly gone to bed with a goblin-badger.)

"How do I know you're really Gaki-san?" I said, after he had apologized for the lack of refreshments. I was dying for a cup of hot green tea, but I told myself there would be plenty of tea in my future, assuming I survived this weird night. "I mean, I'm very grateful to you for rescuing me, but your voice doesn't sound right at all, and you won't let me see your face."

"Jo-san," the voice said tenderly, and I felt a little thrill as the memories of that other night washed over me. "Dear Josefuiinu." Had I told him my real name? I didn't remember having done so. "I don't know where to start," he went on, "because you are the best thing that has ever happened to me in my life, or afterward. The last thing I would ever want to do is to hurt or frighten you."

In my life, or afterward? When I heard those words I understood the old cliché about blood running cold, for my veins seemed suddenly to be filled with sherbet. My invisible companion took a deep breath and then proceeded to tell me the most incredible story I have ever heard.

He began by explaining that Gaki wasn't really his name, it was his identity. He was a lowly type of supernatural spirit called a *gaki* (in Sanskrit, a *prêta*), slowly working off the bad karma accumulated in a previous existence. He had been ordained in the late 1880s, at a time when priests of his sect were not allowed to marry or fraternize with women. Because he was a man of "unnatural passions," as he put it, he had repeatedly broken his vow of celibacy with a string of courtesans whom he didn't really love but couldn't seem to live without. ("I allowed myself to be seduced by what we Buddhists call *Bonno no Inu*," he said sorrowfully. "The mindless, insatiable Dog of Lust.") He had died young, at thirty-six, of a wasting disease contracted from one of those purchased lovers, and since then he had been slowly working his way up through the horrific ranks of gaki-dom. When he met me he had reached the point where he could take human form one day a year, on the tenth day of the tenth month. On the day we first met he had been in the town of Kawanaka doing good works and collecting alms to pass on to the poor, not even looking at the women he met along the way.

And then I had appeared at his lonely door and he had fallen in love for the first time in his entire life, or existence. He had decided in that first instant that it would be worth it to be the lowest sort of gaki, living on moldy excrement for the next ten lifetimes, just to spend a single night with me. Because love was present along with the most sacred sort of lust (his sweet words), he had hoped to get away with that breach of the rules. That was why he'd made the optimistic promise to see me again in a year, before abruptly resuming his nonhuman form the next morning, when he told me he was going on a pilgrimage.

As for what happened in the hot-spring bath, he had changed into his true form ("albeit somewhat magnified") in order to scare away the chambermaid's ghost. The sutras he painted on my skin were to protect me, on general principles, and because he had always enjoyed calligraphy when he was alive. And then he confided with a squeaky, sheepish laugh that he had just wanted me to paint the Sanskrit "ahs" on him for fun. "Fun isn't even a word where I live now," he added somberly.

When he said it would be fatal for us to make love, he meant lethal for him because of the effect it might have on his slow climb up the karmic ladder, but he also feared that it could be dangerous for me in some unknown way. He explained that there were a lot of shape-shifting foxes, snakes, and badgers in the surrounding mountains. The amorous tanuki must have known about our relationship, and when it saw that Gaki-san wouldn't be able to keep our date tonight in human form, it had decided to step into the romantic breach for purely bestial reasons.

"Of course, he *is* a beast," Gaki-san added drolly. "But that's no excuse."

Once the initial terror and bewilderment wore off, I was fascinated. I asked all sorts of questions about logic and logistics, as if I were interviewing a source for a story. Gaki-san kept saying, "I can't possibly explain all these things to you, and I pray you'll never have to find out firsthand. Let's just say that the afterworld makes life on earth look like a garden party. Enjoy it while you can."

Trying to keep up my end of the conversation, I told him that my grandmother Leda's last words had been, "It's all right, my darlings. All the best people are dead, anyway." He chuckled at that but it was a thin paltry sound, nothing like his old robust face-splitting laugh.

Once when I addressed him as Gaki-san, he said, "That isn't really my name, as I said before, but it's good enough for tonight."

"What is—I mean, what *was* your name?"

"Mutai. Mutai Maboroshimon."

"Really?" I asked suspiciously, for I knew that *maboroshi* meant "phantom."

"No, not really," he said. After that I just called him Gaki-san, which I realized later was the equivalent of Mr. Hungry Ghost. I was intrigued by the whole concept of a shadow world filled with tormented souls, and I asked him to tell me more about gaki.

"Well," he said cheerfully, "there are thirty-six different kinds, most of which, as it says in the old books, are associated with 'disease, putrescence, and death.'"

"Sounds delightful," I said, but I wasn't scared. In a weird, journalistic way, I was even enjoying myself. "Please, tell me more."

"Well, it's exceedingly complicated, and after a hundred years I'm still learning my way around. The afterworld isn't exactly as it's sketched in the Buddhist books, but it is true that the realm of the gaki is one step below that of the animal kingdom, and one step above Hell. I hope someday to be a full-time human being again, perhaps in a century or two if our foolish species hasn't made itself extinct by then. But even being a hungry ghost is better than burning in the Eight Hot Hells, or shoveling nightsoil all day while being flogged by demons."

"Tell me more about the hungry ghosts," I begged.

"All right," he said in that reedy voice. "Briefly, there are the *Muzai-gaki*, who suffer from perennial, unrelieved thirst and hunger. Then there are the *Shozai-gaki*, who get to feed occasionally on some bit of rotten garbage. Above them are the *Usai-gaki*, who eat the leftover food of humans and the offerings that are made to the gods or to ancestors, at household altars. At the other end of the social scale are the *Jiki-niku-gaki*, the Eaters of Human Flesh; the *Jiki-ketsu-gaki*, or Blood-Eaters; the *Jiki-doku-gaki*, or Poison-Eaters; the *Jiki-ke-gaki*, or Eaters of Nasty Smells; the *Shikko-gaki*, who devour maggoty corpses; and the *Jiki-fun-gaki*, or Feces-Eaters, to name a few. Then there are several forms whose torments are directly connected to the misdeeds they committed while they were alive. For example, there are the *Jiki-ko-gaki*, what the old books call 'incense-eating goblins.' They are the ghosts of men who either made or sold bad incense for mercenary reasons, and the only thing they are allowed to ingest, to assuage their endless hunger pangs, is the smoke of incense. And then there are the *Jiki-man-gaki*, which can live only by eating the mildewy toupees that adorn some religious statues. Those gaki were once people who stole valuable objects from Buddhist temples."

I had seen a few of those musty old hairpieces, and I couldn't help shuddering at the thought of munching on them for eternity. Marveling that such a topic even existed, and that I was casually discussing it while the so-called normal world went on outside, I said matter-of-factly, "And what sort of gaki are you?"

"Oh," sighed my invisible companion, "I was hoping you wouldn't ask. I'm what's called a *Yoku-shiki-gaki*, a Spirit of Lewdness. The reason I have some supernatural powers, like being able to take human form on occasion, is because I was given karmic credit for doing good while I was alive. In fact, aside from violating my vow of celibacy at every turn, I believe I lived quite a virtuous life from the age of twenty or so. What it comes down to is this: I'm being punished for the sin of lust."

"Is lust always a sin?" I asked.

"Only if you think it is," Gaki-san replied.

We talked all night and it was unexpectedly comfortable, and comforting. As long as I didn't start italicizing my thoughts (*Eek! I'm shooting the breeze with a hungry ghost!),* I didn't feel afraid or imperiled. At one point I suddenly remembered my close call with the concupiscent tanuki. That made me a little nervous, so I offhandedly murmured "★★★★★," that magical, secret word. To my relief, no radical transformations seemed to be taking place in the deep shadows across the table, and I covered up by remarking casually, "That was the word I said to make the goblin-badger return to its true form, by the way. I was just wondering, was that what brought you running?"

"No," said Gaki-san, apparently buying my subterfuge. "It was your screams. Tonight I had just planned to watch you silently from the rafters, and let you think I wasn't home. I thought I would go to Kyoto and find you the next time I was able to take human form, and explain my, ah, situation. I had no idea that blasted tanuki was going to interfere."

"I'm glad he did," I said. "This talk has meant a lot to me."

"To me, too," said Gaki-san. I sensed that he was standing up, and I could just make out a tallish loose-robed form, quite a bit thinner than I remembered, its face invisible beneath the big inverted-basket shaped hat. "You'd better get to bed," he said. "I'll say goodbye now, because it wouldn't do for you to see me by daylight." He sounded very sad.

"Thank you so much for the kind offer," I said, thinking how different that was from what I had hoped to be saying tonight. "But I think I'd better be going now. I can sleep at an inn along the way. I hope you understand, but there's no way I could fall asleep in this temple after all that has happened." And all that *hasn't* happened, too.

"Of course I understand," said Gaki-san, sounding even sadder than before. He didn't shake my hand but I could sense that he was bowing. I returned the bow, dropping a tear on the *tatami* as I bent my head. He murmured "*Saraba*," that poignant old-fashioned farewell, and I said "Let's meet again." A moment later I heard ominously light-sounding footsteps moving down the hall, and I knew that our long-awaited rendezvous was over.

I went to the entrance, put on my shoes, and stepped out into the clear cold night, closing the door loudly behind me. I didn't plan what happened next. I don't know whether it was my travel writer's curiosity or just plain snoopiness, but somehow I felt that I couldn't go through the rest of my life without knowing who or what I had made love to the year before, in the corporeal sense. If Gaki-san hadn't been in human form tonight, what form *was* he in? It was none of my business, but I simply had to know.

I ran down the cobblestone slope toward the road as noisily as possible, then doubled back and crept silently through the woods to the temple. It had rained recently so the leaves were nice and soggy, and I was careful not to tread on any brittle twigs that might snap and give me away. "I was just looking for Pimiko and Suzu, to say hello," I muttered under my breath, rehearsing my excuse in case I should be caught. I hadn't seen either of the animals around, and I hadn't had a chance to inquire about their fates, or their true identities.

My heart was thumping as I threaded my way through the woods. It wasn't that I was afraid of Gaki-san, in any form, for I felt that he was a good soul who was being punished much too harshly for having been a passionate man. But I didn't relish the thought of meeting that randy tanuki again, or any others of his ilk.

I tiptoed past the glassed-in corridor, past the bathroom, past the guest room where we had spent that wondrous night a year before, past the sitting room, past the kitchen. Finally I came to what I thought must be Gaki-san's room. The windows were closed, but I found a small hole in the paper screen and peered in.

As my eyes grew accustomed to the darkness I saw Gaki-san with his back to me, kneeling in front of an altar. A match flared briefly as he lit a stick of incense and began chanting a sutra in that odd but now familiar voice. After a few minutes he stood up with his back to me, looking so much like himself (only thinner) that I wanted to burst through the door and throw my arms around him. But then he turned to face me, and as I watched him shed his garments I had to put my hand over my mouth to keep from shrieking out loud.

The tall slender body hidden under the robes and hat was that of a gigantic insect. It didn't resemble a cockroach or any other bug that I had ever seen or squashed; it was like a grotesquely distorted dragonfly (if a dragonfly could stand on two long legs) with the thick, solid armature of a beetle. The beast's segmented torso was a shimmering greenish-blue, and it had translucent gilded wings. And the face—oh God, the face. It was the most hideous, nightmarish visage I had ever seen, with mirrored eyes, a demonic snout, and an unspeakable maw of a mouth. While I watched in horror, the thing in front of me began to glow like a firefly, and by that eerie bug-light I saw that there was a leather cord around its stumpy insect neck. Suspended from that cord was my missing Zuni earring. This monstrous creature—I could no longer think of it as Gaki-san—was *wearing my colors*!

I screamed uncontrollably and ran off through the woods. The sharp leafless branches scratched my face and arms, but I didn't care. After a moment I heard a door slide open in the temple behind me, and then there was a sinister whir of wings. Putting my terror to use, I pretended I was sprinting to the finish of a crucial cross-country race back in prep school, and the adrenaline bore me along ahead of my winged pursuer. Somehow I reached the car and got my key in the door. With my heart pounding at an alarming rate I fell into the driver's seat, locked the door behind me, and started the ignition. Steam poured from the tailpipe as the cold engine warmed up and then suddenly, wreathed in the ghostly steam, I saw that huge, horrible bug-face right in front of me, practically glued to the windshield.

I shrieked, long and high and loud. I couldn't help it, and I couldn't stop. Through terrified eyes I saw the creature moving its gruesome mouth-aperture, and my stomach lurched as I remembered the kisses we had shared. At first I found it difficult to read those grotesque lips, but after a moment I realized they were saying "Forgive me," and then, "Forget me."

How can I forget you if you won't go away? I thought giddily, but I can't say I wasn't touched, in an odd way. Then the beastly insect put two of its spindly arms up to its neck, untied the cord that was attached to my missing earring, and hung the cord over my side mirror, very gently. I sensed that it wanted something from me, some sort of resolution or closure, but I simply couldn't bring myself to meet those ghastly alien eyes. I just nodded my head, hoping that would be sufficient, and after a long moment the creature flew off. It seemed to be shrinking before my eyes, and by the time the insect-ghost vanished through the temple gates it appeared no larger than a normal dragonfly.

I jammed my foot down on the accelerator and sped down the road until I found a turnaround. As I careened past the temple going the other way I glanced up the path and wasn't even slightly surprised to see that there was no building there at all, just a pile of rubble and ruins. I think I must have been in mild shock from all the weirdness and unreality, because I drove like a madwoman on those deserted roads, swerving abruptly whenever I strayed into the opposite lane, or onto the gravelly shoulder.

My mind was going even faster than the car. I spent the first hour or so trying to understand what had just happened, and striving in vain to convince myself that it had all been a dream, or a nightmare. I simply wasn't ready to deal with the realization that I, Josephine Lilio-Leda Stelle, entomophobe *cum laude*, merciless nemesis of cockroaches and pulverizer of mosquitoes, had just spent a year of my romantic prime being faithful to a supernatural insect. But I knew perfectly well that it hadn't been a dream. There was an abundance of proof: my lost earring dangling from the side mirror, Gaki-san's "ah" calligraphy on my notebook, the stripes of soreness on my shoulders where the lust-crazed tanuki had gripped them with those knife-like claws.

If those thoughts were the not-terribly-palatable main course of my mental meal that night, dessert was finally allowing myself to think about the future. The Gaki-san I had loved so dearly, and whom I now pitied with all my heart, had turned out to be an illusion. That fact struck me as a perfect metaphor for all my romances to date, except for one. I knew, with the absolute certainty born of romantic epiphany, that the immediate future of my heart lay with Raadi Ulonggo. Just saying his name filled me with joy, and I felt incredibly fortunate to have someone so remarkable waiting for me. I would tell him everything, and the frustrations of our last meeting would only make our love stronger, our passion more intense. I could hardly wait to call him and say, "I'll be on a plane tomorrow, if you'll have me."

"So you went to the temple, after all. I thought you might. Well, how did the big reunion go?" Amalie asked warily when I called her the next day.

"You needn't have worried," I said. "He wasn't there." Well, it was true in a way. Maybe someday I would share the whole story, but I wasn't going to tell anyone until I understood it more clearly myself.

"It's probably just as well," said Amalie, obviously relieved. We chatted a bit about autumn leaves and Japanese soap operas, and then I heard a jovial male voice calling out in a mock-Australian accent, "Ahoy, mate, permission to come aboard?"

"The elusive Brian?" I said.

"Um, yes, more or less." Amalie laughed nervously. "He couldn't get away to meet me for lunch today, so I'm going to cook him a bite of dinner here."

Aha, I thought, that old ruse. But I just said, "Well, in that case I'll let you go. Have fun, and don't do anything I wouldn't do." Like carrying torches for the living dead, I thought.

The curious thing was that I felt quite calm, even sanguine. What happened, happened, and I would deal with it. I had been intrigued to learn that there really was an afterlife, even though it didn't sound quite as pastoral and forgiving as I might have hoped. Now I began to wonder whether there might be some sort of god or gods, as well. (You know the old joke: I was raised to be an agnostic, but I always had my doubts.)

"Don't call, just come," Raadi had said on the Night of Flowering Flesh, but I couldn't wait to talk to him. That evening, after a long and blessedly dreamless nap, I calculated the time difference, then dialed the number of the school where he taught. He had told me never to call him there, but there was no telephone service on the Moth Clan's island. Besides, I felt that this qualified as a medical emergency. That is to say, I wanted to hear his voice so badly it was almost a physical affliction.

"Hello?" I said eagerly when the ringing stopped.

"Hallo, Seagull Island School," said a woman's voice on the other end. She spoke clearly, with that peculiar island lilt to the vowels.

"May I please speak to Raadi Ulonggo? It's sort of an emergency, in a way." God, that sounded lame. There was a long silence, and then the woman said, "Pardon me for asking, but when did you last see Mr. Raadi?"

"Just a week or so ago, at the festival," I said.

"Ah," she said. "Well, I don't know of any easy way to tell you this, but our dear Mr. Raadi was shot and killed in 1995 during the clan wars, bless his soul."

"But I saw him," I said. I was about to add "I kissed him" when I realized that wasn't true. I had fantasized about it so often that it had become a sort of counterfeit memory.

Another long silence. "Do you believe in spirits?" the woman asked.

"Spirits?" I echoed. For some reason, perhaps because I was the teetotaling daughter of an alcoholic mother, I thought she might be talking about beer, or whiskey, or Mai Tais.

"Spirits," she said. "*Zozollio*. I believe you call them ghosts?"

"Oh, absolutely," said the former card-carrying nonbeliever, and I couldn't help thinking what a short journey it was from "absolutely not" to "absolutely." The Japanese understand such fluid ambiguities; they have a word, *zenzen*, that encapsulates both those meanings.

"Well, then," the woman said, "I can tell you that on the Night of Flowering Flesh, even those who are no longer flesh may walk among us, and dance, and fall in love. Please don't ask me to tell you any more, this is the most secret and dangerous information."

A well-kept secret indeed, I thought. There was nothing about ghosts becoming flesh in any of the numbingly objective anthropological studies I had read.

"It's strange," I said, fishing for more. "My guide didn't mention anything like that." I think I was doing my reportorial fact-finding thing because I wasn't ready to accept what she had told me about Raadi.

"Who was your guide, if I may ask?'

"Her name was Sigella Klamm, and she was at least seven months pregnant. I think she must have been from the Blue Snake Clan," I added authoritatively, remembering the scaly hair-ribbon.

"Ah, Sigella. No, she wasn't from the Snake Clan, she was a Cricket. She died in 1975, from a snakebite. The snake dropped from a tea tree and bit her right in the abdomen, so the child couldn't be saved, either. A Brown Mamba, I think it was. Exceedingly poisonous. As God's creatures go, a rather nasty piece of work."

"Wait. You're saying my guide was a ghost?" I thought I was unshockable by now, but this news sent a major quiver down my spine.

"It was very tragic, to die so close to delivery, but at least they're together forever now, the mother and child."

I digested this information for a moment. Then I said, "But Raadi explained everything to me in such convincing detail, all about how he was wounded, and in a coma, and then he recovered. And his fingers were warm!" His fingers on my lips, as he said goodbye.

"Ghosts do not necessarily realize that they are ghosts," said the woman. "Life is not as simple as it appears, and neither is death."

"So are you saying that the only way I can see Raadi again is to come back next year for the Festival?"

"I'm not saying anything," the woman said, her voice suddenly cold. "As far as I'm concerned, this was a wrong number." There was a click, and the phone went dead.

I was stunned by this latest revelation. *Holy cow*, I thought wildly, as I stared unseeing at the filmy blue dusk that hung over the fields like an indigo-dyed mosquito net. *I really know how to pick them. If I could just come up with a few more once-a-year supernatural lovers, it would almost add up to a normal social life*. And then I remembered the sperm bank in San Jose, where Raadi said he had sold his sweet tropical seed to pay for textbooks. Maybe someday …

Just then the phone rang and I snatched it up, hoping it would be the woman from the Seagull School, calling to spill more secrets or to tell me she had been joking, that Raadi was alive and well and full of desire, standing by the phone. "Hello?" I said eagerly.

"Hello, Ms. Stelle," a smooth Japanese voice said in English. "This is Shibako Suzuki from *Tabigarasu* magazine. Thanks so much for turning in your Boston stories on time. We were quite pleased with the way they turned out. I realize this is sudden notice, but I was wondering whether you might be free to fly to Oahu tomorrow to do a story we're calling 'The Best Hotel Brunches of Waikiki.' You'd be staying at the Royal Hawaiian, by the way."

She didn't say that I would be flying first-class; that went without saying. I pictured myself on the plane, watching miniature two-star movies among the fragrant Rolexed moguls, checking into my opulent room, sitting down to plate after plate of eggs Florentine and caviar-and-shallot timbales, and I thought, I don't think I want to do this anymore. And definitely not right now.

"I'm sorry," I said, "but I'm totally booked up through next year." After I had hung up I began wondering what the karmic punishment would be for telling an off-white lie. It's a sin if you think it is, Gaki-san had said. I didn't feel that turning down that cushy assignment was morally wrong in any way, so I was probably all right there. I sighed as I realized that from now on I would no longer have the comfort of believing that everything ended at the grave. As if life hadn't been complicated enough when all I had to do was worry about the immediate consequences of my actions …

Again, the jangle of the telephone interrupted my ruminations. "Sheesh," I said. "Who on earth could *that* be?"

"Hello," said a nervous-sounding female voice, familiar as my own and yet somehow different than I remembered. "This is your prodigal progenitor. Remember me?"

"Mom!" I said after a long speechless moment. Then, with the automatic nastiness born of lifelong resentment: "Sorry, I mean Lilio. I know how you hate to be called anything that smacks even faintly of the maternal."

"Don't worry about that," said my mother. "'Mom' is fine now. In fact you can call me anything you want, as long as you don't call me late for 'Masterpiece Theatre.'"

I started to chuckle politely but then I said, suddenly suspicious, "What's this about, anyway? You sound weird. Have you been drinking?"

"As a matter of fact, I've been seriously sober for a year, exactly. I've been marking off the last month on a calendar, day by day, just waiting to call you, as my reward. I've missed you, Jojo, and I'm so sorry I wasn't always the mother I should have been."

"That's all right, Mom," I said, as the room suddenly blurred before my eyes. "Actually, I think I might sort of need you now." She's finally off the booze, I thought with cautious jubilation. That's why her voice sounds different.

We chatted for two hours, catching up, crying quite a bit but laughing a lot as well. I invited her to come visit me, but she said she had a part-time job working on a newspaper in Mendocino, so she couldn't get away for more than a long weekend. "All right," I said, "I'll go there." I didn't tell her what had happened to me; that wasn't telephone talk. But I did ask whether she had ever visited my grandmother's grave in Maine.

"No, I haven't," said my mother. "You know perfectly well that to me it's just a heap of dirt in a very inconvenient location. I wouldn't mind seeing that nifty statue again, though."

"'There are more things in heaven and earth ...'" I began, but my mother interrupted.

"Please, spare me the schoolgirl Shakespeare," she said. "How many times have I told you: this life is all we have, the rest is silence, so you have to seize the moment. My problem was, I somehow got the moment confused with a bottle of bourbon." She gave a rueful laugh.

"Did Leda, I mean did Grandma believe that death was an eternal void?" It had never occurred to me to ask my grandmother about such things, even on her deathbed. At ten, I had been more interested in hearing about her affair with Mr. Pancho Villa.

My mother laughed. "Oh, you know what an incurable romantic your grandmother was," she said. Her tone was fond, but patronizing too. "She had some naïve idea that her soul would turn into a butterfly after she died."

I hung up with a feeling of relief, for my immediate future, at least, was clear. I would go to visit my mother, and then I would travel to Maine and put some of my grandmother's favorite wildflowers on her grave. Beyond that, I didn't have a clue.

I was as confounded as I had ever been, not just by my brushes with a realm I never dreamed existed, but by my sudden feeling that much of my work, which had seemed so exciting and enjoyable, was not what I ought to be doing. It wasn't that I didn't want to go on writing, but I felt a new and overwhelming need to expend the remainder of my quota of words (sublime, miraculous, wonderful words) on something more significant than a plate of overpriced cold cuts, or the sunset view from some elite hotel. Like most revelations, this one was both alarming and exhilarating. Yet in spite of my nervousness I felt absolutely certain that I would find a way to live in the world, to do good work, and to put my love to use: one human foot in front of the other, one earthly day at a time.

The November sky above Deer Hill Island was a startling cobalt blue, but it wasn't nearly as blue as the butterfly that rested lightly on my grandmother's grave. Unlike the usual gloomy gray geometric tombstones, the marker was a rose-colored marble statue of the Hindu goddess Sarasvati that my grandmother had brought back from a tea-drinking pilgrimage to Darjeeling. The lissome, voluptuous statue stood out amid the somber geometric obelisks like a half-clothed temple dancer at a meeting of the Daughters of the American Revolution. Leda wasn't a practicing Hindu, but she liked their lenient attitude toward earthly passions (at least where their deities were concerned), and she used to say that if she could have any job in the world, she would choose Sarasvati's. "Goddess of art, beauty, and eloquence," she would declare. "I'd take that over penny-a-word journalism, any day."

I had always loved that statue, with its elaborate headdress and graceful lines. It seemed like a perfect memorial to my brave, uninhibited grandmother. On this late-autumn day the surrounding woods were still tinged with gold and crimson, and the maple leaves seemed to echo the deep rosy hue of the marble. I put my hand on the statue's bare arm, and found it surprisingly warm to the touch, as if blood were flowing beneath the surface. The iridescent purplish-blue butterfly was perched on the tip of the goddess's elegant aquiline nose; it fluttered slightly when I approached, but it didn't fly away.

"Look, Mom," I said. "That butterfly is exactly the color of Leda's eyes." And of mine, too, I thought. It suddenly struck me as unutterably marvelous to be human, and to have ancestors. Being on speaking terms with one of them, after such a long cold silence, seemed like an unbelievable bonus. Over several long lunches and dinners in Mendocino I had shared my stories, somewhat expurgated. With perfect predictability, my mother had insisted that everything that happened to me in the Japan Alps and on Kulalau Island was an elaborate hallucination, brought on by overwork, accretional jet lag, and a serious deficiency of Vitamin L. ("By the way, what does the L stand for, anyway?" I asked. I had always assumed that it stood for Lust, or Libido, or Liaisons Dangereuses, but I thought that I might as well ask. "For Love, of course," replied my mother.)

When I drew my mother's attention to the butterfly, which was still hovering around the statue of Sarasvati, she sniffed, "It's just a coincidence. A very pretty coincidence, I'll admit that, but nothing more." I gave her a skeptical raised-eyebrow smile.

"Sheer coincidence," my mother repeated. "The world is full of coincidences, and butterflies." But when I returned later from a solitary hike down to the rocky beach, she was crouched in front of the Sarasvati statue, gently holding the blue-violet butterfly in her cupped hands, and I could have sworn her lips were moving.

"That's the spirit, Mom," I whispered, and then I tiptoed away, silent as a footless ghost. A bloodthirsty trio of beach gnats began buzzing around my face, and as I prepared to silence them with one deadly clap I suddenly thought of Gaki-san, that lovely, passionate, sweet-souled man imprisoned in a wretched insect's body. "Hey, little bugs," I said in a friendly voice, "won't you please go away?" And to my very great surprise, the gnats flew off into the blueberry air.

THE UNDEAD OF UGUISUDANI

A woman drew her long black hair out tight
And fiddled whisper music on those strings
And bats with baby faces in the violet light
Whistled, and beat their wings,
And crawled head downward
Down a blackened wall …

—T. S. Eliot
The Waste Land

The Tokyo district of Uguisudani has long been known as a picturesque place to visit, and a pleasant place to live. Until the beginning of the Edo period the area, which lies in a verdant valley between two corrugated purple hills, was a dense forest of cryptomeria and gingko trees inhabited primarily by exuberant nightingales. Hence the name Uguisudani, or Nightingale Valley. Even at the beginning of the twenty-first century, the trees still outnumbered the buildings, and Uguisudani remained one of the greenest, most countrified sections of the great gray labyrinth known as Tokyo.

In one of the charming old tile-roofed buildings amid the birdsong-filled trees of Uguisudani, a young Francophile named Mikio Makioka ran a specialty coffee shop called, in homage to two of his favorite artists, Café Delaunay. Mikio had fallen in love with the idea of *la belle France* as a result of watching the Jean-Luc Godard film *Breathless* five times in one fateful, intoxicating week. After graduating from a small liberal-arts college in Sendai, Mikio continued his education by reading French books, frequenting museums and libraries, attending lectures, and listening to language tapes. Mikio had never been outside Japan, but his dream was to go to Paris and sit at a zinc-topped table at a bistro in Montmartre, drinking Sumatran coffee laced with absinthe (or some less corrosive substitute) and eating *pissaladière niçoise*, surrounded by the antic ghosts of Valéry, Huysmans, and those amazingly artistic Delaunays: Sonia and Robert, *sœur et frère*.

Next door to Mikio's coffee shop there was a handsome mock chalet with whitewashed walls, dark brown half-timbered trim, and beveled-glass windows. In the ten years since Mikio had moved to Uguisudani, this building had housed a series of businesses—restaurants, boutiques, florists—several of whose proprietors had gone bankrupt, or mad, or both. The most recent occupant, an upscale butcher, had been found hanging upside down from a large hook in his own meat locker, pale as uncooked sweetbreads and frozen stiff.

The local police, who were more accustomed to dealing with runaway poodles and birdflesh-craving cats stranded in trees, declared the death a suicide. The coroner attributed the disappearance of every drop of blood from the body to "gravity and evaporation," and the case was quickly closed. The building's heavy wooden doors were padlocked, the diamond-paned windows were boarded up, and everyone, including Mikio, assumed that it would be a very long time before the landlord would find another occupant for such an obviously ill-omened space.

But one bright, cool morning in late September when Mikio strolled past the empty building on his way to work, he noticed that the crisscross boards had been removed from the windows, along with several months' accumulation of urban grime. Peering through the sparkling glass, he was amazed to discover that the medium-sized space had been transformed overnight into an opulent restaurant, with striped-satin wallpaper, poppy-colored velvet banquettes, and hand-carved tables of rich dark ebony under gilt-and-crystal chandeliers which might have come from a garage sale at Versailles.

"They must have worked all night," Mikio muttered to himself as he hosed down the sidewalk in front of his shop. There was no sign of life inside the restaurant next door, although it appeared ready to open for business. The heavy tables were laid with fine white linen and sterling cutlery, and each was adorned with a single red rose in a crystal bud vase. Mikio had gleaned these details through a triangle of leaded glass, under the nonchalant pretense of studying the hand-lettered menu posted in the front window. The offerings struck him as Continental, with an Eastern European accent. There were cassoulets and organ-meat patés, blood sausages and goulashes, peasant soups and skewered meats. For dessert, there were tortes, trifles, puddings, and the inevitable *tiramisu*.

"Persimmon pudding," Mikio read aloud from the menu. "I'll have to try that sometime." He loved persimmons in any form: in ink paintings, on leafless trees, in wooden boxes at the vegetable stand, or (best of all) sitting ripe and waiting on a glossy black-lacquer tray next to a small, sharp knife, on a slow dreamy September afternoon. To him the persimmon was the very soul and symbol of autumn—and autumn, with its pale sun, crisp evenings, and painted leaves, was the most exhilarating of all the seasons.

Business that day was unusually brisk. Mikio had just introduced a new specialty coffee called Café Voltaire (Costa Rican Tres Rios mixed with chicory and cinnamon) and, coincidentally, his shop had been written up in Tokyo's leading English-language newspaper by a columnist who lived in the neighborhood. On the day the column ran, and every day thereafter, the shop was deluged with high-spirited foreigners, exclaiming with delight over the originality of the menu (all the coffees were named for famous figures in French art, letters, or history) and the decor (Toulouse-Lautrec *Folies Bergère* wallpaper, Degas' *L'Absinthe* on the covers of the hand-lettered menus, bowls of fruit assembled in the manner of Cézanne, flower arrangements inspired by the luminous paintings of Odilon Redon). They raved about the "morning set" menu: a quartered hard-boiled egg, a warm baguette with shallot-chive butter, and sliced tomatoes—grown without pesticides in a little green-staked garden behind Mikio's shop—drenched in a Dijon-mustard vinaigrette and garnished with fresh basil. Indeed, they seemed to love everything about the shop, from the music (Couperin, Poulenc, Piaf) to the napkins of Basque border-printed cotton in bright primary colors. One effusive American woman even gushed at embarrassing length about the outfit Mikio was wearing: blue-and-white striped fisherman's jersey, baggy white canvas trousers, red espadrilles with suspenders to match, and a navy-blue wool beret.

The columnist whose article had precipitated this radical upswing in Café Delaunay's fortunes was a handsome chestnut-haired woman in her late thirties named Rebecca Flanders. She was originally from Boston but now, after nearly two decades in Tokyo, she was often called "more Japanese than a Japanese"—the ultimate compliment an ethnocentric *Nihonjin* can pay to an Occidental interloper. Rebecca Flanders had been frequenting Mikio's shop since it opened four years earlier, and they had gradually become friends.

Rebecca worked at home, but being sociable by nature she found telecommuting via e-mail too isolating. Unless there was a typhoon or a rail strike she traveled every weekday to the newspaper office in central Tokyo to turn in her copy, read galley proofs, and pick up her mail. On this day, as usual, she had stopped at Café Delaunay for a cup of coffee on her way home around three P.M., but Mikio was so busy with a polyglot horde of customers that he hardly had a chance to talk to her.

"It's all your fault," he joked as he served Rebecca's customary order: a cup of Café Colette (café au lait sweetened with Tahitian-vanilla syrup) and two of his cousin Sanae's addictive marzipan macaroons. "If you hadn't written so glowingly about my shop then I wouldn't have so many customers, and we'd have more time to chat."

"Sorry about that," Rebecca Flanders said in mock apology. "I promise never to do it again." She spoke excellent Japanese, the result of years of faithful listening to radio call-in advice programs like "Romance Counsel" and "The Love Doctors." "I do wish you weren't quite so busy, though. I wanted to talk to you about the new place next door. It's like a toadstool—it just sprouted overnight!"

"I know," Mikio began, but just then the bell above the door jingled and a pair of tall, blond, dark-suited Dutch bankers came in and sat down at the counter. "We'll talk later, Rebecca," he promised as he rushed off to tend to his perking pots, his thirsty customers, and his overflowing till.

Around nine that evening Mikio went outside, ostensibly to water the dwarf persimmon trees, strung with tiny white lights, that flanked the front door of his shop. In truth, tending his trees was just an excuse for peering discreetly through the window next door. The restaurant was completely filled with elegantly-dressed foreigners, drinking and laughing and talking. Something about the scene made Mikio feel like an intruder, and he quickly turned away, though not before forming some rather disturbing impressions. "*Il y a quelque chose qui cloche,*" he told himself. "Something isn't quite right."

Mikio could hardly wait to share his thoughts with Rebecca Flanders, but he was inundated with customers for the rest of the week, and it wasn't until late Sunday evening that the two friends finally had a chance to sit down and talk.

"So, what do you think about the place next door?" Rebecca asked as she sipped her cup of foamy Café Colette.

"Well," Mikio said thoughtfully, "there's something kind of strange about that restaurant. To begin with, they've been totally busy, from the first night, even though I don't believe they've advertised at all."

"No, they haven't. At least not in any of the English-language papers."

"And the hours are odd: they're open from eight P.M. until four A.M. Usually I close at around eleven on weeknights, twelve at the latest, but the other night a friend from my hometown stopped by and we ended up talking until two. On my way home, I looked in and the restaurant was filled to capacity with sophisticated-looking foreigners, all very stylishly dressed, and everyone was drinking the weirdest thing."

"What's that?"

"Well, wouldn't you expect them to be drinking wine, or beer, or cocktails?"

"Not necessarily," said Rebecca. "So, what *were* they drinking?"

"They were all drinking tomato juice, in big tall glasses!" Mikio paused dramatically, and Rebecca laughed.

"Those were just Bloody Marys," she said. "They're all the rage in Europe now, and they've always been popular in the United States. They're made with vodka, tomato juice, Worcestershire sauce, Tabasco sauce, and lemon juice, as I recall. Some people even drink them for breakfast after a wild night—hair of the dog, they call it."

"Oh," said Mikio sheepishly. "I've never heard of such a drink. To me it looked more like … well, never mind."

"What else seemed strange?" Rebecca prompted.

"Well, I just wonder why they aren't open for lunch."

"Maybe they don't want to work that hard. Or maybe they're already wealthy and are just running a restaurant for fun."

"Yes, I suppose you're right," Mikio said. The conversation turned to other topics then: the phenomenal boom in his own business, the wonderfully low price of persimmons, the lucid loveliness of the weather. Still feeling a little foolish for not having known about the Bloody Mary craze, Mikio decided not to mention his other concern about the restaurant next door: namely, that in spite of the restaurant's perpetual fullness, he had never seen anyone entering or exiting by the front door. No taxis or cars or limousines ever seemed to pull up in front of the place, either.

Rebecca Flanders went away for ten days, to research a story for an American travel magazine about the health-giving properties of *rotenburo*—open-air hot-spring mineral baths. In truth, she confided to Mikio, she had taken the assignment primarily because her most recent love affair had ended badly and she was in desperate need of what she called "a little working vacation, with the emphasis on vacation."

One day during Rebecca's absence Mikio was at the vegetable stand buying peridot pears and glossy red apples to replenish his Cézanne-inspired fruit bowls. He casually remarked to the proprietor, who always wore a jaunty porkpie hat over his wispy white hair, "Say, Mr. Kaneshiro, it looks as if that restaurant next door to my shop is doing a pretty good business. Have you ever eaten there?"

The elderly greengrocer couldn't have looked more aghast if Mikio had suddenly begun foaming at the mouth. "You must be joking," he said, shaking his head. "It would take an entire month's profits just to buy a bowl of soup at that place!"

"What do you mean?" asked Mikio.

"Haven't you looked at the prices on the menu? They're outrageous! I don't know anyone in the neighborhood who's eaten there. Of course we'd all like to try the food, out of curiosity, but there's no way we're going to pay ten thousand yen for a simple bowl of soup. I mean, even if it does have a fancy foreign name like gazpacho"—he pronounced it ga-su-pa-cho—"soup is soup, right?"

Mikio thought Mr. Kaneshiro must be mistaken. It was only natural for the old man to become confused about numbers at his age; just the day before he had accidentally overcharged Mikio for a dozen tangerines.

"Ten thousand yen for a bowl of soup? That sounds unlikely," Mikio said diplomatically. "Maybe it was a misprint."

"No, it wasn't," retorted Mr. Kaneshiro, polishing a long purple eggplant on his green cotton apron. "I mean, even a glass of water costs a thousand yen there. I know because Uncle Baseball—you know, the fellow with the scruffy beard who sleeps in the park? Anyway, he told me that he went to the back door looking for work, and they said he could come back the next night and wash dishes. Then he asked very politely if he could have a drink of water, because he was thirsty, and they told him it would cost a thousand yen!"

Mikio's mind was racing as he hurried back to Café Delaunay with his bag of fruit. There had been no prices on the menu that first day. He was positive of that.

Mikio dashed past the florist, the fishmonger, and the stationery store. He didn't pause to check out the clientele of the musty little coffee shop called Happy Days, which was his only competition in the neighborhood. And he only shot a quick glance at the community bulletin board, with its heartrending notices of runaway children, vanished pets, and lost wedding rings.

When he reached the restaurant Mikio stopped and looked at the posted menu. Sure enough, prices had been written in, in ornate Gothic calligraphy, and what prices they were! An appetizer was five thousand yen, an average *à la carte* entrée ten thousand yen, and a complete *table d'hôte* dinner cost an astounding thirty thousand yen. Even the persimmon pudding, which Mikio had been looking forward to sampling, was listed at four thousand yen.

Mikio was incredulous. His first thought was, They must be making a fortune, since they're packed from eight P.M. on, seven nights a week. His second thought was, Those foreigners must really be well paid, to be able to afford to eat out at those prices. But his third thought, which didn't come to him until several hours later, as he was brewing a batch of Café M. Antoinette (a dark-roasted Viennese blend, subtly flavored with rose petals and served with a piece of Sanae's airy Parisian pound cake) was the most dramatic of all.

"Wait a minute," he said to himself. "Maybe those aren't the real prices at all. Maybe they're just posted to keep regular people out!" But then he shook his head and chided himself for having an overactive imagination.

Business had been good, better than ever before, and Mikio was turning a tidy profit. So on the day that Rebecca Flanders was scheduled to return from her hot-spring tour, he took twelve ten-thousand–yen notes out of his cash register and put them in his wallet. Then he telephoned Rebecca's house and left a message on her answering machine: "Please have dinner with me tonight, I think you know where. You might want to wear red, in case you spill some tomato juice. Just joking."

Rebecca called him back around four that afternoon. "Mikio?" she said. Her voice sounded hoarse and weak.

"Rebecca, welcome home. Are you all right?"

"Do I sound all right?"

"No, actually, you sound awful. What's wrong?"

"Well, I've heard that prolonged soaking in hot mineral water can bring all the subterranean toxins to the surface, and I think that must be what happened to me, because I caught the most horrendous cold I've ever had. I can barely speak, or breathe, or think. I'm going to fall into bed right now, so could I please take a rain check on your very generous and tempting offer?"

"Of course," said Mikio. "Sleep well, and I'll give you a call tomorrow to see if there's anything you need." He hung up the phone feeling mildly disappointed. He had been looking forward so eagerly to having dinner with Rebecca at the restaurant-without-a-name (that was another odd thing about it) that it had never occurred to him that she might decline. Since the restaurant seemed to attract mostly foreigners, Mikio would have felt more comfortable going there with his American friend, but after a moment's chagrin, he turned to Plan B: dinner for one.

He had already arranged to have his cousin Sanae watch the shop from eight until ten P.M., so at 7:40 he went into the little curtained-off room behind the counter and changed from his loose black linen trousers, saffron-colored turtleneck, and moss-green suspenders into his most elegant black-and-gray chevron-patterned silk kimono. He combed his shoulder-length black hair, put on a black cashmere beret, wrapped a rust-colored *obi* around his hips, and ducked back under the curtain into the coffee shop. To his surprise, the small audience—regulars from the neighborhood, and a few foreign students hoping to practice their Japanese—greeted him with a standing ovation.

"You look utterly dashing," said Sanae, who was busy behind the counter making a chocolate mocha latte.

"Yes, indeed," agreed a Japanese customer, a wiry-haired martial artist and aspiring novelist who taught Urban Self-Defense classes at a nearby women's university. "Like a *tanka* poet or a famous ink painter."

"That's exactly the effect I was hoping to create," said Mikio, trying not to let the praise go to his head. "You see, I'm going to try to get into the restaurant next door without a reservation."

"And pray tell what restaurant might that be, if I could be so bold to inquire?" asked a shaven-headed medical student from Kenya in ultra-polite Japanese.

"You know, the classy-looking one with the ridiculous prices," said a statuesque young Brazilian-Japanese woman who was studying classical *buyo* dance, and giving samba lessons on the side. "It's a wonder they can stay in business, even if they do cater to rich foreign executives and their mistresses, and fat bankers on expense accounts. At least, that's what I've heard."

"Well, wish me luck," said Mikio. He slipped a pair of black leather-strapped geta clogs over his pristine white cotton split-toed socks and strode confidently out the door. With the comforting warmth and light and camaraderie of Café Delaunay behind him, though, he felt suddenly apprehensive. "Don't be silly," he told himself sternly. "It's a public place, and I'm a cash customer."

It was ten minutes before eight when Mikio stationed himself in front of the mysterious restaurant. He peeked through the window and saw that there wasn't a single guest, although a couple of tall, thin, light-haired waiters were putting the finishing touches on the formal place settings. Another foreigner, of similar physical type but with an air of authority (probably the maitre d', thought Mikio) was standing by the kitchen door, reading a newspaper.

The solid-walnut door was locked, as Mikio discovered when he gave it a discreet push, and there was no doorknob. So he waited patiently outside, and on the stroke of eight o'clock he knocked on the door. A small sliding-wood window in the top of the door slid open almost immediately, and the lower half of an angular, thin-lipped face appeared.

"Can I help you?" said a deep male voice in well-enunciated but rather brusque Japanese.

"Yes, please, I'd like to have dinner this evening."

"You have a reservation?"

"No, I would have made one but there was no telephone number on the menu, and I didn't know the name of the restaurant."

"This restaurant has no name. And no telephone. Nor, I might add, does it need them."

"Oh, is it like a private club for foreigners?"

"A private club?" The man seemed to find the notion amusing. "Yes, in a way."

"Then why do you have the menu posted?"

"It is a custom," said the man in a tone which seemed to suggest that cross-examination would be not only unwelcome, but perhaps even dangerous.

"So are you telling me I can't have dinner here?" Mikio had never before been so persistent or so confrontational, and he found the sensation oddly exhilarating.

"That is correct," said a voice at his ear, and Mikio almost jumped out of his clogs. Standing next to him was the tall, thin man whom he had identified earlier as the maitre d'. The man had a long, narrow, sharp-featured face and the slick patent-leather hair of an American silent-film star, except that instead of being glossy black his hair was platinum beige, like champagne mixed with heavy cream. Mushroom-colored, Mikio thought, visualizing the woven baskets filled with etiolated foreign fungi at Mr. Kaneshiro's vegetable stand. He glanced back at the opening in the door just as it was sliding shut.

"I'm sorry," he said to the maitre d', who was wearing large dark sunglasses with silvery rims. "I just assumed the restaurant was open to the public."

"Members only," wheezed the man. He appeared to be out of breath, although he had only walked a few feet. Mikio noted this evidence of cardio-vascular flabbiness with some satisfaction, for he himself had been a devout jogger since junior high school.

The maitre d' wore an arrogant, condescending expression, almost a sneer, and Mikio couldn't help noticing that there was something awkward about his mouth in repose, as if his lips didn't quite fit over his teeth. The man's features were regular and handsome enough, in a cold, ectomorphic way, and he was impeccably turned out in a black tuxedo with a pin-tucked white shirt, red cummerbund, shiny black dress boots with high flamenco-dancer's heels, and white gloves. He exuded a not entirely symphonic mix of twentieth-century scents: minty mouthwash, musky aftershave, polyurethane hair fixative, and something else, some vaguely unpleasant underlying odor—a slightly funky undershirt, perhaps?—which Mikio couldn't identify. The man had something tucked under one of his long, thin arms. Mikio mistook it at first for a menu, but then he realized that it was a folded copy of the *Tokyo Tribune.*

"You work at the little coffee stand next door," the maitre d' said dis-dainfully, as Mikio was turning to go. So much for masquerading as a famous artist or poet.

"Yes, I do," said Mikio. It didn't seem appropriate to point out that it was a thriving shop, not some lowly pushcart, and that he was, in fact and in deed, the owner—along with the Mitsubishi Bank.

"You might just want to forget that we're here," said the man, still panting as if he had just run a 10K. It was not so much a suggestion as an order, and Mikio felt another shudder travel down his spine.

"Sure," he said. "Whatever you say. I'm sorry to have bothered you." As he walked away, his wooden geta clicking on the pavement, he thought he could feel the man's eyes boring into his back like a spinal tap, but when he turned around the street was empty.

Rebecca came by the next morning for a cup of slippery-elm tea. "No coffee for me for awhile, I'm afraid," she said between bouts of coughing. She had dragged herself out of her sickbed to deliver a perishable souvenir from the last hot-spring resort she had visited: a confection of caramelized chestnuts encased in a semi-sweet dough, glazed with egg white, then baked to an almost ceramic sheen. Touched by this considerate gesture, Mikio opened the artistically-wrapped box and offered the first dumpling to Rebecca.

"I'll pass," she said. "I'm ashamed to say that I ate an entire box of these on the train, all by my greedy little self, so I've had more than my share. I never feel like eating sweets when I'm sick, and I couldn't taste anything now anyway. But please do share them with your charming cousin, the baker. I know she'll appreciate the flavor, and the artistry. And now, tell me all about your adventure last night."

Mikio related his experiences, omitting only those details which he felt might make him appear less than samurai-like, such as his unseemly levitation when the ominous-looking, heavy-breathing waiter appeared beside him.

"Hmm," said Rebecca when he had finished. "I don't like the sound of it at all. I wonder if they might be doing something illegal." That was all she said, but when she left her face wore a familiar reflective look. I'll bet she's going to write something about that place in her column, Mikio thought. Maybe I should stop her.

He rushed outside, but Rebecca was nowhere in sight. Oh well, he told himself, she's not likely to go back to work while she's not feeling well, so I can talk to her tomorrow. But Mikio had underestimated Rebecca's Yankee resilience, and by the time he got around to calling her the next morning, she had already left for the office. She didn't come by after work, nor did she respond to the increasingly anxious messages he left on her machine. Around five, Sanae dropped by, waving the late edition of the *Tokyo Tribune*. "The plot thickens," she said cryptically.

Rebecca's column was usually on page three of the newspaper, but on this day it had been moved to the front page. SOMETHING SHADY GOING ON IN NIGHTINGALE TOWN? the headline asked, in extra-large, boldface type, next to a rather glamorous photo of Rebecca Flanders, with her hair up. The article that followed chronicled, in vivid, opinionated prose, the coming of the unorthodox restaurant with the exorbitant prices to a quiet little street in the Tokyo district of Uguisudani.

"Perhaps," the piece concluded, "this may be a matter for the licensing board to look into. It is one thing to exclude the public from what appears to be a public restaurant complete with posted (albeit unconscionably overpriced) menu. It would be quite another to be serving alcoholic beverages without a proper liquor license, or to be staying open until four A.M. without a cabaret license."

Oh, dear, thought Mikio after Sanae (who, conveniently, had been a member of the English Club through high school and college) had translated the entire article into Japanese for him. They're not going to like this at all.

Rebecca Flanders first came to Tokyo as an exchange student, and she liked the city so much that she decided to return after graduating from Boston University with a double major in Japanese literature and journalism. The first time, she stayed for nine months; the second, for eighteen years. Every time she went out in public, Rebecca was subtly reminded that she was and always would be, undisguisably and irremediably, a foreigner in her adopted homeland. But that didn't faze her in the least, because she had always felt a little like an alien even in her hometown of Newton, Massachusetts.

Rebecca had moved a number of times since settling in Tokyo, but the place she finally found in Uguisudani suited her perfectly. The small but airy house, once the servants' quarters of a sumptuous mansion, had been converted into a single-family dwelling when the mansion burned to the ground ten years before. Now there was a small Shinto fox-shrine on the grounds where the mansion had stood, so Rebecca's house was surrounded by a double zone of greenery: her own tiny garden on four sides, and the tall trees of the shrine beyond that. The house had been remodeled in half-Western, half-Japanese style, with tatami mats and sliding *shoji* doors on the first story, while the second level had large glass-paned windows and parquet floors. Rebecca loved the duality, and the balance. She could sit downstairs at a low table and drink tea while looking out at the lush, mossy garden, then go upstairs and work at her roll-topped desk while nightingales and bush warblers crooned and twittered in the tall lacy-leafed cryptomeria trees outside her window.

That night, Mikio closed the coffee shop just before midnight. He thought briefly of crossing the street to avoid passing the nameless restaurant, but some combination of defiance and habit made him decide to take his usual route. He did, however, vow to keep his head down until he had safely passed the disquieting windows. Mikio usually walked with his head held high (which in his diminutive case was right at window level), so he had never noticed the way the light from the big chandeliers was filtered through the beveled edges of the glass, splashing a prismatic plaid of intersecting triangle-rainbows on the sidewalk.

"*Courage, camarade*, you're almost there," Mikio reassured himself as he came abreast of the big wooden door, for there was just one more window to pass. But then something made him stop, raise his eyes from the kaleidoscopic pavement, and glance into the restaurant—a move which was entirely contrary to his plan, and against his better judgment.

The tables were filled, as usual, with splendidly dressed foreigners toasting one another with tall crystal glasses filled with tomato juice, vodka, Worcestershire sauce, and so on. Hah! Mikio thought. They're all drinking the same thing again. And they call *us* conformists!

But then his attention shifted to another detail that had hitherto escaped his notice. Although the weather was still quite warm, all the guests were wearing gloves: black leather or white cotton for the men, long formal satin gloves in bright spring-flower colors for the women. Perhaps that was another of the club's odd customs, like posting a menu and then refusing admittance to the general public. Mikio's gaze traveled slowly around the room, and when it finally came to rest on the red-enameled double doors that led to the kitchen, he understood what had caused him to stop in his tracks.

There in front of the kitchen door stood the supercilious maitre d' from the night before, looking exactly the same: formal dress, pale slick hair, white gloves, folded *Tokyo Tribune* under one arm. But while his expression the previous night had been remote but neutral, now he was staring straight at Mikio with an angry, electrifying glare. Mikio felt his own eyes go wide at the sheer hostile force of the contact.

Instinctively, absurdly, he bowed his head in automatic greeting and hurried past the window. He half-expected to hear the menacing click of flamenco footsteps behind him, but there was no sound, all the way home, except for the cacophonous wails of cats doing battle in the trenches of territorial lust, and a surprisingly harmonious trio of blue-suited expense-account drunks singing the mournful ballad "*Tsugaru Kaikyu no Fuyu-Geshiki*" as they stumbled home from another long night of overpriced Scotch-on-the-rocks, sycophantic small talk, and compulsory *karaoke*.

When Mikio got back to his cozy little apartment he made himself a cup of chamomile tea, took a bath, and put on his mail-order French silk pajamas. Then, as was his habit, he took down a book to read himself to sleep. Mikio had an entire shelf of books written in French; some had been gifts, others he had found at used-book stores in the Jinbocho district of Tokyo.

To add a bit of surprise to this bedtime ritual, Mikio liked to close his eyes, spin around twice, then pluck a book off the French-language shelf at random. On this evening the result was more than a surprise, it was a shock. The book that ended up in his hand was entitled *Une Histoire Complète du Vampirisme*, and Mikio was startled not only by the sensational subject matter, but also by the fact that he had never seen the book before in his life.

It was an antique, obviously, bound in weathered Malaga-colored leather with the title in tarnished gold. But where had it come from? Had someone—some evil slick-haired enemy with a skeleton key—been in his apartment while he was away?

After a long, paralytic moment of terror, Mikio suddenly remembered that Sanae had mentioned finding an old French book with unusual illustrations at her favorite bookstore in Kanda, and had promised to drop it off when she came over to return his VCR. "Whew," Mikio said out loud, exhaling enough pent-up breath to inflate a large balloon. So there was nothing sinister or supernatural about the book's appearance on his shelf, after all. Still, it was an extraordinary coincidence, given the nature of his percolating suspicions about the restaurant-without-a-name.

As Mikio skimmed through the vampire book, a number of alarming phrases leapt from the pages and lodged in his mind. "Unnaturally long fingernails"; "dreadful odor"; "heavy breathing, except when asleep"; "insatiable thirst for fresh blood"; and, perhaps most disturbing, "supernatural ability to assume any form they wish." Toward the end of the book there were several pages of eerie, old-fashioned illustrations. One in particular caught Mikio's eye.

It was a grainy pen-and-ink drawing of a half-man, half-bat creature hanging head downward from the parapet of a haunted-looking black-walled castle. When Mikio turned the book upside down to get a better look at the bat-man's face, he couldn't suppress a little cry of surprise, for the face bore a striking resemblance to that of the malignant maitre d'. Mikio's heart was pounding as he put the book back on the shelf. The time had come, he realized, to give voice to his wildest, most preposterous fears—fears which had been growing in the darkest recesses of his subconscious like (to borrow Rebecca's analogy) toadstools in a damp mildewy basement.

"I strongly suspect that the fancy restaurant next door is a private club for vampires," Mikio said, slowly. It sounded so ludicrous, and so melodramatic, that he almost laughed out loud. But then, out of nowhere, an image came to mind: the maitre d', last night and again this evening, with a copy of the *Tribune* tucked under his arm. Since Rebecca's sensational column was splashed all over the front page of the paper, it was very likely that the creepy host had read today's article. And since he had no doubt seen Rebecca entering Café Delaunay on numerous occasions, he was probably aware of her association with Mikio. That would explain the anger and hatred in his eyes.

"Oh, no!" Mikio said out loud, as his mind pursued this unsettling hypothesis to its unthinkable conclusion. "Surely they wouldn't—" he began. And then he thought: of course they would.

He jumped up and quickly replaced his burgundy silk pajamas with what Rebecca called his "ninja jogger" outfit: the black hooded sweatshirt and matching sweatpants he wore when he went running three or four times a week. Not bothering with socks, he put on his black and silver running shoes, grabbed his lucky talisman, and dashed out the door. "Please, please, please," Mikio repeated to himself as he sprinted through the silent streets, "Don't let me be too late."

Rebecca Flanders, too, had drunk some chamomile tea that evening, and it had made her exceedingly drowsy. Without removing her ivory silk dressing gown or turning back the covers, she lay down on the big four-poster bed in her upstairs bedroom, wrapped herself in a multicolored afghan, and immediately fell into a deep sleep.

In her first dream, someone was knocking at her door. But when she went to the door, there was no one there. The noise continued, and as she slowly swam toward consciousness Rebecca realized that someone actually was knocking, not at the door but on the window.

Probably one of the neighborhood cats, she thought as she sat up and switched on her bedside lamp. The bulb sputtered and flared out, and the room was dark once again. "Oh, terrific!" Rebecca said. One of these days she would have to write a wry, rueful column on why lightbulbs always seemed to choose the worst possible time to burn out.

Fortunately she had a candle next to her bed, a relic from the vanished days of languid, sensuous evenings with her departed (but by no means forgotten) lover Philippe—an aristocratic, twice-divorced black sheep who, if he didn't get himself disowned first, would eventually inherit an enormous chateau in the Loire Valley, along with some of the finest vineyards in the world. Rebecca lit the candle and shook her head to clear the cobwebs, then concentrated on listening.

It was a slow, steady tapping, the purposeful sound of human knuckles on glass; definitely not the random percussion of some fleabitten stray cat scratching itself next to the window. Rebecca wasn't frightened, for she was a great believer in rational explanations, and she knew there had to be one for this. She walked over to the window, but all she saw was the trees in her garden swaying slightly in the wind. The knocking came again, this time from the other large window. Rebecca turned around, then gasped in amazement and delight.

Standing at the window, dressed as if for a high-society ball in black tails, white gloves, black top hat, and long red silk scarf (and sporting the racing sunglasses he always affected, even at night) was the man she had loved so much—and still loved, against all common sense. Rebecca had been deeply hurt and bewildered when he had abruptly terminated their torrid relationship on the flimsy pretext of "needing to spend some time alone living like a monk, to find out who I am without a woman." The man smiled his familiar full-lipped, sardonic smile, and Rebecca's heart filled with joy as she ran over to the window, opened the latch, and slid it open.

"Philippe! Darling! You came back!" she cried. Philippe stepped silently into the room, still wearing his international-seducer-of-women smile. Rebecca sat down on the bed, feeling suddenly dizzy and disoriented. "Did you climb a tree in your white tie and tails?" she asked, her heart pounding wildly. "How impulsive of you! And how romantic!"

Philippe went on smiling, but didn't speak. He seemed to be breathing rather heavily, no doubt from his arduous climb. Or perhaps, Rebecca thought with a frisson of pent-up passion, he's just excited about the prospect of being with me again.

"Take off your sunglasses, my darling," she murmured. "I want to see your eyes." Ignoring her request, Philippe began walking toward the bed. The closer he came, the more Rebecca's vertigo and confusion increased. Her sight grew dim, her breathing became labored, and she seemed to be on the verge of dissolving into a molten puddle of desire. Being ill had always made her feel uncommonly amorous, but this was the most extreme attack of purely carnal craving she had ever experienced.

Philippe stood over her, still breathing audibly, like an out-of-shape jogger being pursued by wolves. Rebecca, too, was all but panting with arousal as she lay back on the bed. "Why don't you say something, sweetheart?" she asked between shallow inhalations.

If only he would say what she wanted to hear—"I've missed you terribly, and I know now that I want to marry you and make you my last Duchess"—then she could close her eyes and lose herself in the rapture of the reunion. But even in the throes of feverish lust, it was beginning to bother her that he hadn't spoken a single word. Philippe's lovemaking had always featured the most elaborate verbal foreplay: lyrical compliments, intimate declarations, tantalizing previews of the ecstasies to come. Silent seduction had never been his style.

Philippe bent down, and Rebecca watched in wonder as his handsome, decadent face—the face she thought of every hour, and had been afraid she might never see again—came closer and closer to hers. Even in her dizzy libidinous swoon, she couldn't help noticing that there was something abnormal about his breath; it smelled of raw meat and organic decay, like a cannibal's compost heap. Philippe liked his steak *tartare*, but he had always been conscientious to the point of obsessiveness about maintaining perfectly pristine breath. He carried a miniature folding toothbrush with him everywhere he went, and once, after Rebecca had served him some crudités with a super-garlicky *aïoli* dip, he had asked her for a sprig of parsley to chew, in order (as he put it) "to disarm the garlic fumes." But disgusting as his halitosis was tonight, it did nothing to diminish Rebecca's passion. In a way, it made the almost supernaturally flawless Philippe seem a bit more human.

"Please, say something," she pleaded again, although she could sense that he wasn't in a chatty mood. She was actually quite excited by the prospect of a bestial, wordless coupling, for like many highly intelligent women, Rebecca Flanders occasionally fantasized about being treated like a mindless medieval wench by the rough-bearded, leather-jerkined (or black-tuxedoed) man of her dreams.

We can always talk later, she thought, closing her eyes and preparing to surrender to the thrill of this erotic dream come true. And then, just as Philippe's strangely cold, dry lips brushed against her neck, there was a loud crash. The door to her room burst open, and the next thing she knew there was a struggle going on above her. Rebecca opened her eyes and saw Mikio, her sweet little friend from the coffee shop, flailing away at Philippe with a small, shiny object.

What on earth? she thought. Her lovely lustful mood was shattered, and she sat up in bed just in time to see the man she adored climbing out the window. Rebecca ran to the window and called "Philippe, come back!" but he had already vanished among the trees. She turned slowly to face the panting, sweat-soaked Mikio, who was standing in the middle of her room dressed all in black and holding, of all unlikely things, a silver crucifix.

"How dare you burst in like this, in the middle of the night!" she said angrily. "I know jealousy makes men do crazy things, but this is really going too far."

Mikio's jaw dropped in astonishment. It was true that he had been secretly attracted to Rebecca ever since their first meeting, but jealousy had absolutely nothing to do with his behavior tonight.

"Rebecca," he said gently, "who was that just now?"

"That was Philippe," she said curtly. "The man I love." Mikio winced. "He finally decided to come back to me," Rebecca went on in an uncharacteristically peevish voice, "and now you've chased him away. And knowing him, he won't believe me when I tell him that you're just a friend, because he's the most jealous, possessive man I've ever known."

Mikio knew he had some explaining to do, but he wasn't sure where to begin. "Listen," he said, taking the roundabout approach, "I know you're angry at me, and I know it must have seemed incredibly rude to burst in here like that. But I was trying to protect you from something far worse than an overdressed playboy with vulture-breath. There's something weird going on around here, and I believe you may be in danger. Will you please let me try to prove it to you?"

"Okay," said Rebecca wearily, twisting her disheveled hair into a loose braid and tossing it over one shoulder. Mikio had never seen her with her long reddish-brown hair down, and he thought she looked seriously beautiful, and infinitely desirable.

"Could you give me the phone number of the, uh, person who was just here?" Mikio said, struggling to focus his thoughts on the matter at hand. "And then will you go listen on another extension while I call him?"

"I don't see the point," said Rebecca. "He wouldn't have had time to get home. Even in his Turbo Carrera it would take at least half an hour to get to Roppongi at this time of night."

"That's exactly the point," said Mikio. "By the way, what did you say his name was?"

"Philippe duBois de Sansonnet, le Duc de Loup-Lyon," said Rebecca lovingly. She had always relished saying Philippe's name; it seemed to have the same mesmerizing cadence as the first line of "Kubla Khan." She went into her study and waited until Mikio had dialed the number (it was still number one on her auto-dial), then picked up the extension. The telephone rang ten or eleven times, and Mikio was on the verge of hanging up when a young female voice said "Hullo?"

"Hello," said Mikio, who still remembered most of the basic telephone English he had learned in high school. "May I speak please to Mr. Philippe?"

"Aye, 'old on," said the young woman, in a breezy Yorkshire accent. "It's for you, luv," she called. After a moment's wait, during which Mikio could hear Rebecca's anxious breathing on the extension, a man came on the line.

"*Allo*? Who is this?" he asked brusquely, in a deep voice with an upper-class French accent. Mikio was silent. "Don't you know it's rude to ring people in the middle of the night?" demanded the Duke of Loup-Lyon.

Mikio hung up and waited for Rebecca to come back into the bedroom, but she didn't appear. He found her sitting at the old-fashioned desk in her study, still holding the buzzing telephone in one hand and brushing away tears with the other. Mikio felt a powerful urge to put his arm around her, but he didn't dare.

"It's okay," he said, timidly patting her shoulder. "You're safe now."

Rebecca looked up at him with brimming eyes. "That lying bastard was in bed with another woman!" she wailed. "Oh, I feel like such an idiot. He was going to have a midnight fling with me, and then go back to her! I should be grateful that you burst in when you did."

"You still don't understand, do you?" said Mikio, kneeling in front of Rebecca and gazing up at her winsomely tear-streaked face. "This is about something far more serious than romantic betrayal. Think about it: you said yourself that there was no way he could have gotten home so quickly."

Rebecca looked baffled. "But how—"

"That wasn't Philippe who was here just now."

"Then who on earth was it?"

"Rebecca, you can't possibly find this any harder to believe than I do, but I think it was a vampire." Rebecca gasped. "They can take any form they want to," Mikio continued. "And they're incredibly strong. And they have terrible breath. It's so weird; even though I'm a sort of lazy Buddhist myself, I've had this crucifix in my pocket for ages—I found it one day when I was jogging around the park and I thought it might bring me luck. But if I hadn't had it I would have had to stand here helplessly and watch him suck your blood." Rebecca's hand went up to the side of her neck.

"Oh my God," she said.

"It's okay," Mikio reassured her, "there's no break in the skin. A few seconds later, though ..."

Rebecca began to cry again. No wonder, thought Mikio tenderly, she's just been saved from a fate worse than death. But when she looked up at him a few moments later it was to say not "Thank you for saving me from living unhappily ever after" but rather: "That girl sounded so young. And so pretty. And so English—oh, how could he?"

"Never mind that now," said Mikio. "We have work to do."

Fortunately, Rebecca liked to cook Italian, so there were several strings of garlic in the kitchen. They festooned the windows with the aromatic bulbs, and when Mikio left, Rebecca was sitting at her desk drinking echinacea tea and busily tying bamboo skewers into makeshift crosses. At least she believes me, Mikio thought as he said goodbye. But now that *they* know I'm an enemy, the real battle begins.

Jogging back to his apartment house, Mikio kept one hand on the crucifix in his pocket. Tomorrow he would go out and buy a strong chain, and begin wearing it around his neck. He would buy a little silver cross for Rebecca, too. His mind was churning with a chaotic jumble of thoughts and emotions: relief at having arrived in time; disappointment at finding out that Rebecca didn't see him as a possible romantic partner; amusement that a woman could be more concerned about discovering that her former paramour had found another lover than about being the target of vengeful vampires; and under and over and around it all, the growing chill of pan-systemic, cell-deep fear.

When Mikio awoke from a fitful sleep the next morning, it all seemed like a bizarre dream. He lay under the futon for several minutes, trying to puzzle out an explanation for the strange behavior of the man who had invaded Rebecca's bedroom—that is, some explanation other than the one that had seemed so obvious the night before. Perhaps it really was Philippe; perhaps he had moved somewhere closer to Uguisudani, but had kept the same phone number. Maybe he had fled not out of fear of the crucifix, but because he thought Mikio was Rebecca's new boyfriend (no chance of *that*, Mikio thought with a sigh) and he wanted to avoid a confrontation.

Just as nighttime is the natural habitat of supernatural evil and elaborate suspicions, so daylight seems to bring with it a sense that there's nothing to worry about, that whatever was glimpsed by the evocative light of the moon or the suggestive glimmer of a candle wasn't really real. In the fresh pragmatic glow of morning Mikio no longer felt completely certain that the place next door was a private blood-drinking club for busy urban vampires who didn't have time to prowl the streets looking for fresh prey. Maybe it really is a gathering place for well-to-do sophisticates, he thought. And maybe the red fluid in their glasses was nothing more than tomato juice, vodka, and flavorings.

Still, there was no reason to take unnecessary chances. So before going to work Mikio went around the neighborhood buying up all the fresh garlic he could find—strings, bags, loose heads. After draping the six small windows in his apartment with garlic strings and hanging several bulbs of the "stinking lily" above his door, Mikio stuffed a few leftover cloves in his pockets and set off for his shop.

He walked past the mysterious restaurant as quickly as he could, although he knew there would be no one inside. I wonder where they sleep, he thought. He couldn't help shuddering at the idea of hordes of well-dressed undead dreaming unquiet dreams in creaky-lidded coffins, all over Tokyo. Did they go home at dawn, to various places around the city, and then converge on the restaurant after dark, in the guise of bats or nightingales, flying down the chimney one at a time? Perhaps they took the form of cats and dogs and went slinking through the alleys. Or maybe—Mikio gulped—maybe they slept in the back of the restaurant, in the meat locker, right next door!

Mikio was surprised to find Café Delaunay already open. A fragrant pot of Ethiopian Yergacheffe was steaming on the counter, and his cousin was sitting inside talking to Rebecca. It was a reassuringly normal scene, and Mikio's heart swelled with love: for his family, for his friends, for his customers, for his sweet simple life.

"Oh, there you are, sleepyhead," said Sanae in her playful way. "Rebecca was just telling me that you interrupted her romantic *tête-à-tête* last night, dropping by at an ungodly hour to see how she was feeling." Mikio gave Rebecca a quizzical look. Was it possible that she, too, had awakened to the reassuring sunrise with a feeling that the outlandish events of the night before had been a surrealistic dream?

Sanae excused herself and went off to work at the bakery, and Mikio went behind the counter to begin his chores. While he boiled eggs, sliced lemons for tea, and pulverized cinnamon sticks for the inevitable onslaught of orders for Café Voltaire, he talked to Rebecca. "What did you tell Sanae about last night?" he asked.

"I don't know," Rebecca replied vaguely. "I'm feeling very confused, as if I had a really nasty hangover. But all I drank last night was some tea. I remember that Philippe came to the window, and then you burst in, and he left, and then you called his number and he was at home with some, some ..."

"A woman. And he was definitely there. Is there any chance he could have moved somewhere closer since you last saw him, and still have the same phone number?"

Rebecca shook her head. "I know for a fact he hasn't moved," she said. "I mean, I just happened to be walking by his apartment building one day last week and I saw his car. It's the only purple ragtop Turbo Carrera in Tokyo, as far as I know. No, he still lives in Roppongi, and you were right. He couldn't possibly have made it home, except maybe in a helicopter." Rebecca laughed at the absurdity of this thought, but Mikio froze, with his lemon-cutting knife suspended in mid-air.

"Oh, no," he said.

"What is it?" Rebecca asked urgently.

"This is just conjecture," said Mikio, "but think about it. Remember I told you they can take any form they want to?" Rebecca nodded. "Well, I just assumed that your visitor last night was one of them—maybe even the maitre d' I talked to, the one who had the newspaper—who had taken the form of your, uh, friend." Rebecca smiled sympathetically, as if she understood why it was difficult for Mikio to say the word "boyfriend" in this context.

"Yes, and—?"

"And it just occurred to me that it might really have been what's-his-name, Philippe. I mean, maybe he's one of them now, and maybe he flew to your place from Roppongi, in the form of a bat or something, and then flew back in time to answer the phone when I called."

Rebecca's mouth had dropped open, and her face wore an expression of pure horror. "Oh my God," she said, "do you mean I might have been involved with a … with a *vampire*?"

"Well, we don't know that, it's just another possibility. And even if he is a vampire now, maybe he wasn't one of them while you were, uh, hanging out together. Did you ever see him during the day?"

"Not too often," said Rebecca. "He worked as a commodities broker—that is, when he worked at all—and the market is open only at night, so he slept late most mornings."

"But did you ever have lunch with him?"

"Yes, maybe once a month at some posh hotel, the Okura or the Imperial. I always ended up paying the bill, for some reason, and then afterwards we would go to his place—"

Mikio didn't think he could bear to listen to an account of these diurnal trysts. "Okay," he interrupted briskly, "then at least we know he wasn't a vampire when you were seeing him. Listen, I have an idea. Why don't you go check around his building and find out if anyone ever sees him during the day? You could wear a disguise of some kind so no one would recognize you."

"Oh! What fun!" Rebecca, exclaimed, clapping her hands like a child. "I have a frowzy black thrift-shop wig and an old black dress, and I'll wear dark glasses and one of those heavy gauze flu masks."

"That sounds perfect," said Mikio, "but don't start thinking of this as a lark. We may be dealing with matters of life and death." And the nightmarish realm that lies between, he thought, but he kept that melodramatic notion to himself.

"Okay, I understand," said Rebecca. As she was going out the door Dieter Heimlicht, a German student who lived down the street and stopped by every morning for a cup of Café Perroquet (Arabian Mocha Sanani coffee with a scoop of livid green pistachio ice cream), came in, breathless with excitement.

"Guess what?" he said. "The restaurant next door has gone out of business! Everything's gone, all the furniture and the crystal chandeliers and everything. I knew they wouldn't survive for long with those insulting prices!"

Mikio and Rebecca exchanged a wide-eyed glance, then rushed out the door together. Sure enough, the space next door was completely bare. The striped wallpaper had been removed, the red velvet banquettes were gone, the heavy carved ebony tables had vanished. The only proof that the establishment had ever existed was the overpriced menu still posted in the window.

Rebecca studied the menu for a moment. "Oh, my God," she said.

"What?" Mikio was still so shocked he could hardly speak.

"I'm surprised you didn't notice this, Mr. Supernatural Detective."

"Notice what?"

"That under 'Beverages' the menu lists wine, beer, *aquavit*, tea, and coffee."

"So?"

"So there's no mention at all of tomato juice, or Bloody Marys!" The two friends looked at each other and began to laugh the peculiarly mirthless, snorting laughter brought on by incredulity and alarm.

Rebecca went happily off to spy on Philippe (whom she insisted she was completely "over" now, since whether or not he actually sucked people's blood he was, as she put it, "a major-league lout, and a lousy rotten liar"). Mikio, meanwhile, was busy dealing with a polyglot avalanche of customers and trying to devise a plan of action. Slowly, like Turkish coffee seeping through a sugar cube, an idea began to emerge. It was a dangerous, risky, and quite possibly foolhardy idea, but it was the only idea he had. And so, at six P.M., approximately an hour and fifteen minutes before dark, Mikio put out the "Closed" sign and got to work.

By 6:30 he had completed his secret preparations. It was a balmy September evening, breezy but not too cool, with the sweet smell of burning leaves mingling with the scents of chicken on the grill and rice in the pot. The people on the street were dressed in shirt-sleeves and light dresses, and Mikio felt very conspicuous as he emerged from Café Delaunay wearing long underwear, blue jeans, two sweaters, a thick knee-length down-filled coat, and warm woolen gloves. He was carrying his equipment in a large shopping bag decorated with a colorful silk-screened portrait of the cartoon characters Tom & Jerry, but there was nothing unusual about that. Japan is the land of bizarre and incongruous carrier bags, and the only way that even an "I ♥ SATAN" bag could attract attention on a Tokyo street would be by bursting into spontaneous sulfur-scented flames.

As Mikio approached the back entrance to the restaurant, it occurred to him that perhaps he should have left a note. But there was little enough daylight remaining as it was, and he couldn't afford to take the time to run back to his shop and scribble an explanation. Besides, what could he say? "Gone next door to take care of some business. XXXO, Mikio"?

The restaurant's back door was latched, but it proved surprisingly easy to open with the blade of a pocket knife. Once inside, Mikio found a light switch, turned it on, and looked around. He was in a narrow hallway, with doors on all four sides. The door behind him led out into the alley, while the door straight ahead appeared to connect with the dining room. The windowed door to his left, he determined by peeking through the glass, led into the dark, quiet kitchen. That meant that the door to his right, a heavy metal door with a large handle, should open onto the room which had served as the florist's refrigerator, and as the meat locker of the unfortunate butcher.

Mikio rubbed his silver-cross pendant once for good luck, and grabbed the handle of the door. He felt a strong urge to run away, back to the comforting warmth and sanity of his own little universe. But then he remembered why he was here: not just to protect his own right to live a normal life and die a natural death, but to safeguard the humanity and existential birthrights of Sanae, Rebecca, his neighbors and customers, and hundreds—perhaps even thousands—of other innocent people.

Taking a deep breath, Mikio slowly opened the door. The meat locker wasn't nearly as frigid as he had expected, but it was considerably larger. He couldn't find the light switch, so he reached into his Tom & Jerry bag and pulled out a big plastic flashlight. When the cone of bright golden light illuminated the room, Mikio saw exactly what he had been afraid he might see: rows of wooden boxes, each the length and width of a human (or inhuman) body, laid out neatly along both sides of the room. There wasn't time to take a census, but he estimated that there must be close to thirty of the ominous-looking boxes. Shivering more from dread than from cold, Mikio set out to find the thermostat.

His mental five-point checklist for this expedition was very simple:

1. Enter meat locker.
2. Turn thermostat down to Maximum Chill.
3. Kill sleeping vampires.
4. Run home as fast as possible.
5. Drink large quantities of Irish coffee.

The thermostat was high on the wall in the right-hand corner of the meat locker, and Mikio had to stand on one of the coffin-sized boxes in order to reach it. For some reason, this didn't bother him. The prospect of what he might find inside the boxes, and of what might happen if he didn't finish his loathsome task before dark, was so unspeakably horrific that he seemed to have transcended ordinary trepidation. His heartbeat was accelerated, but steady; his mind was calm; and his resolve was absolutely firm.

Now there was nothing to do but open the boxes, and see what was inside. There was still a chance that it had all been his imagination, that the coffin-like boxes contained nothing but perishable foodstuffs: truffles, sausages, persimmon puddings. Please let it be food, Mikio pleaded silently to any god who might be listening, and then he bent over the first box and began to pry. The brass clasp yielded almost immediately to the pressure of his miniature crowbar, and Mikio slowly lifted the lid.

He was prepared to find the box filled with food. He was prepared to find it empty. And he was prepared, reluctantly, to find it occupied by a male vampire of the classic Transylvanian aristocrat (or maitre d') type, with wicked red lips and pale skin and oleaginous black or mushroom-colored hair. But he had never heard a Japanese-vampire story, so it had never occurred to him that the box, or casket, might contain someone he could easily imagine falling in love with, under different circumstances.

The box was lined with opulent white satin brocaded with gold, green, and orange chrysanthemums, the same sort of cloth used in modern times for a bridal kimono. Lying on this sumptuous bed with her long black hair spread out over the silken pillow was the loveliest Japanese woman Mikio had ever seen. She had a perfectly oval face with an elegant aquiline nose, incandescent ivory skin, and full, peach-colored lips over which a small, stylized red courtesan's mouth had been painted. Her closed eyes were fringed with feathery black lashes, and her eyebrows were smudges of black ink high up on her forehead. She was dressed in a lavishly gilded kimono, intricately embroidered with promenading male peacocks in all their iridescent gilded-azure splendor, worn over several under-robes of thin, gauzy silk in red, white, and purple.

Suddenly Mikio put it all together: the unusual clothing, the otherworldly face, the shaved-and-painted eyebrows. This was obviously not a woman who had lived as a human being in the twentieth century, or, for that matter, in any of the seven or eight centuries that had gone before. She must have been a high-ranking Kyoto lady of the Heian period who was transformed into a member of the fiendish clan of the undead, perhaps by some seductive vampire courtier. Somehow she had ended up in Tokyo. But had she been prowling the nocturnal streets for hundreds of years, seeking the sustenance of fresh-drawn blood, or had she only recently awakened from her restless sleep? Either way, Mikio thought grimly, the party's over.

He took one of the sharpened bamboo tomato-stakes from his bag and held it high above his head. He was about to plunge it into the exquisite creature's antique heart when something made him hesitate. She was so beautiful, and so Japanese, and she looked so harmless sleeping there, albeit without breathing. Surely it wouldn't hurt to let her rest a while longer. He would work his way around the room and then liberate her (this was his carefully-chosen euphemism for "kill") at the very end. He glanced at his watch; 6:40. Time was running out, and it would be disastrous to become personally involved with the sleeping monsters. That was the trick, he realized: to think of them as pernicious demons, not pitiable mutations of humanity.

Mikio moved on to the next box, which opened even more readily than the first one. Inside lay a homely but pleasant-looking Caucasian man with wheat-colored hair, a nose like a pockmarked dumpling, florid cheeks, and a small, babyish mouth. Mikio remembered seeing him in the restaurant one night, dressed in evening clothes and sipping a Bloody Mary. Even in his coffin, the man looked so unlike the stereotypical image of a vampire that Mikio felt obliged to check his bona fides.

Gingerly, he pulled back the man's top lip, and what he saw made him cry out in horror. There they were: the quintessential vampire teeth, unnaturally white and shining, with hideously elongated, sharp-pointed canines. The sarcophagal smell that wafted from the monster's half-opened mouth was so intensely noxious that Mikio had to fight to keep from vomiting.

"*L'arôme abominable de l'abattoir,*" he whispered, impressing himself by recalling an entire phrase from the French vampire book he had scanned briefly the night before. He reflected for a moment about how quickly the seemingly-farfetched abstractions of the book had been converted into appalling reality, and then he took a deep breath.

"Here goes nothing," he announced in what he hoped was a warrior-like voice. In one swift, strong, unthinking motion, he drew a sharpened stake from his bag, hoisted it as high as he could, and plunged it straight into the heart of the sleeping vampire.

Mikio had expected some bloodshed, but he was totally unprepared for the geyser of warm, foul-smelling gore that shot up toward the ceiling and then fell like slaughterhouse rain, drenching him from head to foot. In a way this macabre shower was almost a relief. Surely it can't get any more gruesome than this, he thought as he wiped the putrid corpuscles from his eyes.

Now that Mikio was positive that the creatures were indeed vampires, liberating them was relatively simple. By the third casket, he had developed a grisly routine: open lid, check teeth, plunge stake through heart, remove stake and discard, quickly close lid to avoid being soaked in blood. To make his task seem a bit less ghoulish, he pretended that it was springtime and he was planting his garden, sticking stakes into the damp earth. He giggled hysterically at the thought of tomato plants growing up the stakes: presto, Bloody Mary time.

One by one, Mikio opened the caskets and drove the sharpened stakes through the hearts of the occupants. Some were wicked-looking men, and some were evil-looking women; those were the easiest. Others were so sweet and fresh and innocent-looking that Mikio had to check their teeth—and their breath—a second time before he could bring himself to perform his grisly ritual of liberation. But there were no cases of mistaken identity; every creature in the room had long, sharp canine teeth and that uniquely putrescent brand of halitosis known in Gothic horror-story *patois* as "the ghastly stench of the charnel house."

Perhaps the most terrifying thing was that they were all so close to waking up and going about their diabolical business—an activity which, Mikio suspected, would eventually have included killing him or turning him into a vampire, or both. He didn't really understand the technical aspects of vampirism, but he felt confident that anyone who offended the bloodthirsty monsters would be hunted down, and punished.

With the exception of two Japanese vampires—the medieval courtesan and a delicate-featured man who appeared, from his velvet suit and ruffled cravat, to have been alive during the dandified days of the late nineteenth century—all the sleeping creatures were adult Caucasians. He recognized quite a few of them from the restaurant, but there were others, including the two Japanese and a dazzling blonde California-girl type (Vampire Barbie! Mikio thought giddily) whom he had never laid eyes on before. It was fortunate that there were no children among them, for he would have found it very difficult to drive a stake through a miniature heart, however monstrous its owner might be.

Finally, twenty-six merciful murders later, Mikio was nearly finished with his unspeakable task. The only vampires left alive (or undead) were the two Japanese and the unidentified occupant of the largest, most luxurious-looking box of all, which seemed to occupy a place of honor at the end of the room.

"Aha!" Mikio muttered. "The senior partner!"

Yawning hugely, he headed toward the big box. The locker had become noticeably colder, and he could see his breath before him, as thick as winter fog on the Japan Sea. He was beginning to feel stiff-jointed and terribly sleepy. The idea behind turning the thermostat to its lowest setting was that it might slow the vampires down if they happened to wake up, but Mikio hadn't stopped to think about the possible effects of extreme cold on his own fragile human metabolism.

To the left of the large casket was a door that Mikio hadn't noticed before. I wonder where that leads, he thought. And while every rational cell in his brain was shouting "Don't open it! Don't even *think* about opening it," he felt an irresistible urge to turn the knob.

The door opened easily, and Mikio found himself in a small, dark, refrigerated room with an unfamiliar and highly unpleasant smell. Spoiled pork chops, or maybe rotting sausage, he speculated as he looked around the room. He shone his flashlight to the left, but there was nothing except a roll of hollow rubber tubing. He shone it to the center; nothing at all. Then he pointed his flashlight at the right-hand wall of the little room. What he saw was so shocking, and so horrible, that he couldn't help letting out a shriek.

"Oh no," he said, when he could speak. "Not this."

There was a stout metal pole suspended horizontally from the high, open-beamed ceiling. Trussed to this pole by the ankles, hanging head downward over large black plastic buckets were two pallid, bloodless, naked human corpses with livid incisions at the pulse-points of all the major veins and arteries. That's what happened to the butcher, too, Mikio thought with sudden comprehension. The monsters must have killed him for his lease, and taken his blood as a bonus. Another phrase from the French vampire book popped into Mikio's head: "*les vaches du sang*"—"blood cows." Clearly, he had stumbled onto the vampiric equivalent of a boutique dairy.

One of the corpses was a man of about forty-five, with a grizzled beard. Mikio felt sick when he recognized him as the homeless man known affectionately as Uncle Baseball. He was a simple soul, a free-lance dishwasher and woodchopper who lived harmlessly in the park, listening to baseball games on a pair of bright red earphones plugged into an ancient transistor radio and sleeping on a stone bench in the sculpture garden. Mikio suddenly remembered his conversation with Mr. Kaneshiro, the vegetable man, about the thousand-yen glass of water. Oh no, he thought as tears welled up in his eyes. If only I had shared my suspicions about the restaurant before Uncle Baseball went there to wash dishes, he might still be alive.

The other body was that of a plump young woman whom Mikio had never seen before—or had he? After a moment he remembered the flyers that had appeared around the neighborhood, tacked to telephone poles and posted on the community bulletin board, a week or ten days earlier. HAVE YOU SEEN OUR DEAR DAUGHTER? the message began, above a blurred photograph of a moon-faced, smiling young girl in a dark blue middy blouse with white piping.

Oh no, Mikio thought, the poor girl, and her poor parents. He felt a strong urge to weep, or flee, but then he remembered that he had very important work to do, and very little time to do it. "This next one's for you two," he murmured, wiping away a stray tear as he closed the door behind him. "I just hope you didn't suffer too much."

All the other boxes were made of brass-bound cedar, but the last unopened casket was polished mahogany, with hinges of what appeared to be solid gold. This has to be the leader of the vampires, the vicious murdering beast, Mikio thought. As he pried open the latch of the casket his heart was pounding with anger and anxiety.

The lid opened soundlessly. Inside, lying serenely against a padded interior of rose-colored satin, was the undead maitre d': the same man who had approached Mikio in front of the restaurant, and had glared at him so hatefully the following night. The vampire was dressed in his familiar black tuxedo with the crimson cummerbund, but he had taken off the white gloves and his pale, slender, blue-veined hands with their grotesquely long, curved, yellowish-purple nails lay clasped across his sunken chest.

"You!" Mikio breathed. To his horror the vampire's eyelids fluttered slightly and his red-lipped mouth opened in a maleficent long-toothed grin, then closed again, very slowly, like a tulip at dusk.

Mikio looked at his watch. Two minutes past seven. Sunset was at 7:00, and darkness would settle over the city ten or fifteen minutes after that, so there wasn't a moment to lose. He pulled a bamboo stake from his bag, but just as he raised it on high, it broke in his hand. "Stay calm," he told himself, reaching into the bag and pulling out another, slightly thicker stake. He raised the second stake and plunged it into the chest of the vampire, but it splintered into three jagged pieces when it hit the creature's chest.

In a panic, for the vampire's eyelids had begun to flicker again, Mikio reached into his bag for another stake. He only had four clean stakes left now, and he needed to save the last two for the Japanese vampires. The book of vampire lore had said that a clean stake was required for each dispatching, so he couldn't risk reusing any of the bloodied stakes that now littered the floor, like stirring-sticks for cans of vermilion shrine-paint.

To Mikio's alarm, the third stake, too, broke off when it struck the chest of the master vampire. Suddenly he remembered an American action movie he had watched recently on video in which the unnaturally muscular, wise-cracking hero was saved from terminal perforation by a bulletproof vest. "A stake-proof vest?" Mikio asked himself incredulously.

Sure enough, when he pulled open the white pin-tucked dress shirt the vampire was wearing under his tuxedo, there was a thickly padded vest. The garment didn't fasten down the front, but after a moment of fumbling Mikio discovered that it was held together at the sides by a sort of primitive Velcro made from cockleburs. As he ripped open the seams and pushed the vest to one side, he could feel the slow, sick throbbing of the vampire's blood-engorged heart.

There was very little time left now, and Mikio was beginning to feel frightened by his increasing sleepiness and slowness of movement. Just as the chief vampire began stirring in the casket, Mikio mustered all his strength and drove an extra-sharp stake through the monster's narrow chest. A malodorous stream of blood shot high into the air, drenching Mikio's face and torso. Suddenly the vampire king's terrible eyes snapped open. Hypnotized by that evil gaze, Mikio stood motionless, staring slackjawed at the frightful sight unfolding before him.

The vampire lifted himself halfway out of his casket, with his ancient heart still spewing blood and his talon-tipped fingers reaching out as if to strangle Mikio, who stood helplessly, unable to will himself to move. Then, with a gigantic shudder and a harrowing wail, the undead maitre d' simply crumbled before Mikio's unbelieving eyes into an unholy heap of dry, mephitic debris. Mikio clamped his fingers tightly over his nose and held his breath. So that's what happens at the end, he thought bleakly.

The execution of the chief vampire had been unexpectedly time-consuming, so Mikio raced over to the caskets of the two sleeping Japanese bloodsuckers. He was feeling extremely dizzy and light-headed, as though he might black out at any moment. In a stupor, he flipped open the lids of the two remaining boxes. Without allowing himself to be swayed by the thought that these two vampires had probably once been kind, sensitive Japanese people, lovers of flowers and writers of verse and dreamers of human dreams, he quickly drove the icepick-sharp stakes into their gently pulsing targets.

For some reason these last two stakes, unlike all the others, were very difficult to pull out, so Mikio just left them as they were, protruding from the chests of his countrymen. My countrymonsters, he thought dizzily. The weirdest, most frightening thing was that he was undeniably attracted to the medieval beauty. He had even wondered fleetingly whether he could somehow rehabilitate her, the way his mother back in Sendai used to clip the claws of raccoons and turn them into nervous, reluctant housepets.

Without waiting around to witness the revolting process of decomposition, Mikio stumbled hurriedly toward the exit. He wanted only to leave the blood and violence and grotesquerie behind him, and breathe some relatively unpolluted air. Halfway to the door, he began to feel so unbearably nauseated and drowsy that he had to sit down on the floor.

I just need to close my eyes for a moment, he thought sleepily, now that my work is done. When he inadvertently relaxed his hand, the flashlight fell to the ground and rolled away. The room went totally dark, and then, out of the blackness, Mikio heard the sound of shuffling feet. He groped groggily for his flashlight, while the strange halting footsteps continued to advance toward him.

After a few seconds of frantic searching, Mikio's hand finally closed around the plastic torch. He pointed it in the direction of the footsteps, and switched it on. There in the sudden illumination stood two terrifying apparitions. The Heian beauty was holding Mikio's bloody bamboo stake in one hand, tottering unsteadily toward him with the peculiar mincing, pigeon-toed gait of the Japanese courtesan. Her almond eyes were open, her splendiferous robes were splash-dyed with blood, and there was an expression of bewilderment and sorrow on her ethereal face. The nineteenth-century dandy lurched along beside her, his ruffled white cravat and lilac-colored shirt stained with blood from the wound made by the stake, which protruded from his chest like a bizarre coat-rack. He, too, looked sadly perplexed by his rude awakening. Mikio couldn't understand why the stakes he had driven through his countrymonsters' hearts hadn't done the job, until he remembered that in his haste he had neglected to check the pair's teeth, and breath. What if they weren't vampires, after all?

Just then, as if divining his thoughts, the wounded demons opened their mouths like lions about to roar, and Mikio knew there had been no mistake. Feral fangs shining, fetid breath fouling the air, the two came closer and closer, while Mikio cowered under the table, paralyzed with fear, weariness, and cold. The expressions on the two old-fashioned faces had changed now, from sorrow to murderous anger, and Mikio suddenly realized that this was it: he, Mikio Makioka, was about to die. Oh, no! he thought deliriously. I never got to drink absinthe in Montmartre!

With his last shred of consciousness Mikio decided to try to reason with the vampires. When no words came out of his dry mouth, he sent a telepathic plea instead: "Kill me if you must, but please, I beg you, don't make me share your awful fate." The Japanese vampires were just a few feet away from him now, and Mikio's terror and exhaustion finally overwhelmed him. He felt himself slipping into unconsciousness, and with his last ounce of strength he switched off the flashlight. I wonder if they can see in the dark, he thought. And then, just as he felt the vampire claws digging into his arm, he surrendered to that same sinister dark.

When Mikio returned to consciousness, his first thought was, God help me, I'm a vampire! He put his forefinger in his mouth and ran it over his canine teeth. They felt completely normal: short, square, and blunt. If I'm not a vampire, then I must be dead, he thought.

He opened his eyes slowly, half-expecting to find himself in some cartoonish Buddhist hell filled with snarling demons and smoldering heaps of dung. But he was in the familiar alley behind the restaurant, propped up against a cool cement wall. Standing in front of him, wearing a ragged black dress and a look of extreme concern, was Rebecca Flanders. Her wavy chestnut hair was piled becomingly on top of her head, and as he stared at her in bewilderment, Mikio felt an overwhelming urge to kiss the long pale parabola of her neck.

"Rebecca, run!" he said hoarsely. "I'm one of them now!"

Rebecca's reaction was hardly what Mikio expected. "No, Mikio," she said with a merry laugh, "you're not a vampire. They never laid a hand—or should I say a tooth?—on you."

"But they were so close, and so scary!"

"So they were, and if I hadn't come in when I did—it must have been just after you passed out—who knows what might have happened." Rebecca squatted down in front of Mikio and he noticed that her dress was covered with patches of something shiny and wet. He touched one of the spots and his fingertips came away covered in thick, greasy blood.

"It wasn't pretty," Rebecca said soberly, handing Mikio a tissue from her pocket, "but it's all over now." And then, while Mikio sat with his arms wrapped around his knees, shivering and inhaling great sweet draughts of the cool autumn air, she began to explain what had happened.

"When I went to stake out Philippe's apartment (no pun intended, believe me!) I figured it might be a long, boring wait, so I stopped by the newspaper office to pick up something to read. By chance, or by fate, I found a book in English on international folklore. It was by someone named F. Vasily Vukavitsky, and it had an entire chapter on vampires. I read the whole book and learned all sorts of fascinating things, like the reason they wear dark glasses is because their eyes are very sensitive to light, even at night. Then when I came back and found your shop closed, I knew right away where you must have gone."

"But what happened to the two Japanese vampires?" Mikio asked. "For some reason, the stakes didn't work on them."

"Ah," said Rebecca sagely, "I thought you'd never ask. According to Dr. Vukavitsky, crosses and stakes only work on Occidental vampires. For the Japanese variety, which are rare but not unheard-of, you have to use a samurai's short sword, called a *wakizashi*—"

"I know what a wakizashi is," Mikio interjected, for his ancestors had been illustrious samurai in Uesugi and later in Sendai, under the great warlord Date Masamune.

"—and it has to have been blessed by a Shinto priest. And you have to stab them in the abdomen—you know, the *hara*—not in the heart."

"But where did you find a wakizashi on such short notice?"

"Actually, I got two of them. I live next door to a Shinto shrine, remember? And fortunately, or perhaps fatefully, the priest collects antique weapons, so I just called him up and he rushed over with two pre-blessed swords and a piece of wood hung with sacred streamers, to keep any stray vampires from attacking me. I must say it worked like a charm, though I'm afraid my little black dress is ruined. No, I'm kidding. I literally plucked it from my ragbag for my undercover-detective disguise. I swear, I'm more Nancy Drew than Nancy Drew!"

Mikio could tell that Rebecca was babbling out of a combination of euphoria, fright, and posttraumatic stress, but he didn't feel ready to indulge in lighthearted banter. "How did you manage to kill them both, all by yourself?" he asked in a serious tone.

"As I said, it wasn't pretty. And it would have been much more difficult if they hadn't been weakened already from the stakes you so bravely drove through their hearts. My job was minor by comparison—just a little parry and jab, so to speak."

"Rebecca, you saved my life. How can I ever repay you?"

"That's easy," said Rebecca. "Just promise me that this whole episode will be our little secret. A lot of people don't believe in the supernatural, you know, and in my position I can't afford to acquire a reputation for being crazy. Eccentric, yes, but not insane!"

"Yes, of course, I understand," said Mikio. "But isn't there something else I could do to show my gratitude? I mean, something major? After all, I owe you my life."

"All right," said Rebecca, "if you insist, there is one thing."

"Anything," Mikio declared, hand over heart. "My soul is yours."

"Well," said Rebecca solemnly, "I wouldn't mind having the secret recipe for your cousin Sanae's celestial marzipan macaroons."

"Oh. Okay, sure, no problem," Mikio said in a subdued voice. He was disappointed that Rebecca hadn't asked him to perform some difficult, heroic task to demonstrate the absolute sincerity of his gratitude and indebtedness. Nor could he help feeling a bit scandalized by what he perceived as the American tendency to be glib and frivolous about matters of life, death, and eternal obligation.

Back at Café Delaunay, after placing an anonymous phone call to the police, Mikio slowly warmed himself with double-strength Irish coffee (technically, it was Scottish coffee, made with Laphroaig's, but the effect was the same). As he looked around at all the familiar, beloved things—the gleaming brass-and-copper cappuccino machine, the Toulouse-Lautrec wallpaper, the colorful fruit bowls, the painterly bouquets—he vowed that he would never again take anyone or anything for granted. In particular, he would always be grateful for the ability to greet the sunrise with joy, and to walk among his trusting neighbors without worrying that he might end up inducting them into the unquiet limbo of the living dead, or butchering them for their blood.

He gazed admiringly at Rebecca, his lovely life-saver, with her cheeks still flushed and her casual pompadour in captivating disarray from her tussle with the Japanese vampires. Mikio felt very tender toward his American friend, and he wanted nothing more than to hold her in his blood-soaked arms.

"We've been through so much together, Rebecca," he said, with the boldness of the recently resurrected. "I wish we could be together all the time—I mean you could do your work and I could do mine, and I could make you pots of extra-strong Café Colette when you had an all-night deadline.

I could even learn how to make those macaroons you like so much."

Rebecca turned to meet Mikio's earnest eyes, and in that ego-shattering moment he knew that he would never marry her or live with her or even kiss her, except perhaps on the cheek.

"Yes," she said gently, "we have shared a lot, and we've become very close friends. I love you as a human being, and I hope that our friendship will last forever. But why is it that it's never enough for men and women just to be good, true, faithful friends? I really don't want to marry anyone, or live with anyone, or even be involved with anyone right now. I'm just too odd in my hours and too set in my ways. You're one of the sweetest people I've ever known, and I've always thought you were very attractive, but with my history of relationships always ending badly I would never risk messing up such a fine friendship with romance. No, when I lose my heart again, I guarantee it will be to yet another worthless, unprincipled, charming Lothario. I mean, why break a perfect streak? Oh, speaking of unprincipled Lotharios," she interrupted herself with a laugh. "About Philippe: he may have been a cold-blooded cad, but he definitely wasn't a vampire. I saw him this afternoon, going out with his new squeeze in broad daylight, so to speak. She's not particularly good-looking, by the way. Oh, I suppose her figure's all right, if you like the Las Vegas showgirl type. But she has brassy blonde hair with charcoal roots, and her face reminds me of a boiled potato with false eyelashes. The funny thing is, I've seen her before—she used to be a cocktail waitress at the Foreign Press Club."

Mikio smiled wanly at Rebecca's gleefully catty description of her rival. "I do believe you're gloating," he said lightly, but his heart still felt as if someone had put a tomato stake through it. My first proposal, he thought, and my first rejection. Does that mean I'm batting a thousand, or zero?

"Oh no, I would never gloat," said Rebecca. "But I admit I'm only human, which means I can't help feeling a perverse sense of relief and vindication when the woman who steals my supposedly monastic man turns out to be a bleached-blonde serving-wench. Oh dear, I can't believe I'm talking this way when less than an hour ago we …" She shook her head. "That's human beings for you!"

"Well, it's only thanks to you that I'm not an *inhuman* being!" quipped Mikio. They laughed and hugged each other, and then they laughed some more. Mikio loved Rebecca very much at that moment: as a friend, as a benefactress, and also (in a doomed, bittersweet way) as a smart, brave, strong, independent, passionate, desirable, and utterly unavailable woman.

That night, after soaking in his small cedar-wood bath for two hours, Mikio went to sleep and had a very strange dream. He dreamed that he *was* a vampire, after all, and that one moonless night he climbed through Rebecca's window and proceeded to do all the darkly erotic things that vampires do to the women they crave. And the strangest, most frightening thing about the dream was that it wasn't a nightmare at all. On the contrary, it was the most delicious dream Mikio had ever had.

Like any stubborn, self-respecting Japanese male, Mikio was tempted to devote the rest of his life to the hopeless but noble task of trying to make Rebecca Flanders see him as someone to love as a man, not just as a human being. But he had read enough Occidental novels to realize that such an approach would ultimately destroy the friendship, leaving him with nothing at all. So he affected a cheerful, casual conversational style with Rebecca, and he made a secret vow never again to mention his foolish proposal, or her gentle but firm rejection.

Once the excitement over the vampires had died down, Mikio started to feel that it was time for him to settle down and share his pleasant, purposeful, hardworking life with someone. One afternoon in October he called his aunt in Okayama and told her to go ahead with the often-postponed plans for an *omiai* meeting—the first step toward an arranged marriage—with the highly respectable daughter of the cousin-in-law of his aunt's tea-ceremony teacher. After the phone call he felt profoundly depressed, especially when it occurred to him that Jean-Paul Belmondo and Charles Aznavour would never have had to resort to a matchmaker. But they were glamorous Frenchmen, and he was just an ordinary Japanese who ran a modest little coffee shop.

Mikio was slumped morosely behind the counter, sipping a tiny glass of Pernod and reading *Grimm's Fairy Tales* in French, when the bell above the door tinkled softly. He looked up and saw a petite, sweet-faced young woman, dressed in a black corduroy jumper over a black-and-white-striped cotton shirt. Her lustrous black hair was nearly waist-length, and she wore a black straw hat with a fresh red rose stuck in the white grosgrain band. Snow White and Rose Red, Mikio thought, but he just said "Welcome," as he would to any potential customer.

"Excuse me," the young woman said in a light, melodious, enchanted-princess voice, "but I was wondering whether you might need someone to help out in the shop, part-time."

"Please sit down, and we'll talk," said Mikio, surreptitiously pinching his elbow to see if he might be dreaming. The visitor sat down, Mikio made her a cup of Café Piaf (Sulawesi coffee, Courvoisier, and, he liked to joke, a pinch of salt to simulate tears), and they talked, and talked, and talked. The young woman's name was Shizuka Takitani, and she had spent the previous year in Paris studying modern dance. Now she was performing with an avant-garde troupe called Vive la Danse! and looking for a daytime job to make ends meet. She loved to read French books and go to French movies and cook simple French food. By the time the sun went down, Shizuka had decided to fall in love with Mikio Makioka, and Mikio knew that he already loved Shizuka Takitani, and always would.

Of course, being Japanese, they didn't put their feelings into words that first day, or the next, or the one after that. The exchange of romantic declarations occurred three months later, on the memorable winter night (full moon, first snow, mulled wine) when Mikio asked Shizuka to marry him.

"Of course I will, you silly," she said, giving him a playful shove. "I would have said 'Maybe' the day I met you, and 'Definitely yes' the day after that."

"*Now* you tell me!" said Mikio, rolling his eyes like a TV comedian. The rejection by Rebecca Flanders had taken a severe toll on his self-confidence, and he had spent the past ninety days slowly working up the nerve to propose to Shizuka.

On the same day that Shizuka appeared in his life, Mikio had called his aunt in Okayama and asked her to cancel the omiai. He didn't mention that he was fairly certain he had just met his soulmate, the person who held the other end of his red thread of fate. Instead, he said that he had been working too hard and simply didn't feel up to the meeting.

"No problem," his aunt said. She possessed the peculiar clairvoyance of the matchmaker, and she could tell by the excitement in his voice that Mikio had met someone special. Perhaps he'll get to marry for love after all, she thought happily as she hung up the telephone.

Four weeks to the day after the massacre in the meat locker, a new restaurant called "Curry House Calcutta" opened in the space formerly occupied by the private club for the undead. The decor was exotic, the food was cheap and tasty, and the turbaned waiters were gracious to the point of gallantry. Night after night, the place was packed with people from the surrounding area, Japanese and foreign. Mikio invited Shizuka to go to dinner there one evening, and on a whim he also invited Rebecca Flanders, whom he had only seen a couple of times since the vampire-killing.

"Be sure to bring a date," he said on the telephone. "I'm going to!"

"That's good," said Rebecca, in a tone of undisguised relief.

Rebecca's date turned out to be a tall, tousled Englishman named Alexander Ludgate. He was a political correspondent for the London *Daily Examiner* who spoke exuberant French and equally fluent, self-taught Japanese—a hilarious hybrid of demurely flirtatious women's speech and guttural gangster slang, which he had picked up by frequenting hostess bars and racetracks, respectively. The two couples enjoyed an antic multilingual meal together, and Mikio felt very proud of Shizuka. Not only did she look enchanting in a long blue-green cashmere dress and matching cloche, but she was able to converse expressively in English, a skill she had never mentioned before.

Later that night, Rebecca called Mikio at home. "You've really found a treasure," she said. "And I think it's terribly exciting that the two of you are going to Paris for your honeymoon. But aren't you glad now that I was so sensible about our not getting together?"

Mikio was, in fact, exceedingly glad. It was a somewhat awkward moment, so he quickly changed the subject. "I thought your escort was a very interesting character," he said, chuckling at the memory of the Englishman's idiosyncratic reinvention of the Japanese language. "He didn't seem like the selfish heartless playboy type at all."

"I know," Rebecca sighed. "Alec really is too good to be true. Masculine, yet poetic; cultured and erudite, but full of fun as well. He doesn't seem to be a compulsive liar or an incurable womanizer, either. In fact, I'm beginning to worry that I may have lost my uncanny gift for choosing the wrong men!"

Mikio knew, for certain and forever, that he had chosen the right woman. In addition to her intelligence, talent, and charm, Shizuka was a remarkably sensitive and understanding person. Even after they became formally engaged and began spending intoxicating pre-nuptial nights together, she never asked Mikio why he always kept garlic around his doors and windows, or why there was a pile of sharpened stakes and a sheathed wakizashi sword festooned with Shinto streamers stashed in the back of the futon closet. She didn't inquire why (since they were both Buddhists, albeit non-practicing) he wore a silver cross around his neck, and insisted that she wear one also. Nor did she ask why he and Rebecca Flanders had exchanged a knowing glance when Rebecca's English boyfriend ordered a carafe of fresh tomato juice, spiked with coriander, at Curry House Calcutta. Shizuka figured that everyone was entitled to a few secrets. In time, perhaps Mikio would tell her exactly what had happened just before their fairy-tale meeting. If not, that was all right too. After all, it wasn't as if she didn't have one or two spicy secrets of her own.

And so life went on in the green-and-golden district of Tokyo known as Uguisudani. The birds still sang in the gingko trees, and the neighborhood cats, seduced by visions of nightingale *tartare*, still got themselves stranded on fragile branches and had to be rescued by the local constabulary. But when night fell, the only creaking was the sound of antique doors sliding closed; the only heavy breathing came from lovers and remedial joggers; and the only beating of wings was by pigeons and doves flying home to roost.

THE SNAKE SPELL

I am willing to taste any drink once.

—James Branch Cabell
Jurgen

It's ironic, considering how I loathe clichés, that I should have ended up living one: the near sighted, celibate, cat-loving librarian, with her hair in a bun and a dun-colored wardrobe. I don't know if it's poor shopping skills or self-fulfilling stereotype, but somehow I always seem to end up wearing sepia, khaki, and ash: colors which may look all right on career soldiers and small rodents but don't do a lot for a brown-eyed girl in her supposed sexual, romantic, and reproductive prime. Oh well—at least I'm not moldering behind the desk of some small-town library in the Deep South, indexing back issues of *Soap Opera Digest* and trying to keep *The Catcher in the Rye* from being tossed onto an all-purpose obscenity pyre along with the collected works of Lenny Bruce, Anaïs Nin, and Deep Purple.

No, indeed, dear Diary. By some miracle of luck, synchronicity, and résumé-gilding, I, Bronwyn C. LaFarge, have ended up as the youngest-ever first assistant librarian at Cosmopolis House in Tokyo, which has several fine collections (Muromachi-period Japanalia, original manuscripts from the French Imagist poets, death-poem calligraphy by famous Zen priests). The library is housed in a dazzling, angular building designed by Madoka Morokoshi and constructed of Kamogawa river-rocks and charcoal-tinted glass. All I do every day is go to work, go home, exercise, eat dinner, study a bit, and read myself to sleep, so in that sense I suppose I might as well be living in Hush Puppy, Alabama. But at least I answer the telephone in fairly fluent Japanese, and take my solitary vacations at idyllic hot-spring inns, and pay my exorbitant rent to a direct descendent of one of the more obscure members of the Forty-Seven Ronin.

Everything went wrong that morning. The alarm didn't ring, the Earl Grey tea spilled on the chocolate mousse, a zipper broke, the cats escaped and had to be hunted down in the leafy little park across the street, Bronwyn missed her usual bus, and there wasn't a single taxicab to be seen on the nearest thoroughfare, which was usually packed solid with nothing but taxis.

Miraculously, Bronwyn was only twelve minutes late to work. She was sitting at her big koa-wood desk in a bright-windowed corner of the library, still panting slightly, when Erica Krill sashayed through the door. Oh, please, Bronwyn prayed, don't let her be coming to talk to me.

But of course Erica Krill headed straight for Bronwyn's desk, dressed in a vermilion leather mini-suit which showcased her willowy, jazz-dance–toned figure. She wore her cornsilk-blond hair in a smooth, thick-banged page-boy, her flawless face was faultlessly made up, her naturally long fingernails were lacquered *à la française*, and her custom-designed gold jewelry was studded with amethysts that reflected her violet eyes. If only she chewed gum with her mouth open or used bad grammar, Bronwyn thought. But no such luck.

"Hello, Bronwyn," Erica said in her perfectly modulated, slightly English-accented voice. She was an American who had spent most of her child-hood at the bucolic East Sussex estate of a titled aunt and uncle; at the age of sixteen she had won a Metropolitan Opera audition, but had decided instead to be a broadcast journalist. Now, two decades and many high-profile assignments and illustrious awards later, she was taking time off to raise two beautiful, gifted children while her dashing husband (when he wasn't writing spy novels, building harpsichords, or racing formula Jaguars) advised multi-national corporations on how to display a "pragmatically idealistic" environ-mental conscience while still raking in the loot. In her spare time, Erica sang in semiprofessional productions of Gilbert & Sullivan, volunteer-edited a bimonthly newsletter for Cosmopolis House, and celebrity-modeled for Pachinko Piaf, the flamboyant Japanese-French fashion designer of unspecified gender.

"Hi, Erica," Bronwyn said glumly, feeling suddenly aware of her disheveled hair, her one-octave singing range, her absolute ignorance of her Personal Color Profile. Was she a Late Spring? An Early Autumn? Or just a Mouse For All Seasons? Of course, Erica Krill knew which colors looked best on *her*: all of them.

"Listen, Bronwyn," Erica said in a stage whisper. The combined aromas of Listerine and Osïrïs (Pachinko Piaf's potent new fennel-and-ambergris perfume) almost caused Bronwyn to regurgitate her hastily devoured breakfast of cinnamon toast and chocolate mousse. "I need a teensy favor."

"Uh, what might that be?" Bronwyn asked warily. Erica had a reputation around the library for trying to turn other women into ladies-in-waiting, or errand girls.

"Well, there's a terribly unusual Shinto festival this weekend. It only happens once every twelve years, in the year of the snake, on the day of the snake, in the hour of the snake. I had planned to go myself, but I have to do some modeling for a couple of charity fashion shows in Kyoto. You know how these things are ..." Erica trailed off and Bronwyn could almost hear her thinking, No, I don't suppose you *do* know, you with your drab little non-designer life.

"Sorry, I don't write," Bronwyn said flatly. This was an unvarnished lie, for she had been keeping a journal since she was eight years old.

"Oh, you won't need to," Erica said breezily. "Just take factual—or, better yet, impressionistic—notes, and I'll turn them into the most convincing first-person prose you ever saw. Please? Pretty please with *crème fraîche* on it?"

"I don't know," said Bronwyn dubiously. "I don't like crowds." This phobia (according to her ex–best friend Pilar Lorenzi, who was a clinical psychologist) was the subconscious legacy of Bronwyn's having been born on a table in the gluten-burger tent at Woodstock.

"Oh, I forgot to mention one thing," Erica said casually. "If you'll do me this teensy little favor, I'll let you use my driver car for the entire weekend; I won't be needing it, so you can jump in and out and avoid the nasty proletarian crush." And so it was that Bronwyn LaFarge, who hated crowds slightly less than she loved riding around Tokyo in chauffeur-driven luxury cars, agreed to attend the Festival of the Snake Goddess at Hebigazaka Shrine, and to take impressionistic (if not factual) notes on the entire experience.

—IMPRESSIONISTIC-IF-NOT-ENTIRELY-FACTUAL NOTE NUMBER ONE: The gates of the shrine were the color of a flashy dresser's leather suit: vivid vermilion. The sky was the purest, most primordial blue, small white birds flew above in parabolas of rapture, and as the ancient cryptomerias shimmied in the breeze, I thought I heard someone chanting: "Spring is here and snakes are near/Shed your anger, lose your fear/Befriend your lovers, love your friends/For nothing ever really ends." I can't help it; ever since I took that silly "Good Riddance to Bad Rubbish" seminar, I seem to hear catchy mantras wherever I go.

Everything had gone wrong on the morning of the Festival of the Snake Goddess, too. Neither alarm went off, the sassafras tea sloshed into the blackberry cobbler, the khaki linen suit lost one of its pewter buttons, and Dewey and Truman escaped once again and had to be retrieved from the park across the street, though not before they had tortured, killed, and partially autopsied a luckless shrew. After coping with all these setbacks, Bronwyn barely had time to pull on a hamster-colored corduroy pinafore over a high-necked silk blouse in gerbil gray before she heard a horn honking outside the little garden cottage where she lived. After hastily stuffing several pens, a loose-leaf notebook, and her "organizer" (which was, more precisely, a corset for chaos) into her satchel, she dashed downstairs in her bare feet, clutching her gray Reeboks and a pair of brown-and-gray checked kneesocks.

Erica's driver-car was a brand-new Infiniti Q45, luminescent platinum on the outside with a custom interior of hand-buffed walnut and ecru leather. The chauffeur was standing by the rear passenger door, holding it open.

"Good morning," he said in lightly-accented English. "*Bonjour. Guten tag. Buon giorno. Ohayo gozaimasu.*"

"Good morning," Bronwyn replied in English, although she was familiar, in varying degrees, with all of the other languages he had touched upon. How typical of Erica, she thought uncharitably, to hire a polyglot showoff to be her chauffeur. Or maybe Erica had taught him those greetings herself, to impress her society-column passengers.

The driver was taller than Bronwyn, and, she guessed, several years younger. It was hard to tell because he had a moustache (unusually bushy for a Japanese) and a scruffy grunge-rock goatee, and his eyes were hidden behind big black sunglasses. He was dressed in a baggy, voluminous jacket of saffron-colored suede encrusted with buttons, buckles, pockets, and paramilitary insignia, worn over a pair of floppy chocolate-brown trousers. His hair was invisible under a large mushroom-shaped beret cut from the same fabric as the jacket, and instead of the customary white cartoon-character gloves worn by most taxi drivers and chauffeurs in Japan, he wore gloves of dark brown leather, and boots to match.

At first Bronwyn assumed that the clownish, outsized uniform was a hand-me-down from the driver's much larger predecessor, but then she realized that the unbecoming get-up must represent the cutting edge of fashion for chauffeurs. Perhaps it had even been designed by Erica's pal Pachinko Piaf. As for the mock-military decorations, they might have been intended as a rueful satire on the battle hazards of navigating the streets of Tokyo.

Bronwyn climbed into the back seat and hid behind her opened notebook, hoping the driver would take the hint and leave her alone. She had been expecting a taciturn, withdrawn older man, and she could feel herself getting nervous, as she always did when she was within three feet of any marginally attractive male—even one as socially inappropriate as a colleague's chauffeur. She thought it might have something to do with her biological clock, which sometimes ticked so loudly that it kept her awake at night, and she had to muffle it with a pillow.

Time to recite your mantra, she told herself.

> All men are beasts
> All men are beasts
> I do not need their fleshly feasts
> A woman can be whole alone
> The devil take your pheromones!

Bronwyn had learned the mantra at a two-day GRTBR ("Good Riddance to Bad Rubbish") seminar she attended in Seattle, just after her purported fiancé Miles had run off with her presumed best friend Pilar. The seminar was subtitled "YES, I CAN!: LIVING LARGE WITHOUT A MAN." According to the brochure, which was written by a self-proclaimed "career celibate" who called herself Boadicea Smythe, "the 'Men Are Beasts' mantra is to be recited without fail whenever one finds oneself feeling attracted to a man. Always bear in mind, my fellow goddesses, that all men are sexual opportunists, and that gleam in his eye isn't love, it's the warning-light of callous concupiscence."

Bronwyn had found the seminar humiliating rather than helpful, but the mantra had turned out to be surprisingly useful. She frequently chanted it at work (silently, of course) when she was called upon to assist some bashful, rumpled, sweetly inarticulate young scholar with his research. It also came in handy when riding in the Cosmopolis House elevator with its usual all-male cargo of raffish writers, turpentine-scented artists, and well-dressed *mensches*-about-town. Bronwyn was emphatically not in the market for a boyfriend, or a lover; she was perfectly happy alone. It was just that blasted biological cuckoo clock, which didn't keep up with current events and thus was unaware that the planet was already overpopulated and no longer required every fertile inhabitant to date, mate, and reproduce like it was going out of style.

The only mildly diverting part of the seminar, besides the mantra, had been the Nickname Drill, wherein the bitter, betrayed, and heartbroken women in the group had been instructed by Boadicea Smythe to invent insulting nicknames for the person or people who had driven them to spend their weekend—and two hundred dollars—at a seminar on how to live without a man. Bronwyn came up with "Piles and Pilaf" for Miles and Pilar, but in the end she concluded that she would have had more fun, and learned more, if she had stayed home and read every word ever written by Ovid, or Gabriel Garciá Márquez, or Irma and Marion Rombauer.

—More Notes From the Front Lines of Serpent Worship:
Well, here I am at Hebigazaka ("Snake-Slope") Shrine, along with several hundred other people. (I really do hate crowds.) In the center of a gravelly courtyard, there is a dirt-floored ring circumscribed by a thick straw rope. Inside the ring are two gigantic Japanese bodybuilders, dressed in red loincloths and straw sandals; they appear to be brothers, with the same full-lipped, broad-featured, strong-boned faces, but one wears his glossy black hair down to his shoulders, while the other has a trendy short haircut with the Japanese ideograph for *hebi* (snake) razor-carved into the back of his scalp. They are meant to represent the Nio, those ferocious-looking, lumpy-muscled guardians who stand in wooden cages on either side of the gates of many great temples. (I learned this from an elderly man in a sky-blue jogging suit named Mr. Shibazaki, who approached me and volunteered, in charming self-taught English, to answer "your any questions" about the festival.) The two bodybuilders are the largest Japanese men I have ever seen—aside from

real *sumotori*, of course—and quite possibly the handsomest, too. The Nio Brothers, as everyone calls them, are taking on challengers from the audience, but no one can begin to match their strength. As they toss even the fittest-looking young men out of the ring, I can't help seeing them as a couple of underdressed *sous* chefs weeding out wilted leaves of lettuce from the salad greens.

Now there is some music coming from the paulownia-wood Noh stage in the main shrine building; I can make out a hand-drum, a wooden flute, and some bells. A dancer in a *sari*-like white costume trimmed in gold, carrying a Japanese *biwa* lute and wearing a beautiful female mask, is mincing around on the stage, making sinuous snakelike movements with her long-fingered hands. I know from my hasty pre-festival research (confirmed by Mr. Shibazaki) that this is meant to be Benten, the only female among the Seven Gods of Good Fortune. Also known as the White Snake Goddess, She is famous for her passionate appetites and caste-blind choice of sex partners, from sublime beings (including the Buddha himself) to working-class mortals. She was said to have a particular fondness for good-looking horse-carriage drivers.

A man wearing a glowering warrior-mask (this is Benten's oft-cuckolded husband, the otherwise powerful God of Good Fortune, Bishamon) has come out onto the stage, leading a large, recalcitrant tabby cat on a thin, gauzy leash. This, Mr. Shibazaki tells me, is meant to represent the god's customary companion, a tiger. Bishamon and Benten are gliding around in a sort of peevish *pas de deux*, and they have just been joined by a dancer wearing a fox mask, and another in a long-nosed, red-lacquer *tengu* mask. Now the stage is being thronged by new arrivals, straight from my book of Japanese mythology: a long-toothed female demon; an oval-faced, slightly ghostlike Noh beauty; the fat-cheeked goddess Otafuku; old man Okina; crooked-mouthed Fire-Blower; an assortment of wild-eyed *oni*-devils; and all of Benten and Bishamon's supernatural colleagues, the remaining five Gods of Good Fortune: Jurojin, Hotei, Daikoku, Ebisu, and Fukurokuju. They are all dancing and chanting, and it's really quite transporting.

There's a great wave of excitement as sixteen sturdy young men wearing nothing but white loincloths and blue monkey-masks (Hanuman's Japanese cousins?) come marching through the woods into the clearing, bearing an elaborately-gilded red lacquer palanquin which, I am told, contains an enchanted thousand-year-old white snake from another Benten shrine, two or three miles away. The snake will be set loose in the dirt ring, and the first person it touches as it darts toward the forest will win some prizes, and will supposedly be inhabited by the spirit of Benten in some mysterious way. Mr. Shibazaki (who is hard of hearing, and has a disconcerting habit of shouting the titles of American musicals for no apparent reason) just told me—after yelling "Paint Your Wagon!"—that "romantically undernourished" men will push their wives into the path of the fleeing snake, hoping that it will make them more passionate, while jealous, possessive men hold their wives back, fearing it might make them promiscuous. It sounds hilarious. I must admit that I'm really glad I ...

Before Bronwyn could finish the sentence, a jostling middle-aged couple bumped into her, knocking the pen from her hand and dislodging her shoulder bag. It fell to the ground, and out tumbled her most private belongings: her hairbrush, her little bottle of cinnamon mouthwash, her makeup kit, her canister of pepper Mace, and her precious organizer, which she called, without a trace of irony or hyperbole, "my life." Business cards, unpaid bills, and irreplaceable scraps of paper scattered onto the ground, and Bronwyn crouched down to retrieve them, while the crowd above her swayed and screamed and jockeyed for position.

Just as she picked up the last business card, Bronwyn became aware of some movement behind her and the next thing she knew a long, thin, dry white snake had passed lightly over her hand, like a rolled-up summer cloud. Bronwyn gave a little cry of surprise, but she didn't realize the significance of the encounter until she stood up and discovered that everyone was pointing at her. "Congratulations, Guys and Dolls!" shouted Mr. Shibazaki. "You are winner of Snake Spell prize!"

After that, things happened very quickly. Bronwyn was led to the shrine stage by a priest dressed in long, stiff azure culottes, and a whispered argument ensued about whether a foreigner should be allowed to win the sacred contest. A tall, white-haired priest wearing four-inch clogs and something that looked like a black-lacquer yarmulke finally said, "Benten-sama was a foreigner, too, you may recall; she came from India, where they called her Sarasvati." And so the matter was resolved.

My parents always used to rhapsodize about the "natural high" that comes from living in and of the moment, although I couldn't help noticing that they seemed to be quite partial to unnatural highs as well. In any case, I don't think I have ever been so aware of the vivid, pulsating essence of every instant as in the hours that followed my fateful brush with the snake. Fortunately I already had plenty of notes for Erica's little story, because from the moment I had my close encounter of the ophidian kind, everything became a giddy exotic blur.

After the priests decided that it was permissible for a mere foreigner to be the recipient of the Snake Spell, as they called it, two *miko* shrine maidens dressed in long vermilion culottes over white kimono took me into a small room. Swiftly and silently (except for one outburst of giggles at the sight of my Occidental breasts), they removed my clothes and dressed me as Benten, with flowing Indian-style robes and a gorgeous antique mask of enameled wood, complete with black center-parted wig and caste mark. I had heard about the transformational power of masks, and I suppose I may have glimpsed it once or twice, on Halloween and at costume parties, but this was something utterly strange, wonderful, and mysterious.

The miko led me into a large *tatami*-matted room, where a double–life-size wooden statue of the goddess herself reclined on a sort of tapestry-covered cot, surrounded by vases containing painted metal flowers, hundreds of red and white candles, and pyramids of bananas, apples, and tangerines. The masked dancers were there, a virtual *tableau vivant* of Japanese myth. There was music, bells and drums and flutes, and the air was loud with chants and thick with incense. I felt intoxicated and vertiginous, and this was *before* I started drinking the supernatural saké.

As Bronwyn sniffed the heady, aromatic air of the Benten shrine, she was suddenly reminded of her faithless fiancé Miles. Or, more specifically, of the odor that had permeated the bedroom of Miles's bachelor pad on Queen Anne Hill one Saturday afternoon when Bronwyn, after getting off work at the University of Washington's East Asia Collection library several hours early, had dropped by to surprise him with a very special gift.

After quietly letting herself in, Bronwyn found her two best friends—Miles and Pilar—together in the bedroom, in the most graphic *flagrante delicto* imaginable. The details were too painful to recall, but Bronwyn could never forget the way the apartment had smelled. As she analyzed it later, it was a sort of sexual joss—a decadent combination of pheromones, sweat, musk-scented toiletries, and intimate secretions.

Bronwyn had fled without saying a word, and no one came running after her to apologize, or explain. The following Monday Miles called from his law office—on the speakerphone, the bastard—and said, "Look, Bron, I'm sorry you had to find out that way; I'm sure it must have been super-painful. But I'm only human and, let's face it, I did put up with your anti-quated attitudes about preserving your virginity for two very long and frustrating years. I mean, you're a great person in many ways, and it probably isn't your fault that you have a underactive libido and an archaic attitude toward sex. I know you tried to make me happy within the limits of your weird neo-Nietzschean philosophy of abstinence, but still—I mean, let's face it, I'm a healthy adult male, not a cenobite, so why should I have to suffer just because your parents were a couple of dimwit free-love hippies and you've decided to spend your life overcompensating for having been born at a rock festival? As for Pilar, it's not just the incredible, astounding, unbelievable sex. She and I are on the same wavelength in every way imaginable, and it's just really unfortunate that she happened to be a friend of yours. Okay, let's face it, your best friend. Okay, okay, your best friend since kindergarten. But anyway, I really do hope you'll find someone someday who will ring your bell and dance to your tune, too—a monk, perhaps, or a eunuch, ha ha. No, seriously, we both wish you all the best. Uh oh, sorry, there's another call coming in!" Miles hung up without having permitted Bronwyn to say a single word, and she never spoke to him, or to Pilar, again.

As if it hadn't been humiliating enough to walk in on that tired old torch-song cliché (my fiancé in bed with my best friend, tra la), the excru-ciating truth was that Bronwyn had let herself into Miles's apartment that day with the intention of "giving herself" to him at last. She had even taken the library's gift stamp (used for book bequests) into the ladies' room and had stamped GIFT on her pale, slightly convex abdomen, just below the navel. That evening, as she scrubbed the stubborn purple stamp-pad ink off her stomach, Bronwyn looked up at her tear-ravaged face in the mirror and said: "Okay, that's it. No more men for me. From now on I'm going to be a Dewey Decimal nun, married to my work."

This distressing memory triggered an automatic silent recitation of the GRTBR mantra: "All men are beasts/All men are beasts/I do not need their fleshly feasts …"

Just then the dancer in the Benten mask appeared at Bronwyn's side and led her into another room. It was smaller, darker, cooler, and scented, to Bronwyn's relief, with a blissfully non-mnemonic strain of incense: a heady combination of frankincense and myrrh. "Please sit down," said the Snake Goddess, and she handed Bronwyn a gold-lacquered cup of something sweet, warm, and viscous. The liquid in the cup was thick and milky, and there were some gray flecks floating on top, like powdered fog. "Drink," the woman said, in a surprisingly deep voice and, obediently, Bronwyn drank.

I had never tasted saké before, and it wasn't at all what I expected. I had heard that it was smooth, dry, and diabolically intoxicating, but this drink was sweet, thick, grainy, and diabolically intoxicating. I drank it without question, for I didn't want to be rude and spoil the magic. Besides, how could I tell a stranger that my parents had abused drugs and liquor and that therefore I didn't drink, and indeed had never had a full glass of alcohol in my life? Almost immediately I began to feel singularly strange: dizzy, reckless, disoriented, and filled with desire—undiluted, undeniable sexual desire, far stronger than anything I had ever felt for Miles (who, let's face it, never really lit my fire). To my surprise the object, or objects, of my startlingly graphic fantasies were the two Nio Brothers—either one would have done, although I felt more drawn to the short-haired brother, for some reason. Fortunately, they were nowhere in sight.

After I had finished drinking the saké potion, all the masked dancers stood in line and spoke to me, one by one. Each person bent over and whispered "*Omedeto*" ("Congratulations"), then passed his or her joined palms through my slightly open palms, as in a game of "Button, button." I couldn't help noticing that the blue-faced monkey-men all reeked of saké and seemed a bit unsteady on their feet; one actually kissed me wetly on the corner of the mouth, darting his tongue through the opening in his mask and leaving a slug-trail on my cheek. I was too shocked and appalled to protest, and then he was gone.

After each visit I would surreptitiously check my palms, but they were always empty. The last person in line was the Benten dancer, and I could tell by the position of her palms that she had something for me. Sure enough, she deposited a cool, chunky object in my hands, and then stood back. "Look at it," she ordered, in that deep, disturbing voice. I looked down and found that I was holding a gorgeous necklace made of oblong carved-silver beads, with a curious charm or amulet suspended from the center: a circular silver snake, evidently in the process of eating its own tail (the Worm!), which formed a frame for a tiny painted-porcelain replica of the Benten masks we both wore. "It's beautiful," I said. Then Benten took one end of the necklace, and Bishamon took the other. They gently placed it around my neck, and fastened the old-fashioned hook-and-eye clasp at the back. It was a short necklace, almost a choker, so the Benten-snake image rested comfortably in the hollow of my throat. I know this probably sounds like wishful nonsense, but the moment I put the necklace on, I felt like a different person.

When Bronwyn walked out into the pale sunshine, she couldn't help blinking. She felt like a mole, or like Rip Van Winkle, or perhaps (for she did look very fetching in her Snake Goddess costume) like Sleeping Beauty. There was no handsome prince in the vicinity, though; just the two shrine maidens in their red culottes and, to her surprise, for she had forgotten all about him, Erica Krill's chauffeur. He was leaning against a vermilion-painted *torii* shrine gate in his incongruously modern uniform, holding Bronwyn's satchel and her neatly-folded clothes—including, she noticed with a rush of back-to-reality embarrassment, her non-matching underwear: a lavender lace brassiere and a pair of red cotton bikini-briefs (printed with, of all childish and unseasonal things, grinning snowmen and candy canes), which were the first two garments that had come to hand as she was rummaging frantically in her anarchic underwear drawer that morning. Bronwyn took the pile of clothes, muttered "Thanks" without meeting the driver's eyes (which were in any case concealed behind his oversized Ray-Bans) and followed the two miko into a small tatami room. They gently removed the

Benten robes, wig, and mask, and then, with only the briefest squeak of schoolgirl giggles, left Bronwyn alone to change back into her drab pinafore, mousy blouse, and ludicrous undergarments.

When Bronwyn emerged from the dressing room, still feeling dizzy and bewitched, the long-haired Nio Brother, looking smashing in a cape-shouldered green trenchcoat over a yellow-orange silk suit, was waiting for her. "Hi," he said. "I'm Kosuke Kuchinawa. You were great."

"Thanks," Bronwyn said, "but I'm feeling a little dazed, I guess from the saké. I'm not much of a drinker, you see. But what's the Snake Spell, and what am I supposed to do now?"

"The Snake Spell is a gift from the gods," said Kosuke Kuchinawa cryptically. "And what I would do now, if I were you, is go out and buy a couple of cases of Samurai Stamina Drink for your boyfriend."

"But I don't have a boyfriend!" Bronwyn protested.

"Really?" Kosuke's handsome face registered a sudden increase in interest. "What a waste! Why don't you give me a call later on, and we'll get together, okay?"

He handed her a card, which read "Kosuke Kuchinawa, Director of Artists & Repertory, Varuna Records." There were reams of addresses and phone numbers for the company's Tokyo, London, and New York offices, but Kosuke turned the card over and scribbled something on the back in purple ink. "Call me on my cell phone, anytime, day or night," he said. "I'll tell you all about the Snake Spell."

"Oh, I'd like that," Bronwyn said, for it had just occurred to her that everyone—the masked dancers, the priests, the shrine maidens—had vanished without telling her what, if any, her duties might be, or when she should return the necklace, which had the look of a valuable antique. The shrine maidens had given her a "goodie bag," as well, which contained a paper-wrapped book, a small bath towel printed with the name of the shrine, and a box of sweets of some sort, but Bronwyn assumed those things were hers to keep.

Kosuke Kuchinawa was standing very close to her, and Bronwyn was finding it difficult to draw a normal breath. Not only was she still slightly tipsy, but she felt a sudden resurgence of the tingly feelings of sexual desire that had overcome her after drinking the saké. She tried to remember the GRTBR mantra, but her mind seemed to have become a perfect void.

"So was the other Nio your brother?" she asked.

"Yes, I'm afraid so," Kosuke said humorously.

Bronwyn realized then that her desire was not for the handsome man standing beside her, but for his absent brother. Suddenly she wanted desperately to see him, and to run her fingers over the "snake" character carved into his hair. She wondered if he had a snake tattoo as well. If so, she wanted to see it, right now. "So, is he still around?" she inquired as casually as her labored breathing would permit.

Kosuke laughed. "No, he went back to his monastery," he said.

A sexy bodybuilding monk! Bronwyn was intrigued.

After repeating the invitation to call him anytime, Kosuke jogged off toward a vintage navy-blue Bentley parked illegally at the end of the walkway to the shrine. Bronwyn felt there was something anticlimactic about having been the center of so much attention and then having no one to see her off, but since that was clearly the way it was going to be, she sighed and followed Erica Krill's taciturn chauffeur down the hill to the waiting Infiniti.

"Would you like to go home now?" asked the driver as they were cruising along the highway toward the Mita area of Minato Ward, where Bronwyn lived. She thought for a moment, and realized that the last thing in the world she wanted was to go home. She wanted this strange, unnerving, transporting day to go on, if not forever, at least until the sun went down.

Suddenly, inspiration struck "Where does Ms. Krill get her hair cut?" she asked.

"At Atelier Amadeo, in Aoyama," the driver said.

"Please take me there," said Bronwyn.

My parents almost didn't go to Woodstock. My mother was eight-and-a-half months pregnant at the time and her parents, who were both conservative, well-to-do physicians, threatened to disinherit her if she insisted on going off and camping in a tick-infested cow pasture with a bunch of drug-crazed dropouts. But my parents were idealists (it's in *Roget's Thesaurus*, under "fools") and they set out, defiantly, in their daisy-decaled Volkswagen Bug. When it broke down in Mamaroneck, they blithely hitched the rest of the way, in funky old graffiti-covered cars on bumpy rural roads. My mother went into labor while Jimi Hendrix was on stage, so I should probably be grateful they didn't name me Purple Hazel, though what they did name me wasn't much less weird. (No, not Bronwyn; that's my self-chosen name, legal since I turned eighteen.) It was a very short labor, and I was delivered extemporaneously in one of the food tents by a self-styled "gypsy midwife" from Greenwich, Connecticut. My birth and the subsequently-broadcast congratulations ("Hey, people, dig this!") weren't immortalized in the movie, thank God, but being a Woodstock baby has definitely shaped my life.

Actually, what has shaped (or distorted) my life even more than that squalid, unhygienic beginning was having parents who felt, until the day they died, that those four days in the messianic mud were the high point not only of their lives but of world civilization. They raised me on what they considered to be the sacred behavioral principles of hippiedom, and I have spent most of my post-adolescent life repudiating those principles by being as conservative and un-Bohemian as I knew how to be. Even though my parents aren't around to react anymore, I still catch myself rebelling, unconsciously, against the old flower-child red-lightbulb far-out-man can-you-dig-it clichés I grew up with, and I still become physically ill at the slightest whiff of patchouli.

One of my mother's obsessions was with the moral necessity for everything to be absolutely natural, unsullied, unimproved by subterfuge. She forbade me to wear makeup, and I wasn't even allowed to invite girls who used cosmetics or nail polish home to visit. When I was a teenager, I exercised what I felt was my inalienable right to garish self-adornment by secretly spending all my money at the "beauty aids" counter of the drugstore. I used to go to school half an hour early, hauling a huge satchel full of every product ever manufactured by Maybelline and, later, Revlon.

Stationing myself in front of the girls' restroom mirror, I would make up my face to look as luridly unnatural as possible—azure eyelids, moss-green lashes, burgundy cheeks, lips iced with white lipstick then overglossed with Cinnabar Red, so it looked as if I had breakfasted, messily, on cream cheese mixed with raspberry jam. Then I would waltz defiantly off to homeroom, where even my best friend Pilar, the future boyfriend-stealer, would be hard put to compliment me on my startling appearance. ("You look very, um, *vivid* today, Bron," I remember her saying, once or twice.) After school, it took at least fifteen minutes of painful scrubbing to wash off the layers of color, and I used to curse my mother the entire time.

Later, in college and in library school, I was too busy to spend much time on my appearance, and Miles, I mean Piles, was one of those anti-artifice autocrats who require their women to display the scrubbed-for-surgery look at all times, so I fell out of the habit. When I landed this dream-job in Tokyo, I began to wear a little earth-toned makeup to work since I felt self-conscious about being younger than some of my subordinates, but I usually ended up dabbing it on haphazardly as I dashed out the door.

The point is, I had never had, or even dreamed of having, what the women's magazines call a Complete Makeover. I was just going to Atelier Amadeo to get my hair trimmed, or so I thought. But I didn't reckon with the powerful—no, that's too mild—the atomic personality of Amadeo Gregorian.

Atelier Amadeo was housed in a new building, designed by a rising young architect who lived around the corner. One admiring critic had described the unusual structure as a "house of heavy metal, in the metallurgic rather than the musical sense," for it was constructed of great sheets of hammered copper, brass, bronze, steel, pewter, platinum, and tin, with gold and silver trim, all intersticed with enormous expanses of smoky glass. The floor was carpeted in industrial gray, and there was a huge cylindrical floor-to-ceiling atrium filled with golden monkeys, toucans, rainforest flora, and brown-and-yellow oncidium orchids.

One wall was stacked high with video monitors, each showing a different feature film, or documentary, or musical event. Customers could tune their battery-powered earphones to their choice of monitors while they waited, or while the chemicals sizzled in their hair. Bronwyn was momentarily tempted to tune her earphones to Monitor 27 and settle back to watch the familiar sepia-tinted scenes of Sean Connery clambering through the labyrinthine innards of a medieval monastery. She considered *The Name of the Rose* the ultimate paean to bibliophilia, and to libraries (if not to the moral rectitude of librarians), but she had already seen it at least twelve times.

So instead she reached into her satchel and took out the book which had come with the Snake Spell, and carefully removed the paper wrapping. It was what used to be called a slim volume, perhaps half an inch thick, and stamped across the bottom in bold black letters was the word REMAINDER. Bronwyn was surprised that the print run hadn't sold out, for it was a very attractive book.

The cover featured Benten, a.k.a. the White Snake Goddess, the racy Japanese equivalent of Sarasvati: goddess of music, art, literature, beauty, and eloquence. She was sitting, voluptuously topless, with a lute on her cloth-swaddled lap. There was a jewel-shaped caste mark on her forehead, and her hair was piled on her head under a tiara in the form of a snake. In the background were her fellow Gods of Good Fortune: her oft-deceived husband Bishamon, and the other five eccentric-looking supernatural characters. Cavorting around the edges was a partial roster of her lovers: the muscular Nio, assorted mountain ascetics, several samurai in full battle armor, and a contingent of her beloved carriage drivers.

The Secret Life of the Snake Goddess: Adventures on the Ouroboric Trail of Japan's Most Outrageous Female, read the title. The author was one of Bronwyn's favorite writers: Murasaki McBride, who, some said, was a somewhat outrageous female herself. Bronwyn had never seen a copy of this particular book, but she knew that it was considered one of McBride's earlier, more peculiar efforts, before she managed to navigate her ship of words closer to the literary and mercantile mainstream.

Utterly beguiled by the intriguing little volume in her hand, Bronwyn opened it to Chapter One.

CONFESSIONS OF A TUBULAR TROLLOP

No doubt you've heard the scandalous rumors about me, and I'm delighted to say that most of them are true. Yes, I've had my share of paramours: gods, demigods, samurai, merchants, mountain sages, medieval bodybuilders, carriage drivers, beasts. Yes, I can change into a snake at will; I do it to facilitate a dramatic getaway, or to indulge the ophiolatrous fantasies of depraved human males. Yes, I did spend one sublime night with the Buddha, in the days when he was still Prince Gautama. (He was a beautiful man, and a truly amazing lover.) And finally, no! It wasn't I who incinerated that unfortunate monk at Dojoji. That was a certain randy she-dragon of my acquaintance, whose bedside manner is crude at best.

Some self-righteous mortals have called me a tramp, and a vamp; they say I'm as recklessly promiscuous as a reptile in heat. They don't understand that I'm just a healthy supernatural female, living by the Zen of lust: eat when you're hungry, drink when you're dry, make love when your heart says it's time.

Of course, like any woman, I am prey to attacks of hormonal ventriloquism, and sometimes I realize too late that the hoarse and urgent voice I hear is not my heart, but my hyperthermic loins. Still, why should I suppress the urge to merge? Pagan goddesses aren't prey to petty annoyances like guilt and disease, and snakes have no concept of chastity, or sin.

People call me sex-mad, a love slave, a glutton for seduction. They don't understand that it isn't just the sensation I crave; it's the séance, and the dance. Not just the congruence, but the collusion; not merely the friction but the fiction, too. To me, the interlocking parts of the male and female anatomies are as miraculous as music, and I believe that a tenderly ecstatic sexual union can be the sweetest taste of immortality, and the most rapturous foretaste of death.

Before you condemn me as a shameless slattern or an oversexed anguis in herba, *please read my story. You may still conclude that I am a woman-too-wild, a snake-too-free, a wanton filament of slithering slime, but perhaps you'll end up with a more sympathetic understanding of my pyrotechnic passions. And since every myth is a microcosm, who knows? You might learn something about your own passions and prejudices, as well.*

I was eagerly turning to Chapter Two, when someone tapped me on the shoulder. It was a young woman with a mane of chartreuse corkscrew curls and three silver rings through each eyebrow, wearing a silver lamé apron over her clothes. "Hello, I am Kichiko," she said in a singsong voice. "Please to follow me." A sybaritic, dozy hour of shampooing and head massage later, I was taken to the styling area where, Kichiko told me, in a reverent tone, I would be ministered to by The Man himself.

Amadeo Gregorian turned out to be style personified, fashion made flesh. The artichoke-green kimono-ish jacket (Armani meets Zatoichi?) worn over a black T-shirt and a pair of baggy black pants, the shiny black hair worn in a shaggy samurai-outlaw topknot bound with copper wire: every detail had a unique, easy flair, without being contrived or outré. I remembered reading that Amadeo was half-Japanese and half-Sicilian, which had struck me in the abstract as a curious, even schizophrenic combination, like a

Doberman Pinscher and a Golden Retriever. In the flesh, the sculpturesque Mediterranean features and Oriental eyes added up to one of the most attractive congruencies of genes I had ever seen.

"Hello, Miss Bronwyn," said Amadeo, smiling a sweet, luminous smile. He spoke English fluently, with a very slight, unidentifiable accent, as if his native tongue might have been Esperanto, or Mondolingue, or one of those other "universal languages" that only thirteen people in the universe have ever bothered to learn. "Lovely name, Bronwyn," he added.

Ordinarily I would have just said, "Thank you," but I was still feeling a bit loose from the alcohol I'd drunk: *in saké veritas.*

"Actually," I blurted, "that wasn't my birth name at all." And then while Amadeo snipped away at my wet hair, I proceeded to tell him the provenance of my self-bestowed name.

The name on my birth certificate was Blue-Moon Butterfly LaFarge. My parents claimed the moon was a deep and mystic blue on the night I was conceived, but I decided, as soon as I was old enough to be a judgmental cynic, that that was just another of their sordid psychedelic hallucinations. The butterfly, apparently, was an extra-large black-and-orange Monarch that flew into the gluten-burger tent just at the moment when I popped into the world to the strains of Country Joe & the Fish singing "Don't ask me I don't give a damn/Next stop is Vietnam."

So how did I get from "Blue-Moon Butterfly" to "Bronwyn Cabot"? Easily. Cabot was my mother's surname, and I chose it because it reeked of respectability. As for Bronwyn, I found that in an old reference book called *Proper Names of the British Isles.*

"I like your new name," Amadeo said when I had finished my confession. "But I have to admit I liked your old one, too. It has a sort of American Indian sound to it, very poetic."

"Actually, that was part of the problem," I said. "My great-grandfather was a soldier at Bosque Redondo, and my parents thought they could neutralize that atrocious karma, as they put it, by giving me a vaguely Native American–sounding name, but they just succeeded in embarrassing me."

Amadeo looked a bit bewildered, so I quickly said, "Never mind, that's all in the past. But what kind of a name is Amadeo Gregorian?"

"Actually it's my own invention," Amadeo said, lowering his fluty voice conspiratorially. "My real name is Ichiro Tanaka—isn't that just a hideous turnip of a name, pale and bland and boring?—because my parents got divorced before I was born and I was adopted by my Japanese grandparents. But I decided that I wanted to commemorate my Italian heritage, and of course I adore Wolfie—Mozart, you know. As for Gregorian, I just thought it sounded *molto elegante*."

"Absolutely en-chant-ing," I said, and Amadeo laughed.

"Besides," he added with a candid, mischievous grin, "my new name is ever so much better for business. Speaking of which, I've been talking to Kumo Takatori—"

I must have looked blank because Amadeo said, "You know, Erica's driver."

"Oh, right," I said. It was the first time I had heard the chauffeur's name.

"Anyway," Amadeo went on, "he told me the exciting news about your winning a big contest at a snake shrine—"

"It was nothing," I protested, "just serendipity. Or serpendipity." Amadeo laughed, and I wondered if his English was really that good.

"So anyway," he said, "I would like to offer my congratulations in the form of what we modestly call *il transformazione miracoloso*, compliments of the boss—that's me. No, I insist. I'm going to start by cutting your hair. By the way, have you ever thought of changing the style *un piccolo po'*?"

I must have dozed off again shortly after that, because I was startled awake by Amadeo saying, "So, what do you think of this?" I looked into the mirror and my mouth literally dropped open. My hair has always just sort of flopped around disconsolately; that's why I wear it in a bun. Now it fell gracefully to my shoulders, surrounding my face with an aureole of delicately feathered layers. I had never seen it look so full, or so shiny, or so … red?

"I like it," I said, "but where did the color come from?"

"Oh, it'll wash out in a few weeks," Amadeo said. "It's just a Level Two rinse—the color is called 'Foxy Lady'—that Kichiko put in when she shampooed you." Amadeo worked me over for a few more minutes with a brush and a blow drier, and when he was finished my hair looked exactly like polished copper.

"Voilá," he said, taking a little bow, while I gaped incredulously at the glossy femme fatale reflected in the mirror.

Two hours later, Bronwyn had been worked over by a facialist, a manicurist, and a cosmetologist. (Bronwyn was dying to ask "But how do you handle the weightlessness?" but she couldn't figure out how to say it in Japanese.) She had been given several new outfits by the vivacious Argentinean-Japanese manager of Boutique Amadeo, as a gift from the generous owner, whom she now considered a friend. It was nearly six P.M. when she finally stepped out onto Aoyama Street with russet hair, nacreous nails, and Visionary Violet lips. She was wearing a long-sleeved, scoop-necked, short-skirted purple crepe dress over matching diamond-patterned leggings, with taupe-colored lace-up ankle boots, and she was laden with dress bags and hat- and shoe-boxes.

When Bronwyn saw the driver leaning casually against the double-parked Infiniti, talking animatedly to a willowy, sophisticated-looking young Japanese woman dressed in a pewter silk pantsuit and matching Stetson hat, she felt an odd and totally absurd jolt of jealousy. And when he didn't leap to help her with her burdens, she felt distinctly annoyed.

Still, she couldn't help fishing for compliments. "So what do you think, Mr. Takatori?" she asked coyly, after the beautiful stranger had thanked the driver (for what, Bronwyn wondered, but she wasn't about to ask) and tottered away in her gray Manolo Blahnik stilettos.

"The dress is very nice," said the driver, holding open the door as Bronwyn tumbled in with her packages. "It's a beautiful shade of purple, like starflowers." Thanks a lot, thought Bronwyn, who had been hoping for a slightly more ego-gratifying response. From now on, she decided, it's strictly business. No way am I going to call him by name, or discuss anything remotely personal with him, ever again. And if she ever met up with Kumo Takatori again, after this weekend, she would pretend not to remember. "Oh, good evening," she would say, extending her hand like a dowager duchess. "I'm terribly sorry, have we met somewhere before?"

Bronwyn was planning to say, curtly, "Please take me home," but when she leaned forward to speak to the driver she caught sight of her reflection in the rear-view mirror. She had been visualizing herself as the slightly dowdy Old Bronwyn, but what she saw in that mirror was a knockout. Much too good to waste, as Kosuke Kuchinawa might have said.

"Where would Erica Krill go for a drink?" Bronwyn asked. She was thinking of tonic water with lime, or maybe a Virgin Bloody Mary.

"With her husband, or with her female friends?" The driver put his hand on the passenger-seat headrest and looked back at Bronwyn. He was still wearing the stupid black shades, but she noticed that his hand was large and strong and brown, and she felt a sudden weird stirring in her viscera that she attributed to hunger. No wonder, for she hadn't eaten since breakfast.

"With her female friends, I suppose," Bronwyn said.

"Oh, shall I take you there? It's a very interesting place."

Bronwyn stole another glance in the mirror. It seemed almost criminal to waste so much glamor on a couple of cats, however dear and delightful. Besides, she liked interesting places, and she was thirsty.

"Yes," she said haughtily. "Take me there."

There was a line of cars parked outside the euphemistically-named Harajuku Business Center: limousines, sports cars, and luxury sedans, in shades of silver and gray and black, all gleaming in the white-neon light like freshly-caught albacore. There was a line of people, too, Japanese and foreign, waiting hopefully behind the black velvet rope, hoping to gain admittance to "FaxLoveCity," as it had been dubbed by the Tokyo *Tribune* columnist Rebecca Flanders. After Erica Krill's driver whispered a few words to the doorman (a seven-foot Jamaican bodybuilder decked out in a black velvet three-piece suit, a rattlesnake-hide necktie, and a glistening mop of coconut-oiled dreadlocks), the serpentine rope parted and Bronwyn was allowed to slip into the inner sanctum of high-tech courtship masquerading as Business As Usual.

I'll spare you the technological details, Diary dear. Suffice it to say that the place (which was very classy inside, all cool gray marble and glass and waterfalls and mirrors) was set up to function as an office-away-from-the office for busy corporate types, and some people may actually have used the computers and the fax machines for that purpose. Clearly, though, most people came there to meet others, for purposes known only to them.

My secretary-waitress, Ms. Kuboyama, was dressed as if for a board meeting, in a charcoal-gray pinstriped pantsuit, and she explained the process in mind-numbing detail. Then she helped me fill out a questionnaire, took a Polaroid of me and scanned it into the computer, and explained briskly that I was under no obligation to respond to faxes that might appear in response to the automatic dissemination of my résumé and image to all the other fax machines in the place. My table was inside a smoked-glass cubicle, so I couldn't see any of the other patrons, and they couldn't see me.

After all the data-processing was done, Ms. Kuboyama took my drink order. ("I'll have a Grasshopper," I said, having no idea what that might be; it sounded like something a sophisticated Snake-Spell recipient should order, and Ms. K. assured me that it would be sweet rather than sour). When she brought the drink, along with the plate of assorted canapés that I had ordered, I asked the question that had been on my mind since I walked in.

Ms. Kuboyama looked deeply hurt, and horrified. "No, this is most emphatically *not* a singles bar, or a dating service. We think of it as an arena of multidimensional communication-interface. People find racquetball partners here, or investors, or a fourth for bridge. Of course, romances do sometimes develop, just as they might at work, or at a cultural event. But it makes me want to scream when the media call us a 'pickup joint.' In fact, many of our best clients are married." With that enigmatic remark, Ms. Kuboyama left me alone with my multidimensional communication devices and my bright green cocktail, which was exactly the color of the sleazy polyester lounge suit my father picked up at the Salvation Army, back in the mid-seventies, when his boss told him to go out and buy some respectable clothes.

The first fax was very brief. *Welcome to the jungle*, it read. *Me barbarian, you librarian. As the Paleozoic bartender said when he added a juniper berry to a mammoth's skull filled with fermented-potato moonshine, it could be a very interesting combination.* The note was signed "Mick," and the accompanying photograph showed the handsome, complacent, slightly coarse-looking face of a male in his late thirties. It was, Bronwyn thought, the kind of face that had kissed a lot of women, and told a lot of lies.

The second fax was signed Manju Matsumoto, and the message was superimposed, in carefully hand-written capital letters, on a photocopied image of a serious-looking young man wearing black-framed glasses and a polka-dot bow tie, slightly askew. *Good evening*, it read. *I am aspiring stand-up comedian of Japanese ancestors. I would like very much to talk to (with?) you to try to refine my pork chops, as they say at comedy clubs in U.S. of A. Would you be so kind to speak with (to?) me and cast critical American ear upon my mediocre humor? Thank you very awfully for your free time. See you again, I hope so.* Bronwyn smiled at the ambiguity of "free time," then went on to the next missive.

My dear girl, it began chummily, *yours is the most interesting, intelligent, appealing face ever to emerge from my fax machine, and as a charter member of FaxLoveCity, I speak from broad experience. (No cheap chauvinistic pun intended, I assure you.) I enjoyed your quixotic résumé, as well, especially the bit about your two cats, and the fact that they are not named after the famous duo in American politics, as one might have assumed. Very witty and subversive, my dear. I keep felines myself, although mine are a bit larger—leopards, actually, smuggled back from Pakistan many years ago. In the event, would you care to join me for a drink and some genteel, literate conversation? As Punch said to Judy, no strings attached.* The note, which had evidently been typed on the word processor, was signed *Rupert Y., Litt.D., Durham,* and the photograph showed a man, old enough to be Bronwyn's father (or grandfather), wearing a singularly unconvincing toupee and what appeared to be a glue-on moustache and Van Dyke beard. Under all this hair, whether real or purchased, lurked a face that struck Bronwyn as selfish, soft, and vain.

The fourth message began innocuously enough. *Dear Ms. L.,* (Bronwyn had chosen to use only her initials on her dispatches), *I couldn't help being taken with the loveliness of your appearance and the charm of your words, and I would consider it a privilege to take you back to my place and spend the entire night, if not the whole weekend, feeding each other aphrodisiacal bivalves and rutting like pigs. If that prospect appeals to you, please send as your reply the single word* "Oui" *(as in, "Oui, oui, oui, all the way home"). Sincerely yours, Gianni B. Goode.*

Good grief, Bronwyn muttered, what a creep. To her consternation, though, "Gianni" didn't look at all like a creep, or a jerk, or a sex maniac. He was a dark-eyed, curly-haired young man with an almost cherubic face. He might have been a vicar, or a vintner—but a satyr? This is definitely not my cup of tea, Bronwyn thought. I would much rather be at home, curled up with a good book, in a place where the only males are furry eunuchs with tuna breath. First, though, I need to finish this yummy drink.

I had decided to polish off my third and final Grasshopper and go home, for (*pax*, Ms. Kuboyama) FaxLoveCity seemed to be nothing more than a glorified high-tech singles bar. The truth was, I was feeling uncharacteristically open to romance, but none of the men who had sent me messages really rang my bell. Just as I was about to get up I noticed another piece of paper sitting in the tray of the fax machine.

I looked first at the photograph. It showed a man in his early forties, perhaps ten years older than I am, with a face that was, by male-model standards, a symphony of flaws. To me, though, it was startlingly attractive. In fact, I thought it was one of the most appealing faces I had ever seen, and while my other long-distance admirers had left me cold, this one (even before I read his intriguing message) made me feel decidedly warm.

The message was hand-written in the sort of square, artistic script I associate with architects or graphic designers. *Dear Ms. L.*, it began, *I did not come in here hoping to "meet someone." I was curious about the concept, and the design, so I stopped by to have a drink on my way home from a performance by the Early Music Consort (that's a group, not a clavichord-playing concubine). But when I glanced at your résumé and noticed how many fondnesses and, perhaps more important, how many antipathies we have in common, I felt that I simply must communicate with you. Do you believe in the Red Thread of Fate? Do you believe that magic is still afoot in the Age of Mundanity? Do you believe that I am posing such intimate questions to a total stranger? Maybe this isn't such a good idea after all; I'll probably be gone, home to my cats and books and licorice tea, by the time you read these words. Still, it was nice almost meeting you, and I wish you a life filled with pleasant surprises and sweet revelations.* [Signed] S. X. Q.

Quickly, I shuffled through the stack of résumés until I came to one headed SIMON XAVIER QUIMBY. (It could have been an alias, but Ms. Kuboyama had told me that men were inclined to use their real names.) Scanning the "favorite" categories I was amazed by our commonality of slightly eccentric interests and tastes. Simon Xavier Quimby liked to eat Ben & Jerry's Cherry Garcia frozen yogurt for breakfast while reading Phillip Larkin and listening to Albinoni, he liked to suck on licorice gumdrops while watching videos of films like *Local Hero* and *Truly, Madly, Deeply*, he had nine cats, he was a designer of book jackets and theatrical posters …

The résumé was two pages of single-spaced information (which struck me as strange, when I thought about it later, since he had supposedly just come in for a quick drink), and I suddenly realized that if I wanted to stop the intriguing-sounding Mr. Quimby before he departed in embarrassment, I had better hurry.

I scribbled a hasty message: "Hello, yes, let's talk," signed it, recklessly, Love & Licorice (figuring that the ampersand would neutralize the "love"), and sent it off to his fax number (476; mine was 592). Then I ordered another Grasshopper (it was like crème de menthe ice cream, very refreshing and invigorating and not alcoholic-tasting at all), sat back, and waited.

After a moment there was a beep and a piece of white paper slowly sprouted from my matte-black fax machine, like a time-lapse peony. My heart leapt, but it was just a high-pressure follow-up message from Gianni B. Goode. *Hey pretty lady, you don't know what you're missing. I'm sitting here looking at your picture and getting totally hot—I'm talking terminally tumescent, no computer pun intended. Here's my final offer: I guarantee you the most phenomenal night of your life, or your honey back.*) I was alarmed to find myself becoming mildly interested (for G. B. Goode was a very nice-looking and articulate young lecher, and the Grasshoppers were having an effect by then), so I quickly stopped reading and wadded up the paper. I wasn't sure whether "honey" was a misprint or suggestive innuendo, but I decided I didn't want to find out.

I sat for another ten minutes, and then decided that Simon Xavier Quimby must have left before he received my encouraging message. (Or had he left afterward? How humiliating.) So I got up, paid my bill (sixty five dollars for four little drinks and a few bites of smoked salmon!), and headed for the door. There was a long line of well-dressed people waiting to get into FaxLoveCity, and I noticed several of them looking at me in a disappointed way, as if I had somehow let them down by emerging alone.

"It's not a singles bar, you know," I said defensively to a woman in a white leather trenchcoat. "But they do make a delicious Grash-hopper, I mean Grasshopper."

My driver was nowhere in sight, so I headed down the street toward a parking lot where I assumed he would be waiting. The curb was lined with fancy cars, and as I ran the gauntlet of Ferraris, Lexuses, and luxury SUVs, the rear door of a dark-indigo stretch Mercedes opened into my path.

"Hello," said a deep, wonderful male voice. "I've been waiting for you."

I bent over and peered into the dim, luxurious recesses of the Mercedes, where I saw a familiar face: the faint acne scars, the imposing aquiline nose, the chiseled mouth, the intelligent, humorous eyes.

"Simon!" I said, as if I were greeting an old friend,.

"Simon says, get in," said that marvelous voice. What could I do? I got in.

Later, Bronwyn would reconstruct her misadventure with Simon Xavier Quimby by landmarks and traffic lights. At the first stoplight, she gave him a chaste, tentative peck on the lips. At the second stoplight he kissed her, with authority, ending with a cautious one-step–forward, one-step–back inch of Courvoisier-flavored tongue. As they passed the Meiji Shrine the car phone rang, and Simon cut a long spelunking kiss short to answer it. "I'm telling you, the leveraged buyout is an archaic concept," he barked into the phone, and Bronwyn wondered what a designer of book jackets and theatrical posters was doing discussing leveraged buyouts when he should have been attending to the business at hand: kissing the totally infatuated, passion-inflamed young librarian whom he had just picked up, with very little effort, at FaxLoveCity.

At the third stoplight Simon removed his gray Harris-tweed jacket, at the fourth stoplight he removed Bronwyn's jacket, and at the fifth stoplight the car phone rang again. "Listen, Lucinda, I can't talk now; I'm with a client," Simon said, with one hand on the receiver and the other on Bronwyn's left breast, and Bronwyn felt a slight cooling of her animalistic ardor. Who the hell is Lucinda, she thought, and why does he have to lie to her about being with me? The moment Simon began kissing her again, though, her reservations evaporated, and once again she was as indiscriminately amorous as a snake in heat.

At the sixth stoplight, as Simon was fumbling with the buttons down the back of Bronwyn's dress and Bronwyn (with a blissful, Grasshopper-induced lack of inhibition) was trying to get a grip on the zipper of his gray linen trousers, the car phone rang again.

"Blasted phone!" said Simon, but he answered it on the first ring. "Look, Charisse," he mumbled into the mouthpiece, "I told you it would be later tonight, if at all. I'm in the middle of a very important meeting." He hung up and turned back to Bronwyn with a conspiratorial smile, and Bronwyn could feel her lust and longing being replaced with disgust and resentment.

"This isn't what I had in mind," she began.

"I know exactly what you had in mind," Simon said with an almost cartoonish leer. "You want me to induct you into the Back-of-a-Limo club."

Suddenly Bronwyn remembered that she was a virgin, and that she had always wanted her first time to be lyrical, tender, and sweet.

"Please let me out," she said. "I'm afraid we've had a major misunderstanding."

"No misunderstanding at all," Simon said coolly, as he reached behind her and locked her door. "I know exactly what you want, and so do you." Bronwyn tugged frantically on the lock button, to no avail. Simon seemed to have turned into one of those many-armed Hindu gods; he was grabbing at her torso more aggressively now, and she was getting frightened. When they got to the next stoplight, she did something desperate: she slapped his face to distract him, then catapulted herself out through the open sunroof and dropped into the gutter in a heap. Simon Quimby made no attempt to come after her, and after a moment the light changed and the limo drove away.

What if someone I knew happened to be driving by just then? Bronwyn thought dizzily. She was mortified, and she began to cry as she realized what a fool she had made of herself. I wonder if it's the Snake Spell, she thought. Or is it the necklace, or the alcohol? Or are all men really beasts, however nice and intelligent and witty they may appear (or claim) to be? Or—and this thought sent a chill down her spine—could it just be me? Am I one of those people who's doomed never to find sweet love, or true romance?

As Bronwyn was trying to hail a cab, a sleek metallic car stopped beside her and she saw that it was Erica Krill's Infiniti. "Get in the car," said Kumo Takatori in a stern voice, sounding more like a father than a driver. "I'll take you home." What could she do? She got in.

Dewey and Truman were so glad to see me that I began to cry again. What had I been thinking of, running around chasing strange men and behaving like a promiscuous sixties hippie, or an oversexed snake, when my faithful kitties were sitting at home with lonely hearts and rumbling stomachs? To make amends, I treated them to a huge bowl of kibbles mixed with a can of minced clams and a cup of leftover chopped broccoli. (They adore broccoli, for some reason; I call them the Crucifer Kids.)

I took a quick bath and crawled into bed, with Dewey curled up in the crook behind my knees and Truman on the pillow, tickling my nose with his whiskers. I put on a CD of Dvorak's "Bagatelles" to lighten my mood, and then I looked around for something comforting to read. Suddenly I remembered the Snake Goddess book. That would be a perfect equilibrium-restorer. I rummaged in my satchel, but it wasn't there.

Oh well, I thought, it must have gotten mixed up with my other packages. That was when I realized that I had left all my bags and boxes in the back of the Infiniti. I almost wished then that I had been raised a Christian, instead of a Whatever, so I could have said a fervent non-secular prayer for the safe return of my wonderful book. What if I had somehow lost that rare and possibly irreplaceable treasure? That would be too cruel, on top of the horribly sordid way my Snake Spell day had ended.

The sky outside was pink and blue and silver, like the inside of an abalone shell, when I woke up. My head ached, my eyes seemed to be sealed with Crazy Glue, my tongue had apparently been surgically replaced with that of a large, sickly cow, and my lips were raw and sore from Simon Xavier Quimby's loveless kisses.

I got up and drank a cup of peppermint tea and ate an apple turnover. (I can't help it, I like to eat sweets for breakfast, or any other meal; Pilar always said it was because my mother didn't allow any refined sugar or white flour in the house.) I took a shower and washed my face, and when I still felt terrible, I gave up and went back to bed.

I was awakened around noon by the telephone. "Hello," said an attractive male voice, "May I speak to Miss Bronwyn, please?"

"Humf?" I said.

"Oh, were you taking a nap? I'm sorry," said the voice. "This is your driver."

I sat up in bed. I had completely forgotten about having the use of Erica Krill's driver-car for the rest of the weekend. "I'm in the neighborhood," said the driver, "and I have all of your shopping bags in the trunk, and I wondered if you might like to go somewhere."

"Do you think any libraries would be open today?" I asked, after a moment's thought.

"I know of one," said the driver. "It never closes—it's open twenty-four hours a day, three hundred and sixty-five days a year."

"I wonder why I've never heard about it," I mused.

"Maybe you've been hanging around with the wrong people," the driver said, and then he hung up.

As I got dressed in a new fudge-colored cotton jumpsuit, I thought about what a mess the previous day had turned out to be. If only there were some magical formula for living a well-ordered life, some existential Dewey Decimal System. But chaos is like a malevolent weed, growing wild without water or sunlight, crowding out the fragile flowers of symmetry and tranquility. I love the Dewey Decimal System, and I love Mr. Melvil Dewey for inventing it; that's why I named my cat after him. (The other cat is named for Truman Capote, to remind me not to confuse the singer with the song, or the writer with his words.) I used to have another cat, too, a sweet, strange apricot-colored female who liked to swim in my bathtub; I named her Nimuë, after Merlin's "watery tart." She disappeared at SeaTac Airport, cage and all, two years ago, and I still miss her every day.

The Eternal Library was founded by a popular and successful movie actress who claimed to have been too busy to read a single book from the time she finished high school until she turned fifty and left show business. When she retired, she embraced literature with such an acquisitive passion that by the time she died, at ninety-four, she had amassed a collection of over a million titles. The actress, whose name was Miki Hanamichi, left the books (along with a large sum of money and a spectacular Tudor-style house in Denenchofu) to a foundation bearing her name, with instructions that the property should be made into a library, to be called the Eternal Library in the hopes that it would remain open, and would thrive, forever.

"What a wonderful building!" Bronwyn exclaimed as they drove up the winding, elm-lined driveway.

"Yes," the driver agreed. "I especially like the way they've done the half-timbering in the magpie pattern, though that would make it more Elizabethan than Tudor, of course, and the leading in the windows is particularly fine—the house was bought in England, you know, and then reassembled here."

"That's more words than you've uttered since we met," said Bronwyn. The driver looked sheepish, and Bronwyn suspected that he was blushing behind the dark glasses that he always wore, day and night. "How can you see?" she had asked him once, early on, and he had assured her that the lenses adjusted according to the available light.

Once inside the library, Bronwyn felt suffused with joy as she walked through the graciously-furnished rooms and gazed at the ceiling-high shelves full of books in English, French, and Japanese. This is where I'm happiest, she thought. This is where things make sense, not thrashing around in the back of a limousine with some lecherous liar, however attractive he might look on paper, or by limo-light.

Two hours later, Bronwyn had finished her research. She knew at least three times as much about Benten, Bishamon, and Hebigazaka Shrine as she had when she began, but she had only been able to find one passing reference to the Snake Spell. "There is an old belief," one rather scholarly old book said, "that the licentious spirit of the Snake Goddess dwells in a certain white snake, and that once every twelve years that spirit is passed on to a human female who comes into contact with the snake. It might make an interesting longitudinal study to follow up on the experiences of the women who imagine themselves so 'bewitched,' but no such study has ever been done. It is likely that the snake, far from being a thousand years old as is claimed, is only a few years old, for snakes are not known for their longevity in captivity. Still, it is a colorful and charming ritual, and that seems to be the main point."

There was no mention of the necklace, or of the thick saké drink with the gray flecks floating on top. Bronwyn was disappointed, for she had begun to think that her newly-assertive libido could be traced to the latter. She imagined that there had been some sort of time-release aphrodisiac in the saké, which had been activated somehow by the alcohol she'd consumed later. It wasn't a flawless theory, but it was the only one she had.

On the way out, Bronwyn remembered her lost book. "Excuse me," she said to the reference librarian, "but I was wondering if you might have a book called *The Secret Life of the Snake Goddess* in your closed stacks. I looked in the on-line catalog, but didn't see it."

The librarian was an attractive Japanese woman in her mid-thirties with a gamin haircut, dressed in a heathery rose-colored turtleneck dress and a metallic-silver name tag which read Noriko Perry. "That's a wonderful book," she said in barely-accented English, and Bronwyn wondered whether she had been educated abroad, or if she might be married to a foreigner. "We keep buying used copies from Bibliofind, and they keep walking out the door."

"You mean people steal them?"

"Exactly. They may not be honest, but at least they have good taste. Tell me, though, if you don't mind my asking, where did you get that beautiful necklace?"

Briefly, Bronwyn told the woman, who had an intelligent, quirky, sympathetic face, about the Snake Spell, omitting only the alarming effect it seemed to have had on her hitherto dormant sex drive. To her astonishment, the Japanese librarian responded by reaching into her own high collar and fishing out an identical necklace.

"I can't really talk now," she said, after explaining that she, and the people at the shrine, had bought the *faux* antique necklaces at a funny little shop in Meguro. "But please give me a call if you'd like to come to one of our meetings." She handed Bronwyn a card that read:

~ *Sisters of Sarasvati* ~

Art, Music, Literature, Beauty, and
Sometimes a Bit of Eloquence as Well

"We get together once a month or so and do fun things," Noriko Perry explained. "Art openings, museums, concerts, restaurants, movies, overnight trips to see our favorite flowers in bloom around the country."

"That sounds great," said Bronwyn. "Are you all librarians?"

"No, I'm the only one."

Maybe not for long, Bronwyn thought excitedly, carefully stashing the card in her corset for chaos.

What can I say about Cacao? It's as close as I ever expect to get to heaven, and I didn't even have to die to get there. All I had to do was to say "Yes" when Mr. Takatori—no, *Kumo*—asked if he could buy me a cup of coffee and a pastry at his favorite coffee shop, which was right around the corner from the library. "All right," I said semi-aloofly. I had gotten over my annoyance over his stinginess with compliments, but I was still feeling embarrassed at having him pluck me, literally, out of the gutter after the FaxLoveCity debacle. "Now that you mention it, I am feeling a bit peckish."

"Monty Python undertaker sketch," Kumo muttered almost inaudibly, and I gaped at him in amazement. Since I was still in strictly-business mode,

I didn't launch into a giddy litany of my favorite Python lines, nor did I comment on the fact that the book he was reading when I came out of the library was one of my personal favorites: *Flaubert's Parrot*. He had looked rather picturesque stretched out on the grass under an umbrella-shaped tree, with his beret off and his long hair flopping around his face, but I wasn't about to mention that, either.

I was expecting a run-of-the-mill coffee shop, but Cacao turned out to be something I might have dreamed on a really good night. There was coffee on the menu, and tea, and hot lemonade, but the focus of the shop was on chocolate: *Theobroma cacao*, food of the gods, and my own personal drug of choice.

Calling me a chocophile would be as much of an understatement as saying that Benten had an active social life. Indeed, I often suspected that some wires had gotten crossed somewhere and that the "urge to merge" that I should have felt in the form of free-floating sexual desire had instead taken the form of a compulsion to Become One with a large chunk of bittersweet chocolate, at least once a day. I loved other sweets as well, and other flavors (vanilla, maple, cinnamon, licorice, treacle) but chocolate was my Dark Prince, my demon lover, my direct route to Nirvana.

Once, not long after the shattering debacle with Miles, I actually caught myself talking to a handful of Hawaiian Vintage Chocolate pastilles. "I'm your heroine," I babbled as I tore open the purple-and-gold package. "And you're my dirty needle." Hyperbole aside, it wasn't a real addiction; I was perfectly able to go for hours, even days, without a chocolate fix, but I preferred not to.

Cacao was a beautiful shop: modern wood and glass, on a quiet back street with a garden in the rear. The color scheme of red, black, and ivory set off the deep browns of mousse and tart, truffle and cake. Red silk poppies on black lacquer tables, tricolor striped umbrellas over the tables in the garden, square ivory-glazed plates and cups: everything was a treat for the eye.

I had Kumo pegged as one of those austere non-eaters of sweets, so I was surprised when he said, "If you don't mind, I'll order the sampler. That's what I always get. It has eight mini-confections on it, and that way you can try a few different things. And what would you like to drink? Coffee? Tea? Milk?"

"Hot chocolate, please," I said sheepishly, and Kumo Takatori laughed out loud for the first time in our acquaintance. He had beautiful teeth, I noticed, but I wished he would take off those distracting dark glasses so I could see his eyes.

We ended up sitting there for over three hours, under a cocoa-colored umbrella in the budding garden, tasting, and talking, and laughing more and more. To make a long story short, I learned that Kumo had been an undergrad art major at Columbia during the same years that I was at NYU Library School; that he was saving money to go to architecture school in London, having been inspired by his aunt, the famous architect and artist Madoka Morokoshi; and, more abstractly, that we seemed to have a lively, nourishing sort of rapport, which not even a full transcript of our endless conversation could convey. At some point, I threw etiquette to the winds and asked point-blank if he would take off his glasses, just for me.

His reluctance was obviously genuine, but he reached up and removed the glasses. "Oh my God," I blurted like an idiot. "You look like an Australian shepherd!" For Kumo had one blue eye, while the other was brownish-green. Both were remarkably nice eyes, but it was not a usual look for a Japanese. Finally, after I had pried shamelessly, he explained that he was a quarter Mongol on his father's side. Ah, I thought enviously, that explains the cheekbones.

"That's the reason I went to college in the States," Kumo said, "and that's also why I prefer to work for foreigners. Japanese put a high premium on pedigree, and it's not an easy country to be a hybrid in. The worst I've been called with my shades on is an affected hipster, whereas without them I've been called a mongrel gutter-dog, and a *gaijin* bastard. Those were isolated incidents, and both people were drunk, but I can't bear the constant silent speculation: 'Obviously he isn't one of us, but what the hell *is* he?' So the glasses are my crutch," Kumo wound up. "What's yours, I wonder?"

"Resenting my parents, I guess," I said, and I ended up telling him that whole sad story. By the time we had scraped the last renegade speck of chocolate-espresso *pot de crème* from our sampler plates, I felt that we had gone through something rather intense together and come out stronger, like a sword that has been annealed at high heat.

Oh, by the way: the chocolate sampler was sublime. My favorite thing was probably the warm dark-chocolate cakes with Frangelico ice cream, topped with toasted hazelnuts, but everything else was so unbelievably delicious that I think I'll call it an eight-way tie.

I must have walked down that same street in Asakusa twenty times, but I never saw the window full of snakes. I had asked Kumo to take me home by way of Asakusa (which is like going from Paris to London via Dar Es Salaam) simply because it's one of my favorite parts of Tokyo, and I crave frequent transfusions of the delightfully archaic atmosphere. But when we passed a storefront window filled with live snakes of various sizes swarming all over each other, looking like Medusa on a bad hair day, I had to stop and investigate.

A sign in the window said simply, "Snakes For Health." There was no one in the shop, which was musty and dark and cluttered with a fascinating array of antiquated trinkets, including several crumbling ceramic statuettes of Benten. I could imagine Edo-period merchants and samurai and geisha coming in to purchase a pint of serpent's milk, or a kilo of snake-lox.

Just then a very large head appeared from behind a curtained door, followed by a very small body. At first I thought it was an odd-looking child, but when I looked at the hands (grayish-brown, wrinkled, with curved yellow nails like nicotine-stained ivory) I realized it was an old person wearing a Noh mask of a young girl. "May I help you?" said a muffled, creaky voice from behind the mask.

"Um—" I said, temporarily dumbstruck.

"I see, you have a question," said the masked person. I was pretty sure it was an old woman, but I wouldn't have bet Yasger's Farm on it.

"Well, in a way," I said reluctantly, and then I proceeded to share an expurgated version of what had happened at the Snake-Goddess shrine and afterward. I thought of Kumo Takatori, precariously double-parked somewhere on the manic streets of Asakusa, but I couldn't seem to stop talking. When I finished my story, the person in the young-girl mask nodded sagely and something about that gesture confirmed my hunch that there was a woman behind the mask.

"Yes," she said. "The Snake Spell. They put powdered snake in the saké, and of course you know what that does to the blood of a human."

"No, I don't know! What does it do?" I cried, but the old woman didn't seem to have heard me. "What about being possessed by the Snake Goddess's spirit?" I added. "I've heard that that's part of the spell."

"There is one antidote to this particular sort of bewitchment," she said. "It will remove the residue of the enchanted saké from your system, and free you from the lively spirit of the Snake Goddess. But are you absolutely sure you want to return to normal?"

I thought for a moment. The New Bronwyn's adventures had definitely been interesting, but I was ready to get back to quiet and dull. "Yes," I said, "I would like to try the antidote."

It should have been a fantastic evening. Kumo and I had made such a promising connection at Cacao that when he dropped me off, I had spontaneously invited him to go to dinner at Tintoretto that night—my treat. It would save me the trouble of buying him the requisite gift to express my gratitude for his chauffering services, and besides, I quite enjoyed his company.

"I'd be happy to go," Kumo said. "It's just that ..."

"What?" I asked anxiously.

"Oh, nothing," he said. "I'll pick you up at seven o'clock."

I only had an hour to get ready, and I found myself in a tizzy, as if I were getting ready for a big date. It wasn't a date, of course, just a farewell dinner after a somewhat bizarre weekend. It wasn't even a crypto-date, where you pretend it isn't a date but you both know it is. Still, I felt absurdly excited, and not even chamomile tea and "Sheep May Safely Graze" could calm me down.

I couldn't decide whether to go as my old or new self, so I compromised: I put on about half as much makeup as the cosmetologist at Atelier Amadeo had prescribed, twisted my hair up in 1940s-style side-rolls with a braided bun at the back, and wore one of my new dresses (dark blue polished cotton with a deep square neck, Rapunzel-sleeves embroidered with silver-thread arabesques, a dropped waist, and a very full ballerina-length skirt). I wore pumps, too, midnight-blue suede Charles Jourdans with three-inch heels and narrow ties at the ankles. Around my neck, of course, was the exquisite Benten necklace. It had been more a relief than a disappointment to learn that it wasn't a valuable antique, after all, because that meant I would be able to keep it.

As Kumo's arrival grew imminent, I began to feel a little nervous about this subtle adjustment in our roles. What if we ran out of things to talk about? Would he be wearing his chauffeur's uniform? Did he (God forbid) think that my asking him to join me for dinner was an expression of romantic interest? And where should I sit: in the back, as usual, or up front with him?

Bronwyn was surprised when the doorbell rang at seven o'clock, for in the past the driver had always honked his horn from the street. She opened the door and there he stood, smiling shyly. "Oh, Kumo!" she burst out. "You look wonderful!" She felt that curious dip in her viscera again, and it occurred to her that the Snake Spell antidote really should have taken effect by then.

Kumo Takatori was not wearing his physique-camouflaging Pachinko Piaf-designed chauffeur's uniform. He was dressed in a high-necked purple cotton Cossack shirt, pleated gray pants, and gray lace-up boots; he had combed his shoulder-length hair into a low ponytail, and his moustache and goatee were gone. Gone, too, were the off-putting Ray-Bans, and Bronwyn was momentarily mesmerized by the startling beauty of his mismatched eyes. Good grief, she thought, how could I not have noticed how attractive this man is?

"You look wonderful, too," Kumo said. "I like this glamorous princess look, but I have to admit that I also like it when you look like—well, like a librarian. It's rather mysterious and, um, tantalizing." Bronwyn swallowed. This wasn't the scenario she had imagined at all.

"There was a small problem with the car," Kumo said. "Mr. Krill—I mean Mr. Jesperson, that's Ms. Krill's husband—said they needed to use it tonight, if you didn't mind." He led Bronwyn to a white Porsche 911 Turbo that was parked by the curb, surrounded by a crowd of curious children and admiring adult males.

"Where did you get this?" Bronwyn asked as she climbed in. The back seat was barely big enough for a child, or a couple of dogs, so there was no question about where she would sit.

"Oh, I, um, borrowed it from a friend," said Kumo.

"It's a chariot," said Bronwyn.

There was a full moon that night, a pumpkin-colored beauty, and we both pretended that we could see the rabbit who supposedly lives there, according to Japanese folk belief. The moon followed us all the way to Kamakura, hovering overhead like a benevolent fairy godmother. As we rode along, sitting shoulder to shoulder in the fast, low, car, I abandoned the no-way-this-is-a-date pose, and found myself feeling more and more romantic toward Kumo Takatori. I wasn't sure how he was feeling, although I did hear him gulp audibly, like a snake swallowing an egg, every time I looked over at him and smiled for no reason at all.

Tintoretto, despite its name, was not an Italian restaurant. The chef was a Japanese woman who had studied art history in Florence, sculpture in England, painting in Paris, and neon art in Los Angeles before deciding that what she really wanted to do was to cook. After paying her dues at famous restaurants all over the world, she had saved enough money to buy an abandoned Tendai temple in the country near Kamakura, with a view of the sea. She had gutted the temple and made it into one large room with original murals on all the walls. The murals, which she had designed and painted with the help of her "life partner" (a Frenchwoman who was a textile designer-turned-pastry chef) depicted familiar themes from Japanese folk art: exquisite women with fox-tails concealed beneath their skirts, ghosts with featureless faces and long black hair, saké-drinking badgers disguised as priests, dragon-snakes gone mad with love. As for the food, it was an inspired pastiche of French, Moroccan, and Thai influences, with the emphasis on freshness, seasonality, artistic presentation, and sheer surprise. The music ranged from Rameau to *gamelan*, the clientele was picturesque and eclectic, and the view of sea and pines had already inspired numerous amateur haiku poets to chalk their impressions, in 5-7-5 verse, on a blackboard provided for that purpose. Tintoretto was definitely the place to be, but it was so popular that there was no hope of getting a table if you blithely showed up without a reservation.

So what went wrong? First, they had somehow managed to misplace our reservation, so we had to sit at the "dining bar," looking into the bustling glass-enclosed kitchen instead of gazing out at the tranquil moonlit sea. That wasn't a fatal glitch, by any means, and we were getting along fine until two huge shadows fell across my bamboo placemat.

I looked up and there they were: the gorgeous Nio Brothers, grinning above me. When I stood up, thinking to shake their hands, or bow, they enveloped me in a breathtaking three-way embrace that involved a disturbing degree of groin-to-groin contact. (I remember thinking, Oh dear, maybe I should have worn my flats.) I was aroused and attracted, I'll admit it, and once again I cursed the ineffectiveness of the snake-shop antidote.

As I was chatting with Kengo and Kosuke (and learning that Kengo was called "the monk" as a joke, because he was so notoriously uncelibate), I heard a female voice say "Kumo! I'm so glad to see you! You look good enough to eat! Are you alone?"

To which my crypto-date replied tersely, "It would appear that I am."

I looked over and saw the stunner from Aoyama, dressed in a clingy black minidress, enfolding Kumo in a distinctly un-Japanese hug. It went downhill from there. Kumo spent the entire meal talking to his little friend, who was obviously smitten with him, while I pretended to be engrossed in conversation with my two enormous acquaintances. When I reminded Kosuke that he had promised to tell me about the Snake Spell, he laughed and said, "Oh, it's just a cute little ritual, really. If it makes you feel more liberated to think you're possessed by the spirit of the Snake Goddess, that's great. But you don't need any magic potion to turn you into a vessel of pleasure. We can do that for you!"

"Hear, hear," said Kengo, smiling with his tongue between his teeth, and then he stared at me with such intensity that I had to avert my eyes. I had felt strongly drawn to him the day before, when I thought he was a dishy monk, but now I just saw him as another guy on the make.

The Evil Jungle Couscous was supremely delicious and the Nivole Moscato d'Asti was like drinking stars, but I was too upset about my rift with Kumo to fully enjoy the meal. I tried to grab the bill when it came, but Kumo stubbornly insisted on paying for both of us, which made me feel even worse. As we were leaving I saw him giving his business card to the scantily-clad temptress, and I retaliated by saying loudly to the Nio Brothers, "Let's get together soon, all right?"

Kosuke leaned forward and whispered in my ear, "Yes, let's. Have you ever tried a threesome?"

I was shocked. "I haven't even tried a twosome," I whispered back.

"That can be arranged, too," Kosuke said, with what might have been a leer, and Kengo nodded enthusiastically. Suddenly it all seemed very unwholesome. They were enormously seductive, and charming in a slick, practiced way, but they obviously lived in the erotic fast lane, while I was still stuck in the parking lot. I didn't think I wanted either of them to be my first lover, and I knew I would probably never be ready to venture into the carpool lane of the sexual Autobahn.

Kumo and I barely spoke, all the way home. The big orange moon was still visible low on the horizon, but instead of a fairy godmother it now seemed like a searchlight trained on the failure of an outing that had appeared so full of promise.

Back in Mita San-chome, Kumo walked me dutifully to my door. "Won't you come in for a cup of tea?" I asked. I was feeling sick about our lost rapport, and I thought perhaps we might sit down and talk about why the evening had turned out to be such a disappointment.

Kumo looked down at his watch. "I'm sorry," he said, "but I really have to go. Well, please take care of yourself!" And then he was gone, with a roar of the engine and a casual wave of the hand, and I was left standing alone on my doorstep, under a ridiculously romantic moon, feeling as if I had just been punched in the heart.

Bronwyn had once heard someone refer to the telephone as an instrument of torture. As the following week passed, that phrase began to pop into her head every time the phone rang at work, or didn't ring at home. She kept busy, of course. In addition to the usual assistant-librarian tasks, she had had to whip up a page of sanitized, depersonalized notes about the Snake Goddess festival for Erica's newsletter. This required the reading of her journal entries, which yielded a bittersweet epiphany: that her growing fondness for the extraordinary chauffeur was directly analogous with the Snake Goddess's penchant for horse-carriage drivers. Bronwyn had found her own account of the weekend's events amazing, alarming, and, finally, depressing, since the last entry ended with Kumo's abrupt departure—not with a reconciliatory kiss and a promise of future meetings, which was the very least she had hoped for.

Bronwyn couldn't stop thinking about Kumo. She wasn't fantasizing about him as a boyfriend or a lover, exactly; rather, it was his essence, his presence, and his easy conversation she craved. By Friday her longing had begun to teeter on the edge of desperation, and she decided that she simply had to see him, somehow. She timed her departure from the library to coincide with Erica Krill's, and they walked out to the street together.

When Bronwyn saw the platinum Infiniti parked by the curb she felt excited, nervous, nauseated, apprehensive, and happy, all at once. I'm going to see his face, she thought. That's all that matters. Erica tapped on the dark-tinted window of the Infiniti with her gleaming fingernails. "Roll down the window, darling," she said.

Darling? She calls him 'Darling'? Oh my God, Bronwyn thought in horror, *Kumo is Erica's lover!*

But there was an even greater shock in store for her, for when the tinted window slid down, the person in the driver's seat was not Kumo Takatori at all. It was a man whom Erica introduced as "my husband, John-Jacob Jesperson. I call him Jake, but he prefers John."

Bronwyn knew the man in the car by another name entirely: Simon Xavier Quimby. While she stared in disbelief, trying to digest the startling revelation that the charismatic, lying cad who had picked her up at FaxLoveCity was actually Erica Krill's Renaissance-man husband, he continued to smile at her in a polite, neutral way. After a moment it occurred to Bronwyn that perhaps he didn't recognize her, for she was wearing glasses instead of contacts, and she had her foxy hair tucked up under a blue straw hat, She was immensely relieved when the Infiniti finally drove away.

It was just as well that her mind was totally occupied with thoughts of Kumo. Otherwise, Bronwyn might have spent the weekend stewing over the startling realization that if "Simon Quimby" hadn't shown his true beastly colors, she, Bronwyn LaFarge, could have ended up committing inadvertent adultery with Erica Krill's husband in the back of a rented limousine. The man was obviously a faithless spouse, and possibly an abusive one as well. So much for the perfect life of Erica Krill, Bronwyn thought, with neither malice nor glee.

Seeing that odious beast made me appreciate Kumo's good qualities even more acutely, and I found myself missing him more each minute. I felt that if I didn't see or speak with him I would shrivel up and die, like a garden slug on a salt lick. I just needed to hear his voice, even if it was telling me that I wasn't his type, or that he had a girlfriend. (Oh, no! What if he had already gotten together with the sophisticated beauty in the black minidress?)

I toyed briefly with the idea of calling Kosuke, or Kengo, but I knew their interest in me was purely sexual, and I wanted more than that. To make things worse, I was feeling the pesky stirrings in my loins several times a day, whenever I thought about how Kumo had looked lying under the tree at the Eternal Library, or how he had leaned over to brush a bit of chocolate puff pastry off my cheek. Obviously the antidote had been some sort of placebo, and an expensive one at that. Damn that old charlatan, I thought, and on Saturday morning I took the train to Asakusa to ask for a refund.

The shop was just the same, musty and timeless, but the old person in the mask was nowhere to be seen. In her place, behind the counter, was a brisk-mannered young man with a pomaded brush cut and a white lab coat. He introduced himself as the eldest son of the family, and explained that he was studying to be a pharmacist and was thinking about turning the old-fashioned shop into an all-night drugstore after he graduated.

I didn't want to launch into my complaint too abruptly, so I said, "Who was the person who waited on me last time, in some sort of Noh mask?"

"Oh, that was Grandma," the young man said with an affectionate laugh. "She's nearly ninety, and she's still a scamp. No, seriously, she's incredibly young at heart. You know those American male strippers, the Chippendales? When they came to Tokyo last year Granny made my sister Eriko take her, and she sat in the front row waving thousand-yen bills and shouting 'Hubba hubba!' or words to that effect. Eriko was mortified."

"But what about the antidote she sold me, for the Snake Spell, and the enchanted saké? It was this really nasty-tasting stuff, and it wasn't cheap, and it was supposed to make me stop feeling this sort of um, congestion, only it hasn't worked at all."

The modern young man chuckled. "Oh, Granny told me about that. She never likes to turn a customer away, so she has a tendency to improvise a fair amount. Apparently she mixed up some powdered snakeskin with several kinds of Chinese medicine, and added a little wormwood, just to make it taste convincingly foul."

"Snakeskin? Is that like hair of the dog?"

"Hair of the—? Oh, I get it: skin of the snake. That's good," said the young man, but he didn't sound terribly amused.

"So you're saying the antidote was a placebo," I said, serious again. "Do you know of anything that will make me feel normal again? Maybe something I could get at a regular pharmacy, like saltpeter or reverse-Viagra? I mean, I'm supposed to have a underactive libido and I never used to feel like this, so I know something is terribly wrong with my system."

The pharmacist-in-training smiled. "Maybe you don't have a weak libido at all," he said. "Maybe you just never let it off the leash. Or maybe you never met the right person to share it with. Did it ever occur to you that you might just be in love?"

Once she realized that she was a newly awakened woman in love, a sexual Rip Van Winkle who was feeling a normal degree of desire for the object of her affection, Bronwyn felt as though the scales (or the Ray-Bans) had dropped from her eyes. Now all she had to do was to find Kumo, and tell him how she felt, and let the chips fall where they might.

In this determined frame of mind, Bronwyn was skimming the Sunday paper when she noticed that there was an opening on Monday of an exhibit of paintings by Madoka Morokoshi, the famous architect who happened to be Kumo's aunt. Bronwyn knew from previous experience that the private opening party would be held on Sunday night. This is fate, she thought.

She put on her last new outfit, a mercurial aurora borealis of a gown from Pachinko Piaf's Scheherazade Collection, constructed of fifteen separate pieces of two-ply, hand-dyed silk (pinks and oranges on one side, blues and greens on the other). She did her hair à la Amadeo, and applied a moderate amount of makeup, as artfully as she could. Bronwyn remembered reading somewhere that makeup was the modern woman's version of a tribal mask, a way of creating a metaphysical moat, and that seemed to make a lot of sense. For some reason she found that she felt braver and less vulnerable, with makeup on than when her face was bare, and as she set out to confront the man she was now sure she loved, a man who clearly did not reciprocate her feelings, she needed all the courage and invulnerability she could muster.

Bronwyn found Madoka Morokoshi's paintings impressive, but disturbing—huge sea-and-sunset-colored portraits of long-haired, dreamy-faced, beautifully dressed women staring into mirrors from which gazed back images of gorgeously dressed skeletons with long flowing hair. It was an old conceit, but the artist had made it her own by dressing the women not in kimono but in what appeared to be sorcerers' robes, all midnight-blue velvet, gold stars, and crescent moons.

"Intimations of mortality, *n'est-ce pas*?" said a husky French-accented voice at Bronwyn's shoulder, and she turned to find a very tall, thin person with an androgynous worldly-gamin face, elliptical hazel eyes, and short spiky black hair. "By the way," the person added, "that dress looks wonderful on you—you have the height, and the gravitas, and the imagination to wear it."

"Thank you," said Bronwyn. Not only was the stranger very unusual-looking, she (or he) was dressed in a long black battery-powered cape which replicated a starry, moonless night, complete with trailing comets, luminous planets, and opalescent galaxies.

"I love your cape," Bronwyn said. "It reminds me of a trip to the planetarium."

"Bingo," said the French-accented voice, and Bronwyn couldn't help visualizing the word as "*bingaux*." Just then a young Japanese man with waist-length bleached-blond hair, whose bare, shapely torso was completely tattooed with realistic-looking fruit, so that he resembled one of those nineteenth-century *trompe l'oeil* paintings, came up to them and whispered something in the androgynous French person's ear.

"*Excusez-moi*," the person said to Bronwyn. "I'm glad you have the dress, and I hope it brings you luck." And then he (or she) was gone, arm in arm with the young man with the fruitful torso, one long-fingered hand stuck cozily in the back pocket of the tattooed man's black leather trousers. Who was that? Bronwyn asked herself, for the face had seemed somehow familiar.

Bronwyn cast a longing eye at the individual green-tea mousses served in celadon teacups, but she felt that since she had essentially crashed the opening, she wasn't entitled to eat any of the food. She thought of asking Kumo's aunt, a slender, elegant woman of sixty with silver hair worn in a China-doll bob, to give Kumo a message. But what could she say? "I love your nephew madly, and I think he may hate me, but could you please tell him to give me a call anyway?"

Kumo never showed up, and as she stood forlornly waiting for a cab, Bronwyn thought about the person who had talked to her about the dress. It was the first time she had ever met someone whose appearance was so completely ambiguous that she couldn't even hazard a guess as to the person's gender. Yet why, she thought, does everyone have to be ostentatiously male or female in this world? If it's acceptable to stray outside the political two-party system, why shouldn't a human being opt to be a sexual "independent" if neither of the two conventional parties—male, or female—seem to fill the bill? Bronwyn didn't understand why it should be such a big deal if someone chose "undecided" instead of male or female, gay or Lesbian. Like the designer Pachinko Piaf, she thought; all the publicity about "what" he or she is, while undoubtedly good for business, must be very painful. And why should one's sexuality be anyone else's business, anyway?

With a sudden frisson Bronwyn realized what her subconscious had already deduced: that the very tall person in the cosmogonous cloak who had complimented her on her dress had, in fact, been Pachinko Piaf: the person who designed it in the first place. How could I have been so dense? she asked herself. The wild clothes, the French accent, the Japanese eyes, that universal, hermaphroditic face ...

Bronwyn was so caught up in her thoughts that she didn't hear the footsteps behind her, and she jumped at least three inches when a familiar male voice said, "What did you think of the paintings?"

There's a Crosby, Stills & Nash song that I like—yes, I know they were at Woodstock, along with Neil Young, but I have forgiven them that lapse of taste. After all, Woodstock took place more than twenty-five years ago, and a lot of the fresh-faced, pinwheel-eyed freaks in the audience have grown up, gone to law school, voted Republican, and lost their electrified hair. Besides, I've begun to realize, as time goes by, that forgiveness makes a better fertilizer than resentment.

The CSN song is called "Song for Susan," and it contains the lines "Fooling myself about how to exist/All by myself, there was much I had missed/You came and showed me what happiness is ..." Kumo doesn't know it yet, but I think that's going to be our song. Unless, of course, he has a better suggestion.

That was him behind me on the street, of course. He was leaning on an old blue bicycle, looking very young, very shy, and very lovely, dressed in jeans and one of those designer sweatshirts decorated with endearingly incoherent English (his read, in large Gothic letters, POSH BOY PRIVATE BEACH PARTY).

"Hello, Kumo," I said with feigned casualness, for my heart was leaping about like a cat in a hot tub. "Are you going to the show?"

"I was planning to," he said, "but I seem to be late, and underdressed."

"No, you look fine," I said. We went on like that for a few minutes, making excruciatingly superficial small talk, when I just wanted to shout, "I love you! Why don't you love me?"

"Well," Kumo said after our silly conversation had collapsed from its own weightlessness, "I think I'll come back and see the paintings another time." He slowly disengaged the kickstand of his bicycle with his foot; that struck me as a cruelly terminal, dismissive gesture, and I felt deeply, profoundly miserable.

"See you around," he said, and then he climbed on his creaky old bike and pedaled off. I turned away to look for a cab—where were all the taxis tonight, I wondered?—and only by tensing my jaw muscles and opening my eyes very wide was I able to keep from being blinded by tears. To make matters worse, I dropped my bag, and all my cosmic essentials spilled onto the sidewalk: my chaotic organizer, my hairbrush, my makeup bag, the laminated photo I carry around (I'm not sure why). It's a snapshot a neighbor took of my parents—both looking about twenty years old, though they were past forty at the time—standing by their gray Volkswagen bus, just as they were setting out on their annual pilgrimage from Santa Cruz to Jimi Hendrix's memorial on Capitol Hill in Seattle, fifteen minutes before the three-ton refrigerator truck driven by a man who habitually drank large quantities of beer for breakfast ran a red light on Highway 101 and plowed into them, head on.

Just as I finished rounding up my treasures, with unstoppable tears pouring from my eyes for a number of reasons, a big yellow taxi stopped. The automatic door swung open, and as I was about to climb in I heard a voice behind me saying, "Um, actually, if you aren't busy, there's something I'd like to show you."

I apologized to the taxi driver, who muttered something vaguely xenophobic as the automatic door slammed in my smiling face, but I didn't care. I was going to spend some time with Kumo, and even if he was just whisking me off to a quiet place to have The Big Talk (I'm in love with someone else; Foreigners make me nervous; You're not my type, but I hope we can be friends) I was still overjoyed to be in his presence, to bask in his essence, to partake of his conversation again.

Sengakuji Temple at night is an empire of fog. The perennial dry-ice miasma shrouding the temple grounds is actually a thick haze of incense smoke that hovers above the ancient trees and historic tombs like genuine weather. For Sengakuji is the resting place of the Forty-Seven Ronin, revered by all Japanese for their embodiment of the samurai principles of loyalty in life and nobility in death, and the throngs that visit the temple every day show their respect by lighting great fistfuls of sweet and acrid incense in front of the multiple graves.

"Where are we going?" Bronwyn called out as they rode along on the bumpy sidewalks, Kumo pedaling silently while she balanced on the small rectangular book-rack and clung (though not as tightly as she would have liked) to his lean, muscular back.

"I'm taking you to my favorite night spot," Kumo said, and that was the extent of their conversation. Bronwyn was naturally expecting that they would end up at a pub, or a coffee shop, or a bar of some sort, so she was surprised when Kumo rode his bicycle into a fragrant cloud of incense smoke and said, "We're here."

"Sengakuji," said Bronwyn, reading the sign. "I've been meaning to come out here ever since I arrived in Tokyo. But where's your favorite nightspot?"

"Over here," said Kumo, putting his bicycle in a rack and disappearing into the aromatic fog. Bronwyn ran after him and, after threading a path through the incense-shrouded gravestones, they ended up on a little rise. "Have a seat," said Kumo, spreading out a large red bandanna. "There's no cover charge." He explained that he lived nearby and often liked to come sit on this little hill and think about his problems, and possibilities. "I've been spending a lot of time up here this past week," he said, nervously chewing on a fingernail and staring at the ground.

They sat in silence for a few minutes, looking out over the mysterious, hazy graveyard and beyond to the lights of the insomniac city. Finally Kumo spoke. "Do you think men and women can be friends?" he asked.

Uh-oh, thought Bronwyn, here it comes: *I really like you as a person, but ...*

"I suppose so," she said. "It just seems to get complicated when one person wants something more."

"You mean like romance?"

Bronwyn nodded, and they sat in silence for a few more minutes. A crow flew overhead, screeching in outrage; perhaps, thought Bronwyn, it was voicing its resentment over the paving of the fields where it should, by natural right, have been happily night-marauding among the tender lettuce and young corn.

"Well," said Kumo, standing up, "I suppose we should be going."

No, Bronwyn said to herself with a sudden rush of resolve, I'm not going home until I know exactly where I stand. "Wait," she said out loud, "let's just sit here for five more minutes." Obediently, Kumo sat down. "Now," said Bronwyn, heart pounding, lungs pumping hard, "I want you to tell me exactly what you think and feel about me." She was amazed, and a bit appalled, at her own bravery.

"Are you sure you want to know?" Kumo said slowly.

He hates me, Bronwyn thought. He thinks I'm a tramp, he's in love with someone else, he never wants to see me again. "Yes," she said, "I'm sure I want to know."

It was like a dream, except that I seldom have such satisfying dreams. Kumo went back to the very beginning, to that Saturday morning when I came running out in bare feet, carrying my shoes and looking, he said "like the quintessential disorganized librarian." He loved me from that moment, he said, but the more he watched me consorting with glamorous men, the more convinced he became that he would never have a chance. Even after our delightful afternoon at Cacao, he still thought I only liked him as a friend, or as an acquaintance.

When I invited him to join me for dinner on that last Sunday night, he was thrown into a panic, for he had already returned the Infiniti to the Krill/Jesperson garage, and he knew they planned to use it. He felt that I was a woman who expected to go first-class, so he raided his savings account and went out and rented the white Porsche. It would have cost him an extra hundred dollars to keep it past midnight; that was why he had glanced at his watch and then refused my offer of a cup of tea.

"I never wanted anything so much as I wanted to kiss you goodnight that night, even though we weren't exactly on speaking terms on the way home," he said. "But I knew that if you were receptive I would never be able to drag myself away, and I felt that even if you did respond it would just be because of the wine, or the Snake Spell, or some temporary flush of romantic illusion, and the next day you would tell me that it had all been a mistake. Still, even after I drove away I thought of going back, because a hundred dollars didn't seem like a very steep price for a kiss from you, even if it turned out to be the first and last one for me."

"But why didn't you come back after you dropped the car off?" I asked.

"It didn't even occur to me; I was too busy agonizing over all the reasons why you couldn't possibly want someone like me in your life. And to be honest, I was jealous of those two big guys who monopolized you all night, while I was stuck talking to Erica's boring fashion-magazine friend. I felt certain that you were going to get together with one of them later on, somehow. So I came up here, and sat and thought for most of the night."

"If you ever get insomnia again," I said, "promise me you won't waste it on a graveyard. I'll be happy to stay up all night with you, any time."

"Do you mean as a friend?" Kumo asked, for I still hadn't declared my feelings for him.

"I mean as anything you want me to be," I said. "And I haven't been drinking, and the Snake Spell seems to have been a hormonal illusion, and right now there's nothing I want more than to kiss you." And so we shared our first kiss, there above the noble tombstones, with our lungs full of incense and our hearts full of feelings made sweeter for having been in doubt.

"There was one other thing that made me feel I had no chance," Kumo said a bit later, when we came up for breath. "That was the fact that you were obviously quite active, um, sexually, and your partners were such sophisticated men, that I didn't feel I could compete. You see, I'm not really very experienced, although I have had quite a number of opportunities. It's just that I always wanted the first time to be special, with someone I really loved, and I always imagined it would be in some very poetic setting, like high on a hill overlooking the sea, surrounded by wildflowers, with birds singing in the trees."

I shook my head in disbelief. "I know," Kumo said, "that probably sounds impossibly stupid and romantic."

"No, not at all!" I said. "It sounds uncannily like my own stupid, impossibly romantic fantasy."

"Oh," said Kumo sadly, "did you do it for the first time in a place like that?"

"No," I said. "Believe it or not, I'm still a virgin."

"No! Really?" He sounded relieved, and excited. "Still," he said cautiously, "you are much more experienced than I am, so you will have to be my teacher, if we ever ..."

"Dearest Kumo," I said, "when the time comes, I am certain that you will be absolutely magnificent. And so will I."

Back at work, her colleagues began to compliment Bronwyn on how radiant she looked. "Have you been getting facials?" Erica Krill asked one afternoon. "Or is it a new foundation?"

Exactly, Bronwyn thought with a secret smile, but she just said, "Actually, that reminds me of something the makeup artist at Atelier Amadeo said to me. I asked her what was the best sort of rouge to use, powder or gel, and she said, 'My dear, true love is the ultimate blusher.'"

"Yes, I suppose it would be," said Erica Krill in a rather subdued voice, and then she hurried away. Poor Erica, Bronwyn thought. It can't be easy being married to a snake in the grass like Simon, I mean John-Jacob. Maybe she ought to sign up for a GRTBR seminar.

One day just before noon Bronwyn looked out of her office window and saw Kumo, who had the day off from his new apprentice-draftsman's job and had come to take her to his favorite handmade-noodle restaurant for lunch. All men are not beasts, after all, she thought happily as she watched Kumo reach into his bicycle bag and take out a book. She could just make out the title: *Food for Centaurs.* That reminded her of something else that had happened that magical night at Sengakuji: Kumo had produced her *Secret Life of the Snake Goddess* book from his bag, confessing that when he found it on the floor of the car after Bronwyn's visit to Atelier Amadeo, he had decided to keep it for a while so he would have an excuse to get in touch with her again, after the weekend. He was obviously expecting to be lectured or at least chided, but Bronwyn just looked at him with soft eyes and said, "I think you're the dearest man on the planet."

This is really too good to be true, Bronwyn told herself now, as she gazed out the window. It's like a fairy tale, or a Hollywood movie, certainly not the sort of thing I ever dreamed would happen to me. I'm living in Tokyo, I'm having strange if not precisely supernatural adventures, and I adore my job. On top of all that, I have a date for lunch, if not for life, with the man I now love even more than my cats—the man who has promised to take me away this weekend, to a hot-spring inn on a high green hill by the sea, where we may or may not make love, but will definitely have a lovely time.

The garden of Cosmopolis House was famous for its maples in November, for its irises in June, for its cherry blossoms in April, and for its enormous gold and silver carp all year round. During this week in mid-April, the cherry blossoms were at their peak, and hundreds of people passed through the garden every day to marvel at the delicate beauty of the flowers, and to reflect upon the evanescence of human life. Tycoons and laborers, socialites and shopgirls; made equal by wonderment, they would spread out their straw mats, uncork a vat or two of saké, and drink themselves blind while the gossamer blossoms fell around them like feathers from a soft pink dove. As Bronwyn watched tenderly from the window, Kumo took his book into the blooming garden and sat down on a granite bench to wait for her.

She was stepping into the elevator a few minutes later when it occurred to her that she needed a new mantra, something upbeat to replace the spectacularly obsolete "All men are beasts." Perhaps a Lennon-McCartneyish "All you need is love"? But that wasn't true, for her at least. Love was sheer delight, but she needed other things, as well. Work, nature, beauty, cats, friends, delicious things to do and read and eat.

Bronwyn put her finger on the "G" button, and at that same instant a new chant popped into her head, fully formed, as if by magic or inspiration:

Work is pudding
Art is pie
Life is the apple
Of my eye.

Forgiveness is treacle
Compassion is steak
And love is the icing
On the cake.

Mentally, Bronwyn critiqued this little gift from the gods. *Soppy yet sweet. Needs work. I like it.* And then it occurred to her that aside from the unavoidable non-vegetarian rhyme for "cake," it was just the sort of idealistic hippie sentiment her parents would have embraced. But really—Bronwyn Blue-Moon Butterfly Cabot LaFarge thought as she strolled through a diaphanous slow-motion shower of cherry-blossom petals, so thick that she could barely see Kumo at the other end of the garden—really, there was nothing so terribly wrong with that.

NAKED IN THE MOONLIGHT

I ought to tell you that she
has changed her shape ...

—DAVID GARNETT
Lady Into Fox

oncombres au gingembre," said the girl with spiky chartreuse hair to the balding bodybuilder in the cellophane jumpsuit. "Try to say it five times, fast." Tokiyuki Kaminari was standing in line behind the couple, eagerly eavesdropping on their exotic conversation. He could recognize an occasional English word, but he had no idea what the strange-looking foreigners were talking about.

The line was moving faster now, and Toki was beginning to get nervous. He stuck his right hand into the pocket of his rented tuxedo and clutched his new good-luck amulet. Behind him were two young Japanese women dressed in garish flowered minidresses and six-inch platform shoes (probably sexually promiscuous Office Ladies, Toki thought uncharitably) who were singing Beatles songs in phonetic English. "*Obu-ra-ji, obu-ra-da, raifu gozu on,* yeah!" they sang in high, clear voices, but Toki could tell that they were anxious too.

Toki had bought the amulet earlier that day at the neighborhood Inari shrine, from an elderly priest dressed in culottes of azure linen over a white kimono. The old man had large translucent ears filled with intricate seashell-whorls, and in the fleshy center of each lobe there was a black mole, like an onyx earring-stud. Toki was so mesmerized by those rococo ears that he had to ask the priest to repeat his question.

"I said, 'What do you wish to pray for?'" the old man said in a creaky, coagulated voice. Toki felt reluctant to explain why he wanted the amulet; his reason seemed too worldly, and too embarrassing.

"Oh, um," he began, and he was relieved when the priest interrupted him.

"Perhaps you wish to pass an examination?" the old man said. He was holding the amulet in his long, knobby fingers (amber and thick-jointed, like aged bamboo), stroking the rectangle of red-and-gold brocade as if it were a fluffy cat or a new moustache. Inside the brocade casing was a piece of thin paper with mystic writing on it. Peeking at the contents, the priest had warned, could change good luck to bad.

"Yes, that's it, an exam!" Toki said eagerly. He thought of the cruel mascaraed eyes of the doorman, flicking disdainfully from the top of Toki's shaggy head to the tips of his outdated dress shoes before sneering, "Sorry, next!" It *was* a sort of examination, in a way: the entrance exam for the most popular disco in Japan.

"Yes," he repeated. "That's right. I'm hoping to pass an examination."

"Then this will definitely help," croaked the old priest, as he poked the amulet into a small paper bag with the luminous opacity of paraffin and the shrine's name stamped on the bottom in vermilion ink. Toki felt a sudden urge to confide in the elderly man, to share his obsession and his frustration, but then he imagined the puzzled look in the filmy eyes, so he just said, "Thank you," bowed, and walked away. That priest probably doesn't even know what a discothèque is, he thought. He and I aren't just different generations; we're almost like different species. Toki ran down the stone steps of the shrine, oblivious to the dovesongs and the violet shadows and the faint aroma of late-summer honeysuckle, for there was only one thing on his mind: gaining admittance to the inner sanctum of Hell.

As it turned out, the amulet was no help at all. As he had on his first three tries, Toki flunked the entrance examination. Which is to say, the intimidating doorman looked disdainfully at Toki in his rented black-and-white tuxedo and said, "Sorry, next!"

"Okay," Toki said to himself as he headed toward a street-corner noodle stand to indulge in some serious *yakezake*: the ritual drowning of sorrows in saké. "This is it. I'm not going to keep banging my head against that snobbish wall forever. I'll try one more time, and after that I promise I'll give up and start living a sensible life again."

When an international consortium of professional athletes, software tycoons, and semi-famous entertainers decided to buy a former roller-skating rink on a back street in Roppongi and turn it into a discothèque, they expected a certain amount of success. To their astonishment, within a week of its grand opening their club was the single most popular—and profitable—night spot on the Pacific Rim.

The members of NightVision, Inc.—the consortium's legal name—ascribed that phenomenal success to four things: celebrity mystique, location, timing, and distinctive decor. The design was the work of two environmental artists, a brother-and-sister team named Tei and Taya Uno. As it happened, when they got the call from NightVision, Inc., Tei and Taya had just returned from a visit to Hong Kong, where they had been intrigued by the infernal sculptures and murals at Tiger Balm Gardens. So when NightVision's president, a retired period-drama actress named Kesa Kokubo, asked them to suggest a theme for the club, the Unos said, half-jokingly, "What about 'Hell'?"

"That's truly profound," said Kesa Kokubo solemnly, and all the other partners agreed.

Remodeling and redecorating the former skating rink took the better part of a year. The outside was left intentionally drab to contrast with the glossy opulence inside. The peeling celadon paint was unretouched, and the original four-sided marquee was simply outlined with thin tubes of pale-green neon and adorned with appropriate words. HELL, read one side of the marquee, in intentionally crooked black letters; the next side bore the Japanese translation *JIGOKU*; the third read *INFERNO*; and the message on the fourth side was rotated daily among the other major languages of the world.

The night when a tuxedo-clad Toki Kaminari stood in line under a milky half-full moon, sandwiched between the freakish foreigners and the two singing OLs, was his fourth effort to penetrate those drab green doors. (They were red lacquer on the inside, he knew, for he had seen color photographs in a magazine.) The first time, on a whim, he simply put on his best clothes, arrived early, and stood in line, believing naïvely that admission was a matter of space available. The bouncer was a skinny, supercilious, ponytailed *gaijin* whose chilly blue eyes were rimmed with unnaturally black lashes. Toki was stunned when the man barked out, "Sorry, next!" in a vaguely Austro-Hungarian accent, then pulled aside the velvet rope for the couple who had been next in line, a statuesque downhill skier from Sweden and a fur-hatted dancer-choreographer from Vladivostok, now the toast of the Tokyo ballet world.

Toki realized then that admission was selective, if not discriminatory, and at that moment his whim became desire. I absolutely have to see the inside of that place, he thought. It must really be something special, to attract such enormous crowds, and such famous people. He decided that there must be two ways to gain admittance: by virtue of who you were, or by bribing the doorman. Bribery was the fulcrum on which Japanese government had turned for years, and Toki had no reason to believe that the politics of pleasure would be any different.

So, a week after his first attempt, he returned to the velvet-roped entrance to Hell. He was the first one in line, he was dressed once again in his best clothes (gray suit, white shirt, a polyester tie striped in muted shades of green), and this time he had come equipped with a formal envelope—white with an elaborate arabesque of thick gold thread attached to one corner—containing a thousand yen. It was his entire afternoon's profits, but he couldn't think of a better way to spend it. Discreetly, with trembling hands, he tucked the envelope into the breast pocket of the doorman's lilac velvet tuxedo.

"Thank you," said the doorman, without cracking a smile. "How did you know it was my birthday?" Then he added, in a slightly kinder tone than he had used the first time, "Sorry, next!"

Toki's third try was more of the same: a larger tip (two thousand hard-earned yen), a new red silk necktie to spruce up his old gray suit, and a slightly less abrupt rejection. "Thanks for stopping by, but sorry. Next!" the doorman said, and Toki stumbled away feeling angry, embarrassed, and bewildered. On the way home he stopped at a sidewalk noodle stand and gulped down five glasses of warm saké, but they didn't dull the pain at all.

On the train platform one day, Toki ran into a high-school classmate named Shigeo Hinomizu, whom he hadn't seen for at least ten years. Toki was on his way to pick up some snake-medicine for an ailing customer, and he hadn't had time to change out of his work clothes: the baggy blue cotton pants tucked into knee-high split-toed boots made from indigo-dyed canvas, a white V-necked T-shirt, a red *haramaki* (a wide tube of woven wool worn as a belly-warmer, even in summer, by traditional laborers and street vendors), and a blue polka-dotted *tenugui* twisted around his head and tied rakishly on the side. Shigeo was dressed in the elite salaryman's uniform of blue suit, black shoes, and enameled company lapel-pin, and he had looked surprised and not terribly pleased to see Toki. "Well, well," he said, after the reciprocal bows and the long-time-no-sees. "It looks like you ended up following in your father's footsteps."

"Yes," said Toki, "I guess I did." It struck him as a passive, wishy-washy answer, but it was too late to retract it. Besides, Shigeo was talking. "I followed in my old man's footsteps, too," he was saying, a bit ruefully. "Working late, soused every night, seeing my kids once a week on Sunday, and not even then, if I can get a tee time at the golf course."

The train arrived, silent and sleek, with terra-cotta cars and blue velour seats, and the two men sat down together. Shigeo kept glancing around nervously, as if he was afraid someone he knew might see him in the company of a member of the working class, but when Toki asked him where he was planning to go on his vacation he lost his furtive look and began talking passionately about his love for mountain climbing.

"Why do you climb mountains?" Toki asked conversationally.

"Because they're there," Shigeo replied. Toki found that answer highly original and deeply existential, and he parted with Shigeo at Asakusa Station with new respect and a mutual promise to get in touch soon. They both knew that would never happen, but empty promises were a staple of Japanese social interactions, as they are in most advanced, civilized countries.

After his third rejection at the gates of Hell, Toki stopped at a new sidewalk fast-food stand for a glass of saké and a plate of fried *soba* noodles. He had lived in Roppongi all his life, but this vendor was a stranger to him. "Yeah," said the man, after Toki had introduced himself. "I used to set up at Ginza 4-chome, but the competition got too crazy so I thought I'd try my luck over here." After downing his second glass of saké, Toki became talkative.

"Speaking of trying your luck," he said morosely, "I don't understand what you have to do to get into that new disco." He gestured across the street, where the colorful crowd of would-be initiates into Hell wound around the corner and out of sight. "Tonight I was first in line, and I bought a new silk necktie, and I gave the doorman a tip, and he still wouldn't let me in."

The noodle vendor laughed, showing a mouthful of silver teeth. "That isn't how it works," he said. "I read about it in a magazine. They let you in only if you're famous, or if you have an invitation from the owners, or if they think you're decorative, or if you look rich or dangerous or interesting. You can't bribe your way in, so you might as well save your money. But why do you want to go to such a noisy, superficial place anyway?"

Toki started to reply "Because it's there," but then he realized that wasn't precisely accurate. "Because it's a mystery," he said, "and I like mysteries." To prove the veracity of that statement, he went home, climbed under the futon, and read three chapters of *The Demon of Orphan Island* by Japan's most famous mystery writer, Edogawa Rampo. And then he fell asleep pondering his own personal mystery: how, in heaven's name, could he get into Hell?

Every morning, seven days a week, Toki woke up at four A.M. He put on his work clothes, ate a quick breakfast of rice balls and leftover *misoshiru* soup, washed it down with some ginseng tea for stamina, fetched his wooden barrow from the locked shed next to his tiny house, and set out across town on deserted streets, under a plum-colored sky still unleavened by dawn. The schedule, the menu, and the barrow were almost exactly the same as they had been for the past four generations of Kaminari men. Toki was the first one to lock the shed, but he thought his ancestors would understand, sadly, that Roppongi was no longer a rural village where everyone knew and trusted one another. The costume had changed, too. Toki's grandfather had worn wooden clogs and a kimono with the skirt hitched up to his knees, but his father had switched to the more practical shirt-and-trousers and the more comfortable split-toed boots soon after Toki was born.

In those days, the streets had been full of mobile or itinerant vendors. Japan was an agoraphobe's dream, for it was possible to live a sociable, well-fed life without ever venturing beyond one's front gate. All day the air was loud with the competing cries of the vendors of flowers and fruit, of wind-bells and prettily-potted bonsai, of sewing supplies and tofu, of fresh-caught fish and kimono cloth. There were collectors of rags and used paper, there were sharpeners of scissors and trimmers of trees, there were menders of clogs and *tatami*. Every vendor had his own distinctive cry, a drawn-out yodel announcing his wares or services, and some had other sound effects as well. The adults flocked to the horn of the tofu-man or the bell of the vegetable-seller, but there was one vendor's cry that brought every child within earshot running. "*Kingyooo!*" ("Goldfish for sale!") It was one of the magical words of an old-fashioned childhood, along with "seashore," "festival," and "fireworks."

The goldfish-vendor's cry had given Toki goosebumps the first time he heard it as an infant, and now, twenty-six years later, he still broke out in chicken-skin every time he heard that sound issuing from his own mouth. Toki took his craft seriously. He had even taken voice lessons for a year, from a former diva named Ishiki Jingo (known to her fans as La Norma, after her most famous role) who held private classes on the top floor of the Roppongi School of the Performing Arts. At the end of the class cycle she asked Toki if he planned to try out for a place in the chorus of the Tokyo Opera Company—"You have to start at the bottom," she said, "because it builds character"—and it was only then that Toki confessed that he was not planning to go on the stage at all.

"But why not?" asked La Norma, and that was when Toki lost his nerve. Mumbling something about congenital stage fright, he rushed from the room, and never went back. That night he apologized to the portraits of his father, grandfather, and great-grandfather that he kept in the family altar. "I have shamed the Kaminari name," he said. "I will never again conceal my profession, or insult my heritage."

In late twentieth-century Tokyo, being a traveling goldfish-salesman was considered a bizarre and unattractive choice of career for a bright young man. There were only a few goldfish vendors left in the entire country, and most were older men who knew that when they died or retired the barrow would be sold for scrap because their sons had no interest in a low-paying, exhausting, unprestigious job, however poetic it might appear to foreign travel writers. "But the men in our family have always sold goldfish, and it makes the children happy," the old men would say, and their salaryman-sons would laugh out loud and go off to practice their golf swings.

Toki had never questioned his duty, or his desire, to carry on the family tradition, and although he grieved quietly when his chain-smoking father died suddenly of a heart attack at the age of forty-nine, he had been very proud to take over the goldfish route. Toki was eighteen years old then, just out of high school. There had been some talk of his going on to college because of his exceptionally good grades, but when his father died that idea ceased to be a topic of discussion. The physical rigors of the job had taken some getting used to, but what upset Toki most was the discovery that people of his own age, particularly young women, thought it was "very strange and stupid" (as a flighty secretarial-school graduate he once met in a coffee shop had put it) to pursue such a lowly, unprofitable line of work.

Even Toki's sister Biwako, his only living relative, tried to persuade him to find another job—as a cook, perhaps, or a bookstore clerk, or an instructor in a health club. (She seemed to think that having a splendid physique would be sufficient qualification for the latter job.) It was too late to go to college now, even if he had wanted to, but as Biwako pointed out, almost any line of work would be more lucrative and less tiring than pulling a heavy sloshing cart full of goldfish through the smoggy congested streets of Tokyo all day.

Toki would sigh and say, "You're probably right." But he had sworn, first to his dying father and later to his fading grandfather, that as long as there was one child in Tokyo who would rejoice at the approaching cry of "Kingyooo!," Toki Kaminari would continue to get up at four A.M. and pull his barrow through the streets, no matter what anyone said. He was worried about one thing, though. Since women didn't even want to talk to him once they found out what he did for a living, how was he going to get married and produce a child to carry on the tradition? Not just a child but a *male* child, for there had never been a female goldfish vendor, ever, anywhere in Japan. The work was too demanding and besides, like so many things in Japan's male-centered culture, it simply wasn't done.

It was less than two miles from Roppongi to Ebisu, where Toki picked up his day's consignment of goldfish from a wholesaler near the train station. His wooden barrow had two glass sides, and the interior was divided into four tanks. Toki filled the tanks with water, then scooped in the small standard goldfish, the Wakin and Ryukin: the same sort of goldfish that were sold at every shrine festival in the country, the ones that inevitably ended up floating on the surface of the fishbowl after a couple of months of overfeeding or neglect. These fish occupied two sections of the barrow. The remaining tanks held the specialty fish, the higher-priced varieties that were purchased mostly by discriminating grown-ups: fat gilded or silvery beauties from China with diaphanous gauzy tails, and the exotic Sooty Moor, with its lustrous charcoal-colored finnage. Fortunately, many restaurants and homes still had large aquariums, for it was the sale of the larger, more expensive fish that enabled Toki to keep the price of the small, doomed goldfish at a hundred yen apiece, which was exactly what he paid the wholesaler.

The wholesaler, whose name was Saburo Makimoto, had known Toki's father and his grandfather, too. But even he seemed to think it odd and almost improper that Toki had chosen to carry on. "Still at it?" he greeted Toki every morning, and when Toki nodded he would say, "You'll never find a wife, you know. Women want luxury, and status, and glamour." Toki would nod again, glumly. He knew better than to argue with an old man, but in his secret heart he believed that somewhere there must be a woman who wouldn't mind marrying a man who lived a relatively simple life and did what he thought was right.

All day, in rain or sun or snow, Toki pulled his barrow through the streets of Tokyo, from one former village to another. In his grandfather's and even in his father's time, there had been fields and small forests between the villages, but now it was wall-to-wall asphalt and ferroconcrete, with occasional oases of temples or shrines, estates or parks. Toki took a different route every day, to keep from getting bored and also to make sure he visited his regular customers at least once a week. By the end of a typical week he had been as far north as Nishi-Nippori, as far south as Shinagawa, as far east as Tsudanuma, and as far west as Mitaka.

At the end of each day Toki returned to the warehouse, paid for the fish he had sold, and returned the rest to the holding tanks. Then he pulled his barrow home through the darkening streets, cooked his evening meal, went for a soak at the bathhouse, returned home, quietly practiced singing his scales, read a few chapters of a mystery, and went to sleep. That was before he started going out in the evening, of course. Sometimes Toki longed for those simple uneventful days, the days before Hell came to Roppongi and he became a man obsessed.

Toki didn't like to share his secrets with his sister Biwako, because she had a way of making him feel like a fool or a failure. But the day after he had purchased the amulet and rented a very expensive tuxedo with black satin lapels on the theory that it would make him appear both decorative and wealthy, and still received the "Sorry, next!" treatment from the doorman, he went to see his sister in desperation. She ran a small boutique on a back street in Aoyama, specializing in flamboyant leather garments and accessories. Biwako had studied art at the Ochanomizu Institute, and she designed some of the clothes she sold, but if she had not had a mysterious patron (Toki suspected that it was a married man, but he never asked) she would barely have been able to break even in such a competitive business.

"You'll probably think I'm an idiot," Toki began, thus denying Biwako the pleasure of calling him "*baka*," which was her favorite epithet. To his surprise, she was quite sympathetic.

"You had the right idea," she said, "but a regular tuxedo is just too conservative for a place like that." Toki suddenly remembered the foreigner in the cellophane jumpsuit, worn over a dense landscape of tuck-and-roll muscles and what appeared to be a gold lamé jockstrap stuffed with several oversized pieces of tropical fruit. "Of course, you're right," he said, thinking about all the mystery novels he could have bought with the money he had spent on the tuxedo-rental. Hardbacks, even.

Biwako rubbed her hands together. "Let me do a makeover on you, and I guarantee you'll get in," she said. Toki sighed. She had been trying to persuade him to let her make him over for the past five years, and he had always said "I'd rather burn in hell." Now he said simply, "Okay," trusting her to catch the accidental irony.

Two hours later Toki looked in the long oval mirror that stood in the middle of the shop and exclaimed involuntarily, "Hey! Wow! I look really cool!"

"Oh, you're way beyond cool," said Biwako. She had dressed him in a tobacco-colored cashmere turtleneck and a pair of leather trousers in a slightly darker shade of gold worn under a matching ankle-length overcoat with wide lapels and buttoned epaulets. He added brown dress boots and a small eelskin bag, since his tight-fitting slacks had no pockets. His shoulder-length black hair was slicked back into a blunt ponytail and tied with a thick golden cord. Toki had drawn the line at makeup ("Please," Biwako had pleaded, "just a teensy bit of bronzer on those wonderful cheekbones?"), and even though he knew he looked very handsome, he wasn't entirely at ease with his flashy new clothes, or hairstyle.

"Are you sure I don't look like a South American drug kingpin?" he asked dubiously as he pirouetted slowly in front of the mirror, like the tiny dancer in a music box whose batteries were running low.

"Don't worry," said Biwako. "You look hot, and wholesome, and totally irresistible. Speaking of which, I have to get ready for a date," she added, abruptly pushing her brother out the door.

When he got to the disco, Toki noticed that there was a line of illegally parked limos along the curb. The sidewalks were thronged with reporters carrying huge cameras and boom microphones, while a news helicopter hovered noisily overhead. What on earth? Toki thought, and then he saw that the fourth marquee now read not *HÖLLE* or *HADES* or *SHEOL* but CLOSED FOR PRIVATE PARTY. READ ALL ABOUT IT TOMORROW!

Toki took a cab to Aoyama, muttering all the way. Fortunately the driver was immersed in listening to a baseball game between the Hanshin Tigers and the Yomiuri Giants and didn't notice. When Toki returned the leather suit to Biwako she explained with exaggerated cheerfulness that she had been stood up by her date, and when her brother offered to lend a sympathetic ear, she said she didn't want to talk about it. "But what a rotten piece of luck for you, that they would be closed tonight of all nights," she said. "And you looked so terrific, too. Come back tomorrow after work, and I'll fix you up again."

"Thanks, but I think I'm going to take a week off and catch up on my sleep," Toki said. And my self-esteem, he thought. Biwako made a pot of black tea and they ate the fancy strawberry-and-whipped-cream cake Toki had bought at a nearby *patisserie* to show his gratitude. Then he changed back into his own clothes and headed home on foot, to save money.

As he passed the dark, shadowy shrine where he had bought the useless amulet, he heard a whimpering noise, followed by the sound of a human voice cursing. "Come on, you stupid damn dog," said the voice—an adult male, obviously drunk. The dog growled loudly in response.

"Oh, is that the way you want it, sonuvabitch?" snarled the aggressive voice. Toki walked up a short flight of steps and peered around a massive green bush. In the roseate glow of a sodium pole-lamp, a man in a white suit was crouched down, poking with a stick at an animal that was evidently cowering under a stone bench. Toki had been taught from babyhood never to interfere in other people's affairs, but he noticed that the stick the man was holding was very sharp at one end, and he was afraid that some terrible act of cruelty might be about to take place.

"Excuse me," he said, emerging from behind the bush. "May I be of some help?" The man in the white suit stood up unsteadily and turned to face Toki.

"Who the hell are you?" he said, and his cheeks suddenly inflated with a suppressed belch, or hiccup. Toki saw the mirrored sunglasses, the sleazy polyester suit worn over a black nylon shirt, the missing finger joints, and he realized that he had just broken another of the commandments of his childhood: Never, ever, speak to a *yakuza*, much less a drunken, angry one.

"I'm sorry," he stammered. "I just thought you might need some help with your dog."

"It's not *my* stupid dog," said the gangster. "But the bastard stole my blasted box lunch—I had it right here on the bench, and I just dozed off for a minute—and now I'm going to kill it, the thieving mongrel cur."

"Wait," said Toki. "I have a better idea. I mean, you don't want to get blood all over that good-looking suit, do you?"

The yakuza glanced down at his zooty lapels. "Well, no, not really," he said.

"Then come with me," said Toki, "and I'll buy you a nice new box lunch. Or would you rather go somewhere for some grilled chicken?" The yakuza licked his lips, and Toki noticed with horror and awe that he had a snake tattooed on his tongue.

One hour, eight bottles of beer, and innumerable sticks of sweet-sauced *yakitori* later, Toki had a friend for life in the South Central Tokyo branch of one of the largest, most notorious yakuza organizations in Japan. He waved his new pal, whose name he had never learned, off in a taxi, and then he went back to the shrine. "Here pup, pup, pup," he called. Toki had brought some scraps of chicken wrapped in a napkin, and he set them under the bush, sat down on the bench, and waited.

After a few minutes a long narrow rufous snout appeared from beneath the bush, sniffed at the yakitori, then seized the entire napkin and pulled it back into its lair. Toki smiled as he listened to the enthusiastic sounds of gulping and chewing. I'll come back again tomorrow with some more food, and some water, he thought, as he rose to leave.

Toki had only been home for ten minutes—just long enough to change into his *yukata* robe and assemble the supplies he needed for his nightly trip to the public bath—when he heard a faint scratching at the door. He opened it cautiously and was surprised to see the dog from the shrine. "Come in," he said, and the dog walked into the entry hall, limping slightly. Forgetting all about his bath, Toki spent the next two hours cleaning the cut on the dog's leg, brushing its soft auburn fur, and feeding it leftovers from his miniature refrigerator.

The dog was too big to sit on Toki's lap, but it put its paws across his thighs and stared up at him with limpid brown eyes, as expressive as any human's. The dog had a long, slender nose, large perky ears, and a phenomenally bushy tail.

"You look a bit like a fox," Toki said. "I mean that as a compliment, of course," he added, and he could have sworn that the dog's mouth turned up at the corners. "I think I'll call you Inari, since I found you at the Inari shrine, and since foxes are the messengers of the god who is enshrined there." The dog gave a short affirmative yip and wagged its brushy tail. "I'm glad you approve," said Toki, laughing.

Toki made the dog a bed in the corner, but when his alarm went off at four A.M. he discovered that the dog had crept under his covers while he was sleeping, and was curled up in the V behind his bent knees, with its paws on his shoulders. Like a cat, Toki thought sleepily. Or a wife. He put out dishes of fresh water and food, then locked all the doors and windows so the dog wouldn't be able to escape. It (or rather she, for Toki had shyly checked the gender while he was cleaning the leg wounds) was still asleep when he left, and he hoped that she would sleep the day away. He worried a little about leaving the dog unattended, but today was the day he had promised to deliver five black-spotted silver-tailed goldfish to a new Szechwan restaurant in Ogikubo, so there was no way he could take the day off.

Late that afternoon Toki hurried home, stopping on the way to buy some meat as a treat for the dog. He was so excited about his new companion that he hardly thought about the disco all day. As he unlocked the door to his house, calling out "I'm home" even before he stepped into the entry hall, it occurred to him that this might be how it would feel to have a family of his own to come home to. At the moment, though, he was perfectly happy to have a sweet-natured, affectionate dog waiting for him.

"Inari!" he called out, "I'm home!" He had expected the dog to come running to meet him, leaping at him with joyful excitement (especially when she smelled the meat), but there was no sound at all. Oh no, he thought, maybe she died from her wounds! He ran through the house, calling "Inari-chan! Inari-chan!" but there was no sign of the dog anywhere. He checked the doors and windows; they were still tightly locked from the inside. He looked in all the cupboards, he looked under the furniture, he looked in every nook or cranny where a dog—or a flea, for that matter—

could possibly have hidden. Finally, Toki sat down at his low table, feeling depressed and confounded. After a moment it occurred to him that this was exactly like one of the fictional locked-room mysteries he had read about, but that was no comfort at all.

There was no way the dog could have escaped, yet it was gone. Toki spent all his free time for the next several days hanging around the shrine, but he never saw Inari again. After a week of desolation he decided that he needed to do something to take his mind off the loss of his pet, so he decided to make one last, final effort to get into Hell.

Biwako had promised to come over with the leather suit, and she was going to put Toki's hair in the gel-slicked druglord ponytail again, too. When he got home from work there was a note on his door saying that she couldn't make it, and asking if they could reschedule for later in the week. Toki was in a bad mood already—his barrow had run over a nail on the way home, so he had to detour to a tire shop to get the puncture repaired—and Biwako's cancellation was the last straw. Okay, he thought grimly, as he clomped back from the bath in his high wooden geta. This is it. There's still one approach I haven't tried. It's a long shot, and if it doesn't work, I swear I'll never even think about that diabolical disco again, as long as I live.

An hour later, Toki was standing in line. There were five people ahead of him, and when the doorman emerged at five after eight, late as usual, they lunged forward hopefully. "Sorry, next!" the doorman said to the first three people in line (a trio of weedy Japanese high-school boys in identical sunglasses, vintage black serge suits, and Blues Brothers hats). As they slunk away he let a tall, ravishing Korean girl with knee-length black hair and a very short red dress through the ropes, then said, "Sorry, next!" to the next supplicant, an alarmingly busty foreign woman wearing a rainbow fright wig and a red T-shirt inscribed "Samuel 22:45" in fuzzy pink iron-on letters.

Toki was next. He shuffled forward in his geta, feeling sick to his stomach. His brilliant idea of wearing his work clothes as a costume now seemed totally insane, and he wished that the sidewalk would swallow him up, then spit him out again at his own front door. He was staring shamefacedly at the ground, waiting for the inevitable "Sorry," when he became aware that the doorman was talking to him.

"A most unique look," the thin man was saying in his Transylvanian-accented Japanese. "Sort of medieval macho, with a touch of the samurai pirate. Now why in the world didn't you just wear that in the first place? Come along, my friend, you're *in*!"

The music was astoundingly loud. The bass line seemed to usurp Toki's own organic rhythms and he began to breathe, unconsciously, in 3/4 time. "Stayin' alive, stayin' alive," bragged the testosterone tremolos of the BeeGees, for it was Seventies Night in Hell.

Toki had been sixth in line and only one other person had been admitted before him, but the place was already as crowded as the Yamanote Line train platform at rush hour. Toki realized then, for the first time, that there must be a separate entrance for celebrities and their friends. Of course, he thought. The doorman could have turned away every member of the hopeful *hoi polloi* who queued up in front of the velvet ropes, and the place would still have been wildly successful and packed to the gills.

Someone bumped into Toki. "'Scuse me," said a rumbling male voice, and Toki looked up into the massive mahogany face of a legendary professional basketball player, known for his spectacular behind-the-back passes, pickpocket steals, balletic alley-oops, rim-rattling dunks, and philosophical post-game remarks.

"I am sorry!" Toki squeaked in English, awed by the spectacular face, the supernatural height, the platinum sheen of the raw-silk suit. The American giant smiled, and each perfect tooth was like a square effulgent moon, high in the sky.

"It's *all* good," he said reassuringly. "Hey, man, nice do-rag," he added, lightly touching Toki's polka-dot bandanna with one enormous finger, and then he was gone. I should give it to him, Toki thought. It would look good on his shaved head. He took off the kerchief and stared at it for a moment, and then he began to worry that he might be asked to leave if he tampered with the costume that had finally gotten him in, so he retied the tenugui low on his forehead, in the style of a master sushi-maker.

Toki felt weightless and transparent, like a human jellyfish afloat in the alien currents of fame and fashion, and he was relieved when the eddying crowd pushed him into a corner. There was an empty table, tall black lacquer surrounded by red lacquer barstools, and Toki sat down on one of the stools and looked around. He had never been to Tiger Balm Gardens, nor had he read Dante's *Inferno*, and although Buddhism offers some vivid three-dimensional depictions of the topography of Purgatory, he hadn't seen those, either. So the decor of Hell (the nightclub), which amazed even the most blasé parasites of the night and the most esoteric scholars of comparative demonology, struck Toki Kaminari as the single most incredible thing he had ever seen.

Actually, "glimpsed" would be a more accurate description of Toki's visual encounter with the interior of Hell, for the vast ballroom was so clogged with the famous, the glamorous, and the aggressively bizarre that it was impossible to get the full effect of the bas-relief scenes (rendered in the dull cinnabar of nested tables or antique begging bowls) which decorated every wall, from black-marble floor to black-enamel ceiling. Directly across from Toki, broken up by an ambulatory collage of dancers dressed in lurid spandex, synthetic leather, and white sharkskin (for it was, after all, Seventies Night) there was a mural, all in muted Chinese red, depicting a horde of sinners shoveling what appeared to be dung, while a fork-tailed scarlet devil cracked a whip from atop a heap of steaming nightsoil.

Toki had perfect eyesight, but the wall was too far away to make out the details. On a hunch, he turned around and looked behind him at the cool, smooth wall he had been lounging against, and sure enough: it too was covered with an embossed mural of hellish scenes that managed, for all their horror, to be slyly humorous as well. The mural behind Toki's table depicted a huddled bunch of homunculi, crouched around a dense conical mass of what appeared at first glance to be a pile of savory meat dumplings. Some of the little hellions were in the act of stuffing the dumplings into their mouths, while the cheeks of others bulged gluttonously. That image reminded Toki of the dyspeptic yakuza gorging himself on yakitori, and he felt a sudden wave of sorrow at the thought of his vanished dog, Inari.

As he examined the extravagantly detailed tableaus Toki noticed that the pile of dumplings was being replenished by a cadre of squatting devils, naked buttocks glistening in the red-lacquer firelight. "It's shit! They're eating shit!" Toki exclaimed out loud, but the music was so loud that no one heard him. Then he noticed something even more shocking: the features of the coprophagists were not generic evildoers; they were uncannily accurate depictions of a number of prominent people. Toki recognized a rock star, a member of Parliament, the head of a trading company, and a nuclear-power advocate, and after a moment he realized what those four people had in common: they had all, within the past month, been caught engaging in some sort of socially unacceptable behavior (graft, adultery, drug abuse, possession of firearms). Toki looked more closely, and he saw that the heads had been temporarily glued in place, whereas the bodies of the gourmands were part of the flowing geography of the fresco. Musical heads, he thought.

"Would you like to dance?" a voice said, and Toki looked up in surprise. He felt slightly sheepish about being caught with his nose two inches from a mural of famous people snacking on excrement, but when he saw the face that belonged to the voice he lost all self-consciousness. In fact, he nearly lost consciousness altogether, for his brain was unable to process the fact that the loveliest female he had ever seen had just requested his company on the dance floor.

"Okay," he said through dry, insensate lips. As he followed the woman through the laughing crowd and onto the strobe-lit dance floor, he suddenly remembered, with a rush of anxiety, that he didn't know how to dance.

As it turned out, he needn't have worried. Dancing is after all a genetic memory, a molecular instinct as elemental as the sperm-and-ovum gavotte, and Toki was delighted to find that while *he* may not have known how to dance, his body did. His feet shuffled inventively in a cross between an *Obon* promenade and a Navajo dawn-dance, his arms moved as if they had a sinuous snake-mind of their own, his knees and elbows bent and straightened in the kinetic geometry of *hula kahiko*, his head moved from side to side like an Egyptian jackal-god, his torso undulated like an earthworm shrugging off its skin. Toki had felt absolutely Japanese all his life, but as he discovered the secret dancer inside him, he felt for the first time like a true man of the world in the most joyously homogeneous, cosmic, corporeal sense of the phrase.

Once Toki had gotten over his amazement at discovering that dancing came as naturally to him as scooping up goldfish with a mesh-net dipper, he began to stare at his astonishing partner. She was standing very close to him, barely moving her feet, rippling her arms like smoke, or seaweed. Her eyes were closed, but Toki had already noticed that they were green. Not emerald or hazel, but the deep bright green of the topiary tea-bushes at Shizuoka. Her mouth was slightly parted, but Toki remembered her sweet clever smile, and the slightly skewed canine teeth: a dental arrangement much prized in Japan, where vampiric malocclusions are considered cute and orthodontia remains an exotic specialty. There was a pleasing pointed symmetry to her features—the narrow-tipped nose, the bowed mouth, the tapering chin—that made her look vaguely un-Japanese, but what set her apart from anyone Toki had ever known was her gleaming russet hair. He knew the dramatic reddish-gold was probably the result of some high-priced henna treatment, but it looked totally natural, without the unnatural brassiness his sister Biwako's hair had developed when she went through her own wishful "Titian-haired beauty" stage.

They had been dancing to "How Deep Is Your Love," and when the song ended Toki's partner slowly opened her eyes. She ran her small white hands down the front of her shimmery copper-colored dress (Toki gulped when he saw the detour occasioned by the lush convexity of her breasts), as if she were making sure that her body hadn't somehow floated away in the rapture of the dance-trance.

"Are you thirsty?" she said, and Toki nodded. The music had started again ("Disco Inferno"), and he would have liked to stay on the dance floor, watching his beautiful companion swaying in her dreamy kelpish waltz, but now that she mentioned it, he *was* thirsty. He was also very curious about who she was, and why she had chosen him, of all people, from among that sea of glittering celebrities.

The woman led him to a secluded corner of the room, placed a stack of ten-thousand–yen notes on the table, and said, "Order anything you want. My treat."

"Oh, no," said Toki, but she folded his hand over his thin wallet (she was remarkably strong, for a girl) and forced it back into his pocket. "Couldn't we just stay like this for the rest of the evening?" Toki asked, amazed by his own boldness. The woman just laughed, her enchantingly slanted canine teeth snagging briefly on her rosy lips, and gently withdrew her hand. They drank peach Bellinis and strawberry daiquiris and kir with Cassis, they ate shiitake pizzas and pesto timbales and sizzling garlic shrimp, and by the time the plates were empty Toki had told Tsukiko (for that was the woman's name) his entire life story, all the way up to the moment when she had said, "Would you like to dance?"

Tsukiko was less forthcoming. She told Toki that she had grown up in a village in the mountains of Aichi Prefecture, where her father raised nightingales for their dung. Toki thought this was a joke, a dig at him for having been so engrossed in the scatological art on the walls, until Tsukiko explained that nightingale droppings were used to make a traditional facial cleanser called *uguisu no fun* which was favored by geisha and other women who still followed the old ways of beauty. Toki wondered if it was nightingale offal that made Tsukiko's skin so beautifully pale and translucent, but he didn't dare ask.

Tsukiko said that she had come to Tokyo to study acting, and that she was living in her wealthy aunt's house, quite nearby, while the aunt was in Paris taking a course in pastry-making. She offered a great many details of that sort—saying, for instance, that her father had over two thousand nightingales in his flock, and describing the way the sky looked when they flew overhead, as if some heavenly gardener had thrown a handful of sunflower seeds into the air, blotting out the sun—but somehow her story didn't ring quite real to Toki.

Maybe beauty equals unreality, he thought. It was difficult to picture this ethereal woman performing normal daily functions: squeezing into the train amid all the lewd exploring hands, buying turnips at the supermarket, disrobing for her daily bath. Toki lingered on the last image a bit longer than was absolutely necessary, but when he tried to picture her living with him in his tiny old back-alley house the daydream was extinguished like incense in the rain. No way, he thought. The beautiful actress and the goldfish man? Not a chance.

Yet when he told Tsukiko what he did for a living she clapped her hands in delight, seemingly as impressed as if he had told her he was a movie star, or the Chairman of the Board of Kubota Waterworks. "How pure, and how lovely," she said, and Toki's impossible daydream was revived, the incense of irrational hope relit. His little house wasn't that bad, really; it was just run-down. The land it was on was worth a small fortune, he knew. They could sell it and move to the suburbs and build a shiny new house with an Intelligent Toilet and a blue tile roof ...

"Shall we go?" Tsukiko was saying. While Toki was lost in his real-estate reverie, she had paid the bill, and he was shocked to see that the entire stack of bank notes had been used, with the last two left as a very generous tip of twenty thousand yen. Tsukiko stood up and put on a cape made from diagonal strips of metallic gold, silver, bronze, and copper cloth.

Go where? Toki thought. Then he realized he would gladly accompany this woman anywhere, so he just said, formally, "Thank you for the feast," and followed her out the way he had come in. The line of overdressed hopefuls still stretched out of sight around the block, and the doorman was just saying "Sorry, next!" to two sandy-haired American teenagers in full samurai armor when Toki and Tsukiko emerged.

The doorman raised his eyebrows. "Have a good night," he said to Toki as they passed. He looked Tsukiko up and down, then smirked approvingly. "Hey," he added, poking Toki in the ribs with a long purple-gloved finger, "have a *long* night!"

Tsukiko led Toki to an unfamiliar street on the outskirts of Roppongi, although he would have sworn that he knew every alley in Tokyo by now. As they walked along side by side he was aware that people were staring at them, the exotic beauty and the goldfish man, and he felt chosen, proud, and incredibly fortunate. They passed by the dark, shadowy shrine where Toki had bought the amulet, and it occurred to him that perhaps it hadn't been so useless after all. Maybe it was just slow-acting, like his grandfather's Chinese-medicine potions.

In Japan, a modest Western-style apartment is called a "mansion" (the actual word, phonetically transposed from English, is "*manshon*"), but the dwelling where Tsukiko lived was a genuine mansion—in Japanese, an *oyashiki*. Inside, the enormous house was a curious mixture of Western and Japanese style (low tables on Bokhara carpets, *faux*-Monet oil paintings on walls of woven bamboo). There were no electric lights, and the candles Tsukiko had lit cast misshapen shadows on the high walls and the domed ceiling of the room. She led Toki to a big tapestry-covered armchair, and pushed gently on his shoulders until he took the hint and sat down. Then she left the room, saying, "I'm just going to freshen up."

"But you look impossibly fresh already," Toki said, and she laughed.

While he was waiting for Tsukiko to return, watching the wind blow the long white curtains in and out of the open windows, watching the same wind blow away the filmy goldfish-tail clouds that had shrouded the full moon, Toki rehearsed the speech he planned to make. He had no romantic experience with women; he had never gone out on a date, nor had he ever been tempted to patronize the back-street prostitutes he occasionally encountered. It wasn't that he was saving himself for marriage but, while he had never actually put the thought into words, he *was* saving himself for love. And now he had found it, and it was definitely worth the wait.

Toki was running over the words of his proposal, trying to decide whether to use the polite, the super-polite, or the excruciatingly obsequious verb-forms, when he saw a shadow behind one of the curtains. "Tsukiko?" he said, and then the curtain rustled and Tsukiko stepped out into the candle-and-moonlight, astonishingly beautiful and completely naked.

Toki was shocked to the point of speechlessness. I can't believe this is happening to me, he thought. Once when he was very small he had gone to the shrine to play, and had lost track of time. Hurrying home in the disorienting dimness of dusk, thinking about wolves and ghosts and child-snatchers, he had accidentally gone to the house next door, which looked almost exactly like his own house from the outside. When he slid open the frosted-glass door and called out "I'm home," his senses went into shock, for behind that identical door everything was different: the aromas (red meat and garlic), the decorations (dusty plastic roses), the sounds (a raucous television game show and the voices of strangers). For a moment he was filled with a thrilling sort of terror, but then Mrs. Inatari came to the entry and said warmly "Oh, Toki-chan, it's you. Did you come to play with Mitsuo?" Toki realized his mistake then, and without even saying "Excuse me" he ran home as fast as his little blue rubber boots could carry him, home to the comforting smells of miso and incense, the familiar ink-painting of three dancing frogs beside the door, the beloved voices of his grandfather and grandmother, his father and mother, and his imperious tattletale sister.

He felt the same way now, looking at the naked woman in the moonlight: as if he had stumbled through a dream-door into a parallel universe, or into someone else's strange, exciting life. Tsukiko walked toward him and Toki closed his eyes—partly out of shyness, partly out of confusion, and partly because he felt that he shouldn't be seeing his future wife this way, this soon. His eyes were still scrunched shut like those of a child playing *oni-gokko* tag, when he felt her small hand on his shoulder. "It's all right," she said. "You won't turn to stone if you look at me."

I'm not so sure about that, Toki thought, but he opened his eyes and stood up. Tsukiko had let her russet hair down, and the top of her fragrant head came just to his Adam's apple. "You have been very kind to me," she said, "and I want to give you your reward. But first, let's dance." Toki was confused. What had he done? She was the one who paid for the food and drinks, she was the one who invited him to her home. And why had she removed her clothes? It made it awfully difficult to concentrate.

Very formally, he placed his hands on her milky shoulders and began to waltz awkwardly around the moon-splashed room, while Tsukiko put her hands at his waist and hummed "How Deep Is Your Love." She kept trying to pull him closer, and he kept resisting. Plenty of time for that later, he told himself through gritted teeth.

"Uh, what did you mean by 'reward'?" Toki asked. His voice came out sounding strangely high and croaky, like the old priest at the shrine, no doubt because he was in a state of extreme nervous anxiety from trying not to step on Tsukiko's bare feet, or brush against her bare breasts. Their shape reminded him of conical pyramids of incense, and the skin was as smooth and pale as freshly-molded rice cakes.

"Just that I want to make love to you," Tsukiko said, and she stepped forward and pressed her supple white-skinned body against his. Toki dropped to his knees, eyes cast down to avoid seeing anything too stimulating. This wasn't how he had pictured the proposal scene at all, but he knew he had to go ahead now, before things (and one centrally located thing in particular) spun completely out of control.

"I am deeply honored by your generous offer," he said in courtly, stilted Japanese. "But don't you think it would be more romantic if we waited until after the ceremony? That could be first thing tomorrow morning," he added hastily, "if it's convenient for you."

Tsukiko put her hands under Toki's armpits and pulled him up to a standing position. Her eyes were shining, and she was trembling all over with wild excitement. "Are you really asking me to marry you?" she asked.

"Of course I am," said Toki. "Does that mean you will?"

To Toki's surprise, Tsukiko burst into tears. "Oh, you've made me so happy," she said, and he felt a thrill of joy, for he thought that she was accepting his proposal. But then she looked up at him through brimming eyes and said gently, "Haven't you figured it out yet?"

"Figured what out?" said Toki. What was she trying to tell him? That she was married to someone else, that he wasn't of her class, that this was all a cruel and heartless joke?

"That I'm not, how shall I say this, a regular woman," said Tsukiko.

"Oh, anyone could see that," Toki said, feeling relieved. "I know you're much too good for me, too beautiful and too talented and too high-class, but if we truly love each other, and if you don't mind living a simple life—"

"No, no," Tsukiko interrupted. "What I'm trying to say is ... well, let me put it this way. Do you remember that dog you rescued in the park?"

"Of course," said Toki. He felt a sudden premonitory chill.

"Well, that wasn't a normal dog, it was a fox. And it wasn't a normal fox, either; it was an enchanted fox. And—don't you see?—that fox was me, I was that fox, and tonight was going to be my way of repaying you for your kindness. But it turned out that you weren't a normal man, either. You're exceptionally fine and kind, and thanks to your purity of heart I can now become a higher being."

Toki was in shock, and the room around him seemed to be spinning wildly, as if gravity had suddenly taken a sabbatical. Unable to comprehend the larger picture, he focused on Tsukiko's last remark. "A higher being? You mean a human?" he asked.

Tsukiko laughed, and her pointed teeth caught the light. "Oh no, that would be an evolutionary demotion!" she said merrily, and Toki couldn't tell if she was joking. "No, I'm hoping to become a cat, preferably one who lives at a sushi shop or in the Central Fish Market. I would never be hungry, and it seems like a good way to catch up on all the sleep I've lost as a fox, and as a woman. No, seriously, please forget about me, and I promise that someday you will meet a woman, a real human woman, who is absolutely perfect for you. Well, have a wonderful life, and thanks again!"

In a flash she turned into a medium-sized fox with three white feet and a white muzzle—a creature which anyone but a trained vulpinologist could easily have mistaken for a dog—and vanished through the open window. Toki stood for a long time, watching the wind blow the white curtains in and out like the sails of a tall ship or the skirts of an elegant ghost. Then he blew out all the candles and went home.

The next day, for the first time in his adult life, Toki slept through his alarm clock. He slept through the sound of children marching off to school in yellow hats and sailor suits, he slept through the cacophonous rehearsal at the *koto* school behind his house, he slept through the late-afternoon plaints of the tofu-seller, the vegetable man, and the collector of old telephone books. When he finally woke up it was raining and the sky was the color of *sumi* ink. He looked at the clock and assumed it must be five o'clock in the morning, and it wasn't until he discovered the evening newspaper on his doorstep that Toki realized it was five P.M. instead.

He had missed a whole day of work and an entire day of his life. Toki felt horrible, and he felt worse when he remembered the events of the night before. He had a headache from all the potent cocktails he had consumed at the disco; the hangover was soon cured by a tart red *umeboshi* plum in a cup of strong green tea, but that traditional remedy had no effect on the ache in his heart.

Toki examined his psychological options and decided on denial. It was all a dream, he told himself. There was no dog, there was no dance, there were no naked breasts in the moonlight, there was no magic fox. Still, just in case, he decided to go back to the mansion and see if Tsukiko might still be there, in any form.

On the way, weaving through the back alleys where Edo-period wooden houses were gently wasting away in the monolithic shadows of expensive condos frosted with fluffy white plaster, Toki passed the public library. He always bought his mystery novels at used-book stores, and he hadn't been inside a library since he graduated from high school. But when he saw that the lights were on, he went inside. "Welcome," said the librarian, a noble-featured young man with shoulder-length hair and steel-rimmed glasses. "May I help you?" Toki felt vaguely uneasy. I thought librarians were supposed to be matronly women, he thought.

"Well," he said, "I was sort of wondering about *kitsune-tsuki*, fox possession."

"Ah," said the librarian. He disappeared through a glass door and returned several minutes later with a stack of dusty old books. Toki sat down at a cubicle in the back of the library and opened the first book. It was called *Favorite Fables of the Meiji Era*, and in the index under *kitsune* (fox) he found twenty-three listings. Toki turned to the first story: "The Fox-Wife." *Once upon a time,* it began, *there was a lonely wood-cutter in Saitama Prefecture* ...

Two mesmerizing, troubling hours later, the overhead lights blinked on and off, and the voice of the male librarian announced over a crackling loudspeaker, "I'm terribly sorry, but the library will close in five minutes. Please return all books to the front desk, whether or not you wish to check them out. We will reopen tomorrow morning at ten o'clock. Thank you for your patronage, and thank you for reading books."

Toki didn't have a library card, so he returned the books to the desk and nodded to the librarian, who was now almost invisible behind a huge stack of historical-romance novels being checked out by a young girl with a nose ring and a green satin Seattle Supersonics jacket. Something about the girl's body language gave Toki the feeling that she might be attracted to the handsome librarian, and that reminded him of his own lost love.

Outside, the rain had stopped, and a few streaks of toffee-colored sky were visible behind the disintegrating storm clouds. With his head teeming with frightening folktales, Toki retraced the path he remembered taking the night before with Tsukiko. After reading the old stories, he felt less sure that it had all been a dream. The stories of fox-possession were full of convincing details, and one of the books had even reproduced a letter from one of the shoguns, stating that a certain fox had bewitched some female members of his household and offering a reward for the capture or assassination of the mischievous creature.

When Toki found himself on Tsukiko's street, he suddenly became apprehensive. He had no idea what to expect: a rapturous reunion, an abrupt rejection, a house full of strangers? It hadn't occurred to him that there might be a large vacant lot where Tsukiko's mansion had stood the night before, but a vacant lot was exactly what he saw when he came around the corner.

"That can't be," he muttered. He circled the block four times, thinking he might have overlooked some crucial landmark. But the gate was intact—he remembered the roses—and behind the gate there was a great empty patch of earth, and the remains of a Western-style garden.

In a daze, Toki sat down on a bench in the garden. The vanished mansion was consistent with the stories of fox-bewitchment he had read at the library, but it had all seemed so real the night before. He could still see the tall windows and billowing moon-bright curtains, he could still smell Tsukiko's almond-scented hair, he could still feel her lithe slow-dancing body in his arms.

"Meow," said a voice, and Toki looked down to see a gingery cat rubbing against his muscular legs, imprinting him with its scent and absorbing some of his in return. "Meow to you too," he said, and then he felt his stomach drop like an runaway elevator. "Tsukiko, is that you?" he whispered. "Niao?" the cat replied quizzically.

Tsukiko had said she wanted to become a cat, and this cat was definitely the right color. There were no white markings on its feet or its face, but surely the artists of transmogrification wouldn't be so literal-minded as that.

"Listen," Toki said urgently, while the cat sniffed his toes with an ecstatic expression and its mouth slightly open, like a tiny vampire. "I don't care what form you take, I still love you. I know we can't get married, but won't you at least come home and live with me, and sleep behind my knees?"

There was a rustle in the bushes and an old woman holding a muddy spade in one hand and a clump of iris bulbs in the other came crashing out of the underbrush. She gave Toki a horrified look as she rushed out through the gate, and he could hear her wooden clogs clattering along in the direction of the shrine, where she would no doubt pray for purification after the perverted conversation she had overheard. Toki laughed, and then he realized that he was alone. "Kitty, kitty?" he called, but the cat was gone. Toki poked around for half an hour or so, meowing disconsolately, and then he went home.

After a week spent working, sleeping, and feeling so depressed that he couldn't even read his new crop of mysteries, Toki decided to go to the disco again. Maybe she'll be there, he thought. He didn't care if Tsukiko turned out to be mischievous or even evil, like some of the foxes in the stories. He just wanted to see her again, in any form. Absentmindedly, he pulled on a black turtleneck jersey, a black beret, and a rumpled pair of black and gray shadow-plaid trousers with a matching three-button vest that had belonged to his father, for he was far too distressed to worry about the dress code.

"Ah, my main man," said the doorman, when he saw Toki. "We've missed you. It's the retro look tonight, I see. Very hip, very fifties. You look a bit like a beatnik tax-accountant, I must say. But what has become of the beautiful redhead?"

"Oh, you know how it is," Toki said in Japanese, trying to sound sophisticated and debonair. "Easy come, easy go."

The doorman nodded knowingly. "Don't worry," he said. "There are plenty of foxes in the sea."

Toki was startled. "What did you say?" he asked.

"I said, 'There are plenty of fish in the sea,'" said the doorman. "Now have a good time, and try not to break too many hearts, okay?"

Toki took a seat in a corner, under a mural which depicted a deposed Cabinet member skewered longitudinally on a rotisserie spit, over a tall flame. He raised his hand when he saw a waiter coming in his direction, but to his surprise the waiter said, "The manager would like to see you in his office, sir." I wonder if I've somehow violated the dress code, Toki thought. But then he saw a shapely blonde wearing a pink-flowered sarong the size of a small dishtowel, dancing with a Caribbean-looking man in a loincloth made of molded tinfoil, and he thought, No, that can't be it.

The manager's office was a large octagon with white walls and a white carpet. The only color in the room was the single red apple in a vaguely Cezanne-ish still life on the wall, dwarfed by an ornate gilded frame. The manager was a stern, spidery-limbed man with round rimless glasses. "I'll get right to the point," he said, after the obligatory discussion of the subtleties of the season. "Do you know how we can get in touch with the young lady you were with the other night?"

"No, I'm afraid I don't," said Toki. "I wish I did," he added.

The manager explained that the crisp ten-thousand notes that Tsukiko had used to pay the bill and to tip the waiter had seemed perfectly all right at the time but that at the stroke of midnight they had turned into a heap of dusty gingko leaves. Toki shivered involuntarily, for he had read in a book called *Antique Tales of Curious Things* that supernatural foxes like to make lavish purchases with money that later turns into leaves.

"How did you know it was those particular bills?" he asked.

"Because those were the only ten-thousand–yen tips the waiter received, and because we file each bill with the money used to pay it," the manager said. That's the final proof, Toki thought.

"Well, then," said the manager, tenting his hands and putting his fingertips together, and Toki suddenly wondered whether he was expected to make good on the bill.

"How much was the bill, by the way?" he asked.

"Ninety thousand yen," said the manager, and Toki blanched. It would take him several months to save that much money, even if he went without food and neglected to pay his property taxes.

"Oh, no," said the manager, evidently sensing Toki's concern, "we don't expect you to pay it. We realize that you were just a casual acquaintance of the young, uh, lady." Toki thought of his earnest marriage proposal, of Tsukiko standing in the moonlight with her hands outstretched and her foxy face aglow.

"Yes," he said sadly, "that's all I was."

As he pushed his way through the boisterous crowd, Toki wondered why he had ever wanted to be inside such a noisy, smoky, exclusionary place. I'll never come here again, he thought. This part of my life is over. From now on I'll devote myself to my work, and to reading, and to improving my voice. He went out by a fire exit so he wouldn't have to make smirky small talk with the doorman, and then, on a sudden whim, flagged down a cab and told the driver to take him to Tsukiji, site of the famous Central Tokyo Wholesale Fish Market. He couldn't very well check out every sushi shop in Tokyo, but there was only one Central Fish Market.

Two long slow weeks had passed since Toki's last visit to Hell. The days were still warm and clear (except when it rained; then they were warm and cloudy) but the nights were crisp with the promise of fall. Women began to exhume their autumn kimono from cedar chests, along with *obi* patterned with chrysanthemums or maple leaves, and occasionally, in the distance, the cry of a mobile vendor of roasted sweet potatoes would float over the city. "*Yakiiiiiimo*!" Toki loved that sound and sometimes, even if he wasn't working, he would poke his head out the window and call "Kingyoooooo!" in his mellow trained-baritone voice, on the chance that someone somewhere would hear the counterpoint of archaic human sounds and think, Ah, good, the old ways aren't completely dead after all.

Toki had slipped back into his hardworking-recluse routine. Biwako had closed her shop and taken a temporary job managing a large boutique in Hong Kong, so he was more alone than he had ever been in his life. Occasionally one of his customers would invite him to play mah-jongg or go out drinking, but Toki always made some excuse. His summer obsession with getting into Hell, his strange and undeniably supernatural encounters with the dog, the girl, and the fox: these all seemed fantastic and unreal, like something that had happened to another person in another life, on a different planet.

Several long strolls around the antic fish market at Tsukiji had yielded no results (although he did get to sample some of the freshest sushi in the world), and Toki had given up actively searching for Tsukiko. Still, he couldn't help doing a wishful double-take every time he saw a foxy dog, or a rufous cat, or a girl with coppery hair. He began to read an entire book every night, not just mysteries but folklore, science, philosophy, travel, even cookbooks. He bought a set of dumbbells because he had noticed that his legs were much more muscular than his arms, and he planted perilla, spearmint, and trefoil in blue-glazed pots on his sunny windowsill, to use in miso soup and fruit compotes. He also began to do some serious window-shopping at pet stores, trying to decide whether he could make a better home for a dog, or for a cat.

One day in September, just after the first persimmons had appeared on the elegantly leafless trees, Toki was pulling his barrow down a narrow back street in Wakamatsucho. "Kingyooo!" he yodeled, automatically, but he was thinking about something he had read the night before in a book by the great medieval general Uesugi Kenshin: "In possession of an infallible technique, the individual places himself at the mercy of inspiration." I've got my goldfish-peddling technique down, Toki was thinking. Now all I need is some inspiration.

Suddenly he was startled from his reverie by the sound, almost like an echo, of a light, high voice calling "Kingyooo!," not far away. Toki stopped and listened. In all his years of peddling goldfish, he had never once encountered a colleague, or a competitor. He knew there must be a few out there, but there was no goldfish-vendors' union, no newsletter, no annual picnic, so he had gradually begun to think of himself as the Last Goldfish Man in Tokyo, if not in the entire country.

"Kingyooo!" The high, pure cry came again, and Toki got gooseflesh from the ethereal sound. It must be a countertenor, he thought. He felt suddenly curious and eager to meet another man who was living the same hard, humble, lonely, old-fashioned life that he had chosen for himself, and it suddenly occurred to him that he really didn't have any friends, aside from his sister and the vanished fox-woman.

Toki headed down the street at a rapid trot, then took a cross street, following the sound of the other vendor's falsetto voice. Behind him, water sloshed from the barrow and the goldfish darted from side to side in alarm, for they weren't accustomed to traveling at such high speeds. Toki came barreling around a curve on a crooked residential street and almost collided with the other vendor, who stopped in mid-cry and stood staring at Toki in wonderment.

Toki stared back. The other man was pulling a barrow exactly like Toki's, except that it was painted with stripes of green, white, and mauve. The vendor was shorter than Toki and he was dressed in a most untraditional way, or rather in a daring parody of tradition. His puffy pantaloons were glittery silver, his belly-band was woven from metallic threads of gold, silver, and bronze, and his *happi* coat was of gold cloth with a silver logo of interlocking squares on the back. Instead of a tenugui bandanna, the vendor wore a sort of Arabian Nights turban of cloth-of-gold, and his split-toed rubber boots had been painted gold to match.

Toki bowed, and the other vendor bowed back. Then the stranger reached up and removed the turban, and Toki was shocked to see that his colleague was not a man at all. It was a young woman with brown eyes and a charming heart-shaped face and a shoulder-length fall of reddish-brown hair. Toki's heart seemed to have stopped beating. The other vendor said "You're working very hard," or some such preordained pleasantry, and Toki responded mechanically, "You are, too."

It has to be Tsukiko, he was thinking. The hair, the occupation, the metallic clothes: it was too coincidental to be coincidence.

"Why are you looking at me that way?" said the young woman in an accusatory voice. In a more friendly tone she added, "Oh, by the way, my name is Yayoi," and as she spoke Toki somehow knew that it wasn't Tsukiko, after all.

Toki bowed deeply. "I'm Tokiyuki Kaminari," he said and then, in a sudden reckless rush, he told his new acquaintance about the fox-woman. He thought Yayoi might laugh at him, or be angry about his initial suspicions, but instead she stepped forward and looked him in the eyes, very seriously. She wasn't exactly pretty, but she had an endearing face and warm golden skin, and her eyes were alight with sympathy and intelligence.

"I've met a few foxes, myself," she said. "But *I'm* not one. My hair is dyed with henna, just because I got bored with my appearance." She paused and lifted up her bangs and showed Toki where the hair was growing back, a deep raven's-wing black. "As for my costume, it was donated by one of my best customers—she's a costume designer who has a huge aquarium in her studio—because she thought a change might help my business. I didn't plan to be a vendor; I was trained to teach school but my brother died in a bicycle accident and there was no one else to carry on. If you need more proof that I'm not going to turn into a fox, you could come over to my house tonight and look at my baby pictures, and meet my parents," she said with a mischievous smile.

"I'd like that," Toki said, and he realized that he didn't care if she was a fox, or some other supernatural illusion, as long as she didn't run away and leave him. "Um, it's awfully hot today," he said. Actually it was delightfully cool and breezy, but Yayoi seemed to understand what he was getting at.

"It is hot, isn't it," she agreed. "I wouldn't mind something cold to drink."

They parked their glass-sided barrows side by side, while Toki's goldfish peered curiously at Yayoi's baby carp, and swished their gauzy tails. Then the two vendors started down the hill in search of a coffee shop, talking animatedly as they walked. "You like Edogawa Rampo? So do I!" "You like to cook? I do, too!" "You live in Roppongi? I'm in Moto-Azabu, that's walking distance! I mean, of course, that is, if you ever wanted to."

They passed a sushi shop that had a dark green *noren* curtain over the door advertising its wares, with the "shi" in "sushi" depicted by a wriggling eel. On the front stoop, next to a flowerpot of purple starflowers climbing a bamboo pole, lay a sleek, plump, russet-colored cat with a bell attached to its neck by a scrap of red-and-gold brocade, exactly like the wrapping of Toki's shrine-amulet. Yayoi bent down to pet the cat. "Hi, kitty," she said, and then she looked up at Toki and added, "I love cats. We have three at home, all disgracefully fat and totally spoiled."

Toki squatted next to the cat and said, softly, "Niao?" The cat stood up and stretched languidly, two impossibly limber legs at a time, and Toki saw that it had three white paws and a feathery plume of a tail. As he gasped in recognition the cat caught his eye, and he knew that this time there was no mistake. Clearly, this was the latest incarnation of the dog, the girl, the fox. But even as he was rejoicing over finding his friend and almost-lover alive and well, Toki realized that he didn't feel any trace of his old romantic obsession with the mysterious Tsukiko. He smiled at the cat and flashed a quick victory sign, and the cat blinked at him in a most un-catlike way.

The two goldfish vendors walked down the street toward the peppermint-striped awning of a shop called, in English, "Coffee & Cake Wonderful World." After a moment Yayoi said, "You know, I could swear that cat winked at you just now."

"I can see you have a vivid imagination," Toki said. "I like that in a woman."

When they got to the coffee house Toki held the door open for Yayoi with a gallant Western-style bow, like Albert Finney in *Tom Jones*. As he followed her inside he sneaked a quick look up the street, but the copper-colored cat had disappeared.

EPILOGUE

Superstition is the poetry of life.
—JOHANN WOLFGANG VON GÖETHE
Sprüche in Prosa

Not so long ago, on a mother-of-pearl morning in early spring, I was strolling with an American friend—a first-time visitor to Japan—through the foggy, luminous grounds of a small Shinto shrine in the Kiyomizu district of Kyoto. It was just after sunrise, and there was no one else around except an elderly woman in a mauve kimono who was clapping her hands, rattling the ancient brass bells, and praying to the monkey-god for some miracle, or favor. As I listened to the pigeon sutras and inhaled the cryptomeria-scented air, I was suddenly reminded of the old Japanese folk tales collected by Lafcadio Hearn—stories of rebirth and transmogrification in which the strangest, most fanciful things begin to seem not only plausible but possible, too. Beautiful women bewitched by foxes, shape-shifting *tanuki* disguised as tipsy priests, footless ghosts and faceless goblins, disembodied heads that feed on human flesh; some of the stories are grisly and bleak, but they can be tender and earthy and elegant, as well.

Just then, like an Ouroboric memo from the gods, a small eggplant-colored serpent slithered across the silvery gravel of the shrine and vanished into the fairy-tale forest. At precisely the same moment the old woman clapped her hands three times, and somewhere across the vaporous valley a temple bell began to ring.

"Holy smoke!" exclaimed my awestruck friend. "It's, like, Epiphany City!"

"Welcome to Japan," I said, with a snakish smile.

My first encounter with the work of Lafcadio Hearn was the film version of his famous book *Kwaidan: Stories and Studies of Strange Things*. I saw the movie in a tiny, crowded theater in Shinjuku; it was in rusty black and white, but the terror was vivid and unforgettable. After trembling through two consecutive showings, which gave me sleep-with-the-light-on nightmares for days afterward, I went out and bought a copy of the book. Some contemporary cynics now sneer at what they see as Hearn's overly rapturous, exotica-smitten reaction to Japanese culture, but for me, at twenty, it was pure delight and revelation. I loved Hearn's dreamy rococo prose, and I was enchanted by the shadow world he sketched. I felt that I had found a kindred spirit, one who clearly believed in "Maybe, Perhaps, and the Benefit of the Doubt"—my personal trinity of the open mind where matters of the supernatural (and the natural, too) are concerned.

Lafcadio Hearn, in his later, less effusive writings, also seemed to share my perception of Japan as a place that increasingly conceals its medieval magic beneath a dreary modern veneer, yet can still reward the patient explorer with some of the most poignant and illuminating experiences of a lifetime. I eventually went on to formulate my own complex, ambivalent opinions about the Land of the Rising Sun, but the sensitive amateur ethno-mythology of Lafcadio Hearn gave my first small adventures in that country a lyrical resonance and a depth of sympathy for which I will be forever grateful.

I did not set out to write a compendium of supernatural tales. The stories in this book occurred to me one at a time over a period of seven years, and I simply wrote them down—and then rewrote for a thousand hours or so. They are intended as escapist pleasure-fare, to be sure, but I hope that they also convey my affection for what I think of, wishfully, as "real Japan": the soulful, mysterious, sentimental Japan of country fox-shrines, torchlit masked processions, and eerie, poetic superstitions. Only in retrospect, as I wandered through that Kiyomizu monkey-shrine at dawn, did I realize that my light-hearted venture into the realm of the Japanese supernatural was also an oblique tribute to the memory, the legacy, and the benevolent ghost of Lafcadio Hearn. Epiphany City, indeed.